BEEN THERE DONE THAT

The Leffersbee Series Book #1

HOPE ELLIS

www.smartypantsromance.com

COPYRIGHT

This book is a work of fiction. Names, characters, places, rants, facts, contrivances, and incidents are either the product of the author's questionable imagination or are used factitiously. Any resemblance to actual persons, living or dead or undead, events, locales is entirely coincidental if not somewhat disturbing/concerning.

Copyright © 2020 by Smartypants Romance; All rights reserved.

No part of this book may be reproduced, scanned, photographed, instagrammed, tweeted, twittered, twatted, tumbled, or distributed in any printed or electronic form without explicit written permission from the author.

Made in the United States of America

Print Edition
ISBN: 978-1-949202-43-4

"There are years that ask questions and years that answer."

— ZORA NEALE HURSTON, THEIR EYES WERE WATCHING GOD

CHAPTER ONE

Nick

12 Years Ago

"They should be here soon," Sheriff James said.

The hospital intercom overhead came to life, squawking something undecipherable.

I didn't stir. Now that the adrenaline had worn off, I was numb. Numb to the squeaking of nurses' soft-soled shoes that passed outside the open doorway of the family consultation room. Numb to the dreaded hospital smells—both the antiseptic and what they wiped away. Numb to the updates from the doctor with the pitying eyes and the heavy weight of Sheriff James's stare.

Even the torn, bleeding flesh of my fingers and knuckles no longer stung. I'd entered an alternate universe, a different reality that mercifully blunted the pain of this one. I could almost believe that my mother wasn't several hundred feet away in a hospital bay.

Maybe the past three hours hadn't happened . . .

It was an empty hope.

Just as well. It would be a shame if I had no recollection of the first and only time I'd gone apeshit and done exactly what I wanted to do.

I could claim I hadn't known what I was doing—temporary insanity—but the truth was I'd relished every downward swing of that bat as it shattered mirrors, bent chrome, dented metal. I'd been euphoric as I braced myself and tipped over the row of motorcycles, using my legs to finish what the bat started.

The jarring impact of each blow singing through my arms had almost compensated for an entire year of feeling helpless as I watched my little family capsize into dark waters.

"They should be here soon," Sheriff James repeated. He'd sat in the corner for the last hour or so, mostly silent. His face was expressionless, but his voice was warmer than I would've expected considering he'd had to fish me out of an enraged mob of Iron Wraith bikers.

I grunted. I didn't have the energy to work up any other response. All-consuming rage and sorrow had wrung me out, left me empty.

As if on cue, there was a flurry of activity in the doorway.

Ezra and Ellie Leffersbee, faces full of worry, skidded to a stop. They were bizarrely dressed. Mrs. Leffersbee was as undone as I'd ever seen her outside her home. A dark scarf covered her usually perfect hairdo. Grooves from the fabric of a pillowcase imprinted across one cheek. The hem of a frilly nightgown peeked out from under her coat. Mr. Leffersbee wore mismatched sweats, socks, and sandals. It was not the attire anyone would expect for a bank owner and one of the richest men in the county.

Seeing them here, people who knew me and cared, brought huge relief. And shame.

Mrs. Leffersbee said my name in a sleep-roughened voice and started forward, but Sheriff James stood up, raised a hand.

"Ezra. Ellie. If I could have a minute with you first."

Both Leffersbees shot one last glance in my direction before they followed Sheriff James out into the hallway. I lowered my head, unable to meet their gaze. The sight of my bloodied hands filled my vision again. Revulsion churned in my gut. A distant memory pulled at the back of my brain, then registered.

My father.

I hadn't seen him in many years. Not since my mother had finally had enough of him and the tirades that usually accompanied the end of his workday at the mill. Since then, it had just been us, thank God. But I could remember my father in this very position, head bowed with regret, fists bruised. Telling us he'd finally lost his job after getting into a fight with another millworker. Again.

I spent my entire life fighting against any comparisons to that man and his temper, proving to myself that I would be a better man, *was* a better man, and had a better future in store.

And here I was with the same bowed head, mouth salty with the same regret. I'd have to atone for what I'd done, while my mother was at her most vulnerable.

I didn't deserve the life I'd planned with Zora. I couldn't be sure now that I was actually any different than my father before me. And there was no way, after what I'd done tonight, that I'd make it out of Green Valley unscathed. Never mind the plans we'd made together. Eighteen years old, and in one night, I'd ruined my future.

Our future.

How could I even begin to pick up the pieces for my mother, to take care of her? Would I even be able to?

And what *were* these hands capable of?

I had to do the right thing. And I couldn't let doing the right thing hold Zora back.

The Leffersbees rushed back in, mouths set in grim lines. Mrs. Leffersbee blinked back tears as she settled in the seat next to me. Her arms went around me, but I was a block of ice—too cold, too stiff to lean into the embrace. Mr. Leffersbee came to a crouch in front of me. His bloodshot gaze met mine.

"What do you need, son? We're here for you. Whatever you need."

I worked to bring the words up. "Is Zora with you? Does she know?"

They exchanged glances. "No," Mrs. Leffersbee said, very quietly. "We didn't tell any of the kids, we just left as soon as we got the call. The sheriff just filled us in."

I nodded, returning my gaze to the floor. Good. I couldn't do what had to be done with Zora here. If I set eyes on her, I wouldn't be able to leave her. I had to do what was right.

The inevitability of this moment and the decision I had to make finally burst the bubble. Suddenly I felt *everything*. The pain in my ribs, ache in my jaw, hitch in my breathing, dull ache in my chest.

I couldn't see Mr. Leffersbee anymore when I finally lifted my gaze, not with the film of tears in my eyes. Someone's hand rested on my knee. I took in a breath and relished the resulting burn. I welcomed the pain. I hoped it stayed with me forever. It would be all that I had left of Zora.

I ran my forearm against my eyes and met Mr. Leffersbee's eyes like the man I had to be, and I said the words that would seal my fate.

Our fate.

"I need your help."

CHAPTER TWO

Zora

Present Day

My brother called the musky, tangy, sharp body-smell after working out *eau de sweat*, and this description usually cracked me up. Everybody sweats. Everybody stinks after working out. No big deal. I'd like to think I had a good sense of self-deprecating humor about life's inescapable imperfections.

Usually.

But usually, I wasn't sitting in my office at the university post-gym, wearing my rattiest workout clothes, grimacing at my computer screen like an angry, sweaty, grimacing shrew. And yet, here I was, reading the latest message in my email inbox, and feeling—deep in my bones—all hopes for new grant funding plummet and then die a gratuitously violent death in the canyon of despair. *Again.* So, the fact that I could smell myself—*eau de sweat*—filled me with a strange and unreasonable amount of irritation.

My Grandmother Leffersbee used to say, *"Life isn't perfect, but that's* what makes it so interesting." Then she'd wink before adding, "*Do you want interesting? Or do you want boring?*"

Right now? I could use some boring perfection. Just a little. Just a smidge. *Please.*

"Zora." A vaguely familiar-sounding voice said my name from someplace in the vicinity of my office doorway. I ignored it, hoping they'd take my silence as an invitation to go away.

You're almost out of time.

My eyes stung, but I wasn't going to cry. There is no crying in clinic communication research; there is only more research, more grant applications, more trying, more doing. But, *damn*, I really thought we had this one in the bag. Folks' livelihoods depended on it. My tenure, my job, depended on it. Not to mention the research itself was important—so incredibly important.

"Zora," that voice said again, firmer this time. Closer.

Given my present state of mind and *eau de sweat fantastique*, I can't help barking out, "Now isn't a good time."

The man didn't respond for a beat, but then once more said, "Zora," this time with a hint of grit and impatience.

My glare cut away from the offending rejection email and I opened my mouth to volley something scathingly polite and dismissive, but then every nerve and muscle in my body seized. The clouds outside my office window parted at that very moment, emitting a biblical shaft of light that illuminated my overstuffed bookcases—and the breathtaking specimen of man standing in my office doorway on the fifth floor of the medical research building.

What the . . . ?

Shock choked me. I couldn't breathe. The cracked vinyl of the office chair's armrests bit into the tender flesh of my palms.

I recognized him immediately even though he looked very, very different. All the awkward lankiness and unformed promise of his youth had been ruthlessly fulfilled in the intervening years. But after twelve years of empty, aching absence, of wondering and worrying, of resignation and sadness . . . he was here.

Was he real?

"I thought . . . I thought you were dead." The whispered words left my mouth at the same time they formed in my brain.

Nick Armstrong stood silent and unmoving, a stolid sentry, looking at me. Just . . . looking.

The width of his shoulders filled the doorway, leaving scant space between his head and the door frame. I couldn't help devouring the sight of him, half-wondering if he were a mirage. Despite being as fashion challenged as I was, I easily identified the perfect fit of a bespoke suit, noting how the high-quality fabric closely followed the muscled bulk of his shoulders and arms. The unassuming dark jacket, white dress shirt, and trousers did little to hide his tapered waist and well-developed thighs.

His hulking presence alone ensnared my attention, but his face arrested it. He was striking. Thick, ink-black hair just starting to curl over his collar matched the dark stubble shadowing his square jaw. His slightly off-center nose, likely the result of a break, ruined the pure symmetry of his features. But his eyes were a startling shade of green, the same showy, verdant hue of summer leaves under an ominously gunmetal sky.

So unsettlingly familiar. *And yet* . . . No, it couldn't be him. There was no way it was Nick. Not after all these years.

This isn't possible.

I lurched up and made a spectacle of myself as I struggled to stand. Panic weighted my feet. Disbelief severed any connection with my brain's higher processing, leaving me stuck to my chair with my mouth hanging ajar. *"Letting in flies,"* as my Grandma Leffersbee would have said.

I blinked back confusion as I stared at him, captured by a whisper, an echo of a memory. "Who . . . ?"

His mouth moved, like maybe he was going to introduce himself. But instead, he repeated my name for a fourth time, "Zora . . ."

This voice was different from the Nick I had loved. Deeper. But the way he said my name, slowly, as if savoring the taste of something rich? I could never forget that.

It is him.

Any remaining oxygen in the room dissipated. A carousel of memories whirled though my mind at a blurring speed. We'd known each other our entire lives until we didn't, until he'd disappeared. We'd planned to elope, to make what we knew in our hearts official. Legal. There'd been a time when I was incapable of imagining a life without him.

I still remembered our last words. I remembered the last time he kissed me.

Why now?

"You thought I was dead?" Nick's dark brows inched toward his hair line as he finally spoke something other than my name. "Or you wished it?"

That statement, and the familiar smirk kicking up one side of his mouth, gave me the strength to push to my feet, to come back to myself somewhat. No, I hadn't wished him dead, but seeing him here now, alive and obviously just fine? I didn't know how to feel.

Trembling, I braced myself against my desk with one hand. "What . . . what are you doing here?" I managed to iron some of the breathy quality from my voice.

His confidence seemed to slip for just a second at my wavering. He took a small, hesitant step forward. "Z. Are you okay?"

I held up my hand to halt his progress. My mind was stuck between gears, backfiring, unable to acclimate to this new truth. The current reality. That it was indeed the Nick I knew, standing there, nonchalant, as if an ocean of time hadn't passed. As if he hadn't just disappeared.

Why now?

"All this time," I managed to croak, "and now, *years* later, you just . . . show up." I bit the inside of my lip. *Hold the line, Zora. You will not fall apart over this—or any—man. Not now. Not here. Not ever.* "You disappeared," I said, mostly to remind myself of his betrayal, and my voice grew stronger, underlaid with the faintest bit of steel. "Without a single word. Nothing but that stupid letter."

I'd thrown it away and discarded any thoughts of that past. I had moved on. *I've moved on. He means nothing.*

Perhaps reading my thoughts on my face, he looked away, his jaw working, but whatever he'd planned to say was interrupted by muffled footsteps and voices echoing in the corridor. Nick glanced behind him and then back to me. A tic pulsed under his right eye. "Zora." Air seemed to seep from him as his shoulders sagged. "I didn't mean for this to happen. Not like this. I tried—"

"*There* you are!" Over-bright chirping I recognized all too well reached us, accompanied by the strident staccato of high heels.

Baffled, I craned my neck to see behind him. *What in the world is going on?*

Nick leaned forward. "I wanted to talk to you. Just the two of us." His voice was tight, his delivery urgent.

"We thought we'd lost you, Mr. Rossi." The owners of the disembodied voices materialized at my office door, as three of Tennessee State University's highest-ranking administrators stood in a half-circle behind Nick.

"Dr. Leffersbee, you're here!" Nellie Abrams, Director of Development, stepped forward with her customary toothy grin. "We were just taking our new friend on a tour."

This couldn't get any worse.

Nick flinched as her red acrylic nails settled on his sleeve as though they were talons. She gifted him with a blinding smile. If I wasn't already convinced that God had blessed her with more teeth than the standard set of thirty-two, that smile would have cinched it.

"Yes. Here I am," I said the words robotically, my chest filled with cement. I'd seen this dog and pony show before. Hell, I'd *been* the pony. But what were they doing with Nick?

What alternate universe had I stumbled into?

Nellie's smile wilted at my deadpan tone. "Well, we certainly didn't intend to interrupt. I didn't expect you to be here." Her gaze traveled over my third best pair of exercise leggings and the faded Tennessee State University lettering on my oversized shirt. "Campus is always a ghost town this time on a weekday." She flicked a sidelong glance at Nick. "Just goes to show you how hardworking our faculty is." She nudged his arm with her own, a somehow intimate gesture.

9

I blinked. I would have laughed at the muted look of alarm Nick aimed her way if my intestines hadn't crawled up my throat.

"Mr. Rossi, this is Dr. Zora Leffersbee." She gestured to me with a grandiose wave of her hand. I wondered if it was just my chronic sleep deprivation that made her smile and widened, wheeling eyes seem vaguely frightening. "Zora is faculty here. Her research involves improving communication between patients and their physicians. She's done a lot of really interesting studies with our patients, and she's done great work training our docs. I just know she'll be able to help."

What? Help?

Nellie turned back to me. Outside of Nick's line of sight now, she further widened her eyes at me as if imparting something significant. Here it came. Most development officers I knew were a little slick, but Nellie's delivery reminded me of a used car salesman.

"Zora, this is Nick Rossi. His company is at the forefront of really exciting, cutting-edge health care technology. You know how you can take your EKG at home, or on your watch? His company pioneered that technology. He's been telling us about his newest venture into telemedicine as a way of further providing better accessibility to health care. We here at the School of Medicine and our partners at Knoxville Community Hospital are interested in adopting his program. We've been talking about having him partner with our surgical departments to pilot the app, but we're still working out some of the details about communication protocols. So, we thought you might be able to help us think through some of that." She threw him another sidelong glance, followed by another nudge that startled him and broke the connection of our gazes. Nick turned his attention to her, lips thinned.

"And, if that wasn't enough," Nellie continued, "he's indicated an interest in making a gift to our medical school. Isn't that exciting?"

I only registered half of what she said. My gaze moved over him. "Rossi?" He'd changed his last name?

"That's right. Nick Rossi." Nellie nodded.

My pulse came to life in my ears, thrumming loudly. *Slow down, Zora. Proceed with caution.*

Nick's chest visibly lifted with a sigh as he leaned against the doorway. The sight of him shoving his hand through his hair ignited a memory. Impressions streaked across my brain like quicksilver. Nick as a kid, looking away, scowling, mouth pinched when he was scolded. Nick as a teenager, raking his hand through the thick waves of his hair as we both sat silent, hip to hip, sobered by the realization that life had become more complicated than we ever could have imagined. Nick as a young man, his lanky arms pinning my back against his chest, the hollow reverberation of his sigh filling my ears.

I'd known him long enough, intimately enough, to detect the regret in his current downcast expression. But it was done. *He* had done this, somehow maneuvered us into this situation.

But why?

Was this really *happening*?

Under different circumstances, I would find many things funny about this moment. For years, when I'd conjured this scene in my imagination, there had been accompanying music. The reel in my mind's eye always played at half-speed, the better to display the bliss blanketing both our faces as we ran toward one another through a field of wildflowers, or in an airport, or someplace dramatic. We'd be delirious with joy, relieved to be together again.

Somehow, some way, he'd explain it had all been a mistake. Or he'd had amnesia. Or he'd been taken hostage by flat-earthers.

It was hard to imagine a scene that contrasted more sharply than this present moment. The reunion I'd yearned for with Nick featured instead a burned-out, shrewish, confused, funky version of me wearing the sharp tang of *eau de sweat*.

Nick and I stared at each other. As strangers. All under the prying eyes of folks who had no idea of what we'd once been to each other, who had no idea we'd once promised our futures and hearts. They had no way of knowing that, mere months before he vanished like smoke, Nick Armstrong slipped a ring on my finger and asked me to marry him. The uncomfortable silence and blank stares from my colleagues grew to the point they became unbearable. My ears filled with the sound of my own breathing. Acid seared the walls of my belly.

There had to be a script. This had to be a sick prank. Somewhere, there had to be rules and expectations for hideous moments like this. I was expected to say something, to behave in accordance with social rules, when that was already one of my greatest weaknesses. They expected me to slap on a polite mask and perform while blood drained from the ripped-open fissures in my heart. I couldn't help the brief, desperate glance I sent around the room and over their heads. Was this the part when a benevolent puppet master would show up, take over and animate me through the niceties?

Lord knows, I had absolutely no idea of how to proceed, of how to survive this moment.

I'd heard of silence being described as "thick." This was definitely it. This was molasses. The other two people in the room shifted from foot to foot as Nick and I continued to eye each other.

"Thank you for allowing us to drop by unexpectedly," the dean of the medical school interjected through our tense standoff. Peter Gould, or Ghoul, as many called him, attempted a smile. The expression was unnerving on his perpetually pinched features. Erin Soller, my department's chair, looked on with widened eyes from the relative safety of the hallway. We exchanged a quick glance, a nonverbal "What the hell?" Erin's shoulders lifted quizzically.

Dr. Gould inched closer to the doorway and Nellie moved aside to make room. "Dr. Leffersbee," he started sternly, his tone dripping with *meaning*, "Mr. Rossi mentioned wanting to meet you at some point during his visit. Of course, we knew you'd be happy to oblige."

Oh? Is that so?

"We thought he'd gotten lost when he went to the men's room." Nellie's sunny smile countered her chiding tone, as did her chuckle.

"Seems he's good at disappearing," I quipped, unable to dial back the sarcasm.

The muscle at Nick's jaw flexed. I ignored his half-lidded glare, instead glancing away, studying my overstuffed bookshelf.

I wondered how Nick had eluded her, even briefly. Nellie was a bloodhound when it came to sniffing out donations. The greater the potential, the deeper her commitment to the trail. Donors never escaped her clutches. *God bless her.*

Nellie cleared her throat. "Yes. Well. Anyway. We plan to get our surgical residents on board as part of the team, and we're approaching some of our primary care physicians."

My mind was working on a delay, mere moments from shutting down in light of this crisis. "Team? Surgical residents?"

Nellie frowned at me—like *I* confused *her*—as her head tilted to one side. *Clearly, I'd missed something.* But when I looked to Nick, he'd wiped his face of all expression. I continued to stare at him, distracted, searching for some sign, some flicker of who was inside. I wondered if there was any trace of *my* Nick—the one I would have died for—in this devastatingly handsome creature with empty eyes.

The silence acquired weight, settled further.

Nellie divided her attention between the two of us. "Uh, Mr. Rossi, I don't want to delay the rest of our tour. I know you're hoping to complete your business and fly out tomorrow evening." She turned toward me. "Zora, we're counting on you to spare a couple of hours tomorrow morning to host our guest. Introduce him to the work you've done so he understands what we require from his team." She gave me a pointed look. "We can make arrangements if you happen to have class."

She knew I didn't have class. I was a research professor; I didn't teach. Whatever the plot, Nellie must be convinced the university stood to benefit from the so-called Mr. Rossi.

It wasn't an unusual request for a donor to speak with faculty members, though not one I'd personally fielded often. Folks with the real money didn't find working with cancer patients sexy enough to merit a visit with yours truly. That honor went to the magicians over in Engineering who built electric cars, or the biomedical wizards who coaxed miracles from their beakers.

Thank God.

I read the tension in the line of Nick's jaw, the fists balled at his side, the artificial stillness in his stance, while he waited for my answer.

"I'll have to check my calendar, but I doubt I'll have time."

Nellie wore an expression resembling the one my mother had often worn when I'd been in trouble as a kid for not toeing the line. *"Zora Elaine Leffersbee. You are out of order."*

"Perfectly understandable," Dr. Gould said a little too quickly. "We've already imposed on you and now we're making assumptions about your time. I know you're incredibly busy, and you clearly have a lot going on. But I'd be grateful if we could work something out, Zora. Mr. Rossi is leaving tomorrow night. Perhaps you could check your calendar for us, now?"

The barest of smiles hovered over Nick's lips before it disappeared. I knew that self-satisfied smirk.

Somehow, they'd already checked. They already knew I was free, and now I was cornered, with no option but to comply. For now.

Turning, I shifted through the mounds of files stacked on my desk, searching for my mouse with frustrated movements, my neck flaring hot. When I slapped a pile of scattered papers, the mouse emerged and crashed to the floor in an apparent suicide attempt. The tiny battery door shot across the room like a projectile while the AAA battery rolled underneath my desk. I dropped to my knees and clawed for the two items in the darkness. Above me, my computer decided to come alive with audio from an educational module my research partner and I had developed for doctors and gynecological patients. Every muscle in my body locked in horror as my recorded voice broadcasted to the occupants in the room and hallway beyond, *"When I have sex with a partner, I never orgasm."*

Jesus. *Kill me. Kill me now.*

Now I remembered. I'd been reviewing an early draft of an educational video before I'd gotten absorbed in another task, one of several hundred that were still undone. The mouse had simply picked up the replay where I left off.

Adesola Rojas, my research partner and real-life gynecologist, resumed her scripted lines. *"Your sexual health is important. Learning your body and identifying the things that bring you sexual satisfaction are a priority."*

The damning dialogue continued as I groped in the dark under my desk, my speakers spewing an embarrassing recital of information. Adesola's voice was perfectly calibrated between urgency and encouragement. *"It should be just as much a priority as your partner's satisfaction. Many, if not most women, are unable to orgasm from penetration alone. Try prioritizing clitoral stimulation during your physical intimacy. Relax. Don't put pressure on yourself. Either you or your partner can—"*

"Dr. Leffersbee?"

I froze, startled to hear that deep voice so close. Casting a glance to the side, I seized at the sight of the creased seams of trousers over highly-shined dark shoes. "Yes." I hissed the word.

"—find different positions which lend themselves to stimulation. For example, if your partner—"

"Spacebar," Nick said. "Hitting the spacebar will pause the video with this program." A definitive click sounded from above.

The video came to a stop, just as Adesola started to extol the virtues of mutual play during sex.

I shook my head, my cheeks on fire. "Thank you," I said tightly.

Dear God. How had this happened? I hardly experienced disasters of this magnitude anymore. Not since Nick and I . . .

I'd regressed. Lost control. This moment? It ranked high on the list of my most embarrassing moments, and that was saying something. *Get it together, Zora.* After having safely backed out from under the desk without banging my head and adding to the list of embarrassments, I became aware of Nick offering his hand. He appeared to be biting his lip, magenta staining his upper cheeks.

For just one moment, I regarded the hand I'd once known as well as my own. That hand had held mine, resided on my thigh when we were alone. That same scar still stretched across the length of his index finger, from that camping trip when the fishhook caught under his skin. The scar was old, faded white, a remnant of forgotten pain. Had it been so easy to forget me? To forget what we'd had? Had he moved on from that pain so easily?

I turned away, planted my hand on the height of my desk and hauled myself up without assistance.

Now upright, I took in the expressions of the peanut gallery in my doorway. Dean Gould looked like he'd swallowed his tongue. Nellie clutched her throat. Erin was red-faced and stifling her laughter.

I cupped my forehead in one hand. "Young adult cancer patients typically don't get enough counseling about reproductive health and fertility, or their sexual health. It's a training video. One of my projects uses videos to train clinicians on how to discuss some of the stickier subjects in these areas. It also helps other patients know they're not alone with the questions or concerns they may be too afraid to ask their own doctors. We took a poll to see what other topics our patients wanted featured with the remaining funds we have on hand. And... this was a popular suggestion among our female patients. This is the rough cut. We're going to have it shot professionally with actors next month."

Nellie stepped forward, her face frozen. "How interesting. We'll discuss this later. Erin, why don't Dr. Gould and I continue on with Mr. Rossi?" She rearranged her features before turning back to Nick. "I'll let you know if Dr. Leffersbee is able to find some free time tomorrow." She flicked a brief, venomous glance my way as she steered Nick and Dr. Gould out through the doorway and into the hall.

I gave their backs a thumbs up. "Thanks for stopping by," I said, injecting my voice with the syrupy sweetness my mother used with guests who had worn out their welcome. My knees shook, but I stayed standing until the office door closed with a resounding thud. Only then did I allow myself to plop into my office chair with a pained groan.

God. What a *disaster*.

If life was kind, if fate was fair, this haunting should have resembled a Dickensian specter: weighted with the chains of disappointment, groaning with the misery of past heartbreak, moldering with the stink of indifference.

Not something straight out of my private fantasies. And yet, Nick

Armstrong was back, had only improved with time, and was now one of the hottest men I'd ever seen. Given what he'd done to me, it was patently unfair.

But life is not fair. And fate, I'd long since learned, is a calculating bitch. *That bitchy bitch-faced bitch.*

Erin shut the door behind them. "Well. That was exciting. The most excitement I've had in some time."

I huffed. "I'm glad you got a charge from it."

"Zora." Erin said the single word with great solemnity, then dissolved into unrestrained laughter. "What the hell just happened?"

I lowered my face into the cradle of my hands, noting the faint tremor in them. Now that the immediate danger had passed, my heart settled into a jitterbug rhythm that tripped up my breathing.

What the hell *had* just happened? I shrugged my shoulders. "Maybe you can tell me."

"Never mind." She waved her hand in the air. "Tell me what's going on with you and Mr. Rossi. You two are acquainted, clearly." Erin stated the fact as she perched on the edge of the couch. "I knew he was full of shit. He tried to appear off-handed when he asked about you, but he didn't quite pull it off. Something about the way he looked and the specificity of his questions. I'd planned on asking you about him," she said, lifting her hands as if in supplication, "but he managed to find his way to you sooner than I thought he would. Are you going to meet with him tomorrow?"

I was surprised by how hard it was to answer that question. I bit my lip, attempting to calm my riotous thoughts. Did I want to see Nick? Spend time with him, even under the guise of supporting a vendor, or even entertaining a potential donor?

No.

Did I want answers?

Yes. I wish I didn't care at all, but I wanted answers. *But only on my terms.*

"We had a relationship years ago." I tried to sound dismissive, annoyed rather than flustered and shades of heartbroken. "One day he walked away. But I don't care if we meet." That wasn't precisely a lie.

"You don't care?"

I didn't meet her gaze. "I don't care, but I am irritated that he pulled strings behind the scenes, forcing the issue. It should've been for me to decide when or whether we meet."

She nodded. Dying sunlight lit the glinting gray strands of her bob. "I agree, but there are some things none of us can run from. And your Mr. Rossi seems hell-bent on a reckoning."

"Yeah. He does." I curled my fingers into a fist. "That doesn't mean he's going to get what he wants. I'm almost inclined to just say no and let him continue on his merry way."

"I don't know, Zora." Erin ran an agitated hand over her brow. "You might want to take time to talk to him. See what he has to say. I hate to sound mercenary, but the man is richer than God and suggesting he'll invest some of that wealth in the university. Development is salivating over the potential of a strategic relationship like this. He doesn't need us, not really. For him, the advantage is getting to pilot his app. If he pumps a sizable donation into this place in the process . . ." She shrugged. "God knows we need it." She rubbed the worry lines on her brow, her gaze moving to mine. "Have you heard anything about the NIH grant?"

I sighed and aimed my thumb at the computer. "Yep. Just before you all stampeded into my office. The answer is a big fat *no*."

Erin shook her head, looking distraught. "Your research staff won't have jobs anymore if something doesn't hit soon."

"I know. You don't need to remind me. Trust me, it's getting to be all I think about. I had to tell my community health coordinator that I didn't have many more new leads on funding. It's a terrible feeling, being responsible for someone's livelihood and coming up empty. I *hate* feeling helpless."

It was the same kind of helplessness I'd felt when I took a semester off school for my mother's breast cancer diagnosis. But this situation, I could do something about.

I *would* do something about it.

"In that case, it's worth hearing him out. Seeing what he has to say."

"Is that the usual speech you always give faculty members you're about pimp out?"

She made a dismayed sound. "Zora!"

"Well, that is what you're suggesting!" Poor Erin. She probably hadn't bet on this roller coaster of an interaction either, and God knew I probably seemed bitchy and unreasonable to her. It wasn't her fault that I was living my own personal hell in a very professional setting.

"I'm just *saying*," she insisted, "what would it hurt to have a conversation with him?"

"Erin, that money would not go anywhere worthwhile, like to the med school or the cancer program. You know how this place works. The money would go to buy new uniforms for our piss poor football team, or to—"

"He wants to know more about your research, what you do. It aligns perfectly with what we're asking his software and staff clinicians to do for us, and how you've trained our docs in the past."

"Well, I already know about *him*. And while there was a time when I would've wanted to see him again, after this . . . I just don't know. I've been screwed once. I don't need to be screwed professionally by him, too."

Erin laughed. "You're smart as hell, Zora. And you're not a quitter. He has no idea of the woman you are today. What makes you so certain you won't come out of this on top?"

Suddenly, I decided I didn't want to spend any more time with New Nick than I had to. It'd be easier to hide, to carry on with my lukewarm life in peace. But the problem was bigger than me. I had to consider the loss our research staff when all the grants expired in three months. There was no guarantee I'd be able to scrape together enough other funding to help everyone.

More and more, it looked as if I wouldn't be able to save everyone myself.

Erin frowned. "I know this isn't easy. I'll back you, either way."

"Thank you." I rubbed my eyes. "I need to think. If I decide to see him, I'll let you know."

We exchanged more words before I could finally usher her out of my office. Closing the door behind her, I slid to the floor and hugged my knees. I thought of the brief, self-satisfied smirk on Nick's face when Nellie mentioned his involvement with the surgical residents.

This was fishy. What scheme was he planning? What part did he expect me to play? And after all these years?

I hypothesized that they, like I had, would soon learn Nick couldn't be trusted.

CHAPTER THREE

Nick

"Whatcha thinking, handsome? What'll you have?"

Startled, I looked up. The waitress frowned, hands on her hips, head tilted when I didn't immediately respond. "Haven't had a chance to look at the menu yet. It changed much?"

"Since when?" She took a few steps forward. The amount of space left between us could only be classified as intimate.

The strings of her apron cut into a figure more ample than I remembered. She'd been a landmark in my childhood and teenage life, and as much a part of Daisy's Nut House as the ancient light fixtures and gently worn booths. A sigh fought its way out of my chest. I shrugged. "You got any recommendations?"

She went still. Her expression approximated the one on Zora's face earlier that afternoon. "I know you," she said, her face inching closer to mine. "Just can't figure out how."

I gave it up then and met her gaze straight on. "Yes. We once knew each other very well, Miss Rebecca. You'd sneak me free doughnuts 'cause you said I needed filling out. You were always good to me."

I was surprised by the sudden hitch in my breathing. What the hell was wrong with me? What was this place doing to me?

See, this here? More evidence of my recent rash of questionable judgement.

What had possessed me to pull the rental car into this place's parking lot? To actually go inside and fold myself into the now ill-fitting booth?

I wasn't known for having bad judgment, let alone succumbing to it. Cautious experimentation and careful strategy had served me well since my Green Valley days.

Something like recognition crept across Rebecca's face in slow degrees. Her lined face broke into a grin as she let out a whoop. She plopped down beside me on the booth and surrounded my upper body with her soft arms.

"Nick Armstrong! Oh, God! I can't believe this!"

I cleared my throat, attempting to surface from her cleavage. "Yep, it's me."

The hugging continued, her arms tightening even more around my shoulders. "Why didn't you say anything? You come in here like you're just *anybody* and just *sit there*. What are you doing here?"

She pulled back, holding me at arm's length. *"Does Zora know you're here?"* She whispered it, with a reverence reserved for the quiet intervals in church.

I thought of Zora. Holding on to her desk, legs unsteady, eyes wide and glistening with hurt. "Yeah. I've seen her."

Rebecca tapped her foot on the black and white checkered linoleum tiled floor.

I smiled. There was little I could say to satisfy her curiosity. I didn't want to inspect my motives for returning to Green Valley too closely.

"I can't believe you're really here."

I pulled out of my thoughts in time to see Rebecca swiping a tear away with a shaking finger.

"God knows I missed you. I prayed for you after you left."

Left. Well. That was a polite, sterile word for what had actually happened.

"And *look at you!*" she said, taking a step back to accommodate the all-encompassing sweep of her gaze. "I guess you filled out, huh?"

"I guess so," I said, giving a half-hearted chuckle.

"What did Zora say? When she saw you?" Her voice lowered. "You know, that girl just adored you. Thought you hung the moon and stars. I always figured you two would end up married young, no matter what anyone had to say about it. Couldn't keep the two of you apart since you were kids. I used to think you could read each other's thoughts. I wouldn't be surprised, y'all knew each other so well."

She wasn't wrong. The plan had been to get married, to elope right out of high school. Go to the nearby university. Live in married housing. Finish our degrees. My gaze darted to the corner of the restaurant. Our favorite booth.

We'd come here all the time. Zora's second cousin Daisy owned the place, and we'd often crammed in that same booth with her cousins, Dani, Poe, and Simone. But the best times had been when it was just the two of us. When we were kids, Zora had mischievously kicked my leg under the table. When we were older, she'd run her leg against mine more slowly, her eyes lit with dark, delicious intent. I closed my eyes, thinking back to those halcyon days.

They'd also been difficult times. I'd been more than aware of my mother's growing problem. Hell, the whole town had an inkling at that point, despite all my efforts to hide it. But I'd had the backing and support of the Leffersbees. And I'd had the love of the most loyal, intelligent, beautiful girl in the world.

And it all changed. Overnight.

Rebecca chewed her lip. "You know what you want, hon?"

I couldn't quite work up a smile. "The usual?"

She nodded and turned, seeming to understand I needed space. "I think we can handle that."

"Appreciate it," I said, noting that the accent I'd worked so hard for so many years to exorcise had reared its head within just a few hours of being home.

I sighed when Rebecca retreated behind the counter, shouting to the unseen person on the other side of the food window.

Zora Leffersbee.

For so many years, I'd wondered about her. Agonized over memories of the soft weight of her hand slipping into mine, those dark eyes fixed on mine, those lips turned up with secret knowledge, a knowing that always made me listen to her, yield to her.

That closeness. Being loved by someone who accepted me with the same wholehearted openness as Zora, even after seeing who I really was? Having captured her love made me feel like a king among men. But I'd lost all that. Twelve years ago.

She'd always been beautiful. I'd had a crush on her in early grade school. My mother chuckled when I came home brimming with tales of Zora's long braids and the colorful, clicking beads punctuating each end. I'd been lured in by Zora's kind ways. She was curious, upbeat, and mysteriously watchful. I'd spy her sitting quietly during playtime, studying our classmates as if trying to decipher a puzzle. And then she'd see me and smile.

Her smile had been an unspoken invitation into her little bubble.

Admission to her private, quirky world was an honor. It was especially sweet because she was so very careful and discerning about whom she allowed in. Other people thought Zora was shy. They thought she was quiet. She wasn't.

And once I'd met the hurricane that was her twin sister, I'd understood Zora better.

God, I miss her.

My phone buzzed in my pocket. Distractedly, I pulled it out, glimpsing the caller ID, and sighed. "Yeah?" I hoped my curt tone would put him off.

"What the fuck, Nick?"

Hearing the frustration straining Eddie's typical California cool made me sit up. "What?"

"Man, where are you? Still in Green Acres?"

I needed this right now like I needed a stab wound. "Valley. Green Valley. Yeah. What do you want?"

His sigh hissed through the phone's speaker. "So. It's true what I'm hearing, then."

"How would I know what you're hearing?"

"Your secretary just told me that you're out of the office *indefinitely*. Helping to oversee some new app, of all things."

"Not indefinitely. A few weeks." I attempted to stretch my legs out as far as the cramped booth would allow. They didn't go far.

"Why do you need a few weeks?"

An image of Zora, as she was now, as I'd seen her this afternoon, flashed in my mind's eye. I hadn't expected to find her office door open. I'd just wanted a peek. Spotting that familiar crown of wild curls had broken something loose inside me. I hadn't been able to breathe.

Then she'd turned.

She wasn't a girl anymore. She was a woman. Dear God, was she ever.

From the moment I'd met her, she'd bemoaned the fact that she didn't share her twin's ultra-slimness. I'd decked a kid in seventh grade for trying to cop a feel of her chest, but the incident ushered in an era of Zora in oversized T-shirts, sweatshirts, and pullovers. No matter what I'd said, she'd remained convinced she was an overdeveloped freak.

This afternoon, I'd almost swallowed my tongue when she rose from behind her desk. Same big doe eyes, flawless amber skin, and a head full of thick curls I'd loved to pull on. The T-shirt and stretchy pants couldn't hide the soft fullness of her stupendous, ripe curves.

The years had fallen away in a moment and I was, once again, that lovesick teenager.

Fuck.

"Uh, hello? Nick? You still there?"

I shifted in the booth, clearing my throat before responding. "We ran into some snags on the development end. Then realized we hadn't thought through some of the clinic issues. It's what happens when you break into a new industry." When I'd heard our marketing department was piloting our new app in a small town with a moderate-sized, university-affiliated teaching hospital, I'd thought it was a great idea. When they'd set their sights on Green Valley and its closest hospital in Knoxville, well, I couldn't stay away.

"Sure. Fine. But why do *you* have to be there?" Eddie's impatient tone cracked through the line.

I evaded the question by responding, "You know why. We're working it out. The hospital and their partners at the university's med school are walking us through it."

My business had brought me to the very same place where the woman I'd once loved more than anything now lived. I'd known Zora was there; I'd followed all the moves of her schooling and career, even after she'd sent me back my ring.

Hardly a day ever passed when I didn't think of her and wonder, *Why had she returned the ring the way she did? And with that cryptic note? How had she known where to find me? Had her parents ever told her why I left? Had they told her anything? And if she'd known where I was all that time, why didn't she ever write me? Call? Reach out?*

Did she even care? Did she ever?

"Give it air so it can heal, baby." That's what my mama had always said, her nimble fingers ripping at whatever bandage I'd slapped over a scab. It was true in this case. This *thing* had eaten at a corner of my gut for years and needed to be aired out. I just needed to fucking *know*, once and for all. I needed to face Zora and the promises never kept by either of us. So, here I was.

But Eddie didn't need to know any of this. "It's essential that I stay. I'm not planning on micromanaging our very capable team. But wrinkles in the implementation surfaced and I needed to be here on the ground. The changes will make it a better product going forward." I spoke the truth, just not *all* of it.

I hadn't planned to see her right away. I'd spent weeks considering what I'd say to Zora when I saw her, and a few more weeks trying to figure out how to maneuver a meeting between us. All it took was the slightest prompting on my part for that Nellie woman to bring up Dr. Zora Leffersbee. Then, Dr. Gould had realized Zora and her research were essential to our app, and they—I—needed her help smoothing out the details, telling us what we didn't know to ask. Suddenly, I had my opportunity much sooner than I'd expected.

I took it.

And then I crashed and burned.

"You think you need to be there? That's all well and good, but I need you in New York. We've got a board meeting coming up—a shareholders' meeting next week. I need you *here*, being the silver-tongued bastard you are."

"I'll fly back for those," I answered easily. "I've got one of the planes in Knoxville. I can get back whenever you need."

"But then you're going back there. For what could be a month?"

"Yeah."

"Since when is this app a priority? Don't you think you're stretching yourself a bit thin?"

I pinched the bridge of my nose. When I'd first met Edward Holt as a freshman at the University of Michigan, he'd embodied all the stereotypes I'd initially had of folks from the West Coast. Having never left Green Valley before, relying only on television and the scornful commentary heard from others, I'd already had a certain stereotype in mind when I finally sat down to a conversation with long-haired, laid back Eddie, who'd sported psychedelic, homemade tie-dyed shirts with slogans such "Make Peace, Not War" and "Find Yourself in Stillness" written in a childish hand. The computer engineering freshman mixer promised an awkward conversation.

But when he mentioned how his mother read auras for a living, I'd felt an unexpected stirring of identification. Here might be someone who understood.

"That can't pay much," I'd said, by then long accustomed to a painful preoccupation with maintaining household expenses.

He'd blinked, resurfacing from his pot-induced haze. "Of course not," he'd responded, his tone implying an unspoken "dummy." "I manage her portfolio."

That was the beginning of a friendship, a partnership, a brotherhood that endured early failures and all the pitfalls of burgeoning success. Eddie was still the same guy. Slow to anger, patient, direct. While growing success had produced a growing sense of anxiety in me, Eddie had only grown more still and stalwart in the face of exploding growth and risky gambles.

"Nick. I know we pumped a lot of money into this app, but—"

"That's right. I'm gonna make sure we see a return on our investment."

No. There was no way I could tell him what had really brought me here. I'd done my best not to think about this town. Not to look back. And I for damn sure didn't discuss it with Eddie. Let him think it was solely about the business and the money. Maybe, on some level, it was.

The lies you tell yourself...

"At some point, it's just money," Eddie said, stating a position I'd heard from him many times before. It annoyed me every time. If money didn't matter, why the fuck were we in business?

"I'd love to hear you share that philosophy with our shareholders. Oh, that's right." I gave a teasing chuckle. "That's why the PR firm banned you from all public speaking."

He let out a short laugh. "Listen to me. It's not worth having you live out in the sticks indefinitely, just for a better quarter. It's not like we don't already have enough money. We're swimming in it. We're already doing well. How many houses and cars do you need to buy?"

"There's no such as thing as too much money."

He'll probably need to meditate for hours after this conversation.

"Nick, listen to me." Eddie's tone gentled. "I don't know what it'll take for you to finally realize it's okay. You're not where you were. You're in a vastly different position. We're not struggling to get this thing off the ground anymore or dancing for investments. The wolf isn't at your door anymore, man. Hell, the wolf could never get past all your gated security, even if he could figure out which house you're in for the moment. Let go of the past."

Not for the first time, I reflected that only those who'd never had the opportunity to gain a healthy fear of the proverbial wolf made those kinds of statements. I doubted I'd ever get Eddie to understand how a lifetime of only just escaping that wolf, of always hearing its menacing growl in the background of every pleading phone call to the landlord or utility company, had fundamentally shaped me.

Fear of returning to the wretched uncertainty of poverty had rewired my DNA, imprinted on my mind, wound me up. Nothing was a given. Ask any person, any family living on the margins of survival and they'll tell you: All it takes is one roll of the dice, one ill-fated turn on the wheel of fate to reduce your life to ruins. One missed check, one unexpected expense, one badly timed crisis.

I doubted I could ever tell Eddie about the shame I'd felt after my mother went missing for four days before she resurfaced. My shame hadn't solely grown from the cause of her absence. I'd been ashamed because my first thought was wondering if I could afford to bury her if she'd died.

"Nick?"

I shook my head, returning to the present.

"Nick, you okay?" It was hard to miss the concern, the worry in his voice.

"I'm fine. But Eddie—this matters. I'm seeing it through."

"Fine. Are you back for the meeting tomorrow?" Eddie sounded resigned.

"Yeah. I'm flying in tomorrow, late afternoon. I've got a meeting tomorrow morning here. Last minute details."

That was a hell of an understatement. The prospect of seeing Zora again, without an audience, had me suppressing a myriad of impossible desires. I wanted answers from her. That's it.

I lie best when it's to myself.

Eddie exhaled noisily.

"We built this company together, Eddie. Every step of the way. You know I'd never drop the ball or risk our investment. You know you can trust me."

Silence on the line.

When Eddie came back, his voice was quieter. "My concerns aren't limited to business. I want to see this company thrive as much as you do, you know. But we're also friends."

"Here comes the sappy shit." I heaved a pretend sigh. I never missed an opportunity to bust his balls. But he was my friend, and one of the few people I trusted without reservation.

"You've got more money than God at this point, Nick. You're part of a community that appreciates you and all you try to do. If you haven't figured out how to be content with that, I don't know that there's anything I, or anyone, can say to you. I don't know what else you're looking for. I hope you find it, man. You know where to find me if you need anything. Bye."

He hung up.

I sat, phone still clenched against my ear, caught in the echoing vacuum of silence. I lowered the phone to the table and turned to stare out the rain-spotted window. Beyond was the same narrow two-lane road Zora and I had walked all those years ago. The same crack I'd taken care to avoid as a kid still zigzagged across the sidewalk. It was all the same—as if I had never left.

I'd never told Eddie about this town or my life in it before we met. Never told him how being scared and helpless as a kid made me crave stability, predictability. Being in control. And being back here reminded me all too well how it felt to be that kid again.

God, I needed to get out of this town before I lost my mind.

"Alright." Rebecca's voice sounded from the side, and I looked up in time to see her slide a plate of assorted glazed doughnuts under my nose. A cup of hot cider followed. "It's on me," she said with a wink. "Even though you're bigger than the Badcock's barn."

I stared at her. Mr. Badcock had a tiny hen house.

"Oh honey, Badcock replaced that henhouse with something much larger and fancier—a huge, gorgeous, modern barn. That's what I'm talking 'bout." She hit me on the shoulder.

"Ah. Okay."

The waitress leaned a hip against the opposite side of the booth. "You were always tall, but it's like you just . . ." Her eyes widened. "Hulked out."

I laughed lightly and took a bite of doughnut. It was damn good. It tasted like home, but the good memories. "I guess I did, Miss Rebecca. Haven't heard it put quite that way before, but it sounds pretty accurate."

"You remind me of that stripper in the movie. The really big one? Dark hair?"

I coughed. "Uh, stripper?"

One corner of her mouth went up in a sly smile. "Don't sound so shocked. I might look like an old lady to you, but this girl's still got a little oil left in her can."

I choked down the bit of doughnut caught in my windpipe.

What the hell was I supposed to say to that?

"You must take after your daddy's people," she said, lips pursed as she considered me with that same sideways tilt of her head. "God knows your mama was a tiny thing."

There was nothing I could offer in response, and I didn't have a mind to try. Unbidden, the voice of the town's resident gossip, Karen Smith, came to mind: *Do we even know who their people are?*

"Well, I can't tell you how glad I am that you're back. And I'm glad you had an opportunity to connect with Zora. I know she and her family must have been so happy to see you."

Seeing no need to correct her assumption, I only nodded, shoving more doughnut in my mouth so I couldn't answer.

"It's funny the way life turns out, isn't it? Zora and Jackson James are about to be married, and you look like you're doing well for yourself. You got a sweetheart, wherever you settled?"

Wait.

. . .

WAIT.

What. The. Fuck.

I braced my hands on the table, gulping down the entire mouthful of doughnut. "What did you say?"

Because there was no way she'd just said what I just thought she said.

Something in my eyes made her take a step back. "What, Zora and Jackson? They've been together for a minute now. They look so cute together. Both come from good stock." She gave a meek, apologetic shrug. "Families like each other, seems like a good match."

Come from good stock. Families like each other. Good match.

Fuck this town.

CHAPTER FOUR

Zora

"Oh, my God. Finally!"

I jumped back at the shouted words. The front door to my house suddenly swung inward before I had a chance to use my key. My work bag slipped from my shoulder and weighted the bend of my arm before it hit the porch with a heavy thud. I released my grip on the storm door, winced at the pulled muscle in my neck, straightened, and glared at the irritated woman framed in the doorway. In that moment, it was hard to imagine that a world existed where other people didn't live next door to their annoying, intrusive best friend who used her just-for-emergencies key way too freely.

"God, Zora. I was about to go out there and get you. How long were you planning to sit in your car all spaced out? Were you playing that depressing-ass jazz on repeat again?" Leigh pursed her lips. "And you look awful." Her gaze moved over me. "Come inside."

I let out a sigh, casting a pointed look to the other side of the duplex and her designated front door. "How gracious of you to welcome me into my own home. Did you forget where you live? Or did you start out drunk and somehow end up passed out in my living room again?"

Man. I sound like Fate, i.e. a bitch.

Her eyebrows went up. "What crawled up your ass?"

I closed my eyes. "Sorry. I've had a rough day. I'm not at my best."

She turned to head back inside the house. As usual, her short-legged Pomeranian, Felicia, was tucked under one arm. I stepped over the threshold and followed them in.

"I wasn't drunk that time, for your information. But I was tipsy enough to know I'd be better off spending the night with someone who could turn me over if I choked on my vomit in the middle of the night."

"You're my best friend. I'll always be here to turn you over. Even if you work my last nerve at times."

"Back at you, babe. And you best believe you've been sawing away at mine lately, what with your self-neglect and disappearing act."

I turned my back to her and closed and locked the door, fighting the urge to roll my eyes.

"I know you're over there rolling your eyes. And you have some nerve. You still owe me from that time you came over in your swimsuit asking if you could get by without shaving. My eyes still haven't recovered. Would it kill you to wax year-round? Does Jackson bring his own chainsaw when he goes down there?"

Despite myself, I chuckled. "I could've made it work," I said automatically, dropping my bag on the couch as I stepped from the living room to the kitchen. "The bottom was full coverage—" I stopped at the sight of my kitchen. Styrofoam containers, cottage cheese and yogurt tubs, Tupperware containers, and foil bundles covered my kitchen counters.

"What's going on? What is this?"

Leigh parked Felicia on the floor then planted a hand on her hip, head cocked as she aimed a "don't play dumb" look at me. "You should recognize it all. It's from your refrigerator. I've been trying to figure out where the smell is coming from, now that you apparently don't live here anymore."

I sniffed experimentally at the air and, sure enough, detected something pungent and vile. "I live here—"

"You're back to sleeping in your office again. No one's heard from you, your brother is worried—"

"Walker's worried about me?"

"Do you have another brother I don't know about? Stop repeating everything I say. Just listen. Your brother called me because he hasn't heard from you in over a week and he got worried. Said you were supposed to get something with the sink fixed with some guy in town. Then the plumber told him he never heard from you. Then I had to tell him I hadn't heard from you either and your car hasn't been here in three days so he's on his way over—"

I slapped my forehead as cumulative exhaustion settled over me like a weighted blanket. "He's coming over here? God, I feel awful. He's already so busy. Why didn't you just call me? On my cell, my desk phone at work?"

"Your voicemail at work is full. So is the one for your phone. I'd have emailed you if I thought that would work." Her Jersey accent was more pronounced now, as it always was when she was frustrated or angry. "I sent him a text when you pulled up, but he's still coming over to chew you out and fix the sink."

I turned away from her exasperated expression and returned to the living room to retrieve my phone from the work bag.

It was dead.

"Let me guess," Leigh said as I trudged back into the kitchen like penitent child. "You've been working on some super important deadline, probably a grant. So you put your phone on airplane mode. And then you said, 'What the hell? I have some wrinkled-ass pants and shirts here and a shitty couch to sleep on. I'll just stay here 'til it's done.' Even though we all keep asking you not to do that."

I released a sigh and slid onto the stool at the counter opposite her. It seemed the day from hell would never end. The last thing I needed was to rouse the irritation of my best friend and my slightly overbearing older brother.

"I'm sorry, Leigh."

"I don't know what you're trying to do, but you are not going to age me prematurely. Not happening."

I bit back a smile at the defiant tilt to her head. Leigh still looked eighteen rather than thirty. Her posture was aggressively erect and she moved like the graceful dance major she'd been when I'd met her as a transferring undergraduate student at Northwestern. She'd ultimately decided against dancing professionally, but she'd retained all the discipline and healthy habits that kept her lithe and lean. The tiny shorts and tank top screen-printed with the name of a local Knoxville band displayed the figure of someone who had an unhealthy—and therefore very healthy—obsession with working out. Her dark, shoulder-length hair shone from the hair spray that stiffened her roots at optimal elevation. Wide, blue eyes narrowed as she stepped closer.

"I'm glad you're alright, but do me a favor, okay? Invest in some decent self-care. Nothing else will matter if you're dead. I have to tell you that over and over, and you're supposed to be the brilliant researcher."

I shook my head, unable to tear my gaze from the faded Formica countertop. "Today was bad, Leigh."

She picked up a yipping Felicia and settled on a stool opposite me. Felicia stared at me from her perch in Leigh's lap with big, wet eyes. "How is it different from the usual suckitude? What happened?"

"Hello! Man on the premises!" The deep baritone boomed the announcement from the front door, accompanied by the triple chirp of the alarm. "Anyone within the sound of my voice should be fully clothed."

I closed my eyes. "Is there anyone I *didn't* give my key to?"

A small smile tugged at one corner of Leigh's mouth. "He's still scarred from that time he used his key without knocking."

"Why would we have had clothes on in the dead heat of summer, when it was hot as an oven?"

"Because," a familiar voice said from behind me, "civilized people turn on the AC and walk around with their clothes on."

I shook my head at my brother. His quiet brown eyes reflected a solemnity that belied his jocular tone. His gaze moved over me in an all-encompassing sweep. Gone was the crisp suit, his usual uniform as vice president of our family's bank. Instead, he wore a pair of jeans and an old white T-shirt. He set the toolbox and bucket on the floor.

"I don't have air conditioning. You know that."

He folded his arms. "Uh-huh. I also know the plan was not for you to still be in this house. This was supposed to be a revenue-generating property, remember? Dad told you to buy it, renovate it, sell it or rent it out. Instead, you're still here dealing with the same repairs that apparently haven't been fixed. And living with your eternal roommate."

I didn't miss the way his gaze moved over to Leigh and lingered on her bare legs before rising and resting on her face.

I slid down on the stool, weighted from the impact of yet another failure landing on my shoulders. He was right. I'd had every intention of renovating and unloading this house at first sight. My father had pushed, as was his way, enumerating all the reasons why it was a good investment. Fresh off a postdoc and facing the frightening prospect of moving back to Green Valley, I'd thought it couldn't be the worst thing that happened to me, all things considered. Even if the ancient, shadowy house looked like it hosted untold deaths from murder, plague, and consumption.

But sometime between signing the sale papers and exploring the house's large, open rooms with their creaking original wood floors, I'd deviated from my clearly-outlined plan.

Within a few months, I was in love with the house's eccentricities and its little surprises, like the distinctive crown molding patterns and original, untouched woodwork. So when the hospital had an opening for a Child Life Specialist, I sent the job requisition to my best friend, who just happened to be desperate for a change of pace. Of course, I offered use of the house's unoccupied side until she got acclimated with the town and found a place of her own.

After a while, I started questioning why I had to get rid of either the house or Leigh. She was one of my favorite people, she understood me more than most people ever did, her rent checks deposited just fine, and we had fun when I was home. As for the house, I came to accept its deficiencies as part of its character, like an aging beauty queen who, having retained all of her grace and charm, sometimes required assistance to climb off the couch.

Thank God for my brother, who usually supported my questionable choices with a minimum of fussing.

Usually.

Leigh smirked at Walker and leaned against the counter, chin propped up on her fist. "You know you love me. Don't think you're fooling anyone, pretending you're here for Zora. I know you missed me." She turned back to the counter to snatch a piece of paper towel from the roll.

Watching the hungry expression move over my brother's face as his gaze tracked the curve of her backside, I wasn't sure Leigh was wrong. She wasn't exactly covert in her appreciation of him either as she turned back, squinting up at him after conducting her own thorough perusal of his tall, solid form. The air grew thick with sexual tension and I rolled my eyes heavenward.

After the day I'd had, after seeing Ni—*him,* I didn't have it in me to play audience for my best friend and my brother's constant willthey-won't-they (spoiler alert, they never did) flirtation.

"Why are you here again?" I rubbed my forehead.

Walker seemed to rip his eyes from Leigh, his stare softening. "Your sink? Let me help, Z."

A reluctant rush of affection warmed my bruised heart. As chaotic as my brother's life was, he took the time to check on his wayward baby sister. He looked so much like my father: same shade of chestnut brown skin, same deep-set dark eyes, same dimpled jaw. But there was enough of my mother there to soften his otherwise roughcast face. Walker and I shared the same freckle-dotted high cheekbones and fuller bottom lip.

Fortunately, he'd inherited very little of my father's hard-nosed pragmatism and had more than a decent dose of my mother's nurturing streak. My sisters and I all agreed he did his damnedest to hide it, though.

"Walker, I'm fine, and I'm sorry you drove all the way over here for nothing. You didn't have to come over, but I appreciate the sentiment. If I ever think you're dead in your house, I will return the favor."

He ambled over, gaze fixed on mine, and roughly palmed my forehead the same way he'd been doing since I was a little kid and he was the older, annoying dictator of a brother tattling on me for every damn thing.

"It's more likely you'd be dead in your office," he quipped, wrenching my head back so far my neck threatened to snap. "I thought I'd stop here to gather clues first, just in case."

I slapped at his hand while Leigh looked on, shaking her head at our antics. She hopped up, resettled Felicia, and went back to the task of my fridge.

"I've got enough shit on my plate without having to worry about claiming your corpse."

"Oh, please." Leigh turned back to level him with a smirk. "Nobody wants to hear about your so-called hard-knock life, Golden Boy. What, you're overwhelmed with being photographed for billboard ads? You'll need to wait your turn to unburden yourself. Zora looks like she just might win this round of Who's Suffered More."

Walker scowled at her back. "Debatable. But if the way she looks and smells is any indication—"

"Hey! I was at the gym earlier today! I worked out!"

"We'll have to see," he continued, unperturbed by me pinching what little fat I could grab from his side. "Usual terms? Loser buys dinner for all?"

"Might as well." Disgust sat heavy in Leigh's voice as she tossed a container of indeterminate contents into the trash. "There's no chance of salvaging anything from this landfill."

"Deal. Whatever I want?" Walker sounded hopeful.

Leigh swept the contents of the counters into the open mouth of the trash can, throwing an arched look back at him as she did so. Felicia sniffed the air around the trash can before scurrying away, toenails clattering against the hardwood floor as she headed into the relative comfort of the living room. "Confident, aren't you? Why don't you go first? We'll let Zora go last—my money's on her."

Walker let out a shallow sigh, rocked back on his heels as he stared at the ceiling. Leigh folded her arms and smirked.

"So, it's like this," he began, repeatedly running an agitated hand over his low-cut fade. "I, uh—"

"Here we go with some bullshit." Leigh shook her head. "And from the sound of it, it has something to do with a woman."

"That's just part of it." Walker looked as if he wanted to knock Leigh off the stool.

"Okay, Don Juan. What's the problem?"

"This girl I've been, uh, seeing. She wants to talk—"

"Who?" I interjected. "Do I know her?"

"No."

"Let me guess." Leigh's smile was slow, feline, and designed to infuriate. "She wants to have 'The Talk.' To find out what you guys are, where you stand. Because apparently that's not clear to her. Am I right?"

Walker scowled. "More or less."

I studied my brother, hoping against hope he wasn't about to say what I suspected was coming next. "Okay. So, what part of that is difficult for you right now? I mean, do you think you'll have a hard time expressing—"

"She's sweet, isn't she?" Leigh inclined her head toward me, as if sharing some secret insight with Walker. "Still has her delusions about her scandalous big brother. Let's get to the heart of the matter here, shall we? Won't be that hard and shouldn't take too long. Do you like this girl, this woman, Walker? Yes or no?"

He hesitated, tucking his hands into the back pockets of his jeans. "I mean—"

"Yes or no."

"Well, compared to—"

"—That's a no."

I sat upright, agog, as I stared at my brother. "Did you just say, 'compared to?' As in, you can't make up your mind because you've been—"

Walker sent me a vaguely apologetic look. "I just don't have those kinds of feelings for her, Z."

"We're all adults here," Leigh said in a sweet, falsely placating tone. "Let the man speak. I think we'll all learn something. We always learn something when Walker speaks, don't we?" I ignored the mocking grin she sent me.

He glared at her. "No shade, but compared to the other women I've been seeing . . ." He winced.

I shook my head at my brother. "So, let me get this straight. You'd be fine sleeping with her indefinitely, even though you know you don't have those kinds of feelings for her?"

Walker nodded in slow motion. "Yeah?"

God, men could be the *worst*. Even my own brother, apparently.

"I see. Seems the decent thing to do would be to tell her that, then."

"I agree." Leigh nodded at him. "Preferably the next time your dick is in her mouth. You know, so she can give you *her* honest, candid feedback." She bared her teeth, then brought them together with a loud *click*.

He glared at her. "I didn't make any promises. I'm upfront with everyone that I'm just trying to have fun and I don't want anything serious."

"What's the other thing?" I motioned for him to get on with it before Leigh started chewing on his hide again. "You've earned no sympathy from us so far."

"Where's your compassion, Z?"

"I'm at my limit with dicks."

"That statement deserves a few follow-up questions," Leigh said, spluttering with laughter. "Like, how many, and where—"

I threw a balled-up napkin at her.

"The other thing is your sister."

Leigh and I stopped laughing and turned back to Walker.

"Uh-oh." Leigh's eyes were bright. "Trouble in the kingdom?"

"Shut up," Walker spat, and there was enough of an edge to his tone that I leaned forward. He *was* upset.

I held up a hand to Leigh, signaling for her to ease up a bit. My twin sister, Tavia, had been, until recently, content working in New York's financial district, managing a hedge fund. I wouldn't feel so sympathetic watching as my brother's previously uncontested inheritance was threatened if I wasn't so familiar with my sister's bullying tactics. She'd decided to join the family business after all, breezing into town with little warning, announcing her intent to widen the scope of Leffersbee Financial by offering her Wharton-sharpened financial advice to corporations and small businesses. Walker would've been fine with that, if that's all it was, and their separate roles were clearly defined. But we were talking about Tavia. So, the situation was anything but simple. From what I'd heard, each workday brought another challenge, another skirmish, as the two jockeyed for position.

All while my father sat back and watched.

"What happened with Tavia, Walker?"

"Said the decisions I'd been making—with Dad's backing, mind you—made others in the industry view us as stagnant. That if I took risks, was more aggressive about growing us . . ." He broke off, shaking his head. I knew my brother well enough to know that he was beyond angry; he had probably swallowed enough frustration and irritation that it was already bottlenecked inside him.

"I'm sorry, Walker."

"Z, if she wasn't our sister—" he cut himself off, seemed to gather a deep breath. "Anyway, one of the tellers came to the back and said customers could hear the yelling from the lobby—"

My jaw dropped. "Yelling? Y'all were *yelling*? Loud enough that people could hear from the front?"

Walker closed his eyes. "Z. You know I'm not that dude. Raising my voice, getting heated like that."

"That's not you."

"Right. And truth be told, it was mostly her getting loud."

I bit my lip. I considered myself pretty easygoing but I could recount more than a few instances where Tavia had pushed me to the edge and I'd lost my shit.

"Alright," Leigh said, briskly. "Walker gets no points for his general messiness and multiple liaisons. We're issuing sympathy points to the poor woman who obviously doesn't know what's she's gotten herself into. But five points awarded for the usual sister strife."

"You next," I ordered Leigh, sliding down from the stool to head to the cupboards for a glass. "I think I've got Diet Coke. Anyone want some?"

"Don't offer us anything from that fridge unless you're handing out antibiotics, too."

"Ha ha. What's your story for the day?" I filled the glass with tap water and rested against the sink.

Leigh yawned and stretched. Walker watched with rapt attention as her back arched. "Another tit-grabber. I was using my Pete the Patient doll to explain what's going to happen during this kid's surgery next week and this little goober kept grabbing my breast."

Walker looked like he was fighting back a smile. "Sound effects?"

"Worse. He kept saying, 'soft,' in this weird voice. With every squeeze. Mom tried to tell him to stop, started giving him this speech about boundaries and body parts that he's not paying any significant attention to at four years old. And you know what he says?"

Walker bites. "What?"

"He says, 'Like Daddy! See?' and squeezes me again while saying, 'soft.'"

I bit my lip.

"The mom was mortified. The dad got up and left the room. And that's not all of it. The kid's hands had ketchup on them, so I spent the day walking around with bloody-looking, child-size handprints on my boob."

"I will never understand how you ended up working with kids when you eat them for nourishment."

"If only your mother had eaten *you* . . ." Leigh's expression softened as she turned to me. "By the way, thanks for all those Etch A Sketches you left in my kitchen last week. They really helped out. We haven't gotten the usual donations from our toy manufacturers and our stash needed a shot in the arm. You didn't pay too much, did you?"

I waved away her question. "I'm just glad it helped. Let me know what's next on the list."

Walker looked between us. "I wanna help, too. Tell me what's next on your list, Leigh, and I'll get it you. Although," his expression turned smug, "you get zero points. What you've described is an occupational hazard. I'd be willing to throw some points the kid's way, though. He's the one having surgery." He turned to me, his expression expectant. "Ok, Z. You're up. Spill."

I took a sip from the glass, wishing it was something stronger. Like kerosene.

"Well, I had a surprise visit in my office today. Couple of university officials came by . . . with an old boyfriend of mine in tow."

Leigh's head tilted. "Old boyfriend from how long ago?" Her foot beat a frantic beat against the counter island. "Gym Rat Poet? Finnish Foreskin?"

Walker grimaced. "Jesus."

She grinned back at him. "What? Sometimes good things come with uncircumcised packages," her grin widened, "as Zora found out."

I paused for effect, then let the bomb drop. "Nick Armstrong."

It took them both a minute to react.

Walker leaned back, mouth open.

Leigh exploded. "What?!"

"Yes," I confirmed.

"Mr. Houdini himself?"

Walker raised an eyebrow. "You have a nickname for everyone?"

"He's the original disappearing act," she sputtered.

"What's my nickname?"

"Trust me, you don't want to know." She planted both hands on the counter, leaning closer to me. "Oh, he's back is he? Did you tell him we saw him with that red-headed ho—"

"Leigh." Fatigue weighed heavily on my shoulders. "We don't know that she was . . . indiscriminate. It's not fair to pin the blame on her when we don't know what Nick told her."

She waggled her head from side to side. "Fine. Ultimately, it was Nick who cheated—"

"Wait. Pause." Walker held up a hand, eyes closed. "Zora. You had contact with Nick after he left? What do you mean, he cheated?"

Leigh reached into the back pocket of her jeans, producing a leopard-printed hair clip. "Pay attention," she told Walker, winding her hair into knot at the base of her skull. "Houdini disappears one night and leaves behind a letter telling Zora he's sorry, but he has to go. Says he has to get himself together, is leaving for her own good, and he'll fix things when he gets back." She turned to me. "That about right?"

I nodded. "Yep."

"And I know all this already." Walker crossed his arms over his chest.

"So, your sister transfers to Northwestern. Has the good fortune to meet me." She tapped her chest with one of her long polished black nails. "Likes the school, loves the program, but won't go out and play because she's still pining after this guy that just disappeared into the ether. So, I told her we could for sure find him with an in-depth internet search."

Walker's gaze bounced between us. "And you did."

"Yep. My cousin is a librarian. She can sniff out anyone's footprint online."

I picked up the story, seeing the events play in my mind's eye. "It took some doing, but we found a lead. The school paper at University of Michigan was online. There was an article about Nick, something about an engineering contest he won."

"It came with a cash prize," Leigh inserted. "I can't remember how much, but it was a significant amount. Certainly enough for him to afford a phone call back home to let your family know how he was doing, or even a plane ticket."

"And in the article, they mentioned that he worked at a coffee shop near campus. So, Leigh called the coffee shop and found out what hours he worked."

"And then I shoved Zora in my car and we drove the five hours to

Ann Arbor so she could finally see this clown and demand some answers." Leigh grimaced and scratched at the back of her head. "We never spoke to him, but we got an answer."

Even now, all these years later, the memory smarted. Nick, somehow even bigger and even more handsome after just two years. Healthy and whole. He'd worn an apron printed with the coffee shop's logo that emphasized his substantial frame.

He also wore a redhead.

I remembered every single moment of the disastrous afternoon. The shop had emptied of the afternoon crowd. Leigh and I had just made our way over a snowbank and onto the sidewalk. I'd shivered with nerves. Would he want to see me again? Would our connection still exist, or feel the same as before? Would he have a reasonable excuse for breaking my heart by not calling after all this time? Would he finally end the mystery of why he left and just *tell* me what happened, for God's sake?

Then Leigh's hand had captured my wrist, squeezing hard. I'd stopped beside her, my gaze following the direction of her nod. From our angle, we could see inside into the interior of the shop, past the front counter and into the front opening of the kitchen.

Nick lounged against a wall, a tiny red-headed woman plastered against his front. He didn't step away when she reached up and gathered a handful of his shirt. He didn't protest when she pulled him down until the difference in their heights disappeared, leaving his face mere inches from hers.

Leigh's grip on my wrist tightened even more as we both stood, statues on the sidewalk. Waiting.

For the rest of my life, I would forever remember how the bitter chill of winter snatched my breath, turning it to transparent wisps of clouds. How the frigid bite of snow underfoot numbed my feet through the soles of my impractical fashion boots. I would never forget how both Leigh and I gasped when the redhead closed the distance between their mouths.

I'd been waiting for him, for any word from him. I'd put my life on hold, like a dumbass.

Leigh related the story to Walker while I stood clutching my glass of water in a death grip, frozen by the remembered horror. "She cried half the way home."

Walker's eyes grew hooded. His mouth tightened as he flicked a glance in my direction.

"Not half the way," I protested. She was probably right, but I couldn't go down as being *that* pathetic.

Leigh's expression turned fierce. "And I'll tell you now what I told you then. *Screw* that guy. Screw *all* of them, including," she gestured back at Walker, "fuckboys who can't bother to be honest with the women they're dating, let alone *themselves*." She gave a *harrumph* that would have made me laugh under better circumstances. "All while you're sitting in the dorm alone, being a good little girl. All faithful and true while that asshole is Frenching women in the storeroom. And I hope you told him exactly that when you saw him today. Did you?"

When I hesitated, she groaned. "Aww. Shit. What exactly happened?"

I told them all of it, beginning with Nick's sudden reappearance in my office doorway and ending with Erin's exit.

Leigh's mouth hung open. She held up her hand. "Am I to understand this man showed up after all these years, with no warning, and at some point you find yourself ass-up in front of him? While some recording plays about how you can't get yourself off?"

"It's a training—"

Walker shook his head. "Wait until Jackson hears about this."

Leigh smirked, raising a brow at me. "Do we really care about what Jackson thinks? He's never here."

God. My life had finally imploded. And there was even more devastation to come.

"I've looked online." We both turned to see Walker holding his head in one hand.

"You did?" I asked.

"I did. I hated seeing you so upset. But your librarian friend did better than I could. I have never found a trace of a Nick Armstrong."

"He changed his name." I shared a look with my sweet, sweet brother.

"Of course he did." Leigh padded out of the kitchen, then returned with the iPad from my bag in her hand. "What's the turd's last name now?"

"Rossi."

She resumed her seat, fingers flying across the surface of the iPad. Then suddenly, her eyebrow lifted toward her hairline. "Looks like Nick's been a busy boy."

My stomach spasmed at the obvious surprise on her face. I walked over to her on numb feet, barely registering my own movement.

"He's . . . done well for himself. Very well." Leigh turned the iPad around and nudged it in my direction. We crowded in together.

It was a magazine article in Forbes entitled, *"He Did it His Way."* A photo of New Nick topped the page. In it, he lounged on a stone stairwell, elbows braced on his knees, strong forearms resting against his shins. A stunning view of a metropolitan city in the valley below served as the backdrop. From his elevated height, Nick resembled a lord of the realm. I took in the artfully tousled dark hair and the stubborn cowlick I'd stood on tiptoe to rearrange for him so many times. I stared into the depths of those vivid green eyes, searching for some sign, some clue to this man's identity.

"Software engineering," Leigh said. "Huh."

I scanned the rest of the article. Nick had gone to the University of Michigan for software engineering in undergrad. Three years later he'd developed a powerful predictive tool which, with the aid of self-reported patient data and claims information, accurately forecasted catastrophic health events. A leading insurance company had acquired the algorithm for a reportedly undisclosed amount, but Forbes' estimate was downright astonishing. Nick had gone on to establish his own company, working with a team of developers, engineers, actuaries, and clinicians to develop other groundbreaking innovations in health care technology. "The goal," Forbes quoted him as saying, "is to empower patients to take charge of their own health with technology."

Oh, Nick. I realized I had the tablet in a death grip and moderated my hold. I thought of my denied grant application and all the other work I'd attempted at the university. I shouldn't be surprised that the past motivated us to act in such similar ways. Same purpose, divergent roads.

My head was inches away from Leigh's as I leaned closer to enlarge the font and advance the text. Could she hear my heart slamming against my chest?

The article attempted to chronicle his past, which Nick rejected. "I'm from a small town in Tennessee, right outside of Knoxville. Nothing more interesting to report beyond that." The reporter detailed his net worth and investment portfolio in painful detail before the article ended on a promising, almost prophetic note: *Nick Rossi will revolutionize the way health care is delivered*, the author concluded. The sentiment was repeated in a pull-out quote right above a photo of Nick standing in a power pose, legs widespread, arms crossed, face stoic.

Despite myself, I felt a stirring of concern that countered any sense of self preservation. *Who did you become, Nick? And what did it cost you?*

"Damn, Z." Leigh shook her head, eyes closed. "By all rights, this guy should be a stooped-over accountant with the eyesight of a mole. Justice demands it. But no. I mean, I absolutely hate him for your sake. But all this big dick energy . . . even *I'm* getting taken in."

Walker scowled at her. "Do you know what the word 'brother' means?"

"You're not *my* brother." Her eyes burned into mine. "Zora, what are you going to do? Are you going to see him tomorrow?"

"Yeah." I decided there really was no alternative. "I'll find out what he wants, what he needs, so I can be done with this. With him."

"Good." She gave a decisive nod. "Because you need a do-over. And hopefully you can get some closure in the process."

Closure? No. "There's no such thing as closure, okay?" I huffed. "That's just the excuse people use when they don't want to accept something's over. I don't need the redundancy of words to prove what someone's actions have already shown me. We were eighteen when he left. It's old history. Case already closed."

"So . . . you're not at all wondering how it all started? Why he just disappeared into thin air that way?"

"No," I lied. "I moved on, and so did he. Obviously. I'm not that girl anymore. I'm happy. I've reached my goals. I'm self-actualized."

"Alright, Oprah. But tomorrow, you redeem yourself. You make him swallow his tongue. This is *Rocky IV*. Be Ivan Drago and *break* his fine ass."

"This is truly disturbing." We both whirled to find Walker standing behind us, arms crossed. He grimaced at us both. "You do realize that's the movie where Apollo Creed dies in the ring, right? Are all women psychos like you two? Are they all sitting around plotting on innocent men?"

Leigh huffed. "You've never been innocent a day in your life. And neither is this guy."

Walker narrowed his eyes at her. "If what you saw was really what happened, he was wrong. But you know, they *were* a little young to be so serious—"

"Oh, shut up, Walker." The last thing I needed was for my brother to revive an ancient list of our parents' Favorite Talking Points about my past. "And mind your own business."

Leigh whooped and slapped me a high five. "Atta girl. You had a bad day. Your slip was showing at the worst possible time. We'll get you ready, you'll get the upper hand, and this time *you* dismiss the guy from your life. He's yesterday's news. Tomorrow's an opportunity for a new headline."

CHAPTER FIVE

Nick

I trailed Zora down the hospital's hallway, forcing my eyes away from her alluring backside.

Growing up, Zora had never been able to walk in heels. But apparently, at some point, she'd gotten the hang of it.

Dr. Leffersbee met me in the lobby as previously arranged by Nellie. She coolly executed a brisk handshake, and murmured my name as if we were complete strangers.

Gone was the free, unrestrained, Lycra-wearing version of Zora. Her wild curls had been tamed into a fancy bun. Without her usual dark mane, all my attention was drawn to the bittersweet chocolate of her eyes and the lips she'd slicked with something dark red and tempting.

Before yesterday, it had been twelve long years. I don't know what I'd expected, but I hadn't expected this. Hadn't expected my heart to crash around in my chest, or my lungs to stall.

I wanted to touch her.

My fingers itched to tangle in her hair. Was the curve of her lip as soft as I remembered? I managed to stop staring at her gorgeous, full mouth when I realized she'd asked me a question.

"Pardon?"

Zora blinked at me once, her dispassionate stare becoming a glare. "I said, will Nellie be joining us?"

"No."

Nellie scared me. And she had an unnatural number of teeth.

Zora had then turned and walked away, rebuffing any additional discussion. Armored in silence, she stalked down the hallway, occasionally throwing a tersely-worded explanation over her shoulder. I followed behind her, off-balance. As a seasoned CEO at the helm of a billion-dollar empire, I'd made a name for our company by dominating my competitors. And yet, I couldn't work up the nerve to stop Zora and break our momentum. Slow her down. Stop what was rapidly becoming an unfunny farce.

Why hadn't I planned better for *this*? I wasn't prepared for all these old *feelings*, for everything to resurface as soon as I laid eyes on her. I hadn't anticipated the undertow that robbed my mind of all rational thought and stole my power of speech.

I trailed her down the corridors, closing my nose against the all-too-familiar hospital smell, the antiseptic bite, and did my best to suppress my memories of this place.

It was far more pleasant to divert my awareness to Zora's legs in heels.

The engineer in me appreciated how all the disparate components collaboratively powered the engine of her sexy gait. Shapely legs, strong calves, the artificial stretch of her feet, the deep, natural arch of her back. It all produced the hip-dipping, captivating sway of her ass.

Hypnotizing.

I attempted to redirect my gaze. It didn't work. I needed a distraction from the seductive metronome of her hips.

"Which department is your lab set up in, exactly?"

She glanced back at me, her expression flat. "A few places."

Yep. This was going well.

"Listen, it's not my intent to impose. I told Nellie I'd be fine just chatting over a cup of coffee, but she insisted I come see your setup."

Dear God, was I *tattling* on Nellie?

She didn't look back, but I caught the drift of her words as we neared the end of the floor. "It's fine. No problem. I want you to have whatever you need to get your project off the ground."

And leave, was the clear subtext.

I nodded even though she couldn't see me, taking care to avoid the tiny, scrubs-clad woman who detoured around me with a scowl. I wasn't a fan of hospitals. Especially this one. But I could admit that as hospitals went, this one wasn't awful. Abundant light filtered into the hallway through tall windows. High-gloss hardwood floors and framed art of smiling patients contributed to the somewhat cheerful environment.

It was cheery enough that I wasn't immediately reminded of the night I'd rushed to this hospital after my mother's car accident. That visit hadn't been too bad. Scary as hell, but she'd recovered. Although . . . had she? The pain from her bad back had never really subsided. That pain had led us on down a terrible path and another visit to the ER that changed our lives forever.

I shook my head. I needed to concentrate. Couldn't afford to let the past distract me.

Signs marked the end of the hospital and the entrance to the professional building. I moderated my long stride to match her short, deliberate one. After a tense elevator ride in which we both stared ahead at the reflective interior of the doors in complete silence, we finally reached a mostly-full waiting room comprised of women and one lone man. I had a brief impression of brightly colored posters demonstrating various stages of pregnancy and advertising baby paraphernalia before we were on the other side of door, stopping at the nurses' station.

"Hey, Sarah." Zora greeted a slender, red-headed woman in scrubs with a smile.

How easily she thawed for someone else.

"Zora." The woman's eyes widened as she took me in, then moved back to Zora as she approached us. "Hey, girl! Did I miss something? Did you have a patient recording on the schedule?"

"No. I just came by to show off our setup."

Sarah enveloped Zora in a hug. I watched with interest as the hug lasted for more than several seconds with Sarah whispering something in Zora's ear. Zora murmured something I didn't catch in response.

"Well, I'm happy to see you, no matter the reason." Sarah held Zora out at arm's length, grasping her by the shoulders. "No bribes today? Nothing from the Donner Bakery?"

"I'll be ready next time. What do you guys want?"

"Rings of Fire," an invisible voice supplied. I looked around and identified a white-coated man seated at the nurses' desk as the source.

"I'm on it," Zora said.

I had to look away from her smile.

That's not for you.

"Do you . . . eat those?" I couldn't help but ask. "Sounds like something you'd treat medicinally. At the other end."

"They're muffins." Sarah laughed. "Damn good muffins. We keep saying we're going to cut back but Zora keeps bringing them, so . . ."

"Right. Blame it on me."

Sarah's bold gaze dragged from my feet and back up to my face. "And who's your friend here, Zora?" She smiled, slow and sly.

Zora deflated a bit. "This is Mr. Rossi," she said. All warmth evaporated from her voice. "His company—"

"It's Nick," I interjected, feeling irritated that she'd called me *Mr. Rossi*. Reaching out to shake Sarah's hand, I added, "We go way back, Zora and I. We're friends. Were friends."

Zora cleared her throat, not looking at me. "Mr. Rossi's company is working with the School of Medicine and the hospital to introduce a telemedicine app. They are interested in the communication training we do with our docs."

"Well, hiya, Nick." Sarah didn't seem to know whether to smile or frown, her gaze moving between Zora and me. "Let us know if you need any help."

"Thanks, Sarah." Zora gave the nurse a bright smile and they traded another glance I couldn't quite decipher before she peered down the hallway ahead of us. "Six open?"

"Yep, clinic's light today."

Zora made a motion over her shoulder, gesturing for me to follow as she advanced down the hallway.

"Thanks, Sarah." I nodded and Sarah nodded right back, crossing her arms with a smirk.

Down the corridor, turning into the second doorway, I found Zora standing in front of a paper-sheeted examination table. I hesitated as I crossed the threshold to the examination room, suddenly on alert. Were those . . . stirrups?

"So . . . this is . . ."

"What it looks like." She pasted a thin smile on her face, then set her bag on the computer monitor-topped desk.

"Nellie says she told you about the curriculum and the video recordings we do to help coach our docs. I know Legal is addressing the implications of sharing the curriculum with you. Once that's all worked out, I'll provide you with a copy."

I nodded, took a cautious step toward her. "Sounds good. So . . . this is your lab? This is . . . interesting."

Her expression didn't change, but I didn't miss the small step backwards she took. One of her shoulders lifted as she gave a seemingly dismissive wave. "I don't know about interesting. It's not much of a tour. Just these two cameras."

I took a breath. She was finally speaking to me, face-to-face. The two of us were alone. Here was an opening, an entry point. Everything, all that had happened, all that was unspoken between us, weighted my next words.

"Zora."

She didn't look at me.

"Zora, please. We need to talk."

Her mouth twisted. "What do you want to talk about?"

"When I . . . when I left—"

"Let me rephrase that. What would you like to discuss that is appropriate for work acquaintances?"

Acquaintances. Considering all we once were, "acquaintance" had an ugly ring to it. But I'd been the one to create the distance that separated us now. Wasn't it my fault we were practically strangers? I'd walked away, and in those early years I'd stayed away, reasoning that I hadn't wanted to hurt her by being who I was, or who I wasn't, or because of what I didn't have to offer.

And then she'd sent back the ring and told me to stay gone . . .

Admittedly, my sudden reappearance in her office yesterday had been sloppy, rushed—a rookie move. You'd think a twelve-year separation would have given me some impulse control where she was concerned. It hadn't. I hadn't been able to stop myself.

"Acquaintances? Not colleagues?" I asked quietly.

She stepped farther away, now at the head of the examining table while I stood at the foot. She didn't look at me; she kept her head craned at the opposite wall. "There's the camera."

Ignoring the tightness in my chest, I followed her pointing finger to an upper corner of the ceiling. The continuity of the crown molding was broken by a flat, silver panel with a darkened screen. I walked over to inspect it.

I swallowed around the mass in my throat. "I wouldn't have noticed it."

"That's the point. There's the other one." I turned in time to see her nod toward a twin panel on the opposite wall.

I was almost certain they were exactly the same, but I walked over anyway, wanting to reduce the distance between us.

"I'm sorry about the way things happened yesterday. It wasn't my intent to surprise you."

"There's a capture station down the hall. I can get you a copy of the protocol for the study. It details all the nuts and bolts. We educate both the doctor and patient on the purpose of the research and how we're using their data. Then we get consent. Our team can view the interaction between the patient and doctor as it happens. We record it all and turn the camera's eye away during examinations. I can show you the capture station when we leave."

I turned to see Zora's eyes on my face, her gaze full of something

I couldn't identify. Then her eyes met mine and her expression blanked.

"I'd like that. To see it."

Painful silence stretched between us. Zora didn't seem to feel any obligation to fill it. She crossed her arms, kept her eyes averted from mine.

"So . . ." *Damn. That's the best I can do?*

"Any questions?" The brittle, upbeat quality of her voice didn't match her pinched expression. Her grip along her crossed forearms tightened.

I couldn't do this.

"Zora. I'm sorry."

Her expression didn't change. "For what, exactly?"

I hesitated. If ever there was a layered question, it was this one. "For everything. None of this is ideal, it's not the way I wanted things to happen, but . . . It's so good to see you. I—I missed you—"

She held up a trembling hand. "Nick. I'm glad you're alive. That you've been okay all this time. But I'm here in a professional capacity. It's what you asked for and it's what other people determined should happen. So, I'd be grateful if you would just . . . let me do my job. Let me give you the information you requested. Whether you really want it or not, I don't know—and I don't care. I said I would do it." She met my stare full on and concluded, "And I keep my word."

That barb hit its mark. And I remembered.

"We'll get out this town forever, Z. You and me. We won't even look back. And then it'll just be us. Forever. I promise."

I'd been young when I murmured those words into her hair. Eighteen and oblivious to everything that lay ahead. I hadn't kept my promise in the end. And the shame of that never left me.

I nodded, clearing my throat of the continued tightness and working to school my expression. "I do want the information. We're piloting this app for the first time and now we're realizing all the blind spots in our competency team."

She shifted her weight between both feet, coming to a lean

against the side of the nearby sink. Her feet hurt, I realized. The heels had gotten to her after all.

"The actual programming of the app, working out security and identifying ways to merge the datasets is easy. It's what we do, it's who we are." I settled into one of the visitor chairs and slid the little rolling stool in her direction, hoping she'd take the opportunity to rest her feet.

She ignored it, instead shifting to the side and now leaning against the examining table. I looked away, trying not to watch as the stretchy fabric of her otherwise staid black skirt crept higher above her knees. If that little shirt under her blazer rose up just enough . . .

I fought against the wish, frowning as I continued, "We thought we'd accounted for everything else and things would take their natural course. But now I'm aware of the deficiencies. We want our staff clinicians to have the same communication training you've developed for the docs here. I'm new to all of this. I'd be grateful if you could continue to lend us your expertise."

"Fine."

I eyed her grimace of discomfort. Why didn't she just sit down? *Still as stubborn as I'd remembered.* "We should start from the beginning. Are there basic requirements that we need to be watching for? Rudimentary quality assurance?"

"A few. There's the basics. Things one might think are basic, anyway, but are easily forgotten when you're a doc running behind in a stressful, busy clinic. Maybe more so if you're talking to someone through a screen."

I leaned back. At least she was talking to me, and God knew the project needed her help. "Like what?"

She ticked off items on her fingers. "Greeting the person upon entering the room. Using their name. Not interrupting. Then, starting with collaborative goal setting. Not just asking the patient why they came and immediately launching into the diagnostic questions, but inviting them to decide what topics will be covered during the visit. Avoiding medical jargon. Responding empathetically to concerns. Including the patient in decision-making about the treatment plan."

"Okay." This was a good start *and* she was incredibly beautiful.

"You'll get the hang of it. We have a team that manages our coaching here. Once you better understand the expectations of hospitals like ours, you'll know what to expect."

"Fair enough. But why the video cameras? Can't you observe and tick off those behaviors with something less intrusive, like audio recording? Couldn't you get the gist of what's going on without the whole Big Brother vibe?"

"Verbal communication—what's said out loud—is only half the picture. Less, even. The stuff we say only accounts for about ten percent of what we communicate. The other ninety percent? Transmitted nonverbally."

I studied her still-crossed arms, pointedly lifting a brow at the way she'd positioned herself as far away from me as possible on the other side of the examining table. "You don't say."

She ignored this. "Nonverbal communication gives us a window into more subtly expressed attitudes. Shows us what's happening on the conscious and unconscious levels and helps us to study things like implicit racial bias, weight bias, and synchrony."

"Synchrony? I think I read about this in a men's health magazine. They claimed matching nonverbal behavior with a new date could increase the odds of—" Seeing her expression darken I hastily amended, "A happy ever after."

She shook her head at me, with that same disapproving scowl she'd used since we were kids. "When two people are in sync communicatively, mirroring each other, moving in tandem, it's like watching Ginger and Fred dancing. It's an unconscious thing. People are often unaware it's happening. But that's where the magic is. We're more likely to synchronize with others that we're in a positive relationship with, who we want to be in a positive relationship with or who we trust." Something flickered in her eyes, then disappeared. "That matters in a clinical setting like this because we know that synchrony between a patient and clinician is associated with more collaborative decision-making and better recall of information. Studying nonverbal communication tells us the story of that process."

I took a moment to take in our placement. Me, sitting. Her, standing, far away, shifting her weight from one foot to the other in obvious discomfort. Abruptly, she turned away from me, as if the diagram of IUD placement on the opposite wall required all her attention.

Who we *trust*.

An old memory slammed into me. *A younger us. One of the million times she sat in the V of my legs, head tucked against my chest. She leaned back to smile at me, eyes full of trust, as she offered me a bite of her sandwich.*

Today, the look in her eyes had been far from warm.

There was no point in prolonging this. Whatever magic we'd once had was gone. My being here only further destroyed what I'd ruined all those years ago.

"It's okay," I said, studying my hands. "I think I've got what I came for. If you wouldn't mind showing me the capture station—because I am interested in how this is transmitted—I'd appreciate it. I won't bother you anymore, Zora. Not any more than I have to after this."

There was no mistaking the obvious relief that flitted across her features, the way her shoulders relaxed from their hunched position.

"If you're fine with that," she said, but she was already moving, limping, toward the door. "I'll just show you into the closet—"

"I can't say I hear *that* all that often around here," a new voice said.

I turned to see a tiny, dark haired woman in a lab coat in the doorway, arms folded. Something about her was familiar.

"Hey, Zora," she said, taking a few steps into the room once Zora backed up. She studied me. "Who's this?"

"This is—"

"Nick," I said, before Zora claimed I was a stranger who just wandered in off the street. "Zora and I are old friends. She's been nice enough to show me around, explain her work."

"This is Dr. Adesola Rojas." Zora watched me with narrowed eyes.

It clicked. "You're the gynecologist from the video?"

Adesola gave me an alert glance. "What video? You saw one of our videos?"

I gave Zora a quick glance. "Uh, you know. The educational one. For the young adults . . ."

Adesola frowned, her head tilted. "Yeah, all the videos are for our young adults. What was the topic?"

I looked to Zora and realized she'd be no help. She seemed lost in thought, staring into the empty doorway. "It was, uh, about young women making sure they, uh, took care of themselves, uh, empowered themselves—" I broke off, seeing Adesola's gaze now wide and fixed on my hands. Looking down, I watched as my hands nervously twitched at my waist. More than that, the pointer and middle fingers of my right hand were stuck together and drawing small, tight circles in the air.

What the hell? Had I really mimed working a clit?

Fuck.

Heat crawled up the back of my neck.

Adesola grinned at me. "Never mind, I think I know which one now." She threw a teasing look at Zora. "Yep, you two are from the same tribe. Excuse me for butting in. I heard Zora was here and I just wanted to stick my head in and say hello. I heard about the grant. I'm sorry, Z."

Zora's already strained expression tightened further. For the first time I recognized the weariness in her face. "It's okay. Part of life, right?"

"Right," Adesola agreed, lips twisted. "Wanna catch up later, talk next steps?"

"Yeah."

I watched Zora and the new notch between her brows.

Adesola's gaze moved between the two of us before settling on Zora. A grin suddenly spread across her face. "Well. I've got rounds. Nice to meet you, Zora's Friend. You kids have fun in the closet."

CHAPTER SIX

Zora

I can do this. I can do this. I can do this.
 I couldn't do this.

I picked my way down the clinic hallway, feet screaming with each excruciating step. Nick's presence behind me warmed my neck and sent my stomach into aching spasms. But I did my best to slow my stride, trying to shuffle forward at a dignified, measured pace.

I had a feeling I looked like a peg-legged parrot lurching down the hall.

God help me, it was all falling apart. All my carefully constructed walls and boundaries were in danger of crumbling the longer I was around him. I was reassured by the qualities I remembered while also confronted with new data that ultimately proved I didn't know who he was.

Not anymore.

I remembered that same sharp interest, the curiosity that fueled so many of our childhood imaginations. But there was also a new edge to him, a subtle cloak of power that made me vaguely uneasy.

I needed to get away from him. Quickly. Away from him, and that knowing gaze, to someplace with a chair.

I'd arrived at the hospital early, wanting to get myself ready for this moment. I'd listened to a meditation curated by my favorite TV life coach in my car. It was supposed to help me center my energy and prepare to conquer any challenges I encountered. *"You can do this,"* I'd repeated at top-volume, clenching the steering wheel as I screeched and drew startled glances from passersby. *You are strong. You are capable. You are prepared for anything that happens today.* Then I'd freestyled: *It doesn't matter how long he's been gone, it doesn't matter what he has to say. It doesn't matter that he looks like a tree in need of climbing.*

He broke your heart.

You will get through this. Done and over with.

And then, seeing him in the lobby, I'd gone numb.

He'd met me at the coffee shop adjacent to the hospital's entrance. He was in all black, in jeans and a black sweater that looked soft to the touch and did little to hide his sculpted torso. Gripping a coffee cup, he'd fixed an intent stare at the opposite entrance. I was happy to have the element of surprise when I approached him from behind, prompting a startled reaction from him.

The look on his face when he finally saw me, recognized me? Something like relief relaxed his features, followed by a wide smile. It was the Nick smile. The one that once belonged only to me.

And the redhead, I reminded myself.

I had to keep my feet planted in the memories, so I'd endeavored to be strong, to fortify my heart. After less than twenty minutes in his presence, I wasn't feeling all that strong. I bit my lip, cursing the fact that there was another corner to turn, another corridor to walk through.

Why did I wear these shoes?

Don't pretend you don't know why.

Self, pipe down if you only have judgmental things to say.

But yeah, I did know why.

I'd gone on a Googling spree after Leigh and Walker left, unable to stop myself from pouring over images of Nick. Nick at a gala with an actress from one of my mother's favorite soap operas, handsome in a tux. Nick running on the beach with a New York socialite in the Hamptons, defined abs on full display. When Leigh showed up in my doorway with her revered Jimmy Choos, I took them and figured I'd just have to take one for the team.

I'd needed to recalibrate the power differential I'd felt ever since the moment he and Nellie showed up in my doorway and I'd ended up on my hands and knees under my desk.

I *needed* to project cool, professional distance, but I was no longer sure if my feet could carry me to our next destination. I winced, angry at myself and the insecurities that would eventually cripple me. Rage was far more manageable in flats or Birkenstocks.

I'd almost reached the corner when I recognized the woman headed in my direction.

"Hey, Carly." I slowed to a stop to greet one of my research assistants. "How goes it? Do we have a taping today?"

She gave me a cautious smile, her gaze running over Nick behind me. "Hey, Dr. Leffersbee. No, I'm actually working out of the center today. I just stopped by to let the repairman into the capture room. He's all done."

I introduced her to *Mr. Rossi* and listened to his follow-up questions as he queried her about our colon cancer prevention program. Carly was a tightly wound, neurotic woman of few words, known for barking at other research staff if they asked too many questions. Yet she stood patiently, cheeks reddening and eyes wide, as Nick fired off questions about at-home colon cancer test kits.

Great. He charmed everyone in his path.

I half-listened as their conversation meandered through random topics. After a while I realized Carly, who never had more than a few non-work related sentences to share, was telling Nick all about her son, his senior year, and the planned senior trip. They were almost friends by the time their chatter finally ended and I led him to the designated door.

"This is a closet," Nick said, sounding scandalized as I swung open the door.

"It's just the right size," I countered, feeling the tiny room was even tinier than I remembered.

It had been a janitor's supply closet. After its conversion to a "capture studio," it only needed to accommodate a team of two research assistants. A narrow strip of fluorescent light lit the room, but the dark cement walls somehow absorbed any illumination, throwing the room in perpetual shadow. A narrow desk ran the short length of the room on one side, with two chairs tucked under it.

We didn't have far at all before we reached the console in the corner that controlled the examining rooms' cameras. I powered it on, narrating my efforts to demonstrate the cameras' capabilities. The monitor came alive with side by side displays of the room we'd just left. Nick was a pillar at my elbow, peering closely at the screen as I managed the navigation controls, zooming in and changing angles.

"Carly's a single parent?"

The question was so unexpected and the topic so random that I turned in his direction without thinking. He was close, really close, stooped low over my shoulder to see the camera displays. I could see each of the dark hairs dotting his chin, the individual strands of silver at his temples. I looked directly into his eyes without thinking and my heart stopped.

Damn it.

His gaze searched mine. His chest lifted with an audible inhalation.

Damn, I missed him. I'd loved him so much. But that was so long ago. Why wasn't there a button or a switch I could turn off in my brain?

"Carly's my employee," I said carefully. "It wouldn't be appropriate for me to disclose any of her personal information—"

"It's okay, I get it." His gaze stayed on mine, briefly dipped to my mouth, returned to my eyes.

All the nerves along my face and arms tingled, as if I'd stepped into the intense glare of some immense heat or light.

"Zora—"

"Alright, that should do it," I said, hoping he would accept the note of finality I injected in my voice. "So, that's my lab. I hope you found it helpful. Should you have any other questions, Nellie knows how to contact me."

Silence.

I willed myself not to look back, not to get lost in him again. I powered down the console, gathered up my bag and turned to go, intent on shepherding Nick out of the room.

And out of my life.

He stood in the doorway, arms folded, gaze disturbingly intent.

My mouth went dry.

"Uhh..."

"This may be my only chance to get this said. So I'll ask you to just... let me get it out."

"What?" I regretted it as soon as I said it. I'd always been annoyed by manufactured displays of ignorance. Here I'd gone and done the same thing.

However, as of today, I better understood the instincts that fueled these kinds of verbal games. I thought I'd wanted an explanation, a justification of his past actions. But now, more than anything, I wanted to stop whatever he was about say. What if it was somehow worse than what he'd already done? Why was the burden on *me* to relive the pain from all those years ago, just because he'd reappeared on my doorstep?

He unfolded his arms with a sigh and straightened.

I was suddenly reminded of how very small the room was, and how very large he was. Only three of his giant steps and he was directly in front of me.

I held my ground. Looking into those green eyes, I wondered why I'd doubted it was him at first sight.

"I left because I'd wanted what was best for you. And at the time, I wasn't that. I wasn't what you needed. I would've only held you back. When I realized that... I did what I thought was best."

Outside, a knot of women loudly discussed lunch options.

"Could you close the door? Please?"

He nodded and turned to close the door. I took the opportunity when those unnerving eyes weren't prying into mine to settle myself. I'd always hated showing my emotions, specifically the untidy ones. The ugly ones. The cruel irony was this man standing in front of me had once been the only human with whom I'd been comfortable being a mess.

Now I needed to make sure I kept my composure in place and withstood anything he had to say. Because he was also the one person who hurt me the worst.

"Go ahead," I said, hating the cautious, watchful look on his face, hating the hint of smoke I heard in my own voice. But if we were going to do this, then so be it.

I took a step forward and his brows went up. I aimed my next words up, directly into his face. "So, why now? What's the purpose of you coming back, kicking up dirt from the past? You moved on a long time ago. Not long after you left, as a matter of fact."

His Adam's apple bobbed. "I—"

"You *what?*" I hissed. A voice at the back of my brain spoke up, timidly suggesting maybe I wasn't in the right frame of mind to have this conversation right here and now. That the likelihood of my saying something I'd regret was increasing exponentially.

Oh well. *Bite me.* I was done being well-behaved.

Nick stepped back and I advanced into his space, fueled by the fury warming my bloodstream. "What's my part in all this, Nick? Is this the part where I'm supposed to tell you I accept your apology? That's it's all good, it's okay? That we likely wouldn't have stayed together anyway because we were just two dumb kids who didn't know any better?"

His mouth opened, closed.

"And then what's your line, after I say my part? You pat yourself on the back, console yourself, walk away feeling like you're still a good person? Is that what you need? You want my *permission* to feel better about yourself?"

Nick went still, his face stiffening. His gaze didn't leave mine, but I saw the change in his eyes. Saw something lurking there.

There was no way I could stem the tide of emotions barreling out of me. I was as helpless as he was against the force of my own anger, disappointment, rage, and bitterness. "You've apologized. Be happy with that. I don't intend to pat you on the head and tell you I forgive you so you can go on and live your life guilt-free."

"I don't want you to—"

"Don't you?" That wasn't my inside voice. But it felt good, damn it. "Isn't that what you want? What everyone expects of me? To just bury it so we can get to the business at hand and make *you* feel comfortable? Well, I'm not. Not this time. You know why? Because my whole fucking *life* is about doing the right thing. So other people can be happy and okay. And it's not working out too well for me. For once, *just once*, I'm not doing it. I'm doing what *I* really want to do. I'm being true to me. Go find a monk, a priest, whoever fits your belief system. Get forgiveness there. You're not going to make a fool of me, exploit me, and make a profit all at the same time."

His head bowed, hands curling at his sides. "I'm not asking you to do anything, Zora. I just want you to hear this apology. I didn't see another way, couldn't think of another way at the time. And for that, I felt ashamed. I always have. Still do, to this day."

I realized I was holding myself, arms crossed around my body. Each of my hands clutched the opposite shoulder. My chest rose and fell under the bands of my arms, each breath slow. Labored. Watching the cords of his neck tighten, seeing the wash of color drain from his now tightly clenched fists, I held myself even tighter. It seemed we were both somehow adrift, undone, fighting to hold ourselves together. Outside the door, the women's laughter and murmurs from passersby were just audible. Somehow the rest of the world was carrying on as usual, while inside this tiny room time stood still.

"Did you really think I was dead?" His brows pulled together.

The question revived the same inexplicable grief I'd felt yesterday after turning to see him in my doorway. Of course, I hadn't wanted him to have been dead. But I'd never found a trace of him after I sent back his ring, after finding him in that coffee shop, wrapped in a redhead, not even when searching online. The only alternative was a truth somehow just as heartbreaking: That it had been easy for him to walk out of my life without a backward glance, without any attempts at communication. That he'd had so little regard for me that it never occurred to him that he'd gutted me.

Even after knowing how much I'd loved him.

I looked away, fighting to suppress the emotion choking my airway.

Nope. No crying.

Why was this so hard, after all these years?

"I'm not mad that you left, Nick. I'm mad you never came back and didn't have the decency to send as much as flare in my direction before you moved on."

That was far more honest and vulnerable than I'd intended to be.

My ringtone sounded from the depths of my purse. Grateful for the interruption, I fished in my handbag, wondering who was psychic enough to grant this reprieve. Glancing up, I thought I might have glimpsed relief on Nick's face.

I fished for the phone in my purse. "I just need to make sure it's not an emergency."

He nodded, signaling he'd wait.

So great was my agitation, I was hardly surprised when the phone jumped out of my nervous hands and clattered to the floor.

Nick's height folded, his head brushing my shoulder as he bent to retrieve the phone. I jerked away from the accidental touch and backed into the table. His gaze slid over the display of my phone before he placed it in my outstretched hand. His expression soured.

"Jackson James." He managed to make Jackson's name sound like plague.

I turned the phone around. It was a text from Jackson, his delayed response to our previous conversation about meeting up that next evening. It was typical Jackson James: direct and heavy on innuendo.

I'll pick up dinner from the Front Porch after my shift. You just bring that sugar to Daddy.

I barely suppressed an eye roll, noting Nick's gaze was fastened to my face.

He didn't appear to be breathing. "You call Jackson James 'Daddy?'"

Thank you, Jackson, for saving me in this moment.

I managed to arch one brow. "I don't see how that's any of your concern." I shoved my purse back up my arm. "Is there anything else you wanted to say?"

Nick looked away. His Adam's apple bobbed. "Jackson James. You call little, pimply Jackson James, 'Daddy.'"

My spine stiffened. "I care about Jackson. You have no idea who he is now and what he means to our community."

"Is that right?"

"It is."

He took a step closer to me, lowering his voice. "Zora. You and I both grew up with Jackson James. You know—"

I knew the argument currently gathering force wasn't really about Jackson. Not really. It was an opportunity for us both to vent and thrash about something else, something that didn't pick at the scab of our past. Half of me wanted to pursue my line of questioning, wanted to drain Nick of the answers I'd craved for so many years. The other half wanted to avoid it, to walk away from him, forever. To escape before something ugly or cruel was unmasked.

"You, thinking you're the only one who's changed after all these years? It's the absolute height of arrogance."

His head snapped up. "What does that mean?"

A ragged breath escaped me. "It doesn't matter, Nick. If you leave here with only one takeaway, let it be this: Be consistent. You left all those years ago without a single word. If you really want to show me how sorry you are, leave. Again."

I watched his face as I said it. There was a moment, a tiny one, when his expression was unguarded. The hurt I glimpsed countered any triumph I might have felt for finally speaking my truth. I only felt ashamed. I had to fight the age-old instinct to gather him to me, to comfort him.

"I'm going," I told him, suddenly feeling tired. I successfully moved around him without touching him and made my way to the door on unsteady legs, grasping the doorknob before I turned back.

Nick still faced the spot I'd just vacated. "I missed you, Z. *Miss* you."

"Goodbye, Nick."

He straightened and turned to me. "I just want you to know. I loved you, with everything I had. I've never loved anyone that way. And I never would have left you if I'd had the choice. I'm sorry I disappointed us both."

I turned and walked out, before I embarrassed either of us by letting the hot rush of tears blurring my vision spill onto my cheeks.

Carly met me in the hallway, having just left a patient's room. She offered an uncharacteristic smile, brandishing her clipboard. "Got another one!"

"That's great." I attempted a smile, nodding at what I assumed was a signed consent form. "Can you do me a favor, Carly? Mr. Rossi is in the capture station. Can you make sure he makes it out alright and finds his way back to the lobby?"

Her face lit up. "Oh, of course. I'd be happy to."

"Great. I'll see you at the staff meeting this afternoon."

"You sure you're alright, Dr. L.?"

I paused in my tracks and turned back. This time I didn't feel the same strain of artifice in my smile.

"I will be."

CHAPTER SEVEN

Zora

When the email arrived in my inbox early the next day, I realized I'd been expecting it, holding my breath in anticipation of its arrival.

Because you could never really escape the malignant works of fate.

Sitting in my now-partly rehabbed office, I took a deep breath and marshaled all my strength before opening the bold, unread item in my email inbox.

It was short, perfunctory. The invite requested my presence that very afternoon with Dean Peter Gould and several other names I'd never seen before. It was sent on behalf of an administrative assistant outside of the School of Medicine. Dread pooled in my gut with each search performed on the unknown invitee names.

They'd brought in the big guns. They wanted me in attendance.

Shit.

By the time I strolled into the fancy conference room in the one of the hospital's administrative suites, I'd almost accepted my fate.

Almost.

But I sure as hell wasn't about to go down without a fight.

Peter was already seated at the highly-shined wood table, nattily attired in one of the obnoxious bowties in the university colors he seemed to favor, with matching suspenders. He attempted a smile when I entered. It looked like a grimace.

I tacked the corners of my mouth up and made nervous small talk with the other attendees. The Vice President of Patient Experience, Allie Nevers, was there. I'd worked with her extensively in the past and always enjoyed her brash sense of humor and commentary. She made things interesting, at least, and we'd gotten pretty good at teaming up to control the flow of discourse so that it worked in our favor. Our strategic support of each other had helped turn the tide of hospital administrator's sentiments over communication training, and led to the implementation of our wildly successful program. She was a strong support and ally, and I hoped she could throw me a rope.

I could already tell I was badly in need of an escape.

As the meeting started and introductions went around the room, I couldn't help but wonder what merited the attendance of high-ranking hospital administrators. Curiouser and curiouser . . .

"As you all know," Peter began, "our visitor from this last week, Nick Rossi, has presented a solution to integrate new innovation into our patient interactions. This application, and the advent of telemedicine, represent an exciting opportunity to reach patients who might otherwise struggle with access to health care and this hospital. This allows us to extend our reach."

I frowned, wondering when he'd started using commercial-speak. This guy spent most of his time scaring the hell out of medical students. Now he was excited over an app?

"We are by no means suggesting this application will replace face-to-face interactions. I can't imagine a world in which that would ever be possible. But it does allow us to specifically target patients in surrounding towns who are, for example, less likely to come back for post-surgical visits because of constraints with transportation. Our preference will always be for patients to return to the hospital, and we will continue to advocate for that and offer supportive services that accommodate those who require greater assistance. But this application offers the opportunity for earlier, more frequent check-ins. And we can easily identify other applications outside of surgical contexts, say in primary care."

My phone vibrated. I snuck a glance and read a text message from Allie. She sat across from me, nodding along with whatever Gould was saying, her face placid.

I should be back in my office, having my usual fantasy of Idris Elba bending me over my desk. Watch, this meeting will be email-worthy.

I suppressed a snort.

"So, it's FaceTime for patients," Allie said, face deadpan. "It's an app connecting patients with their doctors via video. Sounds like old news to me."

Peter's brows pulled low. "Telemedicine itself is not new, but this application allows for seamless integration with our own medical records. The application and related software would be branded with the hospital's name. The record of the call, any prescribed medications? All indexed on our end, allowing our clinicians access to what transpired while managing that patient's ongoing care."

I heard a few murmurs from the suits at the other end of the table.

Peter nodded. "We're opting for twenty-four-hour support. In the event one of our clinicians is unable to respond to a patient within the specified time frame, someone from Mr. Rossi's pool of highly qualified clinicians will take the case."

His gaze shifted to me. "Mr. Rossi said you were very helpful, and for that we thank you."

Of course he did.

"We agree that your work, and our application of it here in the hospital, has really helped us turn the tide with our declining patient satisfaction scores. We all certainly credit you with that."

He gave a decisive nod, then began clapping. His effort was slow to catch on as others belatedly realized he intended to applaud me.

I didn't react but did brace myself. I'd been in academia long enough to know that flattery came right before being *voluntold*, and ladies and gentlemen, I was just about to be *voluntolded.*

"As we talked to Mr. Rossi, we realized that, while we were

familiar with the nature and quality of training *our* clinicians receive, we have no idea what communication training his pool clinicians have undergone." His voice lowered as he aimed a sidelong glance at Allie. "After working so hard to bring up our scores, the last thing any of us would want is to have our survey scores go down because of unsatisfactory interactions with pool clinicians."

Allie sat up straight. I watched as any last trace of Idris-borne lust vanished from her eyes.

Shit. *Shit shit shit.*

Peter had known just how to hit his mark, how to play this, just what button to push.

Allie and her team in Patient Experience were responsible for ensuring patient satisfaction scores for doctor and nurse communication remained high. HCAHP, or Hospital Consumer Assessment of Health care Providers and Systems, held far more sway than an average Yelp review. The survey measured patient satisfaction among a number of categories, including patients' communication about medicine and their overall communication with doctors and nurses. The scores were public and easily accessible to the discerning consumer. And the results were tied to the hospital's funding from Medicare. Better scores equaled better reimbursement, and that was only one of the many metrics we were concerned about when it came to patient satisfaction.

"We all know," Gould said, "that the hospital is in a precarious position right now. We're a community hospital that prides itself on our outreach. With increasing costs and the record losses we're facing now because of unpaid balances, the hospital is struggling to stay afloat. Offering an incentive like this makes us a more attractive option, but we can't take the risk of lowering our patient satisfaction scores or our funding."

"Okay, wait," I said, fighting panic as I watched Allie's face grow more and more stiff. I saw where this was headed, and if Allie threw her weight behind Peter Gould's not-yet-spoken mandate, with his convincing argument in play, I was done for. I'd have no time to apply for more grants. I'd have no time for my own research. I'd be stuck in training hell. And then what would happen to my staff? To my research team? "HCAHPS are administered to recently discharged patients. Inpatient," I said firmly. "The interactions on the app would not take place on an inpatient basis. This would not affect our patient satisfaction scores."

Allie shook her head. "It doesn't matter, Zora. I hear all the time from our docs and nurses about how patients see a number of different clinicians during a hospital stay, and despite the survey emphasizing who should be rated, if they're upset about something, they might ding the wrong person. If we're agreeing to let other docs treat our patients, whether it's impatient or not, they need to receive the same communication training our docs received in-house. In our patient's minds, it'll all be the same system. And in a sense, they'd be right. If a doc interacts with our patients on behalf of Knoxville Community Hospital, they're representing us." She shook her head again. "They have to be trained."

"I'm so glad you agree," Gould said smoothly. Mentally, I threw my pen at the smug smile he aimed my way. "I think we're all in agreement here."

More murmurs from the other side of the table.

My phone vibrated again. Allie's newest text featured a meme of a stick figure being chased and eventually run over by a school bus, its guts smeared around the broken lines. *I'm sorry,* her text read.

I ignored whatever she was now mouthing to me from across the table.

"We want this done before we close the deal," Gould said, and inwardly, I screamed. "Which means soon."

"How soon?" I couldn't pretend I didn't know where this was going, but I wanted specifics as soon as possible.

"We're prepared to give you whatever resources you may need to help with this request. Mr. Rossi has generously agreed to pay you, and anyone who assists, a consulting fee."

I shook my head. This was an instance where I didn't care how much cash was being dangled about. It was Nick's money. I didn't want it. And besides, I doubted Nick Rossi would agree to pay the salaries of my entire research staff.

"How long?"

He let out a breath. "We'll see. Let's see how it goes. There's an immediate trip to New York involved, and who knows how long that'll be. Fridays are slow clinic days and Mr. Rossi has somehow corralled the folks on his end with hardly any notice, God knows how." I bit back my frustration at the admiration I heard in his voice. "He's prepared to take on any and all costs. But we need you there to ensure their trainers grasp the material and are prepared to train others the right way."

Seven faces all turned toward me. The room grew deathly quiet.

Gould and I eyed each other.

I'd taught others how to use silence strategically. There was no way he was winning this game.

He broke the silence first. "Whatever you need," he repeated. "I don't think I need to tell you how important this is for the hospital."

"We should talk in private," I said, finally. I sat back to signal an end to the conversation. "I'm afraid I can't make a commitment at this moment."

Out of the corner of my eye, Allie's eyes grew huge in her head.

Gould didn't break eye contact with me when he addressed the room at large. "Thanks everyone for coming today. I think we've all got a good sense of the matter at hand. I'd appreciate it if you gave us the room."

I listened as chairs pushed back from the table, scraped along the hardwood floors. *Oooh. You in trouble,* Allie mouthed to me behind Peter before disappearing. Discreet, parting murmurs reached us as everyone else silently filed out of the door.

Gould waited until the door closed again before he spoke. He sat back, mirroring my defensive position.

"I know I've just sprung this on you, and it's not the first thing we've dropped in your lap over the last few days," he admitted.

I said nothing.

"Just tell me: What will it take to make you say yes?"

I met his gaze squarely. "There is nothing you can say."

There was also nothing I could do to save myself, but I wasn't about to admit that to him.

"I know you understand how time-sensitive this is. I'm willing to give you any resources you need, any faculty you need to take with you. I'll make it work. And Mr. Rossi is prepared to compensate you and anyone else you bring along very handsomely."

If there was one thing that pissed me off, it was being maneuvered into a corner by the likes of this guy. And Nick.

Years of pent-up frustration and rage exploded inside me. It was, I realized, an overdue reaction and much more than the result of cumulative stress. I'd had it. I was done with bending over backwards to satisfy everyone else's needs, only to find myself still wanting. I was sick of being unheard and having my needs subjugated to last place. Even now, my entire career, my life, was at stake and I was expected to fully devote myself to another cause.

This man would not use me for his own purposes while my staff was on track to be laid off if I didn't find funding—*long-term* funding.

"You know that Nick and I have a past." I saw no need to be discreet. He'd witnessed our little reunion and he wasn't the idiot he sometimes pretended to be.

His cheeks grew red. "I imagined that was the case, yes."

"And yet you have the temerity to ask me to do this, when you have some idea of how contentious that relationship might be? Wasn't it enough that I toured him around when I clearly didn't want to?"

He sat forward, fingers drumming the table. "I am aware of that, and Nellie and I were both grateful. But, I also know you enough to know that you're a professional, a stellar researcher. While there may be some . . . initial discomfort, I have no doubt that you could interact as two professionals."

I raised my brows. "So, to clarify, you've just said I should have no problem sacrificing my own discomfort for you and the hospital's gain?"

His face took on the holier-than-thou expression he wore when browbeating medical students. "The hospital's gain *is* your gain. The School of Medicine has a unique relationship with the hospital—"

"Peter, I may not be here in in three months—"

"The hospital might not be either!"

Shocked, I took in his reddened face and heavy breathing. It was clear he hadn't meant to make that admission. He ran a hand over his balding head.

"That doesn't leave this room."

"Of course," I said immediately, still battling my surprise.

He studied his hands for a moment, calmed his breathing before he returned his gaze to me. "I know what I'm asking you. I do. And I'm sorry you're in this position. But we are doing everything we possibly can to keep this hospital afloat as the entity that it is now. Do you understand?"

I nodded. "I do understand. But . . ." I shrugged, knowing my next words would make me sound callous, but needing to establish a strong position. "What does that have to do with me? I'm concerned about Carly Sanders, one of my research assistants, who is currently worried that her son won't be able to attend his senior trip. And if I don't get a grant within the next three months, Carly will be worrying about whether or not she can pay her mortgage. Now, I've gotten plenty of grants. Grants that have helped this hospital, our patients, and this community. But not the RoI that's required for my tenure, and submitting more applications will take all the limited, precious time I have left. I've come close. And if I had more time, I'm certain it would happen. Otherwise, I and all the people who depend on me for a living, are done. We won't be here anyway, whether or not the hospital is." I squinted at him. "Seems like we're both in difficult positions, doesn't it?"

The truth was that I cared very much about the hospital and the university community—*obviously* I did. But I owed my staff. They were my responsibility. They deserved for me to be their advocate always, to put them first.

He let out a breath. "I'm not involved in the tenure process, you know that."

"I know that's not true," I countered flatly. My heart hammered against my ribs, but I kept my hands flat on the table, kept my breathing slow and regular.

He hesitated. "I'm not the only decider."

I leaned forward and met his tired blue eyes, because it was now or never. "I guess the real question, then, is how desperate are *you*?" *Play big or go home, Zora.*

He went still.

And then, the absolute last thing I expected happened. A smile.

"Well, I'll be damned," he said, and it was the first smile I'd seen on him that actually worked on his grim face. His gaze turned sharp and assessing, but also appraising, as if he saw me in a new light. "I'm impressed. I didn't think you had it in you, Dr. Leffersbee."

I didn't let him see my relief that this gamble had apparently paid off, even though I couldn't help but think, neither did I.

"The best I can do is a strongly worded letter of support accompanying your application," he said. "And I'll throw all my weight behind it in discussions. But you know, obtaining that RO1 was the benchmark. I don't think it should be in your case, if I'm honest. You've more than demonstrated your mettle as a researcher and you've done this campus a lot of good as a result. But I'm not the only person on the committee, so you understand my letter is only one voice among several."

I nodded coolly. "I understand. But it's a great start." Inside, mentally, I executed a victory dance, complete with cartwheels. *I can't believe that worked!*

His eyes narrowed. "So you'll conduct the training this Friday?"

"Yes." Fine. I'd suffer through more time with Nick. Whatever. It was worth it if my staff all had jobs in three months.

"One more condition," he said.

My internal victory dance halted abruptly. "What?"

"You help Mr. Rossi and his team through the entire process. He needs regional feedback from beta users in our community. We need to anticipate and address any special challenges our community members may experience. He'll need help navigating the university and marketing. And he's committed to overseeing that process until we're satisfied it's done right. You make yourself available to him."

"However, after the training—"

"Even after the training. You make yourself available if any member of his team needs help, Mr. Rossi included. Help him find his way. This is a relationship I—*we*—need to cultivate."

"You're asking a lot of me," I murmured, for once not hiding my discomfort.

"I know. But you're asking a lot of me, Zora." His words and his expression were candid. "Will you do it?"

I lowered my elbows to the table, rested my head on my hands. "Do I have a choice?"

"There's always a choice, Dr. Leffersbee. In this case, the choice is about which is more important to you. Guaranteeing the continued employment of your research staff? Or avoiding a potentially uncomfortable—albeit temporary—interaction?" I listened as he stood, walked to the door, adding, "I think we both know which you'll choose."

CHAPTER EIGHT

Zora

"*L*ook at this spread!" I mimed swooning as I took in the feast assembled on the blanketed bed of Jackson's truck, eliciting a soft chuckle from him.

Cooper's Field was surprisingly empty for a Friday evening and day was slowly yielding to night with a stunning display of pinks and purples along the horizon. It was blessedly quiet, with only a few tentative cricket chirps.

Sigh. I needed this.

Jackson's lips curled with his trademark smirk. "You know I love it when you use the word 'spread' in any context."

I couldn't help my huff of laughter. "You're so romantic. You always know just what to say."

He waggled his brows. "I know." He reached for my arm from the height of the truck, easily hauling me up and over.

"Are these flowers for me?" I smiled at the cellophane wrapped red roses lying next to the battery powered lantern. "Awww. You really *are* romantic."

I settled into the corner while he made his way to the paper bags nestled against the cab. "It's my job to make sure you never forget that, cupcake. I can't remember the last time I bought you flowers."

"Hmm." I pushed aside the plastic, burying my nose in the soft, fragrant blooms. "These are amazing. I will display them proudly. And publicly. Speaking of which . . ." I rummaged through my crossbody knapsack and retrieved a grease-spotted paper bag. It was still warm. "I brought your sugar. *Daddy.*"

Jackson turned with an unrepentant grin, and then he laughed. "Liked that, did you?" Jackson always laughed at his own jokes and I found this hilarious about him. He didn't care if anyone else thought he was funny, *he* thought he was funny, and that was good enough.

"No. You know I don't." I leveled him with a scowl. "Didn't we talk about how creepy that is? Haven't I threatened to disembowel you for talking like that?"

Jackson inched his way over to me on his knees, setting a Styrofoam container in front of me. "Ah, that's just 'cause you haven't been properly inspired. Under the right circumstances, you'd be shocked at what you might be willing to call me."

"Well, I wouldn't know about that."

He arched a blond brow. "And whose fault is that?"

I grinned, rolling my eyes, taking him in as he settled his broad shoulders against the cab and stretching his long legs in front of him. Jackson was definitely a looker. He'd come a long way since our high school days, when classmates called him "shrimp," "metal mouth," and "pizza face." Those classmates were jerks, scum. Bottom dwellers. I'd always appreciated all versions of him.

Anyway, Jackson may not have peaked in high school, but he'd roared into his college years with a vengeance. I took in his flawless tan complexion, warm brown eyes, and close-cropped blond hair, thinking he still had a certain swagger even outside of his deputy uniform.

"Like what you see, right?" Jackson gave me a lecherous wink as he opened the Styrofoam container on his lap. "You could be riding this ride, sweetheart. You're the only reason you're not." He kept his voice light, like it was all a joke, but I knew there was an undercurrent of truth in his words.

We'd been pretending, playacting, for a long while now. This agreement between us was mutually beneficial: his parents stopped harassing him about when he was going to settle down with a nice girl and my parents stopped harassing me about working too much or having no time for a personal life.

The idea had been borrowed from my cousin, Dani Payton, and her multi-year engagement to Billy Winston. After their engagement was broken, it became abundantly clear that the relationship had been entirely for show, a ruse to make both appear more settled, respectable, dependable, trustworthy in their chosen fields. It had also diverted attention away from their personal lives. It had *worked*.

And if it worked for them, then...

I sighed deeply, resting my head against the lip of the truck and stretching my legs out parallel to his. "I have no doubt it's a thrilling ride."

"Really? No doubt?"

"It's just..." I felt myself frown. "I don't know. It's complicated."

"It's never easy with you, Zora." His gaze skated over me. "That's your problem. You'd be a lot happier in life if you learned how to just take what you want without questioning everything." He shook his head when I opened my mouth to object. "Eat your food before it gets cold."

I popped the top, discovering beautifully braised lamb chops bathing in their own juices. Stalks of asparagus and a pillowy biscuit resided alongside.

"Thank you so much, Jackson," I said, strangely feeling a tickle in the back of my throat. "For getting dinner, for making time for me on your rare Friday night off—"

"You brought the fried chicken last time, and I know how you hate fried chicken. This wasn't a hardship."

"That's not the point," I sniffed. "I just appreciate this, and you."

"Hell, we're almost married, according to half the town," he said around a mouthful of steak. "You deserve something, don't you? Well, if you won't let me buy you a ring, have some meat."

Our gazes met and we both collapsed into laughter.

"You're perfect for me, Zora." Jackson's soft smile made me want to hug him. He loosely braceleted my ankle with his thumb and forefinger and gave my leg a gentle shake. "You're the only woman I know who would get teary over lamb chops while barely looking at roses."

"I loved the roses," I protested. "And it's the thought I care about, the effort you put into doing this when we're both already tired. But you know how I feel about lamb chops. They're meat lollipops."

Jackson's eyes narrowed as I slid the first one in my mouth. "Right. Meat lollipops. This is definitely one of those moments when I wonder why we haven't had a bedroom rodeo yet."

"Because you keep calling yourself 'Daddy,'" I teased.

"He saw the text, though, didn't he?" He looked insufferably smug as he forked up green beans.

Yesterday, I'd filled Jackson in about Nick being back in town as well as an overview of our first encounter. I knew that Jackson would hear the news of Nick's return from someone, and I didn't want him worrying that 'Mr. Rossi's' sudden reappearance would jeopardize Jackson's agreement with me. But I hadn't told Jackson about today's morning meeting yet.

Looking up at my continued silence, Jackson pushed, "He saw it, didn't he?"

"How did you know that?"

"Because I know *you*. You told me what time you were meeting. And you don't have it in you to ignore text messages and phone calls. You always look as soon as they come in."

I considered this as I chewed. I hadn't realized that about myself. *Surely, that can't be true, can it?*

"It's true," he said, as though reading my mind. "I figured he'd still be with you by the time I finished the call I was on. Figured he'd likely be stretching things out. I knew you'd pull out the phone. And if it were me, reappearing after all those years, I'd make it my business to find out who was texting or calling my long-lost love."

I speared a stalk of asparagus. "He saw it. I dropped my phone—"

Jackson's rich laughter rolled through the deepening shadows. "Of course you did, Zora."

"Shut up." I couldn't help cracking up at my own usual awkwardness. "I dropped it, okay, and he read it—"

"What did he say?"

"You are enjoying this way too much."

"I'm sorry." He made a half-hearted attempt to wipe the smile from his face with a large hand. "What did good ol' Nick have to say when he saw you were on your way home to Daddy?"

I hurled a crumpled napkin at him. "You don't want to know."

Jackson's fork paused midway to his mouth. "Actually, I do."

"Please don't make me."

"Zora."

I took my time chewing another stalk of asparagus. "He mentioned something about . . . your height in high school."

An unholy light flared in Jackson's eyes. "I blame you," he said deliberately, pointing his fork in my direction.

"Why is this my fault?"

"First you tell all those people I don't make you come—"

"Jackson." I laughed helplessly. "I told you that's not what happened. The computer came on all by itself!"

He shook his head. "So the computer can *come on* all by itself, but you can't?"

Now I was laughing so hard I had to set my food to the side. God, what a crazy few days.

"They heard an early draft of an educational video. We were role playing. Literally no one thinks that video had anything to do with me in real life. It was *scripted*."

He shook his head. "Everyone in that room, from now on, is going to look at you and think, 'No wonder that poor girl is so uptight. It's because Jackson James isn't getting the job done.'"

"I am not uptight."

He scoffed, sawing off another piece of meat. "Please. You're far too self-aware to be pretending you don't know that about yourself."

"So this is about your pride? It's important to you that three strangers at the university think you're a bad lover?"

"Yes. I take that seriously. I don't leave a job unfinished. Ever." He watched me beneath lowered lids. "I'll prove it right now. Take off your pants."

I ignored him. "No, your timing was perfect. He saw it. And his face got all—"

"Jealous," Jackson supplied.

"Yes," I crowed, relishing the memory of Nick's tight expression.

He studied me. "Why do you look like that?"

"Like what?"

"Your face is all scrunched up, like you're confused about something."

"I guess . . ." I thought about it. "He dumped *me*. He left *me*. And I still don't know where he went for so many years or what happened."

"Okay."

"I mean, I know I had unrealistic expectations. I had this stupid fantasy that we'd see each other again one day and it would just, I don't know, work out. I was stupid, naive. Childish." I couldn't look Jackson in the eye. "I'm explaining badly. You wouldn't understand."

"I wouldn't? Are we living in some revisionist version of history in which Ashley Winston did not return after eight years of being gone and immediately take up with Drew Runous?"

I winced. "Yeah, that's right. And you still see her all the time around town. You *do* understand."

He lifted a shoulder before going after more green beans. "Eh. She never made me any promises—not like y'all—and I'm happy for her. I really am. Not how I might've imagined things turning out all these years later, even with me being an idiot at times but . . . what can you do? Can't fight fate."

I watched him, taking in the drawn lines around his eyes and mouth, lines that even the deepening shadows of dusk didn't hide. "You alright, Jackson? You have a hard day? A bad call?"

His sigh originated from the pit of his belly. "Just a crap day. People can't take a speeding ticket with good grace."

I fought back a smile. "You still lighting up anything that moves a single mile over the speed limit?"

He threw me a mock glare. "Rules are rules for a reason, cupcake.

Everyone would do well to remember that. You start letting people do whatever they want, pretty soon there's a car wrapped around a tree."

I nodded obediently. "That's right, I think I remember this lesson from Sesame Street. 'Rules are meant to protect us.' I like your hardcore repackaging of it."

He glared.

"What else?" I pressed. "What else happened today?"

He set his food down beside him, cupping his forehead with one hand. I unconsciously did the same, alarmed. Jackson was an enthusiastic eater, to say the least. It wasn't uncommon for him to eat two entrees in a single sitting, packing it all in with a single-minded focus.

Jackson, not eating? This was serious.

"Call came in from the Piggly Wiggly early this afternoon. Baby crying in the car, mother asleep in the locked car. A shopper came across them and wanted a welfare check after they couldn't wake the mother. Wanted us to check it out." He spoke mechanically, as if reciting a report, but his eyes were fixed intently on some distant spot as he relived the scene. "Knocked on the window, couldn't wake the mother either. I broke the window and got inside the car. The mother was high, overdosed from the baggie in the footwell below. I radioed for an ambulance and administered a dose of Narcan while waiting for it to come." He shook his head. "But that baby . . . God knows how long they'd been sitting there in that hot car. Baby's sitting in a full diaper, screaming her head off. No bottle or formula in the car. No diaper bag with supplies or a change of clothes." He ran a quick hand through his hair. "Some women went in the grocery store and got bottle of formula together. I fed the baby, talked to her, all while they came and strapped the mother to a gurney, took her away. Social Services came . . ." His eyes flicked to mine, then away. "They took the baby."

"Oh, Jackson. What happened to that baby?"

He dug the heels of his hands into his eyes. "Haven't heard."

"Did the Narcan help? Did the mother come around?"

He traced his creased forehead. "Yeah, she did. But who knows if someone will find her in time the next time? I guess I can be glad the baby won't be with her next time, hopefully."

We sat in painful silence. Green Valley certainly hadn't been immune from the growing, deeply entrenched opioid epidemic. The reality was that there likely would be a next time for that woman unless someone intervened.

"Jackson." I scrambled up, crawling until we were hip to hip. I threw my arms around him and he readily returned the embrace. "I'm so sorry," I said into his hair. "I can't imagine what that must have been like. I'm sorry. For everybody involved. And especially the child."

He relaxed into my embrace and his arms tightened around me. We stayed that way for the next few minutes, together. Night came alive around us; crickets, cicadas and katydids all contributed to a nocturnal symphony. It was nice, giving someone comfort, being there and being needed by someone else.

Even though the romance between us was fake, the care for each other was real.

Jackson pulled back enough to look at me, his arms still securely clasped about me. "Why didn't we work, Zora? You never really gave us a chance, you know. Not really."

I let his arm take on the weight of my head as I took in his handsome, familiar face. It was a fair question. About a month into our arrangement, Jackson had made it clear that anytime I wanted to make things real, he'd be willing to give it a shot. So, what was wrong with me? Here was a handsome man, a man of integrity, compassion. Why couldn't I just reach out and take advantage of all that he offered?

But even as I considered it, even as my gaze moved admiringly over the short blonde beard, the line of his jaw, my mind returned to the man I'd sparred with earlier that day. Nick.

Dark where Jackson was all light, complicated and secretive where Jackson was guileless. And even before Nick had reappeared, Jackson and I didn't quite fit. The misalignment, as minor as it might have been to some, would have proved our undoing.

I told him a truth, one of several. "We don't want the same things."

His eyes narrowed. "What does that mean?"

"You know what I mean, Jackson. You're still in your post-high school reject, metamorphosis phase. You're still enjoying your fancy new butterfly wings."

He had the good grace to look sheepish. "You mean all the women."

I traced the bridge of his nose, shaking with laughter. "Yes, Deputy. All the women."

"Awww, Zora. I would try for you, though. I can do better."

I shook my head. "That's just it. I don't want you to do anything differently. I want you to have as much time as you need to find yourself."

"So what do you want?"

"I don't want someone who needs to change in order for us to fit. I want someone who is already right, just as they are, and thinks I'm right, just as I am."

"You want the fairy tale." He turned his gaze to the sky. Orion and other neighboring constellations were faintly visible in the approaching darkness. "Happily ever after."

I shrugged. "Something like that, I think. One day, when I have time. And I don't want one of your conquests to brain me with a can of peas in the middle of the Piggly Wiggly and post the footage online."

He bit back laughter. "I'm always up front with ladies. Although, I prefer it from the back ..."

"Uh-huh," I laughed. "You still sticking to Nashville for your pickups?"

"Yeah. I may have, uh, over-hunted a bit here in Knoxville. I need things to die down a bit. Especially given our relationship."

"I'm surprised it's lasted all this time. We've done pretty good so far, fooling everyone. You think maybe it's time to give up the charade?"

His arms fell from around me. "Are you asking now because of Nick?"

"No. Not at all. But I don't want our little farce to get in the way of you finding true love. It works for me because I don't have my family breathing down my neck—"

"Same here. My dad is so happy that I've settled down, and with a catch like you. He loves you, Zora. And yesterday I overheard my mom on the phone telling one of her friends she hoped we had a fall wedding. Something about a rust-colored mother-in-law dress she found. She's been telling everyone how smart her future daughter-in-law is."

I was torn between amusement and distress. "Oh no. This isn't good."

"Jess told me she was proud of me, and glad that I pulled someone with both brains and boobs. She says I haven't had the most discriminating taste."

I shook my head. I loved his sister, and her candor. "That's not really fair to the women you've dated. I'm sure they all had a good supply of both."

"I told her I liked your boobs well enough. Don't get me wrong, they're amazing from where I'm sitting." Unabashedly, he craned his neck to get an eyeful of my chest in the light knit sweater I wore. "But I'm more of an ass man. Luckily for me, you've got both. You know, you're like that old lady, Sophia something? The one that's still sexy at seventy-something? My mom is always going on about her."

I closed my eyes. "There's about five things wrong with what you just said, Jackson."

He grinned. "That's what's so great about us. We're exactly ourselves. You think you could go on a date and eat a lamb chop the way you just did if I was any other man?"

I reared back. "What are you suggesting? That I should daintily pick at a salad—"

"Nope. I'm saying that when you're yourself, when you're not uptight—"

"That's the second time you've called me uptight—"

"Pay attention," he said with great patience, and I shut up because I could see he was serious. Serious Jackson often had great insights.

"You're sexy as hell. And you don't even know it. Now, I'm not one of those folks who find that attractive, like 'she doesn't even realize what she has, it's part of her charm.' Screw that. I wanna see you embrace that shit. Be confident. You had me turned on over here just from eating that lamb chop."

"That's because you're a horndog, Jackson. It wouldn't take that much to turn you on."

"There's some truth to that, okay. But that's not all of it. You were sliding the bone back and forth between your lips."

"Oh, Jesus," I said, and pushed off of him. "I'm going back to my side now."

"Listen to me. You're more than your brain. You're working with great material here."

I rested a hand against my not-quite-flat stomach. "No, I—"

"Nope." He held up a hand. "Don't wanna hear it. I wanna see you getting ready for our battle of wills with Nick."

"What?"

"You heard me. We're not making anything easy for him. And you're not going to play noble and pretend-dump me from our pretend-relationship while he's circling. I need to get my eyes on him, get a feel for him. What time is your flight to New York tomorrow?"

"Takes off at four p.m. But listen, Nick and I, we're not going to spend any significant time together, let alone battle. I'm there to do a job, then I'm done with seeing him ever again." At least, I hoped so.

"You're smarter than that, doc. Listen. I'm a man. I hunt. Nick didn't come all this way for a stroll down memory lane. He's after something. And I'd guess you're the trophy buck."

"That's a sick analogy. Should I be flattered if I catch an arrow in the heart?"

He studied his hands in glow of the lantern. "We can't know who he is now, after all this time. And I'm not letting him anywhere near you when I don't know his intentions. So, as far as you or anyone else is concerned right now, we're together. Until we sort things out or he's gone. Got it?"

Warmth filled my chest. "I love you, Jackson James. You're a good friend."

He pushed a strand of hair behind my ear, his gaze warm on my face. "I love you, too, Zora. And I know we're just friends. Fact is, even though I loved watching you crawl over here and I can't wait to watch you crawl back, and as good as I think we could be, I would never want to lose your friendship." He nodded to the minimal distance between us. "What we have right here, means a lot to me. There aren't many people I could just unload with like I can with you, you know?"

I relaxed into his side. "I do know that. And you know I'm always here for you."

"I do. And one more thing."

"What?"

He took his time answering, studying the sky. "I know what you're thinking. You're thinking about that baby, and Nick—his history, momma, and childhood. But it's not the same. Not everything can be fixed or saved. Sometimes, when you try to help a hurt bear out of a trap, he doesn't thank you. He bites."

CHAPTER NINE

Zora

"Tell me everything. And I mean *everything*." Leigh's voice blared though the speakerphone, filling the tomb-like silence of the hotel room. I held my phone chin-level as I peered over the balcony railing, staggered by the astonishing view of midtown Manhattan. From my fourteenth-floor perch, Central Park stretched below me as an endless green canopy. Angry traffic noises drifted up to the open window. It was stunning, and what had to be the best view in the entire world. I'd rolled my eyes when Leigh dropped me off at the airport with strict orders to call her as soon as I arrived. "*Yes, Mother,*" I'd sing-songed. But now I was strangely happy to hear her demanding voice.

Considering the task ahead, I was also less confident.

"Tell me again why you turned down a trip in a private plane?"

I sank into the plush upholstery of the nearby armchair. "Flying in Nick's private plane increased the likelihood of a private conversation."

She was silent for a beat, then ventured: "So, you're afraid of being alone with him?"

My fingertips blindly traced the embroidery of the chair's upholstered arm. "I don't trust myself. It's different. He's different. But he's also still very familiar. My reasoning and my feelings aren't talking to each other. So I can't decide if I want to run or—"

"Fuck his brains out?"

"Leigh!"

"Sorry, sorry. I'm projecting. He's evil, but he's sexy as hell. Listen, don't be nervous. You're there to do a job, and you're fantastic at what you do. If you focus on that part, maybe the rest of the hard stuff will fade into the background."

"That's . . . actually decent advice."

"Don't sound so surprised. And if you'd read any of the books I've passed along, you'd have an idea of what to expect."

"I don't have time for bodice rippers."

"Romance novels are a guide to life. I've read enough of the 'millionaire boyfriend resurfaces' trope to know what's next."

"Enlighten me, then."

It was impossible to miss the undercurrent of excitement in her voice. "First of all, expect this guy to be four steps ahead of you at all times. It's precisely that kind of cunning that made them millionaires in the first place."

"Oh, of course." I rolled my eyes.

"Next, he's going to lean hard on the nostalgia, really go out of his way to remind you of the past. Try to convince you he's still the same 'aw shucks' small-town boy he always was. Then . . ." Her voice lowered. "He'll figure out the one thing you really need. And whatever that thing is, he'll throw everything he has at it. You will be so overcome with gratitude, you'll get over your reservations, let him tap it, and settle down in suburbia with a shitload of trust fund babies."

I followed the progress of a woman walking along the sidewalk, pushing a stroller. "If that's the typical plotline in your books, we need to discuss your taste in literature."

"Friend, my experience with love has been the exact opposite of a fairytale. Even though I've been dragged through the mud, stomped on, spat on, and disfigured by love, I still believe in it for others. I still think the men I read about in these novels are the standard by which all mortal men should be judged in real life. It's why I keep insisting that you get Jackson's best."

Nope, I wasn't touching that.

"Besides, I spend my days telling kids what they should expect during the course of their cancer treatment. I'm not exactly in the mood to read NPR's retelling of the world's horrors when I get home. You of all the people would benefit from a good sexy book. A little wish fulfillment, a reminder that happy endings exist, would do you a world of good. Especially since Jackson never seems to be where you are."

"Next subject."

"Where are you staying?"

"The . . . St. Regis?"

"Are you serious?" Her question was breathless.

"Yep. In the Tiffany suite. It's all done up in Tiffany blue. And get this. I have *butler service*."

"Shut up!"

"I'm serious. I don't usually drink coffee or tea, but I let him set up the tea service just because."

"Is there a bidet?" Her voice dropped an octave. "Have you raided the room for everything you can steal? I mean, bring home as rightfully yours?"

I laughed. "I haven't had a chance, I just barely got in the room."

"Okay, tell me everything. I want to know all the details. What amenities do you have?"

"I'm here to work—"

"The amenities!"

We switched to FaceTime so I could take her on a tour of the decadent suite. I showed off the highly-glossed surfaces of the bathroom, the shower large enough to comfortably fit an elephant, and the sleek sitting room furniture.

"Get this," I said, loping over to pick up the small red box on a credenza. "The room came with a 'romance kit.'"

Onscreen, her mouth fell open. "Shut up! What's in it?"

I read off the contents of the box. "Let's see . . . condoms, lube, towelettes, massage oil, breath mints. Huh. Even a 'lover's game.'"

She let out dreamy sigh. "So that's how the rich do it. You gonna save the kit for when you see Jackson?"

I hesitated, caught. Leigh turned her to ear to the camera, a shit-eating grin on her face. "What's that? What do you have to say?"

"I don't want to talk about Jackson."

"I agree, he's not worth discussing. Not if he's not going to at least make a guest appearance in New York while you spend intimate alone time with your old—"

"It won't be intimate or alone."

"Not if you can help it, huh? Thinking about spreading some of that massage oil all over Nick's fine, cheating ass, aren't you?"

Just that quick, my traitorous mind imagined peeling off the black sweater I'd last seen him in and discovering what delicious surprises awaited underneath. Nick was more solid, substantial now. Bigger. I wouldn't mind smoothing a little massage oil all along firm terrain, letting my tongue follow where—

ALERT!

"Definitely not." I fanned myself. Great. Now I was hot. "And I don't need Jackson here. Even if he didn't have to work, I'm more than capable of—"

"Hey, what's that?"

I laughed. She had the attention span of a gnat. Her face filled the screen. I was treated to a close-up of her nostrils. "Behind you? Are those flowers?"

I walked her over to the desk where a massive profusion of tropical blooms took up fully one quarter of the desk.

"There's an empty floral shop somewhere."

"It's huge," I acknowledged.

"What did the card say?"

"It's a thank you from his company, Rocket Enterprises. Standard, boilerplate language on the card."

"Uh-huh. And what's that other thing?"

I turned the phone to face the direction of her craned neck. "It's a basket."

"Of what?" I hesitated again and one of her brows went up. "What are you hiding, Z?"

I let out a sigh. The flowers were beautiful. And plentiful. I'd never cared about flowers, not really, but I appreciated the gesture for what it was. But it was this, the contents of this medium-sized wicker basket with the blue and white checkered lining, that had made my breath catch when I first spotted it earlier.

Inside was candy. But not just any candy. It was the candy Nick and I had eaten as kids, bought for each other, traded, smuggled into movies, left for each other even as young adults. My favorites: Mike and Ike, Hot Tamales, and Boston Baked Beans were all artfully arranged around a few bags of Flaming Hot Cheetos. The kicker? A rainbow assortment of Now and Laters, already unwrapped in a Ziploc bag and tied with a bow.

"You don't eat candy." Leigh's brow furrowed.

"I haven't in a while." My dentist made me choose between sugar and my tooth enamel over ten years ago. I'd chosen to hang onto my sensitive enamel.

"But when you did, these were your favorites. When you were with him?"

"Yep."

"Are those Starburst? Why are they already unwrapped?"

I couldn't help the smile that pulled at my lips. "They're Now and Laters. Those were Nick's favorites. I liked them well enough, but I always struggled to get the pack open and unwrap them."

"Huh. We used to call them 'teeth crackers' back home. I don't know how anybody liked those things."

"I used to say the same thing, but I'd still eat them once Nick got them free of the paper."

I picked up the plastic bag and gently squeezed a pink taffy square. It was soft. He'd gotten the soft kind.

"Hey, Z?"

"Yeah?"

"Don't let him mind-fuck you with Flaming Hot Cheetos."

I groaned. "I'm not."

"Just be prepared. Remember, as a swoony millionaire, he's four steps ahead. Has he offered to solve any problems for you yet?"

I considered this. "No. Well, not for me, no."

Loud pounding sounded from her side. "Details! What are you not telling me!"

"Well, you know my research assistant, Carly?"

"Short, dark haired? Some relation to Attila the Hun?"

"Be nice. She's . . . stressed a lot. Well, she's been anxious about her son's upcoming senior trip. She really wants him to go but I heard from someone else on the staff that the kid's dad didn't come up with the half he promised. We were debating taking up a collection to help but—"

"That could backfire." Leigh winced. "It's a nice gesture, but she seems super private—"

"Right. So, we were a little unsure of what to do."

"So what happened?"

I walked back to the balcony railing. "This morning, before I left, she showed up in my office. Euphoric. Seems some anonymous benefactor took care of the trip. But not just for her son. For the entire senior class."

Silence.

"Anonymous, huh?" Leigh drew out the word *anonymous*.

"Yep."

"Does she suspect it's him?"

"I don't think so. She doesn't even know who he is. She mentioned the trip in passing to him, I don't know how he knew the details, but—"

"You're in trouble."

"Stop saying that!" I waved my free hand in the air. "Aren't you supposed to be reassuring me right now?"

"What he's doing, that random act of kindness thing, that's catnip for you." Leigh clicked her nails against some surface on her side. "If this were me, there would be no question of what I should do. In fact, you would've already clubbed me in the head if you sensed I was weakening. I've known you forever. You're not a dummy or a pushover, but I can sense you weakening and you are not the weakening sort."

"I'm not weakening."

"You are."

"You don't understand."

"Help me. It's almost like Nick has some invisible force field around him that makes you not yourself. We'd practiced what you would say when you saw him for your meeting yesterday, remember? But you admitted afterward that you went all the way off-script."

I closed my eyes, savoring the slight breeze, wanting to forget about my last conversation with Nick. "I tried. I really did. Something just came over me."

"I'll say. You were supposed to project, 'I'm living my best life and haven't thought about you in years, bitch. I'm so damn happy without you I never gave a thought to where you were.' And then verbally cap it off with prayer hand emojis. But no. You went all scorched earth. Showed him just how much angst you still have about it all. Which shows how much you still care. Which gives him all the power."

"It's because I do care," I whispered, feeling ashamed. "Still. It's hard to love someone that much and then just . . . feel nothing." I shook my head at myself and the absurdity of what I'd said. "And there's a lot you don't know about him. And our past."

"Okay. Tell me something I don't know."

"Alright. When we were kids, his mother got in a car accident. A really bad one. I think she almost died. Nick was terrified. Traumatized. His mom was all he had at the time. His dad had split, and his mother had to stay in the hospital for a while. Nick stayed with us, in Walker's room, until she was discharged and could get around. I still remember my mother sitting him down and explaining he'd need to be patient and treat her very gently when he went home."

"That's his trauma? That excuses him for cheating on you?"

"Just listen. I thought everything was fine, that his mom got better and it was over. But apparently, that wasn't the case. She got hooked on the opiates she was taking for pain. It happened over time. We were teenagers when it really became clear to Nick. Then she started getting the pain meds other places when her doctors wouldn't prescribe them anymore. *Illegally.* By the time I realized what was going on, it was out of control. You know how people in town gossip."

"Lord, yes," Leigh said. She'd created quite a stir when she'd arrived in Green Valley with her colorful language and endless animal prints.

"Well, one day Nick and I went to the grocery store after school to get snacks. And we heard Karen Smith holding court, telling everyone within sight that Nick's mother was an addict, that they were both trash, and that my parents were probably horrified by our connection—that we were *involved.* She claimed to have caught Nick's mom in some compromising position." My throat tightened as I was transported back to the market. Watching all the emotions flit across Nick's face. Horror, anger, fear, *humiliation.* "She was crowing about it, going into awful details, saying how I deserved better than someone like him."

On the screen, Leigh closed her eyes. "That's just . . . awful. The two of you heard all that?"

"Yes."

We were both silent for several beats, the only sound coming from the cacophony of traffic below.

"I still want to shank him for your sake," Leigh said, scrubbing a hand across her eyes. "But that had to be shitty. No kid should have to hear that about their parent or live through it."

I spoke around the knot in my throat. "It was terrible."

"So what happened then?"

Thinking of what came next made me smile. "He got revenge."

Her face filled the screen. "How?"

"He spent over a month perfecting candied apples to leave on her doorstep for Halloween. Only he did it with whole onions, then used packaging from the Donner Bakery after swapping out the real thing."

Leigh gaped at me. "Are you serious?"

"Yes. He went through a whole bushel of onions and a million of those sticks when he was perfecting his technique."

"A mouthful of onion for a notorious gossip," she murmured. "It's fitting. Hell, that story even makes me like him a little. Not enough to make up for watching you break down and cry after the coffee shop incident, but a little."

I let out a sigh and rubbed my eyes, suddenly feeling fatigue from the flight catching up with me. "Yeah, it's not simple. There's no easy answer. This all would be a lot easier if he'd just go away."

"All you can do is your best as a professional. Share your expertise and fulfill your promise to Dr. Gould so you can be free of Nick as soon as possible." Her eyes widened to emphasize her words.

"Right. I'm going to go to dinner with his team, be pleasant, get through the training tomorrow and then move on from this. There'll be other people, other buffers, from now on. If I'm not alone with him, it'll be easy."

"Fine. Yes. Exactly. Play your part. Without burning down the restaurant. Easy. Smile. But just remember—he'll always be four steps ahead."

CHAPTER TEN

Zora

*J*ohn's on 12th Street was located in the heart of the East Village, situated on an unassuming corner. The cozy interior immediately reminded me of the charming, authentic Italian restaurants I'd seen in old movies and my repeated viewings of *Lady and the Tramp* as a child.

"We've been around for over one hundred and ten years," the waiter informed me as he led me to the back of the restaurant. "Everything's original. All the woodwork's unchanged."

"It's wonderful," I said, thoroughly charmed by the old-world ambience. I sent a wary eye over the other diners' attire, suddenly glad I'd taken a moment to freshen my curls and mask my travel weariness with light touches of makeup. The lightweight, floral dress I wore would've been fine on its own, but I'd added a cardigan in deference to my professorial, consultant role. At the last minute, I'd swapped my borrowed espadrilles for Birkenstocks. They were better to run in or kick ass with if this went poorly.

I was so distracted by the waiter's explanations of the original artwork that I didn't notice when he came to a stop outside a private room.

"Your other diner is here."

I followed the waiter in, only to stop short at the sight of one person—and only one person—seated at the single occupied table in the room.

Nick.

I turned to the waiter, unsure of what to say, when I heard Nick's voice. "Zora. Hi."

I bit my lip, working to pace myself, to dial back my temper. "Nick."

The waiter looked between us, his eyes comically wide. He pulled out my chair while his eyes darted to Nick, then to me, then back again.

I stared at the chair, unwilling to sit, to be managed. Yet again. Hadn't Leigh said it? *He'll always be four steps ahead.*

"Please."

I looked up at the word. Nick stood, eyes hot on mine.

The waiter stood at my elbow, eyes huge.

Fuck it, I decided. The sooner I slayed this dragon and confronted the past, the sooner I'd be back home.

Right. To all the fun and grant-related failure that awaited me there.

I lowered myself into the seat, obliging the waiter's attempt to push in my chair with awkward forward shuffling. Nick and the waiter released an audible sigh together. The waiter fled to safety while Nick folded his impressive height back into his seat.

Glancing at him, I noted that he looked tired. More dark stubble covered his square jaw. Flickering candlelight caught the dark shadows under his bright eyes. I averted my attention from the tuft of dark hair peeking from the open collar of his white dress shirt. One of his long legs straddled the outside of the table. I didn't miss the way his trousers strained with the definition of his quads.

Grandma Leffersbee had always told my siblings and I that we had to be good for our parents. That we should always do the right thing. *"Be wary of the devil,"* she'd warned us. *"He's tricky."*

Watching Nick in the flickering candlelight, fighting an ancient instinct to slide my hands through the unruly strands of his dark hair,

I realized Grandma had left out rather important details about the dark lord. I wished I could update her, or add a codicil to her time-worn speech.

You left out an important detail, Grandma. The devil is tricky, but he is also one sexy bastard.

Nick's gaze moved over my face and settled on my mouth.

"So," I said, mostly to distract myself from his unsettling gaze as it drifted from my mouth and dipped lower.

What is he thinking?

"Your team is missing," I said conversationally. "And you're here. I feel ambushed."

He sat back in his chair, eyes narrowed as he considered me. "That wasn't my intention."

"This is the second time you've brought up your intentions, as if they somehow make up for the fucked-up reality you create. I don't give brownie points for intentions. Not when I was obviously lied to. There's no team here."

His eyes briefly widened. I suspected he was reassessing me, mentally recalibrating his approach.

Good. I was done being dragged around, even if it was in lovely New York.

"I wouldn't have imagined you'd be the one with the potty mouth all these years later. Wasn't it you that tried to shame me out of my cussing phase? What were we, twelve, when your mother washed my mouth out with soap?" He grinned, the expression briefly chasing the fatigue from his face.

Despite myself, I smiled at the memory. "Yep. She overheard you saying 'shit' in the backyard." I shook my head. "I told you she could hear through that back kitchen window. But you didn't listen." I paused, considering him. "But you've never really known when to stop, have you? Still enjoy testing the limits?"

His expression sobered. "I wouldn't be where I am now if I was worried about testing the limits."

I took in the aura of power in his posture, the simple yet expensive clothing that whispered of his wealth, the predatory light in his eyes. "That may be true. Your bullying tactics may be effective, but that it doesn't make them right, and it doesn't mean I'm going to accept them lying down."

He sat forward suddenly, hands clenched on the table. "I'm not a bully. My team *is* having dinner tonight, with Adesola, at another restaurant. Where they are fine-tuning all the details for tomorrow's train-the-trainer sessions. If you misunderstood—"

"*If?* If I misunderstood? So, that's your line, huh? You didn't *technically* lie."

"I didn't technically lie, correct."

"Technicalities."

"Sometimes, technicalities make all the difference."

I leaned forward. My voice was hushed and angry when I ground out, "Are you saying you didn't try to mislead me? To get me here?"

"Hell yes, I misled you."

My mouth snapped shut and I leaned back, surprised by his admission.

But he wasn't finished. "You are correct. I set out to deliberately mislead you about dinner tonight. *Technically*, I told a lie of omission so you'd come. I fully admit that."

For some reason, his confession cut my anger in half, and that made no sense. I crossed my arms. "And you're not a bully?"

He gritted his teeth in a way that resembled a smile as much as it did a baring of teeth. "If you want to leave, leave." Nick lifted his chin toward the private room's entrance, his eyes flashing with challenge. "I'll understand, and you have my promise that I'll continue with the project. I promise that if you leave, it won't jeopardize my company's collaboration with the university. The collaboration will move forward regardless. But I want to be clear." He leaned forward. "I'm not bullying you. I'm not forcing your participation in the project. That's not me. That's between you and the university, and whatever hold they must have on you given you're actually in New York and sitting at this table."

Glaring at him, I said nothing.

"Now, I know my past behavior has been shitty and you may feel you have cause to believe just about anything of me. But tonight, I believed it would be better if we met separately from the team, to clear the air. If we could, just for tonight, make a distinction between my actual, recent sins and the sins of others, I'd appreciate it. I'm just —I'm just trying to—" He ran a rough hand over his whiskers. "I don't know what I'm trying to do."

I lowered my gaze to the tablecloth and considered his words. He hadn't coerced me to participate in this project; he was right about that. The strong-arm tactics were all Peter, and the school, and the predicament I was hung up in with my lack of grant funding.

Though I didn't feel any guilt for busting Nick's ass over the past, it wasn't fair to lay the blame for all of my current frustrations at his feet.

I risked a glance at him and found him watching me with a grim solemnity. More than a fair amount of salt had invaded the darkened, peppered stubble along his neck. Deep grooves bracketed his lips and his eyes were faintly bloodshot.

"You look terrible," I blurted rather than ask if he'd been sleeping.

He reared back, brows drawing low. We stared at each for the space of several beats before his lips curved in a small smile.

"Still telling it like it is?"

"I don't know any other way."

"I'm glad. Does that mean you'll stay?"

I hesitated before announcing, "I'm hungry."

And then, Jesus help me, were actually *smiling* at each other. I averted my eyes from that roguish grin and worked to gather more righteous indignation before I found my panties around my ankles.

"There's a lot of history between us." His gaze dropped to his napkin as he traced its edge. "My goal here, tonight, is to tell you that I'm sorry, but my apologies don't seem to be going over too well. So maybe I won't lead with that."

I grunted.

"But if you'll allow me to slide a few more in, I do want to say I'm sorry for cornering you in your office earlier this week. And not letting on that we knew each other."

I tilted my head, studying him. "Why *did* you do that? It only added to the pressure, you pretending we were strangers."

He winced. "The moment came and I dropped the ball. I didn't deliberately set out to be deceptive, I didn't know how to handle the moment—" He lifted both palms with a short, humorless laugh. "I don't know how to handle this moment right here."

I looked into the evergreen eyes that I'd once known as well as my own, feeling an unexpected twinge, a dull throb of shared misery.

"Me either," I admitted.

A waiter delivered a basket of bread, providing merciful respite to yet another painful round of silence. I ordered soup, Nick ordered an appetizer, and we both promised to review the dinner offerings before the waiter's departure.

"I want to be clear," I said, drawing myself up to my full height. "Only straightforward, honest communication going forward. No matter how hard it might be for either of us. I can't be an effective consultant if I'm always looking around the corner for the next surprise." *Or back,* I acknowledged to myself. *I can't keep going back to live in the desolation of the past.* Like my mother always said, all anyone has is the current day. I could only make the best of where we were now, going forward.

He nodded, acknowledging my statement.

"And," I continued, "it's clear you've done well for yourself. I imagine there's a host of people that work for you who are trained to jump at your command." I met his gaze. "I'm not one of those people."

He swallowed. "I understand. Completely. I agree. I—"

"And," I continued, "I'm here because my university wants to see this collaboration with you work. That's the only reason. I don't care who has me in a hold—if I decide I don't want to be here, I won't be. If there are any more surprises, I'm leaving."

He nodded again, lips pressed together.

"I will leave," I repeated.

"Got that. Loud and clear."

We both looked elsewhere as silence resettled over the table. A muscle ticked at his temple. I picked at my cuticles.

"I really am grateful," he said finally. "I want this collaboration to work too. It's our first launch of this particular program and we're committed to ensuring it goes well. They set the condition of training our docs before closing, and I'm happy to comply. It certainly goes a long way to improving the service we're selling and providing on our end. I just regret that you got caught up in this."

I stopped myself from saying, *It's okay.*

Because it wasn't.

"So," Nick said, gaze on his menu, "how have you been?"

"God." I laughed. "This is really awful. It's like the world's worst date. Only in reverse. Here, let me raise the stakes, let's see how much more uncomfortable I can make this. How many sexual partners have you had?"

He coughed, color blooming in his cheeks. "Uh, yep. That definitely made it worse." The tension around his eyes relaxed. "Thanks for that." His thumb stroked the base of his water glass, smearing the gathering drops of condensation. My attention was automatically riveted to the slow, methodical movement. "You always could do that, you know? Make things better. I was always grateful for that."

I opened my menu, resisted the words begging to leap from tongue: *I was grateful for you too, and I miss you, and I hate that I miss you. I wish you'd never left. I wish we were sitting on the same side of the table, under far more friendly circumstances.*

"In a way, you're right." He lifted a shoulder. "We are starting over in a lot of ways and getting to know each other again."

I nodded, my gaze moving down the list of entrees in the menu. Was lasagna a good antidote to heartache? Or was that fettucine alfredo? I couldn't remember what my mother had told me all those years ago.

"Although not, I mean, I didn't intend to insinuate it was in any romantic context, at all. Not that . . . I mean, I'm just . . . Jackson—" He cut himself off just as my eyes lifted to his. He swallowed, looking like he wanted to say more.

Interesting.

I hadn't thought he'd made that insinuation at all. What was wrong with him? He'd never been this off-balance, even in the worst of times.

I threw him a rope. "Yes, Jackson. My—uh—partner."

His jaw went taut. "I'm sure he's changed a lot since high school. I just—old habits die hard, I guess. All that matters is your happiness."

Thank God for Jackson and our arrangement. I knew better than to define myself by the presence or absence of a romantic partner. But having a boyfriend prop took some of the sting out of the situation. Having to sit across from Playboy Nick and admit my real relationship partners were my work laptop, index finger, and Harry Potter Nimbus 2000 vibrator . . . well, that would have been in the neighborhood of humiliating.

"I am happy." I smiled widely, taking dark pleasure in the sudden hard glint in his eyes, while also feeling strangely remorseful. "He's a wonderful man." It was the truth. "He's doing a great job as deputy sheriff, and he's a great leader in the community."

"Good parents, right kind of family, good *match*. Right?"

I frowned. Nick gripped his water glass as he studied its contents. His mouth twisted in a bitter line, jaw working.

There was something there, something lurking underneath his words, but I had no idea what it was.

"I guess," I hazarded, searching his face for clues. That was one of the most frustrating things about all of this. How some parts of him, even the smallest gestures, were still familiar. But moments like this reminded me there was a dark side to the moon now, new identities and selves that Nick had cultivated over all these years. I wasn't privy to them.

Watching him during the brittle silence, I frantically groped for what had upset him, what had tripped the wire to some strong, hidden undercurrent of emotion.

"Sounds like he's a perfect fit." His gaze, full of fire now, met mine. "Someone the town, and certainly your parents, like seeing you with."

I'd gone rigid, now fairly certain that I was taking some kind quiz or test, one with high stakes involved. And I was failing.

"I guess my parents get along with Sheriff James, and Janet has always been very nice," I said lamely.

"Sounds like what you deserve then." His tight smile did nothing to smooth the jagged edges of his tone.

I stared at him, feeling lost in a conflict I'd never seen coming.

"How is your family, by the way?" We both sat back as the waiter set my requested bowl of soup in front of me and placed a platter of stuffed mushrooms in the center of the table.

"They're fine," I said, feeling my way around the suddenly unstable, marshy territory.

How had this thing turned around on *me*?

He nodded, as if inviting more.

"My parents are . . . fine. The same. Tavia finished graduate school at Wharton and actually spent some time here in New York doing financial things I never quite understand. Something with hedge funds."

Nick bit back a smile.

"She's back in Green Valley now, working at the bank with Walker."

"The two of them—they're still oil and water?"

I shook my head and let out a slight huff. "Yep. She's currently thwarting all of Walker's attempts to manage the bank and its expansion. Explosions and fireworks every day. All very exciting, from what I hear of it."

"And you're, what, still contributing in an 'as needed' capacity? I noticed you've been representing the bank at fundraisers and events. Couldn't quite break away from the family business, I see."

He raised a brow and I suddenly felt naked, vulnerable, as I remembered all the times I'd bitched to him about getting away. The promises I'd made to us both about overthrowing the expectations, the pressure. The weight.

This dinner was starting to feel like a depressing, subversive version of *This is Your Life*.

This is Your Fucked-Up Life.

"I'm supposed to be a pinch hitter, for the most part. I've been too busy to really contribute meaningfully for a while now. They trot me out for special occasions to network with snobby people, present checks, or extort my relationships at the university." I shrugged. "Not that bad."

Only, sometimes it was.

He nodded, absorbed in smearing the condensation on his glass. "That's good."

I wriggled uncomfortably in my chair, more than ready to turn the bright light of scrutiny back on him.

"And, how about you? How's your mom?"

His entire demeanor changed. His throat worked for a moment before his gaze landed in the opposite corner of the room.

And then I realized my mistake.

I should have proceeded much more carefully, in retrospect. But . . . I hadn't been thinking. And now we were in quicksand.

"She died."

His response, delivered in a near-whisper, seemed to clot any additional words from him. He took a deep breath, then subsided into silence.

I struggled upwards through layers of shock and disbelief. I realized I'd always assumed his mother had gotten better, likely because I'd known her for many years before she'd developed a problem. And she'd hidden it so well, for so long. Had her addiction been the cause of her death? Or something else?

Giving into impulse, I leaned forward and captured Nick's hand in mine. The skin of his palms was rough and callused as if he did manual labor for a living instead of working behind a desk. His oversized hand remained slack and passive for a moment, then tightened around mine.

"I'm sorry, Nick."

"It's okay. There absolutely no reason to be sorry. You didn't know."

"Still . . ." I was mortified to feel my nose stinging. Wetness sprang to my eyes. I swiped at a descending tear. "I apologize for this. I'm sorry."

His grip on mine tightened. His free hand covered mine, sandwiching it. "Why are you sorry?"

I brushed another tear from my cheek. I hated displays of emotion, especially my own. "I just . . ."

"You loved her." His voice was rough. "I know you did. And she loved you, too."

I wanted to ask what happened, but was that appropriate? It would have been years ago, before all the time and distance set in, but now? Probably not.

"It wasn't the drugs. Well, it was and it wasn't. We got her in rehab and it took two tries, but she kicked it. And for many years, I had my mother back again. But in the end, we couldn't escape the consequences of years of drug use. And she died from hepatitis."

I squeezed his hand fiercely, devastated by the grief I saw in his eyes. "I'm so sorry, Nick."

"My entire world changed when she died," he continued distractedly, his eyes growing unfocused. "The cruelest irony was that all I'd ever wanted was to be able to take care of her. To have the means to take away her worries and keep her safe. To be in control of whatever troubles came our way. And when I'd finally done it, when I'd finally made it, all that money, all that influence meant nothing. There was absolutely nothing I could do to save her."

I swiped at another tear.

He released my hand to lean across the table. His features softened as his gaze moved over my face. The sandpaper surface of his thumb slowly wiped at the wetness under my eyes.

"It's okay, Zora," he said, and again I had the feeling that he was answering a question I hadn't asked. It felt as if we were having the same conversation, but on different channels with unresolved shades of meaning.

The waiter returned then.

Nick leaned back, his eyes still intent on my face. I was loathe to release his hand. Too much time had passed for me to share with the same transparency that I had at one time. But I wanted him to feel how badly I hurt for him, for his loss, and for his mother and all that she had been.

Even if all I could offer was a touch.

We ordered and ate dinner quietly, our discussion limited to the upcoming project. His disclosure about his mother left the air heavy and bruised, and neither of us attempted to disrupt that mood with levity or distractions. It was a shared communion of sorts, between two people who had loved the same women fiercely, albeit in very different ways.

When we departed outside the restaurant, Nick handed me up into the fancy Uber while instructing the driver to be careful with me, and I'd felt a shift.

Regardless of whatever had transpired between us all those years ago, there had been a part of me that always loved Nick very much. Though long dormant, it came alive briefly yet again to remind me who Nick had been and the struggles he'd endured. How he'd prospered in spite of it all. Looking into his handsome face, seeing the tired set of his shoulders before he closed the vehicle's door, I'd reminded myself to be angry with him.

I couldn't trust him, not ever again.

Even if I wanted to.

CHAPTER ELEVEN

Nick

My phone rang just as I'd crossed the threshold of our building's lobby. I'd made it as far as the elevator bank when I recognized the customized vibration. My aunt was one of the few people in the world I'd always answer for, no matter what.

I stepped away from the elevators and strode to a quiet corner of the foyer where I could take the call with reasonable privacy. While accepting the call, I frowned at the time on my wrist. Hopefully this would be short.

"Hey, Aunt Nan."

"Don't 'hey, Aunt Nan' me, you little shit. Emily said you were in Green Valley. Is that true?"

I groaned as I set my bag on the marble floor at my feet. This would not be short, and I was going to murder my younger cousin the next time she hit me up for cash.

Aunt Nan was immune to bullshit—especially mine, and especially about this topic.

I decided to stall. "Is that what Emily told you? Well, I'm not."

Silence. "Don't play games with me."

I leaned against the wall, prayed for patience. "I'm in New York right now, at our offices. But yes, I was in Green Valley very briefly. And I'll be going back."

Silence.

"Did you call just so I could hear you breathe into the phone? Because—"

"Why?"

I could easily imagine her standing in the kitchen doorway of her Ann Arbor bungalow, worrying the cord to the wall-mounted phone. I'd bet money, good money, that she was scowling at the opposite wall and chewing on her lower lip.

What I'd hoped would be a stealth trip—one she'd never learn about—had turned out to be anything but. I sighed, feeling resigned. I sat on the nearby plastic chair, rested my elbows on my knees, and searched for the perfect words to reassure her. *Perfect words don't exist.*

"It's for a deal." I took a breath. "An important deal."

"A deal that just happens to be in Green Valley."

Classical music played in the background on her end. My uncle Steve was likely in the adjoining study. He preferred Bach when mulling over his engineering puzzles.

I felt an unexpected pull, a sharp pang of longing. I missed them. I didn't see Aunt Nan and Uncle Steve often; I typically spent my time between New York and San Francisco. But something about being here made me miss that connection, that feeling of belonging somewhere.

"I talked to Eddie," she said.

Shit.

I wiped at my tired eyes. This shouldn't have been a surprise. Eddie and my Aunt Nan had been co-conspirators for years.

"Okay."

"He's worried about you. And so am I."

"You shouldn't be. It's business, that's it."

"You're my sister's son, and she raised you. But I know you. Whatever this is, it's not about money. Now, tell me the truth."

I turned to face the sun's glare against the lobby glass. A procession of cars and taxis inched down Fifth Avenue, their indignant horns blaring. I wished I were back outside and far away from this conversation.

"Why would you want to be go back there?" she pressed. "Eddie told me you took point on this project, rushed it through and barely told him anything about it. And you sure as hell didn't clue him in to your history with that place."

That place. That was how she'd referred to Green Valley ever since my mother and I had shown up at the Detroit Metropolitan Airport separately, worn and defeated. She hated all that Green Valley represented. That my mother had left Michigan with my father all those years ago and settled there, so far from home. That so much had happened in the space of her estrangement with my mother, without her ever knowing. It was just the way of grief, I supposed, the desperate casting about for answers, the way you assigned blame to just about anything to make sense of the loss, to cope, to find peace. She and I both knew the blame for all that happened couldn't be attributed to a location, even if it'd all taken place in Green Valley. But in the end, did it matter? She'd lost her sister. I lost my mother.

"I don't know, Aunt Nan," I said, gripping a handful of my hair. "I guess I've never really found a perfect time to tell my business partner the nitty gritty about how my mother got addicted to drugs. Just never came up, you know?"

Music continued on her end during her silence. Something with strings, with a driving beat. Yep, it was Bach alright. Nan probably thought the music would drown out her side of the conversation, but Uncle Steve was smarter than that. I'd get a call from him soon.

"I don't know what to say," she said, and I bolted upright when I heard the threat of tears in her voice. Aunt Nan did not cry. She grabbed life by the horns, pinned it, and dared it to get up again. She'd never allowed me a moment to stop, to feel sorry for myself or about what had happened. In fact, Zora reminded me of her, especially the remixed, adult version of Zora. Aunt Nan had always been behind me, pushing, prodding, heckling with coarse language. It was a far different style of nurturing, especially compared to my mother's demonstrative, permissive style of parenting. But it'd worked for the snarly, passive aggressive, young adult version of me in Michigan. I knew she loved me and would die for me, just like she'd give anything for her own daughter, Emily.

Now she was crying. Might as well tell on myself. *So much for keeping this close to the chest.*

"Zora's there."

She swallowed back a sniffle. "What? What did you say?"

"I said, Zora's there."

"In Green Valley? What, she's visiting?"

"No. She lives there."

"Since when?"

"Does it matter?"

"I know you know. You've always known where she is. You've always kept track of her. You can't help it." Her tone brightened considerably. "Okay. Zora's there. This is wonderful news. How is she?"

I thought of Zora, dark eyes flashing at me in that little closet back at the hospital. Tears running down her face last night at the restaurant, the bruised indentation in her lip when she'd bit it in a bid to stop her tears. *The silk of her skin beneath my hand . . .*

The way my idiot heart forgot to protect itself around her. All the history, the familiarity, wrapped up in her.

How was Zora?

"She's okay."

"Don't you think it's time?" Aunt Nan's voice was softer. "You won't ever admit it, but I know how much it hurt you to leave her. Watching you always broke my heart, you know that? Seeing the pressure you'd put on yourself to try to take care of everyone. You were just a child, a baby. Eighteen, yes, but in no way equipped to take on the decisions of other adults. Even if it was your mother. There was nothing you could have done to stop your mother from using when she was in Green Valley. I'm proud of you for getting the help you needed—for both of you. It brought you back up here to your family. But I don't think you've ever gotten over leaving Zora. I wish you could see that you didn't have to."

"There's no point in rehashing the past."

"Is she married?"

"What difference does it make? I love you and I'm late for a meeting."

"You're not rushing me off the phone. Sounds like she isn't."

I was relieved to hear more giddiness than tears in her voice now, even if my next words would likely end her improved mood.

"She's in a relationship." I checked my watch again, careful to sound flat and disinterested. "A serious one that will likely end in marriage."

"That's not married," she said, and I was taken aback by the uncharacteristic deviousness in the statement.

"That's the last thing I expected you to say."

"Why? Dating isn't married, and if the young man knew what he had, he'd have put a ring on it already."

"Binging Beyoncé with Emily again, huh?"

"Always."

That made me chuckle. "No, listen. She likes this guy. He's safe. He's the deputy sheriff, his dad was sheriff before him."

"Who wants 'safe?' You know him? Sounds like you don't like him."

I shrugged uncomfortably. "He was a little asshole growing up. But if Zora's with him now, he must have some redeeming qualities."

"I don't care about *his* redeeming qualities. You and that girl loved each other while you were in Pampers, practically. You've been carrying a torch for her for years. You're still in love with her—"

"Aunt—"

"I don't want to hear it. You are. It's why you can't settle down, why you're sticking and moving through all these models, actresses, heiresses—"

My stomach dropped to my shoes. "Please don't ever say that

again, please don't refer to me 'sticking' women. Not like that, not in that context."

"It's true. And you won't ever be able to open your heart to loving *anybody* until you confront what happened all those years ago. It's time to let her in on the truth."

"She's got a life there. She's—" I was about to say *happy*, but stopped, remembering our conversation in the capture station back at the hospital. "She hates me."

"I'm sure she doesn't—"

"She does."

"Well, did you expect her to hug you after all these years? Considering you never came back? Or called? Or—"

"She broke up with *me*. She sent me the ring back with that note. She obviously knew where I was."

"Nick," Aunt Nan said, in the take-no-prisoners tone that meant something hard was coming. "Why the hell didn't you ever contact her? Why are you surprised the poor girl finally sent the ring back after two years of silence?"

I studied my shoes. Put like that, it did come back on me.

"I wasn't ready yet. I kept thinking, 'Let me just get a little more stable, have myself a little more together, then when I came back for her I'd be ready and—'"

"Baby?"

I sighed. "Yes."

"Let me tell you some important things about yourself, so that you can have a better understanding of your own motivations."

"I'm not one of your patients."

"What can I say? You're a lucky you have a psychologist for an aunt. But seriously, here it is—you're a perfectionist by nature. That's served you well in a lot of ways. It's helped you build the career you have today. But growing up, experiencing the things you did—not just in Green Valley, but watching your mother struggle to recover, feeling helpless when she died—it's shaped you."

"I hope it's an interesting shape. Like a quatrefoil."

"I love you, but you can be hard. And controlling. Especially when you *think* you're right, especially when you want to rescue someone you love, and especially when you feel helpless. Yes, you were helpless at crucial moments in your childhood, and that's no fault of your own."

I ran a hand through my hair. "Is this session free? Or should I send you a co-pay through Zelle?"

"I understand this conversation makes you uncomfortable, but listen. Just listen. Being in Green Valley won't always be easy. It's not easy to confront the past, but that's exactly what you need to do. So, I want to give you some homework and I want you to humor your all-knowing aunt and actually do it. Go back to the hard places. Deal with the places and moments you most want to forget."

"I thought you didn't want me to go back there?"

"When did I say that?"

"Just a minute ago!" I caught myself before throwing my hand in the air.

"I said nothing of the sort. Just listen to me, okay? Do your best to embrace that little boy Nick that became a scared teenager, then a desperately ambitious young man. The root of it all is in Green Valley. So take some time to get reacquainted. Heal the past so you can heal the hard places in you. It'll be good for you, and—" She paused and lowered her voice. "It will help you reconnect with Zora. Might do her some good too."

So she gets to hate the town, and yet I need to deep dive into it? "Aunt Nan—"

"And be gentle with Zora."

I huffed out a laugh, certain it sounded frustrated. "You're worried about *her?*"

"Be gentle."

"Zora scares the shit out of me and I'm the one who needs to be gentle?"

Her laugh broke through the line, full and unrestrained. "Good for her! I can't wait to meet her—"

"Aunt Nan, you're not going to meet—"

"Alright, now get busy confronting the past and getting that girl back. I've gotta go, but send the Leffersbees my love." *Click*.

I stared at the display. She'd hung up. What was this, The Twilight Zone?

CHAPTER TWELVE

Zora

The training went off without a hitch. The supervising clinical directors for all of Rocket's staff clinicians were eager to learn the skills they would in turn teach to others. I handled reviewing fundamental communication skills and related literature as appropriate. I'd left Adesola to take over after lunch, knowing our clients would most likely feel comfortable role-playing challenging scenarios with an audience limited to clinicians. My absence would give them room to share sensitivities and admissions they might not otherwise make with a non-clinician like me present.

I hitched my work bag higher over my shoulder, closed the door to the conference room, and smiled at the peal of laughter I heard on the other side of the door. God only knew what practice scenarios Adesola had dreamed up.

I'd only taken two steps out into the hallway when I heard Rocket's receptionist's strained voice. "Dr. Leffersbee! How can I help you? Do you need anything?"

She'd already risen from her desk, looking pained as she began to approach me.

I held up a hand to halt her progress. "No worries, thank you. I'm just taking a break. I thought I might give our group some privacy while they continue working through the material. Would you be fine with me sitting here?" I gestured to the plush waiting chairs arranged across from her. After three hours of standing in the punishing grip of uncomfortable shoes, I was more than ready to collapse into the depths of the overstuffed chairs.

The office was impressive. Modern furniture and floor-to-ceiling windows conveyed a cutting-edge techie vibe, but the rich mahogany woods of the receptionist's desk and floor contributed to a warmer, welcoming aesthetic. My gaze caught once again on the company's name emblazoned over the receptionist's head in oversized, metal letters: Rocket Enterprises.

I felt a stirring of pride for Nick. I could only imagine how fulfilling the sight must be for him each time he walked in that door and saw the empire he'd built from nothing. He'd been a young man who'd experienced significant struggles in his young life, and was now greeted by this sign upon entering this office on the top floor of one of Manhattan's most prominent buildings.

Well. It had to leave him breathless; I certainly felt that way.

"I can find another space for you," she said, "if that would make you more comfortable." The receptionist blended in perfectly with the surroundings. Her flaxen hair was secured in a low French knot at the nape of her neck. Her skirt and blouse were professional yet fashionable, and her makeup had been applied with an expert hand. Taking in her strained smile, I finally read between the lines. She didn't want me lounging in the lobby, if it could be avoided.

"If that's easier . . ." I started to say. The door behind me opened.

"Mr. Rossi." Her posture stiffened. "How nice to see you today."

I turned to see Nick behind me, mouthwatering in a pair of dark jeans. His green polo shirt stretched across his wide shoulders. Abruptly, I found swallowing difficult, as if my tongue had suddenly grown three sizes in the space of that one moment.

His gaze moved slowly over me, no doubt taking in my summery, knee-length dress and matching yellow cardigan. I could find nothing to say as his eyes returned to my face.

"Hey, Samantha," he said, finally moving the weight of his attention from my face to her.

I took a deep, silent breath, as my heart hammered an erratic rhythm. What the hell was wrong with me? I'd been in the presence of truly delicious men before, and without all my body's circuits misfiring. Maybe I needed to schedule some time with my Nimbus 2000 when I got home. It had to be my hormones making me crazy, right?

Right?

Samantha was explaining how she was in the process of directing me to another space when he glanced back at me, that half-smirk in place.

"Bored already? Trying to break out?"

"Adesola's got it covered. They're role-playing now."

One of his ink-black brows went up. "Role-playing?"

I bit my lip. It wasn't suggestion, exactly, that colored his voice. But there was a quality of teasing I hadn't expected. Mere days ago, I'd wanted to rip his head off, skewer him, cauterize his empty words and apologizes. Now a shocking parade of mental images filled my mind's eye as I surveyed his tall, solid frame. We'd never done any role-playing. Hell, we'd been eighteen when we'd parted and still so enthralled with the newness of everything that game-playing hadn't even occurred to us yet. But my imagination was in perfect working order now, likely fueled by my own personal drought. What kind of role playing would we have done, if we'd had time? Nick in UPS shorts, those muscled quads on full display. Or—

Jesus, Zora. You're in public. Get ahold of yourself.

I came back to myself just in time to realize Nick had asked me something. I looked askance between him and Samantha, searching for context clues.

"Tour." Nick's mouth twitched, those clever evergreen eyes alight as though he guessed at the illicit thoughts cycling through my head. "I asked if you'd had one."

Samantha looked between us, a new line between her brows.

"Oh." It was, for some reason, a difficult question to answer. Forcibly, I suppressed my lurid thoughts and concentrated. "No."

"Alright." Nick's hand went to his pockets as he rocked back on his heels.

"Why?"

"Why don't I take you on a short tour?"

"Uh . . . okay."

"Great." He inclined his head, indicating I should follow him, and I complied. I got one last glimpse of Samantha's blank stare as we turned the corner.

"So," I began, mentally kicking myself and my need to fill the silence. "This is a great office."

Nick looked back at me as we made our way down the hall. Raised, excited voices sounded behind the conference room door I'd just exited a few moments prior.

"Our trainings are pretty interactive," I said by way of explanation for the loud chatter, examining the framed photos interspersed along the walls. Some appeared to be staff photos, while others were early press releases chronicling Nick's accomplishments. I paused in my progress, peering closely at a picture of a young, smiling Nick. His arm was thrown around the shoulders of another man with an equally wide grin. They stood at the front desk we'd just left, under the Rocket Enterprises sign.

"That's Eddie Banks. My partner."

Nick stood beside me, his gaze trained on the picture. His arm brushed mine and something like static ran up my arm. Keeping my face straight, I noted the intensity of his gaze, the tension in his folded arms. Had something happened with his partner?

"It looks like a beautiful moment. You both must have been so proud."

He nodded, not taking his eyes off the photo. "We'd just opened this, our second location. Our first office is in San Francisco. I'd argued with him about the cost. I didn't think making such a big expenditure here was a wise move at our early stage of growth."

I scrutinized his strong profile, the tight purse to his full lips. "So what convinced you?"

He shook his head, half-laughing. "Eddie did. Said it would pay for itself, that it would be a drop in the bucket compared to what we were about to bring in." He nodded to himself. "And he was right."

"I'm glad you had the benefit of a partner. I can only imagine how lonely it would have been otherwise, managing those kinds of difficult decisions alone, without the counsel of someone you trust."

"I do trust him," Nick said, quietly, as if to himself. "He's one of the few people I trust completely. Him, and my Aunt Nan."

"Sounds like you would do well to listen to them, then."

He faced me suddenly, his vivid eyes startlingly bright as they searched mine. "Maybe you're right."

This close, I scented the familiar, unique essence of him. He smelled like clean skin, sandalwood, and betrayal.

Get a grip, Zora. You can't trust this man, not ever again.

I blinked at the intensity of his gaze, and then he turned. "C'mon."

His arm briefly extended in my direction and his hand brushed against mine for the barest moment.

I followed in his wake, my fingers tingling from the brief contact of his hand against my skin.

He narrated our progress, explaining the purposes of smaller administrative offices and larger suites, until we came to the mouth of a hallway facing two large sets of double doors.

Nameplates indicated that Nick's office was to the left of his partner's. He quickly keyed in a code and pushed in the door, revealing a massive space that rivaled the first floor of my house in size. The massive desk one would expect occupied one corner, with a separate meeting area and bartender's cart.

But it was the view that stole my breath and left me wide-eyed. Gingerly, I made my way to the floor-to-ceiling window, hypnotized by the streets of Manhattan so far below, the cars and people reduced to tiny specs, everything ant-sized from this vantage point.

"This is amazing," I breathed, unable to tear my gaze away.

"It is, isn't it?" His tone seemed bemused. I caught his reflection behind me in the glass, slowly advancing.

"My first time in here, I don't think I was able to speak for a whole minute."

"You've come a long way from Green Valley."

"Some days I think so. Others . . ."

I snuck a glance to the side, where Nick leaned against this desk.

This version of Nick wasn't at all what I expected, not from reading about him and not from our recent encounters. I'd been distracted, I realized, busy reacting to him and the circumstances that brought us together. But in this unguarded moment, observing his tense perusal of the skyline, I was aware of a heaviness, a burden. Even in the midst of his stunning accomplishments, it was clear he was dissatisfied and unsettled. He was conflicting layers of pride and arrogance . . . and angst. Reflecting light in public, absorbing sullen darkness in private.

Affection and warmth I hadn't imagined could still exist for this man swamped me. He'd obviously worked so hard to put behind the boy, the young man, he'd once been. But watching him now, I still saw that boy I'd known almost all of my life and all the fierce longing and determination that had always been a part of him.

"I'm proud of you," I said, realizing my own self-preservation was somehow at stake as I said it. But I wanted—no, needed—him to hear it. I wanted the statement, the veracity of it, to reach him wherever he was.

He let out a breath and slowly straightened from the desk.

"Thank you, Z."

I held my breath as he continued toward me, towering over me when he finally came to a stop. I fought the urge to step back from the heat of his body and all the danger he represented. "But I want you to know, I would give it all up if I could turn back the hands of time. If I could find a way to go back so that we were never separated."

I averted my face, teeth tightly clenched, fighting to stem rising frustration.

He was the one who left. What kind of cop-out was that? It *had* been in his power to keep his mouth off that redhead. What had stopped him from picking up a phone? Writing a letter? Sending a carrier pigeon?

This supposed regret? I couldn't buy it. And from the look on his face, he believed what he was saying, which ratcheted up my anger by several hundred degrees.

You have to help him, accommodate him as the hospital's new partner. For your own good. Keep it together.

Maybe he really *did* think some cosmic force kept us apart. That it wasn't just him, wanting to pursue a new love while his old one sat waiting to hear from him.

"I'm proud of you, too, Zora. More than you know. Things didn't quite turn out the way we thought they would. But you? What you've accomplished, your research, the way you help people? It's nothing short of amazing. I'm blown away by all that you've built, and how much your work obviously means to the hospital."

Maybe this was the moment Leigh thought I needed. Maybe this was what "closure" looked like. Maybe it wasn't about excavating through all the misdeeds and misremembering until you hit the truth, but more so about telling each other what you needed to hear to keep limping along in life.

And maybe, just maybe, things between us had ended exactly as they should.

Had we stayed together, would he have made these strides? Become what he is today? Would I be the same person or have pursued the same path? Maybe it just hadn't been meant to be. Maybe *we* just hadn't been meant to be.

Perhaps it was just time to accept that.

"I'm beginning to think our paths followed the course fate determined for us, Nick. It's likely that, in the end, that was for the best."

CHAPTER THIRTEEN

Zora

"Cinderella! You're finally ditching your commercial pumpkin to fly in a private coach? Thank God you came to your senses."

Adesola grinned from her seat aboard Nick's private plane, wine glass in hand, as I boarded the small plane.

I was not at my best and fighting to climb out of an abysmal mood. My interaction with Nick had kicked off an endless cycle of rumination that poisoned any chance at a decent night of sleep. I'd finally caught the thinnest current of sleep but woke up after several hours of tossing and turning to discover I'd overslept.

"I missed my flight," I groused. "I didn't have much of choice. I was going to take the next flight out, but Nick's coordinator happened to call and she said he hadn't left yet, so . . ."

"So, you're slumming it back with us." Adesola made a show of leaning back into the cushion of the seat and let out a throaty purr of pleasure. "Good for you! You know, that's the benefit of flying private. Travel is arranged around your schedule and not the other way around."

"Listen to you. You sound like you've been doing this all your life." Carry-on in hand, I surveyed the opulence of the plane's off-white interior: the sleek lines, the rows of paired white leather seats, the rounded windows easily three times larger than the commercial variety.

Good Lord. This was how Nick lived, how he traveled.

"This is crazy," I said, casting another bewildered look around.

Adesola grinned again and made a show of tossing the dark fall of her hair over one shoulder. "It is crazy, but I've decided I'm worth it. I've just got to figure out how I'm going to travel like this from now on." She took a sip of her wine. "You missed out not flying with us here. We had a ball and I really enjoyed getting to know Nick. He's a great guy. Funny how you never mentioned him after all this time."

I shrugged off the weight of gathering irritation. *Sure he is. He's a real prince.* "What, I should tell you about all my childhood friends?" I settled my purse and carry-on bag across the aisle from her and ran a lazy hand over the armrest. The leather was silk-soft with the give of melted butter. I had a feeling this would be a much more pleasant experience than the cramped coach seat I'd purchased aboard the flight I missed.

A glossy, perfectly-groomed flight attendant appeared from the back of the plane to greet me and inquire about my drink preferences. I'd assured her I only wanted water, lamented we couldn't lace it with tranquilizers, and was utterly charmed by her beatific smile. She quickly took possession of my carry-on after I removed the personal items I needed during the flight.

"I like his style. These seats recline, you know. We just have to wait until after liftoff. Listen, can we please keep him?" She peered at me over the rim of her glass, her eyes slitted and sly.

I frowned, unable to follow her logic. "What are you smoking? What do you mean, 'keep him?'"

Her voice lowered to a whisper as she leaned across the aisle toward me. "The man is clearly crazy about you."

"He's crazy about what our curriculum will do to help his company's bottom line."

"Nope. It's you. I see it in the way he's always watching you, the way he always seems eager to touch you, even when it's for the slightest thing." She shook her head, studying the contents of her gently sloshing wine. "You can see the . . . *heat* in his eyes when he looks at you."

"Sounds like you're describing heartburn."

"I know you don't believe that. I think he's a really great guy."

I yanked my headphones out of my travel pouch with more force than was probably necessary. "Do you? All it took was private flight to convince you of that, huh?"

"Of course it's not just the flight. I love talking to him. He's so passionate about what he does. I love hearing his creative ideas about creating easy pathways to health care for the people who desperately need it. And I will admit, this is the one of the sweetest consulting fees I've ever gotten. That didn't hurt. The fee he paid for a one-day workshop with two motivated docs? I call it a win. Let me show you the shoes I'm buying this weekend."

I settled into my seat, trying not to gasp out loud from the glory of the plush seat absorbing me into its soft embrace. Suddenly, I remembered just how tired I was. Maybe I'd finally get restful sleep, even if only for the duration of this flight. It'd been a long week.

Nick, along with the supervising clinicians, had taken us to a fancy steakhouse in midtown the previous night after our training. He and Adesola had kept up a steady banter about the state of health care and the rising cost of pharmaceuticals. They'd debated various health reform plans, all while sawing into aged steaks and downing vodka tonics. I hadn't contributed much, and had been too distracted to take up the thread of tepid conversation offered by the supervising clinicians. I'd been unable to break free from my own compulsive, sleep-hazed loop of thoughts, which demanded to know if I was a coward or passive for not forcing the issue of Nick's disappearance and the Coffee Shop Kiss.

Was it mature to ignore the issue, to bury my own feelings in the name of moving on? Or was that avoidant behavior?

And did it matter, in the end? The guy was only here because he had a product to sell. That was the only reason why he'd come back. Pressing the issue just made me *needy*, right?

See? *Someone, please, turn my brain off.*

"Look at these." Adesola thrust her phone across the aisle. I squinted to make out an admittedly gorgeous pair of crystal-studded heels with the iconic red bottoms. I peered more closely at the caption at the bottom and yelped. "You're going to spend almost four grand on these? Where are you wearing them?"

Adesola gave me the dark, mischievous smile that somehow curled the ends of her lips and signaled the arrival of something naughty. "I like them. And maybe I don't plan on wearing them anywhere. Shoes like these, darling, aren't meant for walking. They're meant to be draped over your man's back. You should get a pair and try it. Oh, hello, Nick."

I jumped, dropping my Kindle in the process.

Sure enough, Nick stood at the entrance to the plane, silhouetted by a halo of bright sunshine. He was casual in jeans and a plain black T-shirt, gripping a carry-on bag in one hand and holding a newspaper tucked under one well-formed arm. He lifted an eyebrow at me.

I threw a horrified glance at Adesola and saw her sly, feline grin grow as she greeted Nick.

There was no way he missed what she'd said.

I aimed a warning look at her, but she ignored me. We both knew what she'd done, and that she'd done it on purpose.

She'd somehow gotten it into her head that Nick and I would be perfect together and hadn't stopped dropping little hints. And now, a bigger one.

"I think you should give him a go, sweetie," she opined after Nick dropped us at the hotel after dinner. "I don't know anything about the sheriff you're dating back home in that sleepy little town. But I never hear you mention him, and this man here seems like he knows what's what. I think he could be the one to wake you up, Sleeping Beauty."

I ignored her as we stumbled onto the elevator, both steeped in exhaustion. "There's ancient history between us. And he screws a different, tight-bodied tax *bracket now,"* I pronounced, then hastily added, *"not that I'm interested anyway."*

Adesola clearly had other ideas. I didn't miss the light that flared in her eyes when Nick advanced toward me, so close his leg touched mine as he stood in the aisle.

Damn he was tall, especially in a plane this small.

He stared down at me with a small little smile, saying nothing. I looked back, silent, determined not to fill the air with all the nervous energy running through me.

"Hi," he said finally, his voice gravelly. "Fancy seeing you here."

"Hey," I returned, neck craned to take in the darkening stubble on his neck, the deeper shadows under his eyes. His hair had endured a marathon of tugging and raking, I deduced as I took in the wild, unkempt strands. He braced a hand against the compartment above, his shirt rising just enough to allow my eyes to play peek-a-boo with the dark whorls of hair on his tightly muscled stomach. God, when had he gotten that *hairy?* Was he that hairy everywhere? Did he have one of those delightful happy trails? And why the hell was it *turning me on?*

I realized I hadn't done a good job of schooling my wayward eyes when his smile evaporated. Something hot and dangerous entered his expression.

"Heard you missed your flight. This is an unexpected treat." His gaze took a lazy course down my seated body, flicked back to my chest and stayed. "I like it."

"Huh?" *Dear God, I sound like an idiot.*

He gestured to my chest with his head. "Your shirt. I like it."

I glanced down. I'd never been one to dress up for a flight. My twin loved to harangue me about it, always going on and on about "the least I could do." Well, today I'd done the absolute least. I wore a pair of dark joggers and athletic shoes. The halves of my cable knit sweater had fallen apart to reveal a pink shirt that said . . . Oh. It said, *Nevertheless, She Persisted.* Now that I thought about it, it might have taken too many turns in the dryer. Maybe it was a little too snug. Jesus.

Heat stung my cheeks as I met his gaze again. He appeared to be fighting back a smile.

I squared my shoulders. "Yep. I like it too."

Who knows how much longer we'd have stared at each other, silently, if Adesola hadn't piped from behind him, her voice overly loud in the cabin of the small plane.

"Hi, Nick!"

He turned, appearing startled. "Dr. Rojas, hi."

I half-listened as they politely chatted about the previous evening and how she'd slept.

And then he was suddenly back in my space, passing in front of me and settling in the seat next to me.

"Uh. You're sitting here?"

He busied himself with pulling an iPad and red folder out of his bag. "That okay?"

No. "Sure."

The flight attendant returned, whisked his bag away and took his drink order.

"So." Adesola's smile was full of mischief, and I swallowed back the impulse to club her with my Kindle as I scented trouble on the horizon. "Nick told me a little about his childhood in Green Valley. I learned things I'd never known about you, too."

I turned and found Nick leaning toward me, his elbow on the armrest between us. "The good old days," he said, and I wondered what was behind his flat tone.

"He said he wanted to be a politician when he grew up. Governor, then president. And you wanted to be a doctor. I never knew that about you. You never told me that."

I nodded. "I did. I wanted to have a free clinic in Green Valley and spend part of the year with Doctors Without Borders."

"So? What happened? You'd be an incredible doctor." Her confusion and curiosity were plain as she propped her chin on a fist, her dark eyes moving between us.

"Life." I shrugged, not wanting to dig that deeply into the past with Nick at my elbow.

Perhaps sensing my discomfort, Nick stepped in. "The plan was that I was going to hold it down at home most of the year, passing legislation that made life better for people in town and nearby Appalachia. But we agreed I'd travel with her, to keep her safe and maybe help with peace-keeping missions."

Well, so much for any attempt to downplay the nature of our past relationship.

I risked a look at him, turning my head on a slow swivel to face him. God, he looked so tired. My fingers yearned to coast along the prickled surface of his jaw, to test the depth of weariness under his eyes.

"We were silly, weren't we?" His smile and his tone somehow seemed too personal, too private for the moment given Adesola was sitting right there. "Just dumb kids."

I looked away. "Yeah. We were dumb."

"Well," Adesola said, in the same overloud voice, "I'm just going to put some music on. So I can get to sleep. I probably won't be able to hear a thing, so don't worry about talking to me from here on out."

Yep. I was gonna kill her. Slowly.

I kept my face in my Kindle until after take-off. When the flight attendant came over to ask if we needed anything else, Nick spoke up.

"Are you sure you don't want anything? You seem tired. Anything you could use to relax?"

I closed my eyes, wondering what I'd done to become fate's adversary. Nick and I were practically fully reclined in our chairs now. The armrest between us was lifted away to allow complete access to the fast-charging ports below. Yes, we were in two separate chairs, but it suddenly felt a lot like sleeping in the same bed together, scarcely more than two feet apart. Those biceps, those shoulders, those wicked eyes, that mouth, all less than two feet away. And he was giving me that concerned look I remembered all too well.

My heart was not fashioned from concrete. I doubted I'd survive this flight, survive *him*. His proximity, the clean smell of him, the ghost of all that had been between us, it all threatened my very existence.

"I'm okay. I don't need anything."

He looked past me to the flight attendant. "Get her a warm blanket, please."

She murmured her assent and disappeared.

I raised an eyebrow at him. "Bossy, aren't you?"

He shrugged. "You didn't know you needed it yet."

I bit back my usual reaction: the impulse to correct him for overriding my wishes. I was tired of fighting. Tired, period.

"You're not sleeping much." He lifted a brow as his gaze moved over my face.

"And you are?"

He ran a hand over his lower jaw before shoving it through his hair. "I don't sleep well in general."

There had been a time when my hands had always been in his hair, rearranging the mess he'd made or taming that stubborn cowlick at the crown. With all that was unsettled and forgotten between us, I couldn't understand my current urge to feel those slick, dark locks sliding through my fingers again. I wanted to close the space between us, to revel in the strength of his chest against my own softness. I wanted to feel the steel of his thighs under mine.

Who said human biology was wired for safety or common sense?

"You used to sleep like the dead. What changed?"

"Life." He said it just as stiffly as I probably had, and I nodded before turning away.

The flight attendant returned in short order, spreading a warm blanket over me that felt like the best hug I'd ever gotten.

I tucked into the romance novel on my Kindle, feeling sleep hovering somewhere in the not-too-distant periphery. The book had come highly recommended by Leigh and sat waiting on my virtual bookshelf for months. It was entertaining from the first page and then . . . I blinked in disbelief as the first chapter unfolded into a highly explicit sex scene.

"What are you reading? You're breathing funny."

I looked up, startled.

"Uh . . . a grant application?"

"Oh, really?" His tone was one of casual disinterest and he flipped through his screen with a stylus. "What's the topic?"

I groped for an answer. "Communication. And, uh, doctors."

"Well, that's specific."

I turned and found him suddenly much closer than I'd expected, his weight fully canted toward my side as he peered at my screen. This close, I could see each of the individual coarse hairs in the growing scuff over his cheeks. He smell was enticing, the notes of clean skin and sandalwood beckoning me closer. I turned away, taking my roving eyes with me, before I did something embarrassing like nosing further into him to chase the elusive scent.

"Yeah, it's interesting."

"I guess so." His voice was laden with laughter. "Especially if they're advocating for —" He leaned even closer, his eyes on my screen. "'The proud, arrogant upthrust of his turgid length?'"

Heat flooded my cheeks. "Get back on your side!"

He cracked up, head thrown against the headrest, Adam's apple working.

My reaction, to throw my elbow into his side, was deeply ingrained, a reflex learned in third grade. I didn't really register what I'd done until he gave a loud laugh-groan.

"I'm not judging, Zora. Hell, I think you've got the market cornered on what makes for an enjoyable flight."

"It's an invasion of privacy, you know, to read someone else's screen."

His color was high from laughing. "You're right. I'm sorry. Why don't we switch? Although I think I'd be the real winner in that trade. I'm reviewing a lease. Nothing fun here."

That got my attention. "Lease? What do you need a lease for? Where?"

"I'm leasing a house in Green Valley. Hopefully I won't need it for more than a month. Just until things are worked out with the app and the hospital is satisfied Rocket has met all their conditions."

"Why lease a house, for something so temporary?"

"Because of Sir Duke. He'll need someplace to run around."

"Sir Duke?"

"Yes." He scrolled through his iPad until he turned it my way.

I gawped at the screen.

It was a greyhound, exceptionally slim, without an ounce of extra fat anywhere on its entire body. Judging from the patch of gray around its snout, it was older.

"This is your dog? You have a dog?" He nodded, and I was both amused and touched to see the same expression new mothers wore when foisting baby pictures on unsuspecting strangers.

"You named him Sir Duke?"

I looked up from the screen. Nick nodded, holding my gaze. "Yes."

And just like that, I remembered all the dance parties we'd had in my parents' finished basement as kids. My dad or Walker playing DJ, spinning our favorites, organizing Soul Train Lines we all boogied down. Stevie Wonder was one of Nick's absolute favorite artists. *Songs in the Key of Life* had been our favorite album, and "Sir Duke" was one of Nick's favorite songs. He loved the driving beat, the exultant lyrics, the infectious melody. He'd played, sang it, hummed it, head bopped to it when he was happy and in the moments when he was desperately trying to get back to happy. I'd once threatened him with death after hearing him hum it all day at school, and then during dinner at my house that evening. He'd agreed to stop with mock solemnity until my mother suddenly started singing back up for him while Tavia imitated the trumpet blare and Walker played the drumline on the table. That song was the soundtrack of our childhood.

And he'd named his damn dog "Sir Duke."

God. I needed to get away from him. Off this plane, and then to whatever half of Green Valley or Knoxville he wasn't in. Spending time with him was like opening a cedar chest of memories that started out sweet, then turned rotten and moth-eaten.

"I always wanted a dog." He grinned at the phone's display of his skeletal dog, and despite myself, something in my heart pinched.

"I know." His mother had not been a fan of dogs.

"And then I kept saying I would get one, whenever things slowed down. And then I realized that there would never be a perfect time and things were never gonna slow down. So I rescued Sir Duke from a racing outfit in Florida. We have a rule, he and I. We don't spend more than five days apart unless I'm traveling internationally."

"Sounds like a celebrity marriage."

"Nah, I can actually trust him." He laughed, then stopped. His gaze flew to mine as he breathed in sharply.

I frowned, apparently having missed something.

"He's my guy. Since these negotiations are taking longer than I'd anticipated, and I hate living out of a hotel anyway, one of my assistants is driving him down."

I smiled privately, imagining the bony dog riding in the back of a limousine with sunglasses. "Sounds like Sir Duke certainly lives a charmed life."

"He deserves it," Nick said, and I frowned at the dissonant note in his voice. "He's had a hard life up until now."

I listened as Nick extolled Sir Duke's virtues. I watched a video he'd taken of the dog racing through the park and collecting thrown balls.

And I wondered if Nick even realized that he was talking about himself.

∾

Nick

This was the flight from hell.

Zora's head rested on my chest. Her hand had started out resting against my collarbone then slowly descended down my side until it clasped my hip. I held my breath, fighting against the tickle of her pineapple-scented curls under my nose, the softness of her hip against mine, the fullness of her breast against my chest.

Bravely, I kept my eyes ahead where a large monitor tracked the flight's progress. Only two and half hours from New York to Knoxville. Only an hour and forty-five minutes to go.

I could not think of a more effective form of torture.

The flight attendant smiled at Zora's snuggle-assault and tucked the blanket more securely around us. Zora tightened her hold on me, nuzzled more closely into my chest. One of her legs intruded between mine.

I swallowed back the sawdust in my mouth, ran through the stats for each of the Yankees. I needed to suppress the lurid thoughts that accompanied the press of Zora softness against the entire right side of my body.

After days of Zora staring at me with accusing eyes, of her watching me with all the caution of a spooked deer, here she was. In sleep she'd come to me the way she had so many times before. Her body still conformed to mine that same way, twelve years later.

Her body remembered my body. My body remembered hers.

But when she woke up, she'd retreat. The spell would be broken. All that separated us before would again divide us again.

I allowed myself to rest my chin against her forehead. Closed my eyes and listened as her breath whistled in and out. I meditated on the little kitten noises, the tiny stretch she made when I slid my numb hand from under her and rested it chastely against her back.

"Does she know?"

I glanced over to find Adesola standing in the aisle between us, learning against the seat, arms folded. I wondered how long she'd stood there. Ever since she'd migrated over to my seat, Zora had been my only reality.

"Know what?" My fingers splayed against Zora's back as I internally assured myself she was real. She was actually in my arms after all these years.

"That you're here for her." Her head tilted, her eyes going soft as she regarded me. "We both know you're not here for that app. I met at least five of your employees yesterday who are more than capable of doing this." She sent me a *tell the truth* look. "You're here for *her*."

I gave my attention to the window and stretches of clouds hundreds of miles beneath us. Zora's chest expanded against mine in regular intervals, her breathing still deep.

"She's with someone." The words angered me even as I spoke them. *Fucking Jackson James, of all people.*

Adesola made a scornful noise and I looked back to see her wave a hand as if I'd irritated her. "I never hear her talk about that guy. She doesn't bring him to functions. He doesn't check on her, doesn't see about her, I don't even know if he knows about the position she's in now—"

What? "What do you mean?"

She hesitated, worrying her lip as she regarded me. "What do you want from her?"

The answer came far more quickly than I'd anticipated. "Everything."

"I like you, I do. I like seeing the two of you together. Zora's . . . different with you. Off-balance. I think that's good for her and I think you remind her of the things she's given up on or forgotten. She deserves to be happy more than anyone I know. God knows she does so much for everyone else." She pinned me in place with a glare. "But if you so much as hurt a hair on her hair, I swear to God—"

"Dr. Rojas—"

"Adesola."

"Adesola. I don't know . . . It's been a long time."

"Just be there for her. She needs that. Especially right now."

This was maddening. "What, exactly, is going on? What position is she in? What do I need to do?"

"Talk to her. And let me say this: That woman is not just my colleague, she's my friend. I'd never speak so informally or even broach the topic if I wasn't so close with Zora, and if I didn't see that look in your eyes. You're not going to stop, are you, until you get what you want?"

I let out a breath, recognizing the truth in her words. "That's right."

She nodded, her eyes on her feet. "Well, then I need to let you know, business relationship or not—if you hurt her, I'll pull your testicles through your throat."

That made me smile. "You know, for a gynecologist, your take on anatomy—"

"Don't be a smart-ass." She shaped her small hand into a fist. "Just remember. *Through your throat.* Got it?"

I nodded, my hand absently massaging a pattern into Zora's back. "I got it."

CHAPTER FOURTEEN

Zora

I hadn't planned on visiting my parents before my morning drive to Knoxville. Even as I turned the corner and piloted my car past the familiar brick homes and waved to dog-walking neighbors, I asked myself what the hell I was doing. I'd been out of sorts and unsettled ever since Nick's appearance, yes, but there was no way I could air any of that out to my parents. Not when I needed to reassure them that everything was fine. Under control. Intact and regularly scheduled as usual. Those were our roles, anyway, and so far, everything about Nick left me shaken and off my game. So, why was I, along with the ball of confused feelings in my chest, headed to my parents' house? What was I looking for?

I let myself in the front door, shucking off my flats at the front door before I headed down the hallway and into the kitchen where my father sat at the kitchen table eating breakfast. He lowered his newspaper to observe my approach, then grinned. "ZoZo! Whoa! This is a nice surprise."

I laughed at my father's exaggerated intake of breath as I padded into the kitchen on bare feet. God, I hadn't expected to feel such overwhelming relief at being home. Lately, I hadn't seen my parents as often as usual, and I had my reasons. It wasn't easy to admit personal defeat to the two people who'd raised me to endure and triumph over any difficulties I encountered in life. Lately my endurance had been badly frayed and any chances of a victory seemed further and further away. And I didn't want to be fussed at or lectured for admitting that I suddenly wasn't sure about a lot of the things I'd always taken for granted. I hadn't realized until Nick reappeared just how far my life had fallen into disrepair. Just how unhappy I was. But now, here in my family's home, I was again a smaller part docked into a larger unit, no longer adrift in the world. I inhaled the scent of cooling cinnamon rolls on the stove and relaxed at the soft bubbling of percolating coffee. I sighed at the quiet rush of reassurance that came from being in this very familiar space.

Both the epic and mundane had occurred at this very kitchen table. My parents had presided over many a scrabble between my siblings and myself, meted out punishments over large and small infractions, and celebrated our triumphs. Memories assaulted me as I stopped and really took in my father, surrounded by all the little tchotchkes and mementos accumulated in our harvest-themed kitchen. It was a testament to the life my parents had built together, a lifetime of loving, fighting, making up, and loving even more fiercely than before. I couldn't help but remember how a younger me dreamed of having this very same life with Nick. I'd imagined meeting Nick's eyes over our own breakfast table every morning, and slowly adding highchairs of squirming children. But it wasn't in the cards for me. My chance with Nick ended years ago.

And I didn't see it happening with Jackson. So the best I could do was choose to be happy in all the other areas of my life. To nourish and build upon those areas that were . . . well, a hot ass mess at the moment. Right? Because ultimately it was far more important to concentrate on real, tangible accomplishments. Things that would stand up over time. Like my research.

Shit.

Fuck my life.

I thought of Nick and winced. He'd once been a permanent fixture in this kitchen. He and I had twirled on those very same dark leather stools at the counter as children, wheedling after-school snacks from my mother. By high school, we'd been pseudo-chefs assembling our own elaborate creations, then disappearing to the basement or our favorite spot in the woods.

I shook my head at myself. Is that why I'd come here? For a highlight reel of all my most gut-wrenching memories with Nick?

"*I love you, Z,*" seventeen-year-old Nick had said, his vivid green eyes fixed on mine as we'd laid side by side on a carpet of crunchy leaves and soft earth, a canopy of gnarled branches stretching over us. "*Forever. We'll always be together. We'll get out of this town. Soon. Together. Just like we planned.*"

But that hadn't happened. By the time I'd transferred to Northwestern for college, Nick had been gone for an entire year. The bleeding in my heart may have slowed, but it never really stopped.

Hard experience had taught me that not every dark corner needed light. I'd learned to suppress much of the emotion and impulsivity that had guided my college years. I was an adult. Firmly settled in the career I'd worked so hard for. I couldn't afford to remember how good, how *normal* it had felt when I woke up in Nick's arms on our return flight. For a moment, just a moment, before I opened my eyes, I'd been awash with a kind of peace and contentment I hadn't felt in *years*. I'd breathed in the familiar smell of him and reveled in his hold. And then I'd opened my eyes and remembered. Remembered all that we weren't, and how much it would cost me to repeat the mistake of trusting him. By the time I finally came to myself, I was practically in his lap. He'd waved away my embarrassment and apologies, then practically fled the plane the moment it landed. And he hadn't ridden back into town in his own hired car with Adesola and I as planned.

Adesola, thankfully, sensed my humiliation and never said a word. But I wanted to wring my own neck. I *knew* better, I did. But my own body had betrayed me.

Dear God, I was a hussy in my sleep.

No more thinking about Nick. I slipped a mental leash around my thoughts as I made my way to my father. Spending any more time thinking about Nick would only uncork a geyser of angst I'd spent years smothering. Judging by how unsettled I currently felt, the seal of that cork was tenuous. Best not to unsettle the already precarious balance. I needed my mind clear and agile.

Especially when dealing with my father.

I planted a kiss on his upturned head. "Hey, Daddy."

Few townspeople would recognize my father in his current state of undress. Instead of a perfectly tailored suit, he wore a fancy blue bathrobe my siblings and I had all chipped in on together to get him for a birthday. Wearing his reading glasses and a blood-dotted dab of toilet paper stuck to a shaving cut, he wasn't quite as formidable a figure. But make no mistake, Ezra Leffersbee was a titan in banking, in Green Valley and beyond. A town for the people, run by its people, he'd always preached to whoever would listen. He'd spent years chasing big box stores and Big Business out of Green Valley, often marshaling the town to pitch in and address the town's individual and collective needs. He and my mother wielded their influence both overtly and subtly, at times simply allowing the strength of their name and the considerable current of power running through our family tree to speak for them. Real power, I'd learned, was silent, stealthy. More times than I could count, I'd watched them mount a campaign or wage war in formal wear, circulating among a room of the state's movers and shakers. As fascinating as it was, I'd never desired to hold those reins, not in the same way my sister did. For me, happiness had always been Birkenstocks and my lab.

That had always been a point of dissension between my father and me. The absolute last thing I needed right now was for him to crow over my career choice and remind me for the millionth time I should be working at the bank. With the rest of the family.

My father held onto my arm, holding me in place. His dark gaze held mine for a long moment. I took in his familiar face, observing the new parallel lines running across his forehead and the deepened trails extending from the corners of his eyes. There was a new, gentle give to his pecan brown skin. I loved this man fiercely.

But I was never really sure of how well he knew me.

"Zora," he said, his voice low and sonorous. "You alright? You sleep okay?"

"Did you?" I gave him a side-eye. "Cause you're not exactly bright-eyed and bushy-tailed yourself."

He rolled his eyes. "Your mother had me out all night at some gala for one of her causes."

I wasn't fooled in the least bit by his off-hand tone. He'd have been briefed long before he walked out the door and would have found some other like-minded person also bent on world domination to talk with.

"Hey, I was shooting the breeze with our neighbor the other day. Said he saw you and Jackson out at Cooper's Field. Reminded us both of our days, squirreling around out there, young, dumb, and in love. I told him how me and Jackson's daddy are expecting a proposal any day now. How is Jackson doing?"

I grimaced and worked to rearrange my features. "Okay, I guess."

His grip on my arm tightened as his eyes narrowed. "You know, if y'all hurry up and tie the knot by—"

"Well, look who's here!"

I breathed a sigh of relief, grateful for the interruption as my mother swept into the kitchen. But it was short-lived. My mother had an uncanny, sixth sense when it came to us kids. I never underestimated her. She had the sharp-eyed acuity and hunting instincts of a bald eagle.

"Hey, Mama."

She was beautiful: face clean, curly hair pushed up in a makeshift bun. She swirled into the kitchen in one of her oldest silk robes, one that evoked some of my most elemental childhood memories. I knew it would smell of her favorite Estée Lauder perfume before I hugged her. She wore that very robe, sitting at the stove, pressing my hair with a hot comb before church when I was a child. She wore that robe as she stood in the kitchen doorway with her arms crossed, her face turned away from my tears after she handed me Nick's short goodbye letter.

God. The history.

"Zora," she said, a smile lighting her face as she drew near. "I can hardly believe it's you. We beat out that university for some of your time today?" She squinted at me. "Did Walker tell you I made cinnamon rolls?"

I laughed. My mother was perfectly aware of Walker's "extracurricular activities" but she'd also learned that a pan of freshly baked cinnamon rolls worked like a homing device for him.

"No, he didn't, but I'll gladly help with the eating of them. Since I'm here and all."

"Anything else going on?"

Uh-oh. Her Spidey sense must be tingling. That wouldn't do. "Nothing much. The usual."

She nodded slowly as she watched me, one eye slightly squinted in a way I knew meant she was working to assemble the errant clues she somehow sensed from me.

"Well, I'm glad to see you, whatever brought you here." She enfolded me in a hug. I closed my eyes at the softness of her slender form, the scent of her floral shampoo, and the deeper, woodsy notes of her perfume. Looking down into her face, I was startled at how much of myself I saw there. I had the same wide, dark expressive eyes, caramel skin, and generous smile. The fuller lower lip. She was beautiful and always had been, but she was also a force. A shrewd businesswoman, a tireless advocate of worthy causes. An exemplary example of womanhood for me.

"I'm going to get dressed and get out of here," my father said, rising to put his plate in the sink.

My mother's eyes burned into my face. I ignored it and went to pull a glass from the cabinet.

"Good seeing you, Daddy. You know, you're getting pretty gray up top."

He ran a hand over his hair. "That's your mother's fault. She was supposed to be tweezing out the gray hairs as they grew in." I turned and saw him level a mock accusatory glare at her. "I guess she's been falling down on the job."

She rolled her eyes, settling in her customary chair at the kitchen table. "Ezra, do you want to be gray or bald? Pick one."

He waved a hand at her, but I saw the trace of a smile. "I'm out. Zora, tell Jackson your daddy's going to come after him soon enough if he doesn't hurry up and pop the question. I'm ready for grandkids, you hear me?"

My laugh was thin and tinny. "I'll tell him."

I watched him make his way out the kitchen, then turned to find my mother leaned against the counter, watching me with folded arms and a smirk.

"Girl, get a cinnamon roll and sit down so you can tell me what's wrong."

"Nothing's wrong," I said automatically. "Daddy said you had an event last night?"

She moved around the kitchen, poured herself a cup of coffee, then switched on the radio in the window above the sink. Al Green's silky voice entered the kitchen, slyly entreating his lover to remember the good times.

"We went to a gala in Knoxville. They started a hot lunch program to benefit children who have difficulty paying for it. It's in honor of that young man who was killed; he was in charge of his school's cafeteria. It's a wonderful foundation. If you know students looking for a worthy cause when they're fundraising this year, tell them about the Castille Foundation."

"That's wonderful. I've been reading more and more about kids being penalized for not having lunch money. It's terrible."

"Yes, it is," my mother said, frowning. "Both for the parents who don't have options and the children who have hungry bellies and no choice in the matter."

My traitorous thoughts jumped the tracks and went to Nick. I couldn't remember exactly how or when during high school I mentioned that Nick didn't have the best lunches. Afterwards, my mother sent me to school with duplicates of everything, snacks and lunches.

I shook my head to clear it, closed and opened my eyes to interrupt the mental stream.

"You headed to the hospital or campus after this?" Mama reached for my father's plate and snagged a piece of plain toast before running a quick eye over me. "You're a little more dressed up than usual."

I glanced down at my dark dress and black blazer.

"Both. I'm giving a talk about implicit racial bias and the impact on patient health outcomes to some of our docs. Then I'm heading over to campus."

She smiled. "That sounds interesting. You know that's one of my favorite talks. I wish I could go today." She took another bite of toast, studied me with a distinctly speculative eye, then added, "Tavia mentioned she's having lunch with you today."

I winced. "Yeah, she sent me a text this morning. Said it was important."

She studied the now empty plate at my father's place setting, but I recognized her carefully neutral tone. "Just remember. She'll always be your sister. Be patient with her."

"Yeah."

I busied myself with plating a cinnamon roll and filling my glass with water before I sat across from her at the table.

"Listen," my mother began, her gaze direct and unflinching on mine. "I want you to know that just because you start a thing a certain way doesn't mean you have to end it that way."

My heartbeat kicked up. "What do you mean?"

"I was thinking about Bethany Winston the other day," she said, biting her lip, and I knew how much it cost her to talk about Bethany without tearing up. Still, after all this time. Probably to be expected when one of your best friends died, I reflected, thinking I couldn't imagine a world where Leigh wasn't around to give me shit.

"I miss her something awful. Not a day goes by when I don't think of her. Other day I was washing dishes and I thought of something she used to say all the time. 'Life is short. Don't dilly dally.' And she was right."

I nodded, unsure of where the conversation was headed.

"I've been thinking about how you came home when I got the breast cancer diagnosis. You got to know the other ladies in my support group and completely immersed yourself in understanding more about communication between doctors and patients. I remembered how you ended up changing your major from pre-medicine so you could learn more about helping doctors have better conversations with ladies like us. And I wondered, would you make that same choice again, follow that same path? Knowing what you know now?"

I stared at her mutely, swallowing against the thickness in my throat. "That was a hard time," I finally said. Actually, it had been a *terrible* time. I didn't take all that much for me to remember sitting next to her in her support group meetings, hands clammy. I'd been terrified she'd end up on the Wall of Remembrance like so many women before her. She'd pulled through it, thank God. But we'd kept going to those meetings. I'd been horrified to hear how helpless those women felt during their clinic visits. How fear clotted their throats and left them mute, unable to ask the questions that burned in their hearts and minds during preceding sleepless nights. How many of them hadn't had anyone to go to their visits with them, and often didn't remember what was discussed afterwards. How they felt small and ashamed in those moments because of their lack of education or ability to articulate their concerns. Even worse, the cold resignation and anger when residents, fellows, and oncologists spent the entire visit with their hand on the doorknob and spouted technical jargon they couldn't understand. Further research exposed me to the dilemma of physician burnout, and all the systemic constraints that challenged physicians' ability to deliver care. I'd been moved by patients' and physicians' stories, and unexpectedly galvanized into action. The experience had changed me, and the course of my life.

I'd thought it was what I wanted. Probably, at the time, it *was* what I wanted.

But it all just weighed on me now.

"Hear me," Mama said, disrupting my inner thoughts. "If the life you've made for yourself doesn't fit anymore, change it. I can't give you a promissory note for how long I'll live, and if you're doing something that doesn't excite you anymore . . . Well, that's not good, even if it's an honorable thing. And," she gripped my hand as she stared steadily at me, "your sacrifice won't keep me here. Your life, this life you have, it's *yours*. Do you hear me? Make the most of it, and do what makes you happy."

Our gazes clung as she stared at me meaningfully.

"Alright, Mama," I said, then busied myself stuffing my cinnamon roll in my mouth and fleeing.

It just didn't feel like the right time to mention Nick was back in town.

∼

I watched my sister's loose-limbed stride across the busy restaurant and marveled that we were, in fact, twins. It seemed inconceivable that we'd once waved to each other across the darkness of our mother's womb with the same tiny, star-shaped hands. It seemed more likely we were from warring intergalactic tribes.

But the force of nature advancing toward me was indeed my twin sister. My younger sister, technically, although she'd been born with a two-pound advantage. Brimming with her usual caged, restive energy, Tavia dropped into the booth across from me.

She wore a stylish, one-piece jumper that flattered her leanness. I'd absorbed enough of her style advice to recognize the outfit and jewelry would easily transition to an evening out. Whereas the idea of nightly networking dinners and empty small talk at parties automatically set my teeth on edge, Tavia thrived on social interaction.

She pushed a hand through the layers of her perfectly coiffed extensions, her dark eyes moving over me as she settled into the opposite side of the booth. I'd barely registered her windblown arrival before she tossed questions across the table like handfuls of bright confetti.

"So, is that what you're doing with your hair now? From now on? Really? Why'd you wanna come here? We could have tried the new Mediterranean restaurant up the street. Walker loves it, but you know it doesn't take much to make Walker happy. Why are you dressed like that? Did someone die?"

I blinked down at my black T-shirt and jeans. "Hello to you, too, Octavia."

She frowned, already perusing the menu in front of her. "You know I don't like it when you call me that."

"Uh-huh. 'Cause I just love your ongoing commentary about my appearance."

Dang. Okay, I fully admit it, I'd thrown a little kindling on what had the potential to become a brushfire of a conversation. But I was just so damn *tired*.

She flicked another glance in my direction. "I'm just saying, you look like the Supremes are about to sing back up for you. Your hair could use some deep conditioning and shaping, and it'd be great to see you in something that showed your shape while not absorbing all the other colors in the light spectrum. But hey. If you like it . . ."

I'm just saying. The three words that most often accompanied her opening salvos.

Ladies and gentlemen . . . we're off.

I suppressed a sigh, one hand rising to pat my wild mane of curls. In truth, I'd noticed my ends were a little frayed from neglect after the briefest glance in the mirror. I made a mental note to have my stylist reshape my growing cloud of hair.

One of these days.

"Thanks for the review." My teeth locked in a grimace that wouldn't pass for anyone's version of a smile. I had a pretty good sense of humor and was self-deprecating to a fault. Of course I knew I looked like a disaster lately, and I didn't begrudge her the honest, sisterly feedback. It wasn't her comments that chafed as much as her superior tone. "How's your day going?"

Tavia's gaze drifted from the menu up to my face. "Damn. You're making nervous small talk. What's happened?"

The waiter, a young man nervously clutching an order pad, chose that moment to wander over.

"Good afternoon, ladies."

Tavia spared him the barest glance before returning her stare to my face. "Not now, come back later."

I suppressed a groan at her rudeness. He blinked at her tone, then wandered away.

"That's not okay. You can't talk to people, treat them that way." *How many times have I told her that, over the span of our lives?*

"What's going on," she repeated, dismissing my words with an imperious wave. "Just tell me."

My shoulders tensed. Interactions with Tavia often left stomach acids climbing up my throat.

"I don't want to talk about it. You wanted to meet. What did you want to talk about?"

She watched me through half-lidded eyes. "Are you sure—"

"Why am I here, Tavia?"

She reared back. Even I was surprised by the bite in my tone. I took advantage of the ensuing silence and signaled to the waiter who still hovered nearby.

Too late, I'd realized I was far too anxious and sleep-deprived to have attempted any conversation with my sister. My normal stores of patience were long gone, depleted. To be clear, my love for Tavia was never in question, but our conversations required painstaking hyper-vigilance on my part. I'd come to understand the barbs and conversational flares she threw out like Princess Peach on a Mario Kart track weren't always intentional. She didn't always set out to start arguments.

I didn't always set out to react.

But we often managed to do just that. Our personalities, our viewpoints, our ways of navigating the world were vastly different.

We weren't yin and yang. Ours was a dangerous, unstable alchemy.

The waiter listed to my side of the table with one watchful eye trained on Tavia.

"Thank you." I worked up a saccharine smile. "My sister may need more time before ordering, but I'd like to put in an appetizer." I glanced in her direction. "I can wait until you're ready before we order our meals."

He quickly noted my order and disappeared.

Tavia scowled down at her phone, nimble fingers flying over the screen. "Can I look forward to a more pleasant conversation once you've eaten?"

"It's in your best interest. I'm hangry."

"You're more than that." Seeing her raised brow and thorough perusal, I cautioned myself to stay calm, not to be reactive.

My mother's voice sounded in my head: *She'll always be your sister. Be patient with her.*

I took a deep breath. I could do that. This was my sister. It wasn't her fault that my life was falling apart. I could be patient and listen to whatever she had to say. Although God knows, I was sick and tired of having to be the patient one all the time.

"You look terrible."

"Yep, that's what I keep hearing."

Her lips flattened. "Is this about tenure? I don't know how many times we have to tell you—"

"I don't want to work for the bank, Tavia."

"It's not working for the bank. It's working *with your family*. This is our legacy, what Daddy and Grandpa built. There's plenty you could do to put your education to use. The way we're growing, the plans I have, we already need your full attention. We're behind in outreach. And if we didn't have to share you with the university . . ."

I closed my eyes and prayed for strength. I'd worked so hard, sacrificed so much, with the hopes of charting my own course and avoiding this very moment. Yet here I was, only a breath away from having to crawl back to my family with my tail between my legs.

"I don't draw a salary from the bank for my outreach work and I'm stretched thin as it is. Let's just . . . leave it alone for right now, okay?"

"Just listen," she persisted, and I closed my eyes, pressed my lips together to bottle the unkind words that immediately sprang to mind. "You're doing some good, I'll grant you that. But it's not like you're fixing the big problems, anyway. I admire the way you're chipping away at health disparities, and trying to help people. You know I do, I've told you that. But it just seems like the game is rigged against you right now. You get grants, but they're not the right ones that count for tenure. You jump through all these hoops, meanwhile, the budgets for grants at the NIH and National Cancer Institute have been slashed. Plus, you're already competing against an insane number of other smart people who are also investigating incredibly important things, all of you fighting for rapidly dwindling funds. It's a losing proposition, Z."

Despite myself, I had to admit that it was a remarkably accurate and astute summation of exactly what had been happening for the past few years. That didn't make it sting any less.

"Please, Tavia. Leave it be." My voice broke. "Not right now."

"Just think about it."

"What did you want? When you sent the text, asking to meet?"

"Well, since we're talking about future plans . . . I might need your help with a few things."

I cracked open one eye. The faintly sheepish note in her voice matched what was on her face. "What have you done?"

Her eyes left mine and settled on the tabletop, her slender fingers drumming a frantic rhythm.

Uh-oh. A speechless, nervous Tavia? Real trouble was afoot. Concern and trepidation gripped my heart in equal measure.

"It's that bad?"

"I may need you to help me with Walker."

God. *Not again.*

"How exactly would I 'help you' with Walker?"

"It's just that he listens to you. He never listens to me."

"And you think *you* listen to *him*?"

She huffed and took an aggressive gulp from her water glass. "I'm thinking about the future of this company. Walker is happy to maintain the status quo. If it wasn't for me, pushing, we wouldn't have expanded past Knoxville. He'd be happy with the same little Green Valley branch. He'd be happy never to leave Green Valley at all."

I considered my sister and the scowl marring her features. "You're not in New York anymore, Gordon Gekko. You went to Wharton and then you graduated to handling multi-million-dollar accounts. Why'd you leave New York, Tavia? You knew the score before you came back. Dad wants Walker in charge, he's drummed that into everyone's heads since we were born. I don't necessarily agree that his Y chromosome automatically qualifies Walker for the keys the kingdom, but then again, I've never wanted to rule from that throne. What are you trying to do, exactly? You can't keep going over Walker's head when you don't agree."

"He doesn't have vision!"

"He doesn't have *your* vision. Doesn't mean he's wrong. Have you tried talking to him about your ideas? Walker's never been unreasonable. I know he'd hear you out."

"Yes, we've talked. And we just don't agree." She selected a piece of bread the from the basket between us and tore it in half.

"So, is browbeating him until he finally goes apeshit the best negotiating tool in your arsenal? How much longer do you think this cycle's going to last before one of you kills the other?"

She chewed on her lower lip. "I know you're the communication expert, but I didn't come here for life coaching."

I rested my head in the cradle of my hands. "You came here because you want something from me, though."

Her nails resumed their drumming again, a dull, successive *click, click, click*. "Walker is mad at me."

Ah. Now she was ready to unveil the mess she'd made. No doubt I'd be expected to grab my hazmat suit and wade in for clean-up. Just like always.

I shook my head wearily. "How mad?" I looked up at her continued silence. "What happened?"

She scratched the side of her face. "He, uh, he swore at me. Told me to get out, that he didn't want to see or hear from me again. Said if I wasn't his sister . . ."

Her throat worked.

I felt a reluctant stirring of sympathy. But I was also exhausted from the whiplash of their moods and the growing volatility of their conflict.

My brother likely wasn't completely innocent. But it was Tavia's way to bulldoze through opposition, to throw her weight around until her relationships were only broken shards of glass. Any demonstration of remorse was always far too late, and delivered long after her opponents' wounds had festered. I recognized that same regret on her face now, and wondered what damage she'd left in her wake this time.

Our older brother was a gentle, patient man. Dad had had the highest expectations for his only son, the firstborn. The successor. He'd been hard on Walker. Yet Walker had somehow emerged with a sense of humor and a soft spot for his three sisters.

Over and over again, I'd warned Tavia not to exploit that kindness.

She never listened. Never.

"What happened?"

The waiter appeared with a platter of grilled eggplant and we ordered entrees. I noted Tavia somehow managed to look smaller during that time.

"I made a move without telling him," she admitted.

I stirred my iced tea. "Again?"

"Are you going to listen or not?"

"Go ahead."

"You know that industrial property, right on the edge of town? The original owners foreclosed on it, and the lien is held by one of our Knoxville-based competitors."

"Okay..."

"And I'd already been eying it, so when I got word that they were doing a silent bid—"

"Tavia. You didn't. Without telling Walker?"

She hung her head. "I know I shouldn't have. But I already knew what he would say, and I didn't want to waste time trying to explain—"

"How much?" I raised a brow at her silence. "That bad?"

She named a figure that made me whistle.

"How could you?"

She dipped a pita point into the eggplant. "It's done now. I won't know if mine was the winning bid until around a week or so from now. And if it is, well . . . We're in business. He'll come to see my point and he'll eventually agree I was right. Now, we just have to move forward. Will you help me, get him to start speaking to me again?"

A month ago, before Nick had reappeared, I likely would have handled things differently. But at that moment, already flattened under exhaustion, worry, and fear, there wasn't room to swallow another emotion.

"No. I will not help you manipulate our brother. I'm not the referee or the clean-up crew. Figure it out on your own."

Tavia gave an exasperated sigh. "Oh, so you decide to retire from your lifelong stint as the bridge builder *now*? When it's really bad, when I'm in this deep? I didn't know it was an option to bail on your family."

"You're not acting like family, and if you think 'family' means anyone can just make asshole, dictatorial decisions that affect everyone else, maybe you need to keep your distance from Walker."

I realized I'd raised my voice only when the couple in the adjoining booth turned to look back at us.

Tavia's head pulled back as if I'd slapped her. We glared at each other in silence.

Tavia broke eye contact first, wrapping her arms around herself. Her jaw jutted, her dimpled chin gained prominence, and I marveled not for the first time how much she was like our father. She was the spitting image of him, yes, but she shared his strength of will and stubbornness. I'd never been successful at connecting with either of them, not in a profound way. Would it always be like this? Would my sister, my twin, always be a stranger to me?

"Tavia—"

"I'm not wrong to want more than *this*," she hissed, gesturing vaguely around the restaurant, and I knew she was referring to Knoxville, Green Valley, and beyond. Some extraordinary emotion took over face, briefly distorting her features as her shoulders fell inward.

Love and empathy for my difficult, headstrong sister filled my chest and stung the back of my eyes. Maybe we weren't all that different after all. I understood her in that moment, recognized myself and my own yearnings in her plaintive appeal. I wanted more too, I realized, albeit in a very different way. It seemed we were both trapped.

"Tavia—"

"I'm not *you*, Zora, and I don't want to be. You want to fight the world so that others can get a chance at a piece of it. Well, I know better, and I'm fighting for *myself*, for my own share, for more than my share if I can help it. For *me*. And no one's getting in the way of that. Not even my brother."

I examined her fierce expression, the gentle flare of her nostrils, the fierce grip of her fists on the table and gentled my voice. I loved my sister and admired her naked ambition, even if it was jagged-edged and bled everyone around her dry. How could you not appreciate the sheer will it took to purse something with such a single-minded focus?

But I also loved my sweet, protective brother.

"It's just the way you go about things. As if there's no chain of command, that you're not accountable to anyone. Walker is not some nameless barrier to maneuver and manipulate. He's our brother, Tavia. Our brother, and he'll be that even if Leffersbee Financial ceased to exist. You'd do well to remember that."

I recognized the moment when she decided to stop, change course. She had the instincts of a cross-examining lawyer, and oh, that's right, she also had an agenda for this lunch.

"I shouldn't have led with my issues with Walker. I should have started by asking how you're feeling."

So much for connecting, for having a real moment. I suddenly wondered if the previous moment, the demonstration of her emotion had been real. Maybe I was just blind and easily manipulated. My shield rose back in place.

"Cut the bullshit. What do you want?"

She was silent for a beat, then, "Two things. Walker and I are going to be out of town for a conference at the same time the American Cancer Society is doing their gala in Knoxville. We need you to—"

"No. You know how much I hate those things."

"Oh, come on. This isn't torture. You get gussied up in a ball gown, press a little flesh, and present a big check."

Press a little flesh. It would be as revolting and as nerve wrecking as it sounded.

"Get Dad to do it. He loves giving those long-ass speeches for a captive audience."

"He's coming with us. *You're* the researcher. You work with cancer patients, Zora. Hell, maybe it won't hurt to have people remember what you do for the community—"

"Tavia—"

"Zora. There's no one else. For once, can you *pretend* to care about our family's business?"

That was patently unfair, and she knew it. "You're about to get a repeat of Walker's performance, when he said whatever he said to get you out of his office. I'm at my limit. I can't take that on right now."

Her shoulders stiffened. "I'm not asking for much, Zora. It's one night, for a couple of hours. Would it be that hard?"

Yes, I wanted to shout in her face. *Yes. Because I'm so tired of going through the motions. I can't take any-fucking-more.* What would it take to get a reprieve? Streaking across campus, followed by a week-long vacation at the psychiatric hospital in Knoxville?

That'd be worth shaving my bikini area.

"Also, I wanted to know how you felt about Nick being back," she added smoothly, and I realized that was likely her real objective for inviting me, what she'd been circling around from the start. "I heard he was back in town."

I studied her and her now empty, inscrutable expression. Was she asking as my sister? Or as a VP at the bank?

"Yes," I said, trying to work the starch out of my voice. "He's back. I don't feel any away about it." I'd never told her all that happened after Nick left; I'd only trusted Leigh with that truth. Tavia would scent blood in the water and pursue the issue mercilessly if I told her about my current entanglement with Nick.

She squinted at me. "Really? I would have thought you'd feel . . . I don't know, something more. You were devastated after mom found that letter from him. I mean, you know I loved Nick but I wouldn't have wanted to get so serious about a guy right before college."

I wondered if Tavia and I would ever grow into a better relationship, once we weren't still so affected by the need to prove whatever the hell we felt a need to prove to ourselves and each other.

"Why are you asking? What do you want?"

She leaned in, eyes bright as she went in for the kill. "Do you care if I contact him, meet up with him? I'm trying to break into some of the same corporations he already has relationships with—"

Why hadn't my mother's uterus stopped at one fertilized egg?

Nick had just gotten into town, I was trying to find a way to manage my feelings while keeping a professional distance from him, and I didn't want to get into why it didn't feel okay to ask him for personal favors for my family.

"And if I say yes? Yes, I mind. Does that mean anything?"

Her mouth twisted. "Then I'd ask you to think big picture and not be selfish. This family, this business, our name, it belongs to you, too. You don't care about the work we do at the bank, and you never have. The least you could do is not get in the way of our future growth and the work we're doing to build on the legacy we all *share*."

I sat back in the booth and slowed my breathing in an attempt to contain the rage buzzing through my skull. I thought of how I'd pretended interest in the bank and its inner workings as a kid, just so I could spend real time with my father. I thought of the times I'd wished I had the same closeness with my dad that Tavia and Walker cultivated by working so closely with him each day. How frustrated I'd always been by the fact that the bank, the business, had come to define our family in so many ways. Just as when I was a child, it was more clear than ever to me that I was outside that circle and I always would be.

Enough. My mother was right. My life, the way it was going, it didn't suit me. It was time to burn it all to the ground.

I stood up, fished in my purse for a twenty and threw it next to my plate. Tavia's startled eyes rose to meet mine.

"Zora—"

"You're right, Tavia. It's time for me to look out for myself, to get my own piece of the world. You're on your own."

CHAPTER FIFTEEN
Nick

I'd made a habit of shoving Green Valley and any related memories out of my brain for years now, but I'd forgotten how beautiful it could be. Life moved slower, more quietly here. After a few days, I no longer thirsted for the relentless pace of our New York and San Francisco offices. Suddenly, I relished the quiet. I caught myself straining to identify birdcalls just as I had as a kid. I took the time to appreciate the perfect weather, the unseasonable warmth of early fall and the stunning perfection of all the late-summer blooms.

Today, however, I was in a majorly fucked up mood and had been all morning. True, I needed to take responsibility for some measure of my ire. It *had* been my decision to take a leave from the office right before a major meeting with our shareholders, and with more than a few crucial irons in the fire. But the sudden ineptitude of our staff irritated the shit out of me. After a series of emails that basically amounted to everyone running around like headless chickens, I'd finally managed to get everyone back on track. Then fielded a call from Eddie asking if I *really* needed to be so rude, and hadn't I said I was going to demonstrate more patience? The staff was only doing their best, after all.

I'd hung up on him and taken my foul mood out to the wraparound porch of the rental house before I permanently burned any bridges. I'd taken possession of a handsome home on Lake Bandit, conveniently furnished by the owner. It hadn't taken much effort to move my suitcase from Knoxville and settle in it.

I should have been thrilled. My mother and I had joked about living out here in this exclusive area all our lives. We'd driven by the houses, mouths agape, and I'd always asked her which one she wanted me to buy her when I was rich. Being here in this gorgeous house should have been a crowning achievement. A milestone.

But I was beyond irritated. Because of Zora Leffersbee. Every time I closed my eyes, every time I attempted sleep, I remembered how easily she'd come to me in her sleep three days prior on my plane. I couldn't free myself from the memory of her open palm against my face, my chest, then mere inches from my zipper. I'd forever remember the moment she finally awoke, her hands reflexively tightening on me before she slowly came back to the world. I wanted her to look at me that same way again, open and unguarded. I wanted her friendship, I wanted her love, I wanted her trust.

I needed to touch *her* again. I needed her touching *me* again.

Luckily my assistant pulled up the long driveway and interrupted my stewing. He opened the back passenger door for Sir Duke, dripping sweat and stuttering incomprehensibly about the switchbacks he'd navigated along the way. I hadn't even heard him. It was an overwhelming relief to see Sir Duke racing toward me at the lightning speed for which he was bred.

I decided to drive into town and take Sir Duke for a stroll. He was eager to stretch his legs after the long drive and I needed to think.

∼

As Sir Duke and I made our way down the tree-lined sidewalk, him stopping every few feet to sniff at curiosities, my thoughts strayed back to Zora. She'd cried when I told her about my mother. She told me she was proud of me, which shouldn't have mattered so much.

But it did.

On an impulse, I decided to stop in the Donner Bakery. Maybe a shitload of sugar would sweeten my foul mood.

The bell over the door heralded our tentative entrance. I shot a wary glance over to the woman manning the register. Sir Duke was a massive dog, and bringing him inside any establishment, never mind a bakery, was taking a chance.

"Hi," I called. "I realize you may not allow dogs inside. I just wanted to—"

"I won't tell if you don't." She beamed a warm smile at me before darting a quick glance over her shoulder. "It's slow today and I'm the only one back here now. As long as you're both well-behaved, I think we could make an exception. Just this once."

"Thank you." I felt worn out and wretched, so I welcomed the kind gesture. I murmured to Sir Duke as we approached the glass counters to examine their contents, doing my best to keep his inquiring nose away from the reflective surfaces.

"Isn't he the cutest thing ever?" She grinned at Sir Duke.

I looked down at him. He was a big dog and easily reached the waists of most folks, so I'd never heard the term "cute" applied to him before. Sir Duke, having just recovered from a cataclysmic case of the shits behind a bush mere minutes before, sent me a guilty expression before looking away.

"He has his moments," I said, noticing my vowels were going softer the more time I spent here. "Got any recommendations?"

"I thought you wanted to try a Ring of Fire," a voice said from the side.

I turned, not at all surprised to find Zora Leffersbee lounging at a side table. She looked beautiful, but her expression was slightly pinched. A mug of coffee, steam still escaping, sat in front of her next to an uneaten muffin. Her hair was slicked back into a ponytail of tight curls, a few wisps framing her lovely face. She wore an old university T-shirt stretched deliciously across her full breasts and matching shorts. I averted my eyes from her shapely legs with some effort. But not before briefly daydreaming about those legs and just how good they'd felt, so many years before, wrapped around—

Shit.

I was in trouble.

"We're fresh out of those, hun," the woman at the register called.

Zora smiled. "Oh, I wouldn't worry. I'm sure you could find some other trouble for him to get in."

I smothered a wholly inappropriate retort about exactly the kind of trouble I wanted in and guided Sir Duke over to her table without another thought. I was unwilling to believe in coincidences anymore when it came to her. I was tired of fighting fate.

Her expression brightened as Sir Duke approached. "So this is the distinguished gentleman."

I hesitated once reaching her, realizing I'd never asked her how she felt about dogs, never mind one as big as Sir Duke. But she surprised me, sticking out her hand so he could scent it.

"He is a sweet old man." She grinned at my hound and I was unaccountably glad.

"He is, although I'll have you know he's still in his prime." I stroked his flank and watched the two of them get acquainted. Sir Duke got bolder, unashamed to rub against her leg and beg for pets. She obliged him.

"You mind if we join you? I won't let him harass you the entire time."

"He's fine. And yes, you're both welcome."

"Mind if I leave him here with you?"

"Sure."

I surrendered the leash to her and headed over to the counter. The clerk helped me select a dozen cookies, some strange creation called a dill pickle muffin, and a fat square of brownie. Remembering Zora's weakness for all things red velvet, I selected a thick slice.

Walking back to the table, tray in hand, I almost stopped in my tracks at the sight in front of me. Zora and Sir Duke, suddenly fast friends. He sat at her feet while she smiled down, baby-talking him.

And suddenly my day was stratospherically improved. What

would it be like to come home to this sight? Would seeing her at the end of the day always lift my burden, the way it did just now?

God. I'd almost had it all, all those years ago.

"Good stuff here," I announced. There was barely enough room to arrange it all on the table. "They even had a dog treat for Sir Duke."

"Really?" She grinned down at him. He'd curled up under the table, resting his mammoth head on her feet. "I was just thinking that he shouldn't be left out of all the fun."

"I'll give it to him at the end of our walk. He's got a sensitive stomach and can't really eat after exercising."

She blinked at me. "I can't believe you went out of your way to adopt a geriatric dog with a sensitive stomach."

I shrugged. "We all come with baggage, right?"

She stared. "I guess so."

"You want any brownie?"

She peered at the contents of my wax paper. "I *should* say no."

I tore off a hunk of brownie and planted it on her side. "It's Sunday. It's not a day for shoulds."

"You too, huh?"

"What?"

"You still look stressed. You've got that tired look you'd get when you were working too much and studying all night. Still not sleeping, huh?"

I watched her, thinking we both needed to put each other out of our misery. If I couldn't sleep, couldn't stop calculating how much better it might be between us this second time around . . . well, I hoped she was similarly afflicted.

"Are you? Sleeping? What's keeping you up at night?"

Her eyes widened briefly before her gaze dropped to the table. "Just a lot on my mind."

"Me too. Feels like I can't quite escape all the memories of this place. I'm realizing now that most of my favorite memories from Green Valley and growing up were with you."

She kept her gaze on the table. "Well, all that was a long time ago."

"Was it? Feels like only yesterday to me. For instance, I know you don't really want that bland, dry-looking muffin over there."

"Watch yourself. *Nothing* is dry or bland here."

I bit back a smile at the playful challenge in her voice, relieved to feel us slipping into a familiar rhythm. "Fair enough. But that's why I got you the red velvet cake." I slid the plate over to her and enjoyed the way she bit her lip in response. "Because I know you. I know you'll always treat someone else, always go the extra mile for someone you love while denying yourself."

"You don't know me," she said, and it sounded like a dare. "Not after all this time."

I decided we were at a place where I could poke back a little. "Are you gonna tell me you didn't just get in a fight with Tavia?" Her face slackened and her expression went blank as she gaped at me.

"How—?"

I swallowed back a smile at her obvious surprise. "You've got the look you always got when the two of you went a few rounds and your post-sugar soother is already in place." I handed her one of the forks. "Might as well indulge in a form of sugar you'll actually enjoy."

Her mouth fell open. One of the curls in her ponytail slid free. I fought the urge to touch it, to test its softness.

"I'm right, aren't I?" I took a bite of brownie. Salt and sugar launched a dual attack on my taste buds.

It was divine.

"You're right."

I shoved more brownie in my mouth. We were going to need another one soon. "Some things don't change, huh?"

"I guess not," she said, and I couldn't interpret the look that suddenly crossed her face. "I guess that's how it is with families."

I felt a twinge of frustration and sadness, sensing her obvious distress. Zora had always been bothered by the fact that she and her sister weren't close, even though she'd come to understand that they were simply very different creatures with sharply contrasting personalities.

"I think so. I've got a cousin, Emily. She's so much younger than me, and really, she's more of a sister. I love her, but I have no idea how we made it this long without us choking each other." I laughed.

"Accurate. Audre's away at UCLA, but I want to kill Walker and Tavia on a daily basis." She fiddled with a crumpled napkin. "I've been meaning to ask you . . . why did you pay for Carly's son? For his senior trip?"

I blinked at the abrupt topic change. "I don't know what you're talking about."

She reached over, lightning fast, and pinched my forearm. I let out an unmanly grunt, then captured her hand in mine before she did any more damage.

And I held onto it. Her gaze settled on our clasped hands and didn't move away.

"Now who's the bully? You haven't changed at all with your schoolyard intimidation tactics."

She tugged at her hand in mine. "I was never a bully. Let go."

"No, you can't be trusted. I'll hold onto this until I feel safe again."

Teasing her, touching her . . . damn, it felt good.

"Why'd you do it?" she repeated, having abandoned her efforts to free her hand.

I heaved a sigh. "I don't know what you're talking about. But if a person were to do something like that, I imagine it's because he or she wanted to help out a single mother. I had a single mother. I remember how hard it was for her, trying to do everything on her own. And I remember what it was like being a son who wanted more than anything to protect and help his mother. For a kid in that position, one of the worst things you can do is make him feel like a charity case. So whatever you do for one, you do for everyone."

Her gaze moved over my face as she bit her lip. "What you did, it was so—"

"Well, isn't this cozy."

Startled, we both looked up.

Jackson James stood at our table, brows raised pointedly at our joined hands.

I relinquished my hold on Zora and sat back to get a good look at him, this man she claimed to love.

Zora was right, he'd changed. A lot. He wouldn't pass for the class shrimp anymore, judging from the way his shoulders filled out the sheriff uniform. I'd never liked the classmates who teased him, and I'd spoken up on his behalf on more than one occasion. We'd never really become friends, though, because Jackson had had more than a little asshole about him for years.

He certainly looked different now. I wondered how else he might have changed, and what the hell Zora saw in him.

Jackson smiled the toothy grin I remembered, but his gaze was flat and without expression as he watched me. Cop's eyes.

"Nick! It's been a long time."

I made a deliberate effort to relax. "It has. Good to see you."

"You did good for yourself, didn't you? I looked you up."

I nodded back at him. "Same can be said for yourself."

"Nah, I don't think I'll ever be on *Fortune's* '40 Under 40' list."

"Who says you need to?" I had no desire to follow this conversational trail.

"You're right." He smiled wider. "Who needs all that money when you've got the love of a good woman?"

He paused meaningfully.

I let silence fill the space he apparently expected me to fill.

From the corner of my eye, I watched as Zora's gaze bounced between us while she rabidly chewed her lower lip.

"I don't know if you'd heard that Zora and I are together. Have been for a while now. I'm not sure how I pulled it off, but . . ." He gave a slow smile, one intended to provoke. "But here I am. And damn sure happy to be reaping the rewards."

I looked down at Sir Duke. He'd lifted his head from Zora's sandal and fixed Jackson with an unflinching stare.

Jackson followed my gaze to the 150-pound dog half-hidden under the table, leaning on Zora's legs. I caught the briefest twitch of the thumbs he'd tucked into his belt loops.

Sir Duke stared back.

I smiled, loving Jackson's obvious discomfort.

Good dog.

Jackson looked back at the register. "Since when do they allow dogs in here?"

"It's good to see you, *honey*." Zora gave him a meaningful glance, her tone full of . . . something.

He whipped around, face lighting with recognition as if he'd just realized she was there. Keeping a wary eye on Sir Duke, he picked his way to Zora's side.

As I watched, he lowered his head to Zora, ostensibly to kiss her. Her eyes widened at his approach. She flicked a wide-eyed glance in my direction, turned her head to Jackson's descending head . . .

The speed at which it all happened made it all the more funny. Their faces met in a collision of foreheads and teeth, both of them pulling away from the ridiculous farce with pained expressions.

It was the funniest thing I'd ever seen, and went a long way toward staving off any irritation I might have felt about this display of affection. Jackson reared back, his hand on his lip. Zora rubbed her forehead, frowning.

"Damn, Jackson," Zora muttered, just loud enough for me to hear.

"You bit me," he stage-whispered, his fingers tracing the inside of his lip. "I was trying to kiss you, not get my lip chewed off."

"It was involuntary, I didn't expect you slam into my head," Zora hissed, her words only just reaching me.

I watched them, fascinated. These were two people who didn't kiss all that often, if at all. They couldn't.

"You're right, Zora," I said, smiling at them both. Their heads snapped back in my direction. "It *is* magic when a couple's nonverbals match, isn't it? That right there? Pure synchrony."

Zora narrowed her eyes at me. Jackson shot me a dark look as he straightened, then one of those sly "aw shucks" looks I'd always hated slithered across his face.

"Well. I keep telling Zora that Daddy doesn't like it when she bites, but, what can I say? She's passionate."

I didn't miss the murderous glance she sent his way at that pathetic and highly inappropriate attempt at recovery.

Yep. Still an asshole.

"Oh, I have some idea," I said, giving him a bland smile. I inspected Zora's set face. "Z, didn't you do a video testimonial about that?"

Jackson's face froze. We both knew *exactly* what video I was talking about.

"Guess 'Daddy' needs a map to find the spot sometimes, huh?"

"Listen," he began, all traces of congeniality gone, "you don't—"

"Ugh." Zora's face crumpled. "What's that smell?"

I sat back, laughing. I knew exactly what it was.

Sir Duke, with his impeccable timing, had launched one of his world-famous stink bombs. My dog didn't spare Jackson the slightest glance, but turned around in a wide circle and managed to back Jackson up a few feet with his perfectly aimed, smelly asshole.

I barked out another laugh.

"He stinks," Jackson grated, hands on his hips. "I—" He tucked his nose into his uniform shirt, audibly choking. "I've got to go anyway." Turning to the empty front counter, he yelled, "Isn't this some kinda public health violation? The big ole dog in here, smelling up the place?"

Sir Duke rested his head on Zora's knee, his eyes big and luminous.

I'd never loved my manipulative dog more.

"Why don't you get some fresh air, Jackson?" I made sure my face was perfectly straight when I added, "We'll be alright in here. I want to hear more about the inspiration for Zora's research."

CHAPTER SIXTEEN

Nick

Retracing my steps to Zora's office a few days later, I couldn't shake the feeling that something was wrong. She was missing right before an important off-campus meeting.

Which wasn't like her.

Nellie had initiated an email sharing details about focus groups for beta users of our app. Zora responded to the first few exchanges where Nellie provided the initial details. Subsequent emails where Nellie asked Zora to take me along with her? Unanswered.

I tried to push aside my growing concern. Zora was an adult, a superhuman at that. She was fine. We no longer had a relationship in which it was appropriate for me to worry about her.

But some habits died hard. Even twelve years later.

By the time I reached her office door, I was kicking myself for going along with Nellie's plan. I didn't need to be ferried around like a guest. I had a rental car in perfect working order. I knew the way to Green Valley.

Not that I'd turn down an opportunity to spend time with her, even if it was just the drive from Knoxville to Green Valley.

Her office door was very slightly ajar. My knock nudged it open in slow degrees.

"Knock, knock."

At first glance, I thought her office was empty.

It was still enough of a disaster area that my gaze caught on several different areas before I could methodically search the room's contents.

A paper bomb had detonated. Sliding mounds of paper covered every possible surface of the desk. Tucked away in a corner, the meeting table and chairs were burdened with towering stacks of stuffed folders. More stacks of paper straddled the entire length of the floor-to-ceiling window. Individual sheets were tacked to a cork board, while others fanned out only inches away from the door's threshold. The printer in the corner had apparently regurgitated more pages than the holding tray could handle.

I shook my head, hand on the knob. Zora had kept her room in perfect order growing up. All of her assignments and syllabi were always organized with color coded folders and binders. She'd created an innovative filing system for all of her college applications.

Sure, time had passed. She might have changed. But this much? I doubted it. This extreme of a reversal was unlikely.

It was hard to reconcile the previous version of her with the chaos I stood in.

What had Adesola said, what had she hinted at? Something *was* going on.

I took a few steps into the room, taking care to avoid the papers strewn across the floor.

Dark curls stood up from one end of the couch.

I eased closer. She was asleep on the couch, legs curled into her chest. It was the first time I'd seen her face completely free of tension. Limp curls obscured the top half of her face. One hand loosely held the dark blanket draped over, under and along the valley of her hips and waist while the other hand propped up her head.

I stood, frozen, trapped in a million memories, remembering all the times I'd snuck into Zora's room and been greeted by this very sight. I wished I could once again run a finger along the rounded curve of her nose, past the generous turn of her lip and down the length of her neck.

If I woke her, we'd resume our current farce of being polite strangers. I'd likely never have an opportunity to see her this way again.

Soft. Unguarded.

I took a moment to drink in the sight, allowed my traitorous thoughts to engage in a dangerous game of "What If." What if my mother had done something different that night? What if I'd responded differently? What if Zora hadn't sent her ring back? What if I hadn't given up? Was there any alternate universe in which it might have been possible for me to wake to those same curves against me, in our own bed, every morning?

Jesus, Nick.

Enough. There was no value in musing about alternative universes; there was only this reality. Where she hated me.

I needed answers, but the last thing I wanted to do was wake her. This had all the signs of a late night work-a-thon: empty bottles of Coke in the trash, a nearly depleted bottle of an energy drink on her desk. There was no point in waking her. The meeting, the focus groups would be just fine without us in attendance. My team was there, and more than capable of running things.

I'd wait, I decided. And then we'd get to the bottom of everything. Once and for all.

∽

Nick

"Nick?"

I froze at the sound of Zora's sleep-rasped voice and checked my watch.

Three hours.

In that time, I'd cleaned out my email inbox and reviewed all outstanding reports while sitting at Zora's disaster of a meeting table.

My team had assured me the focus group sessions were well underway and completely under control. We were expected to attend the next session in two days.

Now, it was time for Zora and me to have our reckoning.

"What are you doing here?"

She pushed curls out of her eyes and pushed to a sitting position. The blanket drifted down, revealed a good three inches of caramel skin below her rumpled shirt.

My breath caught, eyes trapped on the rise of her breasts as she stretched. The shirt stretched higher . . .

What was I reduced to, begging God for just another sliver of that honey skin?

"The better question is, *why* am I here?" The blood in my head rushed south. Thank God I was sitting.

"Answer whatever question you want." She knuckled her eyes, smearing black makeup above her cheeks. "Start with how you got in here and why you decided to sit your happy ass at my table."

"Your door wasn't all the way closed. My being here probably has something to do with the fact our 'happy asses' were supposed to be in Green Valley for focus groups over two hours ago."

"Shit!"

"Yep. It's all in the emails you obviously didn't read."

She threw her blanketed legs to the floor, eyes wide. "What emails? Why didn't you wake me up? God. They're going to kill me!"

I studied her, and the very real fear on her face. Interesting.

"Who's going to kill you, exactly? I'm here with you. We're fine."

"But the—"

"I took care of it. It was more important for you to sleep."

"You can't do that." She pounded her fists against her thighs. "That wasn't your decision to make. You should have woken me up—"

"You were going to be asleep on that couch, dead to the world, if I hadn't wandered by to check on you anyway. This way both our teams think you're showing me something important here on campus. You needed the sleep more than you needed to be there." I allowed a few seconds for a strategic pause before I delivered the killing blow that would get just the reaction I wanted. I hadn't spent all of my childhood and adolescence teasing Zora for nothing. I knew how to get her goat, and I needed her fired up, off-balance, and talking if I was going to pry information out of her. "God knows you're somehow even more gorgeous then I'd remembered. But I think you need a little more sleep. Just to round out a few exhausted edges."

Of course, I knew Zora was beautiful. But I'd also noticed that *something* had diminished her glow and left her obviously sleep-deprived and anxious. I needed her to take care of herself, to turn her attention to herself. It worried me, seeing her this tired and . . . desperate? Teasing her would be the most effective route to persuading the truth out of her, and in short order.

She gasped like we were in some Victorian melodrama. I choked back laughter at her bewildered expression. *Yep. Just need to keep her outraged. Keep her talking.*

There was a lot I needed to know.

"What a shitty thing to say."

"Sounds like you're in a shitty situation. And who are you, Oscar the Grouch?" I cast a look around her office. "Since when you do like living in a trash can?"

"You know what, Nick?" Her eyes narrowed in just the way I remembered and my heart kicked an extra beat. Ah. Just like old times. Back then, this kind of spark ignited the best kind of fun, the most exquisite pleasure.

"No, but I'm sure you'll tell me."

"You can go and—"

"What kind of trouble are you in?"

She hesitated. "I—"

"Start with the truth. Save us both some time, I'll find out anyway. For a modest donation, those thirsty development folks'll sell you out in a heartbeat."

"What do you care?" Her head tilted, flattened curls going skyward as her mouth screwed up. "You couldn't get out of here fast enough all those years ago, you never even looked back. Now you wanna carry my burdens? Now you care so much about what's going on, when you couldn't be bothered, didn't at least have the courtesy to tell me where you'd disappeared to in the first place? Get out. And I mean that."

I leaned forward, paperwork forgotten.

Finally. This was the fight we'd both been spoiling for.

And I wanted it. I wanted to see what awaited us both on the other side.

"I left you a note. I told you I was coming back. *You* sent the ring back, you. That was all *you*."

"It was *two years* later when I sent that ring back," she screeched, and for a moment I thought she would throw her blanket at me in her rage. "What did you think? That I'd put my life on ice until you decided you were ready to start something up again? And you'd *more* than moved on before I even sent the ring back."

What was she talking about? "What the hell is that supposed to mean?"

"Nick." She buried her head in her hands. "I'm not inclined to review your history with redheads in coffee shop kitchens."

What the actual *fuck* was she talking about?

"What are you talking about? I've never even dated any redheads. I don't even know any—"

She pushed back the covers and stood. "I don't have time for *any* of this. I need to get to the community center—" She paused. "What? Why are you looking at me like that?"

My lungs slammed shut. My dick perked up.

You rang?

God was punishing me. That was it. He was using Zora to punish me right now for every broken promise, every misdeed.

"Zora. You're not wearing any pants." The words drifted out on the current of a painful exhale, and I found my eyes wouldn't move from the glorious display in front of me.

She actually patted her naked thighs before she looked down, as if she didn't believe me. Meanwhile, my eyes feasted on the sweet mandolin curves below her wrinkled yellow shirt. The sweetly rounded hips, delicious full thighs, and . . .

Wonder Woman underwear.

She was going to kill me. And my cock.

Her awareness seemed to be on a delay, as if she hadn't quite accepted the reality that she was half-naked. She gaped down at herself for a full five seconds before finally reacting. "Oh, God," she squeaked, and turned back to the couch to tear through its contents.

Which left her ass facing me, allowing my eyes to devour the sight of the underwear that barely contained the glorious curves. Cute dimples just above winked at me. Her cheeks jiggled enticingly as she frantically threw the blanket and an assortment of clothing to the floor in her frantic search.

God, this was the prettiest, juiciest peach I'd ever seen.

So this was how I died. Death by Zora's ass. Not how I'd expected, but still, an amazing way to go.

I gritted my teeth at the insistent throbbing of my cock against my fly. There was no way I could stand, not if I wanted to appear a gentleman.

"Zora." I closed my eyes briefly, reluctant to lose more than a millisecond of the splendid sight in front of me. This woman. Twelve years later and she hadn't changed. She was still as off-beat, as wonderfully awkward as before, and still had the potential to drive me out of my mind with lust. "Why the hell are you sleeping naked on a couch with the door open?"

"The door was closed, or at least I thought it was, I went to the bathroom in the middle of the night. Maybe I didn't pull it completely closed."

"Why are you sleeping without your pants?" *But thank you for doing so.*

"I can't sleep in jeans." She'd moved her search to the back of the couch, as if a pair of pants would magically sprout along the wall. "I usually take them off so I can sleep, really sleep, for a few hours while I'm working on an application and need a break—"

Frustration warred with lust. "Usually? So you do this often. What's so pressing you're sleeping in this godforsaken office?"

"Money," she yelled, turning to face me. "I need money. For tenure. To fund my employees."

"Okay," I said, lost. "How are you making it in this office?"

"Grants, *dummy*." She said it in precisely the same tone she'd used when we were kids and I'd baited her by doing something deliberately idiotic.

She pulled up short and blinked at me.

I snorted with laughter. "Yes. Yes, you did just call me dummy."

We blinked at each other in reluctant amusement, suddenly back to being the children who relentlessly teased and harassed each other.

God, I missed her. God, I missed this.

All things considered, I was making progress. I'd take the bloodlust in her eyes over wounded resentment any day.

"Help me find my pants." Her hands crossed at her crotch. "And stop looking at me."

"While you're like that? Impossible. But I will help you find your pants."

Jesus, how to do this? Well, she was exposed and asking for my help, so maybe it just made us even.

I hesitated, then stood.

"God." Her gaze snapped to my dick, which certainly wasn't going to make it go down any faster. I swallowed a comment, decided I was better than that. I was an honorable man, above asking if it was more than she was used to. Although, fuck honor when it came to Jackson James.

I moved around the table, unable to break my gaze away from her legs, her thighs, which led up to—

"Nick!"

"Sorry, sorry. Shouldn't you know where you left your own pants? How far could they have—"

"There they are." She rushed past me, her soft hip brushing my leg as she ripped a blur of denim from one of the meeting chairs. I looked away as she went through the tortuous process of wiggling and jiggling into her jeans.

I wanted my hands on her, helping. But if I helped, they were going back down.

Good Lord. Was life on her planet always this upside down?

I turned my gaze from the reflection of her glorious ass disappearing into her jeans in the opposite window. As delectable as this distraction had been, I needed to get back on course, find out what was going on.

"Is that what they've got on you, Zora? You need grant money to keep your job?"

Her shoulders slumped. She spoke over her shoulder to me.

"Yes, Nick. Yes. Happy? You've caught me at my lowest. Again. Not only am I half-naked this time, but I'm at the end of my career. I came here—" She gestured at her paper-covered desk and let her arm fall against her side. "Adesola came across a last-minute funding opportunity and I just had to try. It probably won't work. Nothing else has. But I had less than a day to get it done and in."

It killed me seeing her like this. Tired. Broken. Hopeless. "How long have you been doing this?"

"For a while now. A year." She lifted one shoulder.

"My team told me all about your publishing record and your previous grants. Everyone here at the med school and the hospital loves you. They can't say enough for how much you've done. You singlehandedly turned around their Patient Experience office. What's the issue? Federal grant funding nowadays is uncertain, because budgets are cut."

"It's a condition of my tenure." She shook her head. "I had to have a very specific grant by now."

"Or what?"

"What do you mean, or what?" Her arms folded. "I'm not going to have a job. And it's not just me, I'm more worried about my research staff. My existing grants are expiring, and if I don't find new ones, I can't afford to pay them. Which means they won't have jobs because I've failed them."

Her voice broke over the last few words, and I had to shove aside a rising tide of anger. What kind of fuckery was this, and why was she assigning personal blame to herself over it all? God, she hadn't changed.

But I was here now, and she wasn't going to struggle a minute more if I could help it. I reached for my phone. This didn't need to be difficult; it could be easily resolved. "How much do you need?"

Her shook her head, her expression resolute. "No. I don't want your money."

I raised an eyebrow. "Really? Not even to keep your staff employed?"

Her mouth opened. Closed.

"I know you, Z. You're the same. Still setting yourself on fire to keep other people warm. This, really, is what you want to fight for? When you've got administrators stringing you up over a grant? With all you've done for this hospital?"

I took a chance, risked a few steps in her direction. Counted it a win when she didn't back away from my hands on her shoulders.

"I'll take care of it. Rocket Enterprises can easily make a gift that'll keep them on longer. It'll give you time to decide what you want to do, without worrying about everyone else. You're not happy here—"

She jerked away, her face mutinous. "You don't know what I am, and you lost the right to any opinion about my life or what I should do."

Damn. This was hard. How much longer could I go without telling her what had happened all those years ago? Why had I let the deception go on this long? Why hadn't I tracked her down, fought harder when that ring came back in the mail?

Why had I thought she'd be better off fighting her battles alone in this world than with me? Even if I was fucked up?

I wanted her back. I wanted to fix this, and all of her problems. But I didn't want the truth to manipulate her feelings or influence her decision making.

I wanted her back of her own free will, of her own volition. Not motivated by any strings, or by the emotions that had always led her to sacrifice for others. I wanted her to come to me willingly.

Not out of pity.

Not out of guilt.

"It's not what you think." It was hard to breathe past the million cracks in my chest. "When I left, I didn't have a choice, and I did it for you. You have to believe that."

"*For* me? Nick, get out. I can't take anymore."

"What you said before? About me catching you at your lowest? Hardly. I wish you could see yourself the way I do, Zora. I wish you knew how long I prayed for the moment when I could set eyes on the miracle of *you* again. Let me help. Let me set you free from all this so you can be happy."

She backed a step away. My chest squeezed at the moisture in her eyes. "I am happy. Can't you tell? I'm so damn *happy*. All on my own. And I'm going to fix this problem and any other one that comes up. Just like I've been doing, long before you saw fit to show up again. But thank you for offering. Now, let's both get this business between us done so we can get back to our lives."

"I don't wanna go back, Zora." It wasn't me saying it. The words took on a life of their own, slid past my mouth, crawled, arrowed to her. "Not without you. I want you back. I want *us* back."

"I'm trying to be an adult. I'm trying to be a professional, a colleague, your *friend*, as much as it hurts. Isn't that *enough*?" Her voice cracked and she closed her eyes as she sighed out, "Haven't you taken enough?"

"I don't wanna be your fucking friend. And it'll never be nearly enough." I walked past her and headed to the door. "See you soon."

CHAPTER SEVENTEEN
Nick

My palms were sweating.

I knew this house, knew the woodgrain pattern of the big door by heart. I'd gripped the brass lip of the intricate lion head knocker countless times, even helped pick out the four-foot giant brass statue of a honey bee that resided next to the door.

I'd grown up here.

But I was unsure of what to expect. It'd been too long. I didn't know what was waiting for me on the other side of the door.

Several seconds passed, with no indication of movement from inside. I'd just raised my hand to knock one last time, now almost eager to return to my truck, when I heard the tumblers in the lock engage. The door swung inward.

Ellie Leffersbee stood on the other side.

Her face didn't register any surprise. She craned her neck up at me, blinking against the strong, mid-afternoon sun. New lines extended from the corners of her dark eyes. I'd never realized just how much Zora looked like her until this moment.

"Nick Armstrong."

"Yes, ma'am." My voice came out rusty.

"Well, you look like you grew up fine."

"I hope so." My heart beat a little harder. I cast around for the right words to say, to offer to the now painful silence, and came up empty.

A smile split her face. "Get over here and hug me, boy!" She threw the dishtowel in her hand over one shoulder and threw open her arms to me.

Relief and gratitude rushed through me. I bent to enfold her in my arms. That familiar scent I'd always imagined as powered doughnuts surrounded me. And just like that, I was back to all the comforts of my childhood, returned to the origin of all that I was.

"Come inside." She grinned even wider before gesturing for me to follow her into the house. "I was wondering how long it would take you to get here. I imagine you and Zora have tortured each other sufficiently? Needed a breather?"

"Uh . . ." Was she psychic? She'd already known I was here? Had Zora told her mother I'd seen her without pants yesterday?

I followed Mrs. Leffersbee as she led me from the foyer, past the formal dining and sitting rooms to the kitchen. Even now, all these years later, I could navigate this house blindfolded.

"Sit down," she said, gesturing to the kitchen table as she headed to the fridge. "Sweet tea?"

"Yes, ma'am." I looked around the kitchen where I'd taken so many meals with Zora and her family. Much of it was the same, save for new cabinets and flooring. But this wood table, scarred and faded in places, was the same. I lowered myself onto the end of the long bench and my knees only just made it under the table. I ran a thumb across that warped spot I remembered.

And the honeybees were still here, tucked all around the kitchen. Ceramic bees, glass bees, gold bees. When I was a teenager, I'd asked Mrs. Leffersbee if her fascination with bees started after she acquired her husband's last name.

"After, of course," she'd said. "I thought it would be best to celebrate having a new, peculiar last name. As time went on, I learned how fitting it was." Her voice had lost some of its light. "Sometimes being a Leffersbee means taking a few stings before you get any honey."

She hadn't smiled when she said that.

The bulletin board next to the fridge memorialized past events and Leffersbee accomplishments. I took in the pictures and papers jockeying for position on the crammed corkboard. Faded programs for Audre's high school graduation, an award ceremony for Walker's photography. Newspaper clippings about Zora's research. Tavia's new employee bio from an accounting firm in New York. Ah, and the funeral program for Bethany Winston.

Seeing this reminder of Bethany's death made me ache with missing my own mother. I wished there was still a place I could go to see Lila Rossi again, somewhere like this, where we could be surrounded by our history together.

So much had changed.

Zora was right. I'd never looked back.

"Hard to believe isn't it?"

I startled as Mrs. Leffersbee drew near and set a glass of sweet tea at my elbow.

"That she's been gone this long?"

I looked back at the smiling photo of Bethany. *Beloved Mother.*

"Yeah. It is."

She returned to the fridge and returned with a plated cake under a glass dome. "I think about her every day, you know?" She took a sip of her own sweet tea, her dark eyes fathomless and fastened to mine. "But you know what? I know Bethany would have gotten a kick out of you being back." The side-eye she aimed in my direction somehow made me feel she was looking down at me, tiny as she was. "Took you long enough to come see me after you snuck in town."

I ducked my head. "I'm sorry. I wanted to see you. It's just . . . it's just—"

"It's hard." She grabbed my hand. It didn't come close to covering mine. "I know, baby. I can only imagine what's going through your head, being back here. But you made the trip. Your mama said you would."

I looked up at that. "What?"

"Oh yeah." She said it easily, as if stating a simple fact. "She was sure of it. I told her I'd be here to meet you when you did."

This little woman was the first person in a long time to make me feel something close to shame.

"I should have stayed in contact."

She only shrugged. "I understand why you didn't. You were in an impossible position as a young man trying to make his way in the world, figure out who he is. I've kept an eye on you through your mother, then Nan." She leveled a sly glance at me over her glass of iced tea. "I may even have a scrapbook somewhere where I kept track of your accomplishments."

I hated myself in that moment. "I owe you so much."

Her back went straight. "You owe us *nothing*. And don't let me find another check in the mail. You're not too big for me to take a strip out of your hind parts."

I winced, remembering that night. "You paid for everything, for years. Getting us out of town, resettled in Ann Arbor. Rehab for Mom, not once, but twice. My first year of school until the scholarship kicked in. You've got to let me—"

"Excuse me, son." Her eyebrows went up in that smart-ass way I knew. "A few things for you to remember here. First of all, what I do with my money is *my* business—"

"I'm just saying—"

"What, they interrupt their elders in Michigan? Or wherever it is you're laying your head nowadays?" When her eyes went wide with mock shock, I cracked up and she soon followed.

"Dear heart, you can't pay me back. The only reimbursement I've ever wanted was to know that you'd taken care of yourself. You've done that. You've learned a lot and you've done well for yourself. I know Lila was proud as a peacock. But you've got to get through your head that love doesn't carry a balance. We did what we did because we love you, and we always will. All that other stuff? Just money. The love Ezra and I have for you will never change, no matter where you are, no matter how much money you have or don't have. Whether we're in frequent contact or not." She gave me that sneaky side-eye again. "Whether you're with my daughter or not."

I let out a sigh at the mention of Zora.

She continued on, but we both knew she'd just pulled the pin on a grenade.

"I love you, Nick." She gripped my hand again, and I held fast to it, and to her words. "You don't have a choice. So accept it."

I nodded, swallowing back the sudden tightness in my throat.

She had pity on me and changed the topic. "So. You've seen Zora?"

I coughed. "She didn't tell you?"

She sat back, arms folded, her face full of a cat that ate the canary grin. "I think she was working herself up to tell me the other day, but she lost her nerve. Me, I already knew. I know mostly everything going on in this town."

I smirked at her superior smile. "Really, now?"

"Yes. But all I *really* need to know is *you, and I've been knowing you since you were practically in diapers*. Found Zora the first day you were here, didn't you?"

Damn.

"Yes, ma'am."

"And the two of you been torturing each other ever since?"

"Yes, ma'am."

She huffed out a laugh. "Some things never change."

I met her gaze. "No, ma'am. They don't."

"What is it you want with my baby, Nick? She's already turned 'round and confused and trying to work up the courage to make some hard decisions. Don't make it worse, you hear?"

I nodded.

"I know what kind of man you are. I watched you grow up here in my own house and I know who your mama raised you to be. I know why you're back, but do you?"

She busied herself with plating cake slices.

I traced the condensation on my glass, absorbed by her question and my answer. "Yeah, I do. I'm ready to face the past. I'd give everything I have for another chance with Zora." I followed the woodgrain pattern of the table with a finger, unable to meet her eyes while I delivered the naked truth. "When I left here, I left a part of me with her. It's always been her for me. She's all I've ever wanted. She's all I'll ever want."

"Uh-huh." I snuck a glance at Ellie and found a smile that contrasted with the obviously manufactured skepticism in her voice. "And you don't have any of those actresses and models waiting in the wings? Your head's on straight?"

"Yes, ma'am. My head's on straight. *Straight*." A thought occurred to me. "What do you, uh, think about Jackson James in all this?"

She drowned her expression in her glass of iced tea, took her time gulping a bit more down before swallowing. "Y'all are grown," she said when she finally surfaced. "I care about Jackson, too. I watched him grow up and he's become a fine man and is growing into a wonderful sheriff. I don't know that I should have an opinion one way or the other about any of it." I wasn't at all fooled by her philosophical tone, or the mild shrug she sent me. "It's Zora's decision. It'll all work out."

"He's not with her, you know." I made it a statement, but I watched her face for any reaction, any indication of what was *really* going on between those two.

"I don't get in grown folks' business, Nick." Her guileless smile made me certain she killed at poker.

I heaved a breath, unsurprised at the unsteady, gelatinous state of my gut. All of my supreme CEO courage was nowhere to be found now talking to Zora's mother. Not when it was *about* Zora, and when so much was at stake when it came to the future I wanted with her again.

Well, and all the positively filthy things I wanted to do to Zora were never all that far from my mind nowadays. Maybe a little fear was appropriate right now.

"You have any advice?"

"Oh, it's advice you want, do you?" Her smile was like the sun coming out.

"Yes."

She chewed at her lip. "My advice for you is the same advice I'd give her. Trust yourself. Let down your defenses. Trust you'll love each other the way you deserve. All that instinct, that knowing you two have always had about what was best for the other? It's still there."

Then she leaned forward suddenly, her eyes steady on mine. "And Nick, you were never your father. Never. You didn't need to change your last name to know that. You hear me?"

It was, perhaps, the most profound thing she could have said, and lifted and eased a weight I'd been carrying ever since that night twelve years ago. I felt somehow freer as I met her solemn dark gaze.

"I hear you." Several beats of silence descended as we eyed each other.

"Mrs. Leffersbee . . . this won't be easy. She thinks I moved on with . . ." What had Zora been saying? A redhead? I'd meant to pursue that revelation with a line of questioning, but to be fair, she'd been half-naked and my body had been all busy saying "hell yes," distracting me. "And she still doesn't know—"

She cupped her forehand in her hand. "God."

"That's right. She doesn't know what actually happened all those years ago."

"We have to tell her."

"*I* have to tell her. It was my decision. It's my mess. It had to be done, I had to protect her."

Her mouth twisted. "No, we all co-own this. It was our decision then, and I still stand by it. It's just time to pay the piper now." She let out a thin sigh. "When are you going to tell her?"

CHAPTER EIGHTEEN
Zora

"You're on birth control, right? Hand me that black sweater."

I stared at the back of Leigh's head. My mouth fell open.

We'd just completed an exhausting shop-a-thon in Knoxville. Leigh needed the distraction in light of her impending trip back home to New Jersey and no one loved a mall more than she did. The result of our excursion was a bold new haircut for her, new coppery highlights for me, and a dozen new outfits selected under Leigh's supervisory eye. It was only once we were both convinced that Nick would eat his words about my "rough edges," she'd relented and allowed us to leave.

After arriving home, we'd set up camp in Leigh's side of the duplex for movie night. I knew how much she hated returning to Jersey for family events, so I'd plied with her with a few of her favorites: ribs, fries, and pineapple upside-down cake from the Donner Bakery. Now, plates of discarded animal carcass littered her king-sized bed. We'd just finished watching the latest superhero movie, both of us competing to gross the other out with all the kinky things we wanted to do to Superman.

She'd won after suggesting something complicated with beads and I'd drawn the line at letting his rod of steel anywhere near my back door.

Finally, Leigh decided she couldn't delay anymore and lugged a carry-on container onto the foot of her bed. I watched her roll yoga pants and squish them into the suitcase.

I hated the tight set to her narrow shoulders and the grim purse to her mouth. I'd offered to go with her several times, tried to bully her into letting me support her, but she'd resisted all my efforts. It would kill me to drop her off the next morning, knowing how much family gatherings drained her. I'd have given anything to make it easier for her.

My mind had been busy with composing a plan to surprise her in Jersey a few days later, so her sudden question was totally out of left field.

"What are you . . .? What?" *What* had she just said?

"You heard me." She didn't look up as she crossed to her dresser and raided her underwear drawer. "The sweater is on the chair, next to you."

I snatched her favorite cashmere sweater off the recliner next to her bed and fired it at her head. She ignored its impact, calmly rolling underwear into tiny balls.

"I'm a grown ass woman, and quite capable of managing my own birth control, thank you."

She paused in her rolling and straightened to look at me. "You have an IUD, right? The expiration date on that thing still good?"

I looked for something else to throw at her. "Yes, and it's still working just fine, thank you very much. Though I can't imagine why you'd be asking about it."

"It's a valid question. I'm betting you haven't had to think about birth control for a while now. This situation? Fertile ground for the 'surprise baby' trope in some of my favorite romance novels." She winked at me. "Pun intended. But yes, this is the kind of question a woman in your position needs to think about."

"'A woman in my position?' What's that supposed to mean?"

She shook her head, fingers busy on the next pair of underwear. "You're about to sex your ex, even though you know you shouldn't." She flicked an idle glance in my direction before continuing on to the next pair with lightning-quick fingers. "I understand. I've been there before, and God knows I've done it. You're going to do it too, and you'll regret it. But I guess you've got to get it out your system."

I felt almost guilty, trotting out the lie that had to be wearing incredibly thin by now. "I'm with Jackson, you know that—"

"You are not with Jackson. I'm starting to wonder if you ever were. You're my best friend and I live next door to you. You think I wouldn't notice that dude's never here? That you never go anywhere with him anymore? You're not carrying on a torrid affair in your car. You don't have the flexibility—"

"Hey."

"—and I doubt Jackson gets off on dust as an aphrodisiac, so you're not boning in that landfill of an office. Who are you even pretending for? What, for your parents?" She threw the last ball of underwear in the suitcase and aimed a frown at me. "How do you benefit from this little arrangement?"

"We both do. I don't have to deal with the questions from my parents and everyone else around town about what I'm doing. Have I met a nice young man, aren't I getting older, shouldn't I be thinking about kids? Same for Jackson. His family is thrilled we're 'together.' I can live my life in peace."

"What's wrong with just being honest and saying you're content to be with yourself for now? Why can't you just live your truth out loud?"

I chuckled. For all her sensibility, she still hadn't come to understand how close-minded the folks of Green Valley could be, especially concerning this topic. "You haven't lived in this town all that long. You're still doing everything 'out loud' and just about everybody thinks you're a foul-mouthed banshee." I shook my head. "I don't begrudge you—you do you. But you don't know what it's like, living here with my last name. Everyone has an opinion. Everyone, including my parents, have an expectation for what I should be or how I should appear to everyone else. Hell, I think Jackson is the only thing my dad and I ever talk about. He doesn't know what else to say to me. He doesn't understand what I do, he's tired of pretending he does, and he's still disappointed I don't work at the bank like Tavia and Walker."

"Not good reasons." Leigh opened her closet and rummaged through the hanging items. "Sounds more like laziness to me. You'd rather pretend you have an imitation of the thing you actually want, and I think that's sad and pathetic. And friend, you are neither of those things. Why don't you take a chance on someone else? Grab whatever you actually want for once without just going along with the motions?"

"When did you become pro-relationship?"

"A relationship is fine for you," she said, her tone stiff as she returned to the suitcase with a kelly green blouse in hand. "But I'm done with men. Finished. You should learn from my example. I've got to go home now for my aunt's funeral knowing my good-for-nothing ex-husband is going to show his face and somehow make my life hell. You want that kind of grief?"

From what I knew of Leigh's ex, none of it good, Nick wasn't quite as dastardly. True, he'd left abruptly, and yes he had—

"You're over there justifying the cheating, right?" I broke from my thoughts in time to see Leigh staring at me with one hand propped on her hip. "Aren't you?"

"I know how stupid this sounds. Really, I do. But he didn't seem to know what I was talking about, at all. Maybe if I had—"

"What? Should we have waited until he took her to the walk-in closet and got her underwear around her ankles before we jumped out? Just to be certain of his intentions?"

I covered my face with my hands. "You're right. I'm being dumb."

She sighed, planting her hands on either side of the suitcase's halves. "Zora, the last thing I want to do is weigh in on how you should live your life. God knows, I wish you'd take the reins and shock *yourself* a little bit. I'm willing to bet you're going to do that with Nick. I won't judge you if you do. But I just want you to remember that people don't change, not that much. So go into this with a clear head. Know the risk."

"I'm not going to sleep with him."

Her groan reeked of skepticism. "Let's review the data points, shall we? He shows up unexpectedly and you end up face-down, ass-up in front of him. You take a private flight and end up on top of the man. You had a huge fight with him yesterday, all while you were pantsless—"

"Okay. When you put it like that—"

"It's not me putting it like anything!" Her laugh grated on my nerves. "I'm just trying to point out the inevitable here. It's not just you, thinking with your rational mind here. Your body is in on the decision making. You're horny from years of celibacy, and you're not who you were before Nick showed up. I'm telling you, your undercarriage is hot. Your engine is running. Your juice is *loose*."

We glared at each other.

"Fine." Leigh planted her hands on her hips. "Hypothetical question. First thing that comes to mind, say it. If you had sex with him, how would you do it? Missionary? Doggy? Quick."

"No," I said automatically, surprising myself with how quickly the answer and accompanying mental picture sprung to life. "On top." My blood heated at the idea of me on top of Nick, straddling those ridiculously muscled thighs, my bare thighs sliding along the crisp hair of his thighs. I wanted his mouth, his tongue, on my breasts. I needed his hands gripping my back while I rode him. I wanted to follow that captivating scent, whatever it was, all along his neck with my nose, then my teeth. And I wanted my hands in his hair again, finally. I wanted to run my hands through it, grip it, pull it, punish him just a little. Or a lot.

I realized I was staring into space. Cold sweat trickled down my spine as I imagined just how good it would feel to have him inside me again, my walls clenching around him as I came.

Damn.

Leigh looked smug. "You're over there getting off without your hands in your pants. Time to face reality. I put backup condoms in your purse and bedside table."

CHAPTER NINETEEN

Zora

"Thank you for coming."

I slid into the opposite side of the booth where Nick sat, at once both treacherous and delicious in a plaid shirt rolled above his elbows. His dark stubble had taken on an increased volume and depth that made my stomach pitch dangerously. Those unnerving green eyes crawled over my body in a slow sweep, and I couldn't shake the impression that he was somehow collecting data, storing observations that would be used against me in short order.

Meep.

Pull it together. Don't be dumb for a man. Especially one who has already proven he can't be trusted.

I'd pulled on a quick, no-ironing-required paisley dress that showcased my best assets before driving to Kaye's, a cute little coffee shop straddling the Green Valley-Knoxville border. Might as well be cute when dismissing him from my life for the final time, right? I hadn't missed the flare of appreciation in Nick's eyes as I approached the table.

Yeah, this *thing* between us? It had to stop.

"You didn't give me much of a choice," I said in response to his greeting, tossing my purse on the bench seat beside me.

"Actually, I gave you exactly that. I simply made it clear that I had no problem showing up at your house or wherever you were tonight at this time." His eyes burned into mine. "It's time to talk. We have to, without any dramatic exits this time."

"You know, at least one of those exits was yours."

"Regardless." He lifted one well-built shoulder in a shrug.

"Well, I agree. We need to get on the same page."

He nodded at the empty space in front of me. "What, you don't want any coffee? Pastry? Anything? Whatever you want, it's yours."

I suppressed a shiver, internally shocked at my own lascivious read of his very innocent statement. Yep, I was in trouble. "Nope. I just want to get this said."

"Okay. Go for it." He took a sip from his own cup of coffee, looking supremely confident. Watching his remarkable calm, I found myself wanting to kick the shit out of him under the table and make him feel a little of the tumult currently acid-washing my gut.

I'd rehearsed this speech a number of times out in the car, but I found myself suddenly out of words. I looked away from his eyes and out the window to the wet street. After Leigh's warning, I realized I was, in fact, dangling over the precipice of my own ruin. I considered myself a smart, practical woman who usually heeded warnings and steered clear of unnecessary risks. So, I found it unnerving to realize that deep down a part of me wanted to hear the sharp clang of metal teeth closing around me in Nick's trap. A part of me wanted to be caught, wanted to surrender to the dark intent in Nick's eyes. Even though I knew better. After his declaration yesterday in my office where he left no question that he wouldn't settle for friendship, I knew I had to be clear. I had to put distance between us. Permanently.

"I told you I was proud of you. And I meant that. I'm glad you're doing so well in life. It's more than we'd ever dreamed of, what you've accomplished."

"Here comes the but."

"Don't interrupt."

"Fine."

"*But* . . . it doesn't give you license to just walk back into my life like you'd never left. We're not eighteen anymore—I get that. It's not exactly fair to hold you to the promises we made as teenagers. At least, that's what I keep telling myself. But the truth is," I said, letting some of the angst and irritation bleed into my voice, "you owed me more, even at eighteen. A hell of a lot more than what I got. A five-line letter? Some half-ass explanation that you had to go and you'd be back, with no indication of *when*? Even teenage you could have managed a damn sight more than that."

His eyes closed, big hands curling around his coffee cup.

"What would have been wrong with just saying your mother was relocating to Michigan for a job and you'd decided to go with her? I would have understood that. Completely. Agreed with it. Helped you, even. I knew what was going on, what people in town were saying. Of course she would have benefitted from starting over. But you and I still could have made it work, even long distance."

He directed his stare to the table, all while his jaw worked as if he was chewing on unsaid words.

"You just *disappeared, a*nd all I got was that letter from my mother. That's how much I mattered, apparently. Didn't you know, if you didn't want to go through with our plans, you could have just told me? And not planned an escape?"

Anguish, wet and hot, fought for clearance to my throat and eyes. I swallowed it back.

"That's the thing, one of the things, that hurt the worst."

"Zora—"

"No, listen. You disappeared and I waited around like a dumbass, thinking you couldn't have done it without a good reason. Then I drove to Ann Arbor with Leigh—"

His eyebrows shot up.

"Intending to, I don't know, see if you were *okay,* for God's sake. That's how stupid I was." Stupid for *him,* I thought, but didn't say.

He leaned forward, brows furrowed. "And what happened?"

That's right. He wouldn't know.

Even all these years later, talking about it constricted my heart, stopped my pulse. Here I was, thirty years old, near tears remembering the betrayal of a twenty-year-old Nick. How stupid was I? Why was I not using this time and mental space for something that actually mattered?

But at least now, finally, I was able to address it.

Closure, right?

"We went to that stupid hippie coffee shop you worked at, and saw the girl, your coworker. The redhead. Kissing you." My eyes closed against the memory. "And you kissed her back."

He sat back against the booth with a thud, his face blank.

All the promises I'd made to myself to be polite, professional, accepting, a lady á la Ellie Leffersbee's design, flew out the window as I watched the dumbfounded expression on his face. "You were busy kissing your coworker, while I was pining for you, you selfish asshole."

His expression didn't change, but both silvered heads of the occupants in the booth behind him swiveled in our direction.

My breathing wasn't steady. I tried to remind myself of the truth: I was angry at him. Hurt at what he did all those years ago.

But more than that, I was angry at myself. For somehow still loving him.

I *hated* myself for that.

"What you said yesterday." My voice came out steady and I was glad of it. "About wanting more from me? It's completely unfair, and uncalled for. Jackson and I—"

"I didn't cheat on you."

His gaze on mine was direct and unflinching. He shook his head, eyes still on mine, and repeated, "I swear, I didn't cheat on you. It took me a minute to figure out what you must have seen, and I do remember now. That was my coworker, Rebecca, although she wasn't always a redhead. I think her hair was every color of the rainbow in the year I worked there." His hand snaked across the table and gripped mine, exerting warm pressure. "But I did *not* do anything with her. I wish you would have stayed. I wish you would have come inside."

I yanked my hand away, mouth agape. So, this is how he wanted to do this? He wanted to deny what I'd seen with my own eyes? "Are you serious right now?"

"Zora. Listen to me. If you'd come inside, if you'd even waited just a second longer, you'd know I pushed her away. That situation, what happened, it was my fault. She was flirty, and she'd been flirty for some time. I should have shut down her advances prior to that but I just . . . I didn't know. So I kept ignoring her, thinking she'd finally get the hint and stop."

"You had every opportunity to pull away."

He hesitated. "I agree, and you're right. But I remember," he said, his voice straining in earnest, "in that moment, being torn between not wanting to hurt her and disbelief that it was even happening. I should have handled it better, and I should have moved faster. But you've gotta believe me, I stopped it, I did. I'm sorry I didn't do it when you were standing there, but I did."

I folded my arms. "Is that supposed to make it all better? You explaining this is just some soap opera melodrama, a case of 'she kissed me, I didn't kiss her'? If even none of that happened, you didn't so much as pick up a phone to even call me. Or write another letter. For *two years.*"

"I couldn't." He growled it, gripping the end of the table. "Don't you think I wanted to? I'd never been out of Green Valley, never been away from you for more than a week at a time. All of a sudden I was in a completely strange state with a handful of family I barely remembered, finishing college and preparing for grad school. If I'd spoken to you again, if I'd written . . ." He shook his head. "I would have come back. I would have walked away from every responsibility, every obligation just to be with you, and I couldn't. I had to do what was right for my mother."

"Your mother didn't want us to be together?"

"No, my mother was—" He shook his head again, breath whistling between his teeth. I had the distinct impression that he regretted what he'd just admitted. "My mother needed my help."

What was he implying?

"You don't think I wanted the best for her, too? I have *never* suggested you shouldn't do all you could for your mother. I tried to help, but you never let me, and you never told me all that was going on at the time. But what does that have to do with you letting me know you were okay? That you were perfectly fine on campus, French-kissing rainbow-haired girls?"

His face turned to stone.

I studied him, the tightly drawn lines of his upper body, the rigid set of his mouth.

"This isn't supposed to be easy for you. You did a shitty thing. You need to own up to it." I was suddenly weary with all of it, with the both of us, and wanted nothing more than to be back home.

"I didn't cheat on you." His speech was slow, measured. "Please hear me saying it. I didn't sleep with that girl, I didn't sleep with any girl for a while after you sent back that ring. It's true, I've done things I'm ashamed of, but never that. I would *never* betray you in that way. I would never have left you at all, but the question I had to ask myself back then is the same one I ask myself now: whether or not I deserved you. If I was good enough for you."

"What about when you bought that ring? You doubted whether or not you deserved me when you asked me to marry you? Suddenly all that was in question when you moved away?" I gave a derisive sniff. "Okay."

The older couple behind Nick rose from the booth; both snuck furtive glances back at us. The man took his time helping the woman into her jacket. I spotted the quick pat the man delivered to Nick's shoulder as they walked past us toward the door.

"He doesn't need encouragement," I said, scowling. A sympathetic smile flicked across the woman's face before they passed us.

Nick raised a brow. "I don't need encouragement?"

"You're a man about to hide behind a defense as old as Adam and Eve. You're going to tell me you didn't do it and expect me to magically be okay with it, to somehow believe it."

"I'm not asking you to just believe it. I'm asking you to remember what you knew of me, all those years ago. You knew me better than almost anyone else on this planet. If I'd done it, Zora, I'd own up to it. God knows enough has happened, I've already messed up enough, it would just be one more item on the list. Just one more thing for me to confess. But I didn't. If I had, I'd be man enough to tell you. I would."

I watched him, considered his words as I took in his steadfast gaze. There was no denying the sway his words held. He was right; I remembered Nick as a kid. Clever, sly? Yes. But never with me. Never to my detriment. And when he'd done wrong, he'd always confessed. Every single time.

Even when he was afraid of the punishment.

Damn it.

Damn it. I believed him.

I lifted my eyes to him and unknotted my hands, nodding to indicate an acknowledgment of his words. "I believe you. I'm sure I'm a fool for it, and I'll probably regret it, but . . . up until you left, you'd never lied to me. And you're not lying right now. I can tell," I admitted.

His entire body seemed to release its tension. "Thank you, Zora. I know you're afraid to trust, what with all that happened. So thank you for believing me in this instance."

We were silent for several beats in the space of our concession, each of us looking elsewhere before he suddenly asked, "Did you know your father paid our mortgage?"

Startled, I frowned at him. "What?"

"Your dad. The last year my mother and I were here, he paid our mortgage. Every month. I guess he knew my mother had trouble getting another job after she lost hers . . ." He shook his head. He didn't have to remind me what had happened. We both remembered how his mother's access to medication on the hospital floor had ultimately been too much of a temptation. "I had to figure it out. I knew she wasn't paying it, and I'd learned the hard way, before I'd started paying the utilities, that there was no peace in assuming everything was okay. So I went to your father and asked him." His jaw clenched. "And he said—"

"Let me guess. Something about it being grown folks' business?"

A ghost of a smile quirked his lips upward. "He said exactly that. As grateful as I was, as I am still, I hated it. Hated that I couldn't take care of what we needed, she needed. I hated every time someone walked by us and whispered about my mother, and I hated how the town discussed her buying drugs from the Iron Wraiths, long before I even realized it."

Instinctively, I grabbed hold of his hand. "But Nick. You were in high school. You were working two part-time jobs, taking classes at the community college toward your associates degree. No one expected you to take on the responsibility for—"

He shook his head. "You don't understand. My whole life, I was terrified of being my father. Terrified I'd wake up one day and find myself solving conflicts with my fists, drowning my troubles in beer. Leaving behind the people who were dependent on me."

"It's not the same thing."

"I had something to prove to myself. Not just you. I had to prove I could make something of myself, that I could trust myself, that I was better than my father. I told myself I wouldn't come back, not until I had something to offer you. That gave me the fuel, the fight I needed to accomplish all I did those first two years—"

"Nick." I squeezed his hand even harder. "All I'd wanted was you, that was it. That's all I needed to be happy. If we'd lived in a leaky tin shack with only a bucket to sit on and a single can of Vienna sausages to split between us . . . I would have been overjoyed. Because I would have been with you."

"You deserved better than that."

"So, why are you back now? What, you figure you deserve me now? Because you have money?"

He leaned in, pulling my hand further into the heat of his body. His gaze moved over my face and lost its intensity, softened. "Zora, I'll never deserve you. Doesn't mean I'm not going to fight like hell to get you back, though. I just needed to know I had something to offer you, show you I could take care of you—"

"Have I ever given you the impression that I wanted or needed you to take care of me?"

"Of course not."

"All I wanted was for us to have a future where we could take care of each other." I met his gaze square on. "But that time has passed for us."

He didn't blink. "It hasn't. And this has absolutely nothing to do with Jackson James."

"You're right, it's not his decision. It's mine."

"Can you really look me in the eyes and tell me you don't feel this, what's between us?" His voice lowered, but his tone was biting. Urgent. "You're going to tell me there's nothing here?"

"It doesn't matter what I feel or don't feel. I've changed, too. I don't let my heart do the driving anymore."

"I did what I had to do to keep you safe, and I'd do it again in a heartbeat."

"Well, this looks intense."

We both jumped, glancing over to find to Walker standing at our table. He frowned down at us in open appraisal.

"Walker." Nick stood.

It was jarring to see the two men standing together after all these years. Walker had always been the older, taller pseudo-brother to Nick. But even at six feet, Walker had to look up to Nick's towering height.

Nick stuck out his hand. Walker only looked at it, scowled, then fixed Nick with a grimace, an expression of such startling menace that I was taken aback. Nick's eyes widened as he took a step back.

The silence was weighted and deafening.

"I didn't cheat on your sister," Nick said, and Walker glared at him for several more heart-stopping moments before transferring his attention to me. Walker lifted his chin, his eyes travelling over my face as he sought my confirmation.

"I believe him," I said weakly.

"Well, that changes things!" Walker then initiated some intricate handshake that began with him slapping Nick's palm and ending with them loosely embracing in a one-armed hug. "Good to see you, family! Zora, I'm glad you got things figured out. He's a little big for me to whoop now using gentleman's rules. I woulda had to sneak attack him. With a car." He lowered his voice, stepping in closer to deliver the next line to Nick, but I still caught it. "I still can, too, if the need arises."

Nick blanched as Walker cuffed his arm. "Good to see you, brother. We need to catch up while you're still in town."

Nick nodded, clapping Walker back on the arm. I didn't miss Walker's wince. "Count on it."

I peered at my brother. "What are you doing out here?"

"Got a date." Walker inclined his head to a young, smooth-featured woman watching us from the corner of the coffee shop, then looked back at us. "What are y'all doing here?"

"Work," I said.

Nick narrowed his eyes at me, then turned back to Walker. "Yeah, man, we better get back to it."

"Alright. Let's do dinner at Zora's soon."

"Why don't you volunteer *your* house, Walker?"

"Because then I'd have to clean it. Now you get to clean yours. You're welcome. See you both later. Wish me luck." He threw up two fingers and turned away.

Nick resumed his seat in the booth, shaking his head. "Wow. It was good to see that guy." He sounded bemused.

"I guess so." I realized I was grateful Walker had shown up when he did. The conversation with Nick had gotten intense.

A ding sounded from the depths of my purse. I unearthed my phone and found a message from my brother.

Glad to hear old boy there didn't cheat, but you may have other things to worry about. A screenshot followed of Jackson at some sporting game, face painted, mouth open with glee. A woman sat on his lap, equally jubilant. And because it was Jackson, he'd left little doubt to the nature of the relationship: his hand was on her right breast.

Damn. That was Jackson. Sloppy.

I glanced up from my phone to find Nick watching me closely.

"Everything alright?"

"Yeah. Just fine."

I risked a glance across the restaurant and met Walker's stare. He gave me a nod, his jaw set. *Dear God.* When Grandma Leffersbee warned us of all that would go awry when we practiced deception, boy, had she been right. I wished I could signal to Walker that it was okay, that he didn't need to string Jackson up.

But Nick was sitting at the table.

And if Nick got confirmation that Jackson and I weren't together . . .? And he would, the longer he hung around town . . .

I didn't even want to think about it.

Nick sat back, his expression and body language conveying patient serenity.

"There's more we need to discuss, as soon as possible. There's more you need to know. It's important. Right now, all I'm asking for is time, Zora. I'm in no hurry to leave. Why don't we just give it time and see how things sort themselves out?"

Inwardly, I groaned.

Time was the *last* thing this situation needed.

CHAPTER TWENTY
Zora

*T*he community center was transformed.

Almost every Friday night, a good portion of the town descended on the community center to take in great music while scarfing down the county's best barbecue, salads, and baked goods. I'd spent many a Friday here in my lifetime, rotating between different classrooms to hear local musicians produce every variety of country, bluegrass, and folk music imaginable.

Now, the auditorium was filled with enough equipment and lights to resemble a small television studio. I counted nine chairs ringed in a circle with a videographer and light stands parked outside the perimeter. Several suits congregated at one side by the bleachers. The univesity's marketing team huddled on the other side next to a folding table piled high with food.

I spotted Nick, the tallest person in the auditorium, immediately. He stood, arms crossed, scowling at the suits in a semi-circle around him. I forced my eyes away from the tousled hair, the close fit of his jeans, the stretch of his white dress shirt over well-defined traps, the furry forearms.

Damn. Since when did fur do it for me?

If I'd thought I was in danger before meeting at the coffee shop with Nick last night, I was only sinking into quicksand now. True, there was still the issue of Nick's abrupt disappearance all those years ago to reconcile. Knowing, *believing* he hadn't cheated? Well, it changed everything. The information slowly eroded my defenses and left my traitorous imagination free to riot with scenarios I had no business entertaining.

It didn't help that Nick was every sexual fantasy I'd ever had personified, right now.

I needed to give my vagina a full name. I'd need to use her first, middle, and last names when I finally addressed her about the Nick-induced slobbering.

I'd intended to skirt around all the activity and find the designated observation space in peace when a familiar voice sounded behind me.

"Zora! There you are!"

Nellie. Because that's all this situation needed, right?

"Here I am," I said dryly, forcing the ends of my mouth upwards. "And there you are. Isn't this great? We both know each other's locations. Guess our eyes are in perfect working order, huh?"

God, that was bitchy. What was wrong with me? *Let her draw blood first, Zora. Sheath your claws.*

Her smile faltered and she frowned. "Okay. We'll I'm glad you made it in today."

I didn't miss the mild censure in her voice. Yep, that was the Nellie I knew. I kept my expression serene. "It's good to be here."

"What was it, again, that you and Mr. Rossi were doing the other day?"

"Important things." I made my voice deliberately brisk. "Which I'm sure you don't have time to hear about, what with all the little details and everything that could go wrong."

She darted an anxious look over her shoulder. "I think Marketing has everything well in hand—"

"Yes, but's like you always say. 'Every impression matters when a sizable donation is on the line.'" I gave her Ellie Leffersbee's trademarked "I'm-Smiling-But-You-Best-Back-The-Hell-Up" smile.

She stepped back. "Alright then. I'll see you at the break?"

"Yep, sounds good." I'd just made it through the auditorium and rounded the corner when I felt a hand on my arm.

"Zora."

And of course.

Nick.

Who was now—*Queen Beyoncé, please help me*—sporting a full-grown beard.

All that ink-black facial hair made his vivid green eyes glow in contrast. It emphasized the sculpted planes of his face, the high cheek bones, the full lips.

I wanted the insides of my thighs to get a chance at this view.

Don't stare.

"Yeah?" I made my voice neutral.

His gaze moved over my face, then hung heavy at my mouth. "You look good. Amazing, actually. You got some sleep."

Yep. The facial, massage, and $150 haircut I'd gotten the other day hadn't hurt, nor did the cute black surplice dress that handily straddled both the professional and sexy domains. I was looking good, feeling good, and hopefully ready for whatever came my way.

Unfortunately, sleep had the unintended consequence of revving up my hormones. Dear God, had Nick always looked this sexy up close?

"I did, thanks. You look better too." And he did. Still tired, for sure, but lighter somehow. Freer. I wondered if he'd had a positive development with his work.

We stood there nodding like idiots, staring at each other. He still hadn't moved his hand from my arm.

"Listen," he said, his voice pitched low. I leaned dangerously closer to hear him, just as he probably intended. He didn't step back; in fact, he moved forward until I was mere inches away. "We got distracted yesterday, with Walker and all, and you didn't seem much for talking after that. But I need us to talk again. Today. It's important."

He threw a look over his shoulder into the gym, then led me

farther around the corner. We settled against the cool tiled wall. I was trapped in his gaze, unable to move as he edged even closer.

"There's more that needs to be said. There's things I need to tell you."

Jesus, there was *more?*

He glanced over my shoulder. I turned to see what held his attention.

We'd turned out of the auditorium's double doors and into the atrium of the building. His attention was riveted to the massive bulletin board where community members advertised baby-sitting services, posted fliers for lost pets, and advertised work sites for day laborers.

"It hasn't changed." He gave a short bark of harsh laughter. "None of it. Seems like nothing changed around here."

I eyed the board, unsure of how to proceed. "I'm not sure if that's exactly true. But I'm hardly qualified to judge. I've been back a while."

He turned in a slow circle, taking in the arteries of hallways branching off the main corridor. "It feels the same. Looks the same. It's like stepping back in time."

Observing the rigid set of his massive shoulders, I sought to bring levity to the moment. "Oh, so you're saying you remember dropping a whole plate of brisket on this very spot when we were in middle school?"

The tension around his eyes relaxed. He advanced toward me, only stopping when he was so close I had to crane my neck up to see past his whisker-covered jaw. A knowing smile sat on his lips as he captured an escaped curl at my temple, sliding it slowly through his fingers. I didn't want to back away. I wanted to step forward, into him, to rest my breasts against the solid wall of his chest.

I was a smart woman. A thinking woman. A take-no-shit woman.

And my hormones were betraying me in the fight for my dignity.

We who are about to die salute you.

"Are you referring to the incident in which a certain person jostled my arm and knocked said plate to the floor?"

He was so close. Greedily, I inhaled clean skin, expensive musk.

I shook my head, swallowed back a smile. "That's not how I recall it."

"Of course that isn't how you recall it." His hand released the curl. His arm dropped, but those green eyes stayed on my mine. "We had a lot of firsts in this building, didn't we?"

My heart tripped into a dangerous rhythm. I looked away.

"We did."

Oh Lord.

Celeste Solange Leffersbee, you will stop your slobbering right now.

He smirked down at me as if he knew *exactly* what Celeste was up to.

Was I breathing fast?

"Which one of these rooms did you fall in? Opened up a whole gash on your chin. Didn't someone pass out from the sight of all the blood?"

I grinned, releasing a pent-up breath as I took a single, life-preserving step backwards.

Away from temptation.

Celeste whimpered.

"Thirteen stitches, thank you very much. The guitar player propped up the bass player." I lifted my chin, proudly showed off the scar underneath. "Men. So weak."

"God, you were a menace then." Pure appreciation shone in those wicked eyes. "You're even worse now."

"I do what I can. I like to keep people on their toes."

He closed the space between us. I jumped when his fingers slid between mine until our palms met. "I'm glad you're here, you know."

Danger. Danger. "Okay."

"Mr. Rossi?"

A young woman approached, almost running in sky high heels and a formfitting suit. Her hands were pressed into anxious fists.

"Mr. Rossi. Here you are."

I smiled at her hushed, worshipful tone, half-expecting her to genuflect. Her blue eyes widened as she chewed on her lip.

Nick frowned, slid his hands from mine.

Why the hell had we been holding hands?

"Samantha." Nick nodded to the woman. His tone was formal, professional. "Are we about ready?"

"Yes," she chirped, and I saw she was actually wringing her hands now. "They've already started, actually."

"I'd better go, than." I attempted to walk past Nick, but his hand shot up and caught me, rested right against my stomach, slowing my progress.

My not-flat stomach.

"Where are you going? Samantha, this is Dr. Zora Leffersbee. She's been kind enough to consult with us during the developmental process."

"Call me Zora."

"Oh!" She pumped my hand enthusiastically. "Nice to finally meet you in person. We've heard a lot about you."

"Nice to meet you too."

"Samantha heads our San Francisco-based R&D team. She's running point with Marketing at the university."

We nodded at each other like marionettes, neither of us finding anything else to say.

I glanced up at Nick and found him watching me with an odd expression.

"Dr. Leffersbee and I grew up together in this town."

Her eyes widened. "Really? You grew up *here?*"

Nick and I both laughed at the incredulity in her voice.

"Yes, he did." I laughed. "Hard as it may be to believe now."

"I'm sure it's very nice," she said, already back-tracking to the auditorium door. "It's certainly very pretty."

"Everything is handled," Nick said to her, and it wasn't a question; it was a statement.

"Yes. There's a live feed in the next room where we'll all sit since we don't have two-way glass. It will all be recorded, so you and Dr. Leffersbee can take your time." Her voice lowered. "Fourth door to the left."

He nodded and she scurried away.

I watched her departure in bemusement. The last time we'd been in this building together, we'd been college-bound teenagers. I'd been excited to start college and Nick had been eager to finish the last two years of his undergraduate degree. We'd been excited about the unknown, determined to face it together. Now, all these year later, he'd returned as a titan, a leader in a burgeoning industry of health technology.

It was a hell of an accomplishment.

"I'm going to grab something to eat." I sidled away, heading to right of the auditorium where the safety of familiar people and food awaited.

"I was hoping you'd say that. Come on." He inclined his head toward a classroom farther down the hall, in the opposite direction.

"But the food—"

"I ordered in for us."

I jumped at his sudden touch on the valley of my spine. Looking up and up into his eyes, taking in that knowing smile, my stomach fell.

Shit. Shit shit shit.

Thus far, I'd done a terrible of job of keeping a professional distance. My heart was not locked away in the strongest of vaults. It was wrapped in the finest gossamer silk, just waiting to be toppled and trampled.

Again.

I opened my mouth to tell Nick that he had no business looking at me that way. That it was cruel that he could jumpstart my nervous system with the simplest of touches. That it was unfair that we were even in the same room again after all these years, and he looked like my most illicit fantasy come to life.

Okay, it was unlikely I would have I said that. But I did need to get away from him.

Quickly.

A breakfast feast waited for us. Pastries, bagels, lox, spreads, eggs, and bacon were all spread across the raised counter. A huge screen at the front of the room broadcasted the focus group proceedings from the auditorium. Suits were gathered around the screen, watching, taking notes as introductions went around the room. A young man with a charming smile sheepishly informed me he was the "runner" who would hurry any questions out to the moderator, should I or Nick's team have any questions or redirects for focus group participants.

I raised an eyebrow at Nick.

"We're not slumming it with the participants, huh?"

"I had some of Daisy's doughnuts delivered. They're right over there."

I opened my mouth to explain it was a little early for doughnuts, then shut it. I was already in the Valley of the Shadow of Death.

What harm would a doughnut do this early in the morning?

Nick pulled his phone from a pocket and checked the display. "I've got to take this. I'll be right back."

I took a seat, interested in hearing about participants' experiences with using the app.

Onscreen, an older, bearded gentleman raised his hand to speak and earned a nod from the moderator. "I was skeptical at first," he said. "I thought they wanted me to show my naked ass on the phone screen. Figured the footage would be hacked by the Russians and used to blackmail me."

Laughter erupted from the other focus group participants and Nick's staff.

I got up and headed to the makeshift buffet. I listened as the moderator thanked the participant for his candor, then inquired if other group members initially had concerns about privacy. This kind of fun would only be further improved by breakfast.

Huh. Maybe I'd have one of my Aunt Daisy's magical doughnuts, maybe with a little bacon, some protein, to balance it out . . .

Samantha joined me. "This looks like some serious decision making over here," she said through a smile.

"I'm trying to decide how bad I can be," I said, realizing I wasn't only talking about the dilemma of jump-starting my day with sugar and being jittery as a result.

I was also trying to figure out what the hell I was doing with Nick, and exactly how much I'd allow to happen.

Sky blue eyes met mine. "But what's the fun in being good?"

I blinked at her. She smiled again and disappeared.

I picked up a plate, loaded it with a nutritionally balanced meal of a doughnut and bacon, then reached for the coffee carafe just as laughter exploded from the front of the room. Someone shouted something to the runner guy and he responded, scribbling furiously on a sheet of paper.

I returned my attention to the counter and barely caught the flurry of the runner's approach in my peripheral vision, right before his body crashed into mine. That would have fine, if that had been all, but it wasn't that simple as it turned out. Everything—the contents of both my hands, the plate, and the carafe of coffee—left my grip. My shoulder collided with a wall that—surprise!—wasn't a wall at all, but a cleverly hidden doorway leading to a short flight of stairs below. I had a fleeting thought: *Leigh was right, we* are *old bitches now*—right before I descended down into the darkness and was hit with the worst pain of my life.

CHAPTER TWENTY-ONE

Zora

"Zora."

I blinked and opened my eyes.

Nick leaned over me, face tight. His bright eyes gleamed in the darkened interior of the car. "We're here. You ready?"

That's right. I'd fallen asleep in the car on the way back from the hospital. Blindly, I reached for the side lever and raised the passenger seat of Nick's car to a sitting position.

Nick put a staying hand on my arm. "Careful. Slow down."

I winced as the seat raised with a motorized whine. "I'm all right. Just a little sore."

His mouth tightened. "When I get my hands on him—"

"Nick Armstrong. Rossi. Whatever your last name is now, whatever you want me to call you." I was more than a little loopy. "If you say anything more to that man than 'I'm sorry,' I will take a strip out of your hind parts."

"Your mother says that." His cheek lifted a fraction in a smile, then fell again.

"Yeah, well, I mean it. Nothing justified the way you yelled at that poor man. It was terrible."

"You fell down a half flight of stairs. You have second degree burns on your foot."

"In some places," I argued, but even I'd gotten queasy watching layers of skin slide away from my instep. "And it's my skin to lose. That means I'm the only one entitled to do any yelling. I guarantee that poor man has shit stains in his pants. You were awful to him."

"You were on the floor," he said, as if that explained everything. "Practically in tears, clutching your leg. You think I'm not going to seek out who's responsible?"

"It was an accident."

His jaw tightened.

Dear God. What a day.

One minute I'd been mentally fanning my lady parts, the next I'd been bowled over by one of Nick's employees. A carafe of fresh, scalding coffee nosedived off the counter and joined me through the door, down the stairs, and finally on the cement floor. I'd mangled my back and managed to burn the hell out of my right foot.

Just another day in my world.

Meanwhile, Nick absolutely decimated the poor runner in a display of temper I hadn't thought him capable of summoning. I'd worried his head would explode during the drive to the hospital.

It had been a humiliating ordeal, in full view of my colleagues and Nick's employees.

I studied Nick's grim expression in the swath of an outside streetlight, the grim set of his lips, the granite clench to his jaw.

Yes, today's ordeal had been painful. And awkward, especially with him at my side while I modeled a hospital gown.

And abruptly personal. He'd held my hand through all the difficult parts, his arm wrapped around me, lips pressed to my forehead at one point when I couldn't help but whimper.

But I was certain that, somehow, he'd suffered more.

Something about the way he held himself, muscles bunched tight, mouth compressed in a single bloodless line, told me he was terrified.

Or traumatized.

I hadn't realized or remembered he hated hospitals. Maybe I'd never realized how much his mother's car accident years ago might have affected him. I'd insisted he stay with me in the hospital bay, so I could keep an eye on him. Some nagging instinct told me I should not leave him alone in the waiting room.

I eventually texted Adesola and asked her to come down to the ER. Not for me. For him. I discerned the slightest bit of relief in his posture when she pulled back the curtain in our little examining area and came in with her usual shit talk. She'd showed him a picture of the shoes she'd bought, jawed with him over communication training processes for his staff, and kept him otherwise busy.

I'd done my part by reassuring him that I was fine. Several times.

But even now, as we sat in my driveway outside my house, I *felt* the ferocious tension coming off him in waves.

"I'm fine," I said, for what had to be the millionth time.

He looked toward the front of my house. "Your roommate's home, right? I want to go over the discharge instructions with her."

I reached for my seat belt. "No, she's not in town. She had to go home for a funeral."

Not a muscle in his face moved, but his voice was heavy with incredulity. "You *lied* to the discharging nurse."

"Not technically." I pulled up farther into a sitting position, wincing at the pull across my lower back. "My best friend does live with me, in the other half of the house. She just happens to be out of town right now."

"Someone has to be here for you. You can't get around on that foot. You've got meds to get take, to get filled at the pharmacy. You have to take your temperature and go back to the ER if you have a fever."

"I'll be fine." Okay, I hadn't thought as far as filling my prescription for the pain meds and antibiotics. I also needed to get a thermometer.

Maybe I'd call Walker.

He watched me, and I swore I saw the moment when a decision clicked into place. "Let's get you inside."

"If you wouldn't mind handing me the crutches from the back—"

"Listen to me. We need to get inside, up the front stairs. Now, I can get the crutches from the back and you could prove your independence from me by hobbling all the way in the house. But I know your back and arm are hurting. You're already in enough pain. I can make it easier if you let me. You need to let me." His face was calm, but his words rang with an unmistakable finality.

Our gazes clung as I weighed his words. He wasn't wrong. Putting my weight on the crutch would take the weight off my foot, but it wouldn't help the strain in my back.

"Fine." I dug in my purse and handed him my house keys.

He gave a brief nod, got out, and rounded to my side. I unbuckled the seat belt after he opened the door, slowly working to pivot my legs out of the car. My pulse pounded in my right foot. Twinges lit up across my back. His face tightened at whatever was on my face.

And then Nick was *there*.

His wide shoulders filled the interior of the car, one arm going around me to gingerly grasp my shoulder. "Let me do it," he whispered in my ear, and it was so much easier to just let go, to let him. I relaxed into the makeshift hug. He easily lifted my legs to facilitate the turn.

"Good?"

I nodded. He bent forward again and gestured to his neck. "Hold on."

I was taken aback. I'd thought he'd planned to let me lean on him and walk.

My arms circled his neck and suddenly I was effortlessly aloft, my legs automatically winding around his waist. One of his arms formed a secure ledge under my backside. He slammed the car door closed and we started toward the house.

It felt so good to be held this way. Hoisted in his arms, gripping the firm expanse of his back, supported by the unyielding bar of his arm. For the first time that day, after pushing back all that bright pain, I felt safe. He turned his head, his beard pleasantly scraping my face, and murmured in my ear. I yielded the weight of my head to his shoulder as his words went straight into my ear. "I've got you," he repeated.

And I believed him.

It took forever to get settled. By the time I'd changed into my least ratty pair of pajamas and propped myself up in bed, an hour had gone by. The throbbing in my foot had increased to jackhammering.

A knock sounded from the closed bedroom door.

"Yeah?"

"You decent?"

I looked down at myself. I looked a hot mess, and had all day. It couldn't get any worse than it already had.

But what did it matter now? He was already here. He'd seen me get teary when the nurse wrapped my foot in wet bandages.

I'd already lost control, and my composure.

"No, but come in."

He nudged the door open, then stopped in the doorway. Little more than two weeks ago, he'd stood in my office doorway for the first time in twelve years.

Now he stood in my bedroom doorway.

None of it matched what I'd imagined for us all those years ago. But somehow, here we were. Back in the same space, victims of fate.

"These aren't exactly the circumstances I'd hoped to see your bedroom in," he said, his voice gruff. He walked forward slowly, his gaze fastened to mine the entire time. "But I'll take it. Gotta start somewhere, right?"

I patted the space next to me. "Sit."

His brows went up, but he complied, easing down slowly. He planted a hand behind himself, leaned closer. "Comfortable?"

I shrugged and immediately regretted it. "As comfortable as I'll be."

"My assistant is out getting your medication. I gave him your license so he could pick it up. It's a controlled substance."

"Are you okay?"

"Of course I'm okay."

"You just . . ." I let out a sigh. Some habits died hard. I *knew* that look on his face, knew something had spooked him to make him clam up this way. He didn't appear to be breathing. Twelve years ago I would have thrown myself at him, tackled him, made him tell me. Now . . . I didn't know what we were to each other, and I didn't know how to proceed.

"Do you mind if Sir Duke comes here?"

"Of course not. Poor thing. He's been alone all day."

"He'll be okay." He paused, and took in a deep breath. "Listen, I'm staying here with you."

I reared back. "Wait, what?"

"You don't have any food here. You need someone to help you get around. I was there for discharge. I know how to change your dressings, know what to look for in case you get an infection. And I can't go home knowing you're here alone. So. You're stuck with me."

"You can't be serious."

"I am. Completely serious. Sir Duke and I will stay out of your hair. You won't even know we're here."

"But you—"

"I have a very capable team and an assistant that will bring us anything we need. And," he fixed me with a look so absolute, so unflinching, I blinked. "I'm not leaving."

I stared, at a loss for words.

"Food's on the way," he continued, as if the air around us hadn't quivered from him throwing down that gauntlet. "So are your meds. I'll bring them in as soon as they get here. That shot wearing off yet? You in pain?"

"No," I lied. "I'm just going to get some shut-eye."

I needed a break. A reprieve.

"Alright. You want me to help you get comfortable before I step out?" His gaze flicked over me, and all the pillows I'd tucked haphazardly around my back and under my foot.

"I'm alright. You go ahead. Get as . . . comfortable as you can, I guess."

He nodded, slowly. "I won't be far. Just call me if you need me."

He left, pulling the door almost closed.

I stared at the door, brain buzzing.

What the hell had just happened?

~

Sleep proved elusive, even with the blinds closed and the room dark. My television garbled nonsense, keeping itself company.

My foot screamed the tale of dark roast lava on caramel skin.

"Can't sleep?"

I flinched, startled to see Nick suddenly standing in the doorway. He'd changed to a wrinkled T-shirt and gray sweats and his feet were bare. A plastic bag bearing the local pharmacy's logo dangled from one hand and he held a bottled water in the other.

"I don't think so."

He sat on the corner of the bed, frowning. "You're in pain. Why didn't you call for me?"

"I'm alright."

He went still. "Zora. I need you to be honest with me. It's important. Are you in pain?"

"Yes," I breathed. "And I can't sleep. I can't get comfortable."

He quickly administered the pills, dropping them in my hand as if I was a child, standing and watching as I downed it with water.

The tension around his eyes made me suspect he was weighing his next words, so I wasn't surprised when he said, "Can I help you?"

"Yes," I croaked.

He pushed off the bed and picked up the remote on my bedside table. "May I?"

I nodded and he switched off the television.

"Move over."

He was already helping even as he made the order, supporting my back as he removed the pillows behind me. "Hold this to your front and ease over."

I inched to the middle of the bed and rolled over on my stomach to settle atop the proffered pillow. The mattress shifted as Nick's weight settled on the bed, his body following closely behind me. The weight of his hand settled gently on my back, its length spanning the valley of my shoulder blades to the tender apex of my spine. I moaned as his fingertips traced the contours of my shoulders, returning to tentatively knead the painfully tightened muscles.

"Am I hurting you?" I strained to hear his murmur.

"No. It hurts a little, but it's helping."

"You're pretty tight." I sensed his position shifting, finger and thumbs delving into the rigid constriction of muscles at the base of my neck. I winced at the odd mingling of pleasure and pain as he kept kneading. I wasn't sure how much time passed before I felt myself finally relaxing, sinking into the pillow, relinquishing the weight of my limbs.

"Thank you. It feels a lot better." My voice sounded foreign and far away. Maybe the pain meds were working now.

"Good. You're relaxed and loose and ready to surrender to the meds now, I think."

The weight and warmth of his hands disappeared. The mattress dipped and the scent of him left. I stiffened, lifted my head from the pillow. "Nick..."

"Yeah?"

I opened my mouth, grateful I was facedown with my expression hidden, as I willed the words to come. Pride and shame warred within me.

"Zora." I flinched at his sudden nearness, the whisper of his breath along the shell of my ear. The barest touch as he followed the profile of my nose. "You can have whatever you want. All you have to do is ask. You know that, right?" His hand returned, drawing ellipses on my lower back with soothing strokes.

My heart lurched at the words, and the surprising tenderness in his voice. I found the courage to work up the request. "Will you stay? Will you stay here with me?"

His hand paused in its circuit. "I'm not going anywhere. Let's get you comfortable."

Together, we rearranged pillows until I was less inclined to saw off the insistent throbbing of my foot. He kept distance between our bodies, but I *felt* his presence.

And I wanted him. I missed the feel of his body against mine. I wanted to shelter under him, to seek refuge in his strength.

What we had was gone, I knew that. Accepted it.

Don't be weak, came a hectoring voice from the back of my mind.

I shushed it.

Would it be so wrong, just this once, if I chose to remember what was once precious? To take the good instead of fixating on the bad? To relax into the warmth I so badly needed instead of fighting with confusion? To have one night, one bit of sleep, where my mind wasn't buzzing incessantly with all the *what ifs*?

Tomorrow, we could resume our roles. I'd renew my senseless efforts to protect a heart I'd already given away. But for right now, just for tonight . . .

I reached back, my fingers blindly seeking until I encountered his hair-roughened arm. I grasped his forearm, my hand sliding to his palm, then tugged his arm over my waist until he had no choice but to move. He inched forward obligingly, sliding into place until we fit like puzzle pieces. Solid warmth surrounded me. His unique smell invaded my senses. His chin nested in my wild hair.

I didn't want to let go of his hand.

"I'm here, Zora. I'm not going anywhere. Everything's okay, baby." His thumb moved along my knuckles restlessly.

I closed my eyes.

In peace.

CHAPTER TWENTY-TWO

Zora

Sir Duke's unblinking stare woke me. Soulful, wet eyes peered into mine from less than three feet away.

"Good morning, sweet boy." I nuzzled his head and he pushed into my hand, teaching me how he preferred his pets.

I took a moment to stretch and take stock. Nick had woken me up in the middle of the night to feed me more medication, then wrapped himself back around me like a barnacle before we drifted back to sleep. Under the covers, he was curled around my non-injured side. Even in sleep, his grip around my waist was firm, and his prickly chin rested on my forehead.

The bed, the sheets, had taken on the smell I craved.

It was heaven. The best I'd felt in a long time.

Nick and I were in bed together. We'd cuddled all night long.

Yikes. So much for keeping my distance.

Sir Duke nudged me with his nose, more insistently this time. I didn't speak fluent dog but I finally deduced he needed to, as my Grandma Leffersbee would have said, "make water."

Gently, I disengaged from Nick's hold, hopped over to the pair of crutches leaning against the wall and shrugged on the fancy robe I'd told Leigh I'd never have an opportunity to wear. Sir Duke followed me through the house, then exploded out the back door into my fenced yard like a canon. I lowered myself to the steps to watch this fascinating dog-horse acquaint himself with the new territory.

Turned out Sir Duke was particular about where he peed. He sniffed around the perimeter of the yard, sampled the essence of several bushes, nose turned up.

What was the criteria for a good pee spot, anyway?

I leaned back on the concrete pillar, resting my uninjured heel on the edge of the step below.

The sky was gorgeous with a burgeoning sunrise. Weak sunlight strained through the lattice of overcast clouds, dispersing scattered light. I breathed in the damp, chrysanthemum-scented air and relished the quiet, the stillness, all around me and in my mind.

How long had it been since I'd sat on my own back porch and took in a sunrise? Why had I starved my soul of these moments?

And why did these revelations have to coincide with the arrival of the big, sexy beast of a man, the former love of my heart, who still slept in my bed?

Sir Duke raised his hind leg in front of a bush, finally satisfied.

I shook my head. Just when I thought I had things figured out, they kept changing.

Business done, Sir Duke headed over to me, picking his way up the stairs on giant paws until we sat hip to hip on the top stair.

I lost track of how long we sat together in the stillness of morning. The giant dog planted his head in my lap and I stroked his flank, lulled to calm by the perfectly measured intervals of his breaths.

"Well, isn't this cozy."

I didn't turn at the familiar voice behind me, but Sir Duke shot up, tail wagging. The screen door scraped opened and Nick lowered himself beside me several beats later. Sir Duke wriggled his head against me on the opposite side, determined to wedge himself between the porch's stone pillar and my hip.

Sitting like this, all of us in a row? We looked like . . .

Dangerous thinking.

Have a seat, I told my heart. *We're not a family. He's a man you haven't known in twelve years. Maybe he didn't cheat on you, but he sure as hell left. There's no mistaking that.*

I took a deep breath and steeled myself for whatever came next. Nick's lean hip inched closer into my soft one.

"Good morning."

I turned my head and found him closer than I expected, gaze fixed on mine with disquieting intensity. He looked rested. The shadows under his eyes were fainter. Dark strands of hair rioted all over his head in delicious disarray. I wanted to run my fingertips through the hard-scrabbled growth of beard.

"Good morning, yourself. You look like you finally got some sleep. God only knows how."

"Best sleep I've had in over ten years." The quiet intensity in his voice quickened my breathing. "I see you snuck out and hobbled around on that foot."

"I'm still able-bodied. Just a little slow. And Sir Duke has needs," I said pointedly. The dog nudged further into my lap as if validating the statement.

Nick shook his head at his dog. "He seems to be doing alright."

"I wanted to thank you." I stared fixedly ahead into the yard and the struggling summer flower bed badly in need of weeding. "For everything. For taking me to the hospital, sitting there with me all that time. Everything you did afterwards." Heat warmed my cheeks. Thankfully, he didn't jump on that comment. "You were right. I hadn't planned on everything I needed. It wouldn't have been nearly as comfortable a night without you."

Silence.

His fingertip hooked under my chin and steered my face to his. "Don't you understand? There's nothing I wouldn't do for you. Nothing."

My insides turned to mush. *Help me, God.*

"I wish you'd let me do more."

"You've done enough. More than you should. But I'm grateful for you being here. It means a lot. I didn't realize or remember you didn't like hospitals until after we'd gotten home, so this was selfish of me. I know how hard your mom's car accident was all those years ago. I hope being there didn't stir up any memories for you."

Two starlings took flight from the nearby tree, tiny bodies encircling in an aimless, careening trajectory.

I watched their progress until they were out of sight.

Nick was silent, his face averted.

"I'm sorry if I've upset you, bringing it up." I rested my hand atop his hand on the concrete step. Despite our close proximity the previous night, the gesture somehow felt unbearably intimate.

Maybe because it was, now. Things had changed between us; there was no mistaking that.

His eyes, when they finally met mine again, were full of something so bleak and terrible my breath caught.

"Let's get some breakfast in you." He stood, efficiently scooped me off the steps, and herded both Sir Duke and me into the kitchen.

It was a hell of an effective way to change the topic.

Once inside, I watched him as he moved around my small kitchen and acquainted himself with the disorganized contents of my cupboards and drawers. He'd pasted on a smile for me but I read the tension in his tightly drawn shoulders, read the turmoil tight on his face. Something was wrong and he was doing what he'd always done: suppressing some powerful emotion while focusing his energy elsewhere.

"Where do you keep your whisk?"

I rose from the kitchen table and tucked a crutch under one arm.

"Don't get up. Just point."

"It's my kitchen and you don't know your way around. Plus, I wanna watch what's happening. I have a feeling you've haven't cooked for yourself in a long time. You might not know what you're doing."

I wasn't fooled by the wry grin he sent my way. "You don't remember my killer omelets?"

"I do. But when was the last time you made one?"

He intercepted my progress to the sink, cutting me off at the butcher block–topped island. His hands went to my waist and he lifted me, deposited me on a nearby counter.

"You can watch from there. But don't move again."

I pointed out the correct drawer and he retrieved the whisk.

"So, what do you think of my house?" I looked around, trying to see my house, my life, though his eyes.

He hesitated as he reached for a mixing bowl. His head was behind the door of the refrigerator when he finally answered.

"Well . . . it's a fixer-upper, right?"

"Yeah. I was supposed to fix it and flip it."

He squinted at me as he cracked eggs into the bowl. "So, why didn't you?"

I sighed. "I don't know. It grew on me. Then Leigh came to live on the other side and flipping it didn't seem so important anymore. Is it that bad?" I looked around with new eyes, assessing the hardwood floors that probably needed updating sooner rather than later and the worn cabinets.

"It just doesn't look like you. I keep expecting Scooby Doo and the gang to show up and investigate a haunting, that's all."

He passed my Bluetooth speaker and his phone to me. "Be a good sous chef and get these connected."

I blinked down at his phone in my hand, opened, unlocked. Unguarded.

I was pretty sure this exact scenario would be Walker and Jackson's worst nightmare.

"What are you going to play?"

"You'll see. I think you'll like it."

He was right. I did.

He picked one of the playlists from his streaming service, a virtual love-letter to Motown, heavy on Stevie Wonder and Aretha Franklin.

"I see my father's influence had a lasting effect," I said, after we'd both bopped around to Stevie's "Sir Duke."

He smiled from his post at the stove where he waited, spatula in hand, to flip the omelet. "Yes. Although I never picked up his signature Soul Train moves."

"Thank God for that."

"Eh, he wasn't half bad."

"I was similarly corrupted by your mother's Coldplay obsession. I can't hear 'Yellow' without hearing your mother sing it. I still remember her impromptu concerts, singing into the empty paper towel roll in the kitchen."

The song transitioned and Aretha took over, singing, "Ain't No Way."

Nick stared into the skillet, though I doubted he saw its contents.

"Time to turn," I said, fighting the inclination to climb down from the counter to help. To gather him in my arms and hold him close, close enough that I could share his burden and ease whatever put the current look on his face.

He seemed to return from his reverie, shaking his head. "I'd forgotten about that. I remember the time I found her in the kitchen, in the middle of the night, listening to 'Fix You.' Singing along, looking so sad. She turned it off when she saw me. For a while I'd wondered who she wanted to fix. Later I realized it was her. She wanted to fix herself." His eyes closed briefly. "That was right before we left."

He passed by me to grab the plates he'd set aside.

I grabbed the corner of his shirt and pulled him back in my direction.

Surprise bloomed on his face as he allowed me to tug him into my space, in the space between my legs.

"Nick." I hesitated, suddenly at a loss for words and courage.

I almost regretted my moment of impulsivity with him this close. With me on the counter, our height disparity was nearly eliminated. There was no missing the banked heat in his eyes, the way he ever-so-slightly bit his lip when his gaze moved over my face and settled on my mouth. I couldn't ignore how stark fear leaked into my bloodstream and set my heart on a new, galloping pace. But I also couldn't turn from the concern, the deep abiding love I'd always had for the boy who became this hardened man.

"I know it's been a long time. Things haven't been easy between us. But I want you to know . . . I'm always your friend. I'll always care. Whatever's wrong, I understand if you're not comfortable telling me or wanting me to know. No matter what, even if I've wanted to kill you recently, I'm here for you."

His chest lifted. His throat worked. His hand came to a rest against my face. I leaned into it, sighed when his thumb traced a coarse trail against my cheek. My grip on the hem of his T-shirt tightened, exerted more pressure, pulled him farther into me. I gathered the courage to meet his eyes and lost my breath at the raw need, the wanting, in his eyes. His hands slid around my sides and crushed me to him. Relief overcame me when, finally, his mouth lowered to mine.

Nick

I didn't know how to be gentle or gentlemanly now that I was here with Zora in my arms, *finally*, after all this time. After years of yearning for her, of dreaming of this moment, wishing for the day, for the moment that would bring her back and make me whole again, here I was.

Her mouth was soft and warm. I took all she offered, followed the shy invitation of her tongue, and claimed her taste. Her hands slid around my neck, branded me with cool fire, urged me closer. She pressed the round softness of her breasts against me until I was painfully hard and desperate. I was desperate to feel all of her against all of me, to be inside her, to possess all of her, all distance, barriers, secrets removed.

Secrets.

Oh yeah.

The fire alarm erupted with an ear-splitting shriek.

Thank God. I pulled away, worked to reclaim control.

Zora hissed.

"What's wrong?"

"It's okay. My foot—"

So much for displaying my competence. I managed to further mangle her foot and burn our breakfast in the process.

In the time it took to air out the kitchen and get Zora resettled at the kitchen table, I'd decided.

No more putting if off. I had to tell her what happened. Not telling her and acting on my ever-deepening feelings was deceitful.

I had to tell her the truth.

Now.

I turned her chair to face me square on and captured her hands in mine. A sick, queasy feeling twisted my stomach as something like apprehension entered her eyes. God, I was so close. I prayed this moment, this revelation, didn't set us back again. "I need to tell you what happened that night."

Her eyes got big. "What night?"

"The night I left."

She took an audible breath. Seeing the slight tremble in her hand as she pushed her hair behind her ear made me feel like a dick.

I should have done this sooner. But in truth, there really hadn't been a good time.

"So, something happened before you gave me the letter? You weren't just planning to disappear the whole time?"

It hurt that she'd ever believed that was a possibility. "Never. I never would have left you, or our plans, if I could've helped it."

"Then what happened?" She wrapped her arms around herself, a self-soothing gesture that almost broke me. I hated that *I* was the thing that could break her.

But it was time. Time to tell her the truth about the past, if I ever wanted any chance of a future with her.

I gripped my water glass, played a mental edition of Jenga with my thoughts. *Where do I start?*

"I took my mother to Michigan after her first drug overdose here in Green Valley."

She leaned forward, her eyes huge in her head. "Overdose? *What? What happened? Were you with her?*" She closed her eyes. "I'm sorry. Only answer if you can, if you don't mind telling me."

I shrugged. "It's simple and short." *Now you're lying to yourself.* "Won't take long. You remember those days, when Mom was disappearing, not calling? Lost for days?" I closed my eyes against the memories. That time in my life had demonstrated the remarkable elasticity of the human heart, how it accommodated both profound love and profound disappointment. I'd loved my mother and could never adequately articulate the enormity of my devotion to her.

But I'd hated what she'd become, the things that she did for a time.

I'd hated how my anger changed me, how much it had reminded me of my own father.

"I got angry. Lost my temper."

She only nodded, encouraging me to go on. But she leaned forward and one of her small hands captured mine.

It all came back with startling clarity, probably because those memories never left. They had always stayed with me, my constant companions of regret.

The night it all happened, I'd discovered over two weeks' worth of earnings from my job, saved for groceries and the electric bill, was missing. Disappeared. Only thin air greeted me when I'd cracked open the cigar box. I'd been careful. Found a new hiding place. And yet, the money had vanished. I knew where it had gone, and why my mother had left the house again.

When she'd returned home, I'd emerged from my room. It had been obvious there would be no productive conversation. No apologetic weeping or rage that I dared to question her. She was sprawled on the couch, dead to the world.

With a baggie of pills next to her on the coffee table.

I'd stared at the white tablets, reliving our trip to the grocery store earlier that evening. My mother and I were leaving the Piggly Wiggly when one of the bikers called to her. Not in a leering or appreciative way.

In a familiar way.

"Hey, pretty Lila. You ain't gonna introduce us to your son?" He dangled a small bag in the air. "Got a new shipment in."

She ignored the man but there was no mistaking the invitation in the sly, teasing words and I could no longer lie to myself. She'd gotten in deep with the wrong kind of company.

My mother, Lila Rossi—baker of the best chocolate chip cookie, Dr. Who fan, OB nurse, biology wiz, giver of the best hugs, two-letter-word-Scrabble-expert—didn't just have a problem.

She was an addict.

I'd called 911 and the paramedics rushed her to the hospital. She'd narrowly escaped death, but for both of us, our futures in Green Valley ended that night.

I couldn't look Zora in the eyes. "Do you remember when the Iron Wraiths used to hang out at the bar next to the Piggly Wiggly?"

She leaned forward. "Yes. We weren't allowed to go at night. They were dealing."

"They were *her* dealers. After the paramedics managed to revive her and took her on to the hospital, I decided to return her purchase." Deliberately, I flattened my hands against the surface of the table so they wouldn't curl into fists.

"What happened?" Zora looked alarmed. She gripped my hand and the edge of the table.

"I, uh, trashed their bikes. The Iron Wraiths." I kneaded my forehead. I'd replayed this moment again and again in my mind, played with alternate endings.

What if I hadn't lost my temper? What if my mother had resisted the impulse to get high that night?

What would our lives look like now?

"And then what happened?" Her voice was shrill.

I straightened and met her gaze. I needed to be direct and factual for the rest of this story.

"Sheriff James just happened to be on patrol. He waded in and rescued me from an enraged band of bikers, all by himself. Got me back to the hospital where my mother was. I'd known, before I'd left and gone on my mission of destruction, that she was okay. But the doctor and nurse wanted to talk about options for rehab. Getting her out of the environment, away from all her usual dealers and suppliers." Some of the same despair and hopelessness I'd felt that night returned.

It was a terrible thing to be helpless. To be without the resources or the solutions you needed in a crisis.

My choices had been few.

"Sheriff James called your parents. They came down."

She held up a hand. "Wait—what did you just say? My *parents* were there? They *knew* about all of this?"

Yep, this wouldn't be easy.

"Your parents came. They offered to help."

"And how did they help?" Her voice was low and dangerous.

"They asked me what I wanted to do. They offered every option they could think of. I could stay here in Green Valley, they'd take care of her rehab, find her a bed in a residential program a few counties over. Send her to my aunt in Michigan, where she had family and a support system so I could still go to school with you in the fall. But —" My voice broke and I paused to gather myself. "But she was my mother. And I couldn't leave her. No matter what anyone said. Even if she'd become a master at lying to me and manipulating me. She was my *mother*."

I released a breath. God, this was hard. But it was also a relief. Carrying this secret for twelve years had taken so much from me, from her.

From our future.

"More than that, there was also the issue of the Iron Wraiths. Sure, Sheriff James had saved my ass in the short term. But doing what I'd done, wrecking the bikes of the most dangerous gang in the state . . . I couldn't escape those repercussions. While Sheriff James was throwing me in the back of his car, I heard one of them yelling, 'Next time we see your face, that girl of yours is going to pay for what you did.'"

I closed my eyes, sickened by the memory, sickened by the terror and helplessness I'd felt that night. "And if there's one thing we know about the Iron Wraiths, it's that they don't make idle threats. Remember that girl that just 'disappeared' that summer? And that kid who was beat up by his own father and his father's friends after going to the Sheriff's Department for help? I knew they would hurt you to teach me a lesson." Words failed me. I realized I was gripping her hand too tightly and moderated my hold. "I couldn't let my rash actions, my irresponsibility, be the cause of you being hurt by them. I'd have gladly given myself over to be tortured before I let them harm one hair on your head. They knew hurting you would be the one thing I wouldn't survive. So, I knew I had to get away, for your safety, that same night."

She shook her head vehemently, her face frozen in horror. "They wouldn't have done anything to you, or me. My father—"

"Your father thought the same thing, and Sheriff James had to talk some sense into him.

In addition to believing people should 'stay out of grown folks' business,' your father also suffered from a healthy dose of 'I wish a motherfucker would' and felt pretty confident that he could protect the both of us from any threat. But Sheriff James finally got him to understand it didn't matter how much money he had at his disposal. He wouldn't have been able to protect the both of us, not unless we were all handcuffed together under constant guard. It was a mess—a mess I created—and the only thing that would keep you safe from harm was making it clear to the whole town that I'd left. All we could do was hope that would be enough. Fortunately, it was. But I knew I couldn't show up in town again, not for a long while."

She seemed to be in shock as she sat still and unmoving. Her voice, when she spoke again, was a dulled monotone. "So, that's why you left the note saying you'd be back, and never left any word? You didn't think I'd be perfectly willing to find you wherever you were?"

I took a deep breath, unable to look away from her face. "That leads me to my next problem: making sure I did right by you. I couldn't hold you back. I refused to. You so badly needed to leave. All you'd ever wanted was space and breathing room from all your family's expectations. An opportunity to think differently, freedom to consider a different path. Room to grow according to your own desires."

"All I wanted was *you*. I would have—"

I pointed at her with my free hand. "Exactly. I *know* you. Even back then, you were always trying to help people, fix people. Be what you thought everyone else needed. I couldn't bear to see that happen to us. For me to look at you, and not see myself in your eyes anymore. Not as your man, but as your project. Your fix-it mission."

"I never—"

"Zora, it's who you are even now. I'm not knocking it. I think you, and the work you do, it's amazing. But even now, you deny yourself what you really want, and you don't even stop to question what that might be. You always put other's needs, their pain, before your own. And I didn't want to be a part of that."

A glint entered her eyes.

"I'm sorry. I don't mean to hurt you. I never wanted to hurt you. But if I'd stayed, I would have. It wouldn't have been intentional, but it would have happened all the same. Maybe not directly, but I have no doubt the Iron Wraiths would have taken their pound of flesh from you. We were in a terrible cycle of enablement and co-dependency, my mother and me. I thought it would be simple for me to leave; we both did when we made our college plans. I thought I could start over, you and me, at school, away from our families, and we could live life for ourselves. But it never would have been that easy. You would have sacrificed yourself, bled for us, forsaken your own future and plans. And been flattened by every relapse, every disappointment. I had to get our shitshow away from you. Even if it hurt at first—"

"At first?" She looked ready to maul me. "You think that was something I just *got over*? You think it was that easy?"

I shook my head. "It sure as hell wasn't easy for me. I never got over it."

"And all I was left with was that letter," she repeated, and I now had an idea of how much anger and angst my hastily written missive had caused her all those years ago. "A generic letter with no detail, only saying you were sorry you had to leave and you'd be back." She shook her head again. "And everyone else knew what really happened. Everyone but me."

"Only your parents know. And my Aunt Nan. And, of course, my mother knew."

"I still think you should have given me the opportunity to decide for myself. Didn't you understand how much I loved you? Don't you know what I would have given to have made it work between us, even long distance?"

God, this hurt. God, this was so hard.

I gave her the naked truth. "I knew if I told you, you'd have come to me. And I'd have been too weak to stop you. I knew if I saw you, I'd weaken. And I loved you too much to be weak. I didn't want to fail you again. I told myself that when I did go back, I'd go back as a man. In charge, not hiding, with all the resources I needed to change the narrative. Not as a little boy who needed his girlfriend's parents to bail him out of trouble."

"So that's why you're back now."

"I'm back now because I have something real, of substance, to offer you."

"Don't you get it? I don't care about your money. I don't care about *things*—"

"I know you don't. But it matters to me. Because I couldn't be what either of us needed that night. And it cost us everything."

She yanked her hand away from mine. "No, you egomaniac. What tore us apart was you making a decision for the both of us. You took away my choice when you made the decision for me. I didn't get a vote. I didn't get a voice. I just got *left*."

She sat back, arms crossed, face full of a grief I'd fought like hell to keep from her.

I lifted my hands. "I loved you, Zora. More than I loved myself. And when I realized the best thing I could do, the most loving thing would be to stay away from you, I did it. Even though it damn near killed me." I leveled a glance at her. "I know I didn't come back for two years, and that was to keep you safe. It hurt like hell, being apart from you. But your parents had sent word that everything was calm, no one had approached you, and I knew I'd done the right thing in the end. So I focused all of my attention on reaching my goals as fast I could. I worked like hell to get my company off the ground, get funding. I didn't want to come back empty-handed. In my mind, I thought I'd come back, scoop you up, and bring you with me when I'd secured a living for us, a good one. That plan fueled me and helped me reach milestones so much faster. I didn't know that you'd transferred to Northwestern, and I never knew you and Leigh tracked me down in Michigan. But when your ring came back in the mail, with that cryptic, cruel note . . ."

"It wasn't cryptic or cruel. It was matter of fact. I saw you kiss that girl—"

"I know, but you have to understand, I didn't kiss that girl. She kissed me. And if you'd just given me a chance, told me what was going on instead of sending back the ring with that note—" I'd never forget those words, not as long as I lived. *I guess forever doesn't always last.* I cleared my throat. "It was like dying, like losing my life a second time."

We stared at each other. The only sound in her kitchen was the humming of the fridge.

"I know you need some time to process this." It was the right thing to say, the fair thing to say, when what I really wanted was to beg her forgiveness. Ask her for a second, a third chance. Tell her I wouldn't leave until she granted it, not after I'd waited all these years. Persuade her that I'd only been thinking of her safety and well-being when I'd decided to leave so abruptly.

She nodded. "Hearing this, it's devastating. To know we both spent so much of our lives working from the wrong assumptions. It's hard to even think about."

I nodded.

"But, Nick. I'm so sorry this happened to you. I'm so sorry you went through all this alone. If you had let me, I'd have been there for you."

I looked away.

Damn. She was still the woman I remembered.

Then she did the last thing I expected her to do. She opened her arms to me.

I took a moment to collect myself, to shove away the emotion climbing up my throat. My face was still turned away when I heard her chair drag against the floor as she stood. Leaning awkwardly on one foot, she wrapped her arms around me. I reached for her, seated her on my lap so she could rest her foot.

I accepted her embrace.

"I've missed this," I confessed into her neck. "I missed you so much. Is this the part where you kick me out?"

She pulled back to look at me. "This is hard for me right now. It's not okay. I'm not okay. I've barely begun to absorb what all this means. But I think it's important for you to know that I understand, even if I don't agree with your actions. And it breaks my heart that you went through all that alone, without me."

"Where do we go from here?" The words cost me everything, left me paralyzed in anticipation of her response.

Her eyes looked sad. "I guess it's like you said. I think this needs time."

CHAPTER TWENTY-THREE

Zora

*T*here was no air in the ballroom.

Jackson and I pushed our way through the throng of bodies, buffeted on all sides by loud chatter, bright lights, and competing perfumes. I followed closely behind him, grateful my foot had healed enough to allow me to ditch my crutches. Jackson turned back to say something and I shook my head, unable to decipher his words amidst the blaring music. A brass band boogied on a raised platform at the foot of the room. The lead singer, a stunning woman with glittery brown skin and a voluminous curly Afro, led us through a thrilling carousel of Motown tunes as the band provided throbbing, upbeat accompaniment.

Jackson rested a hand against my lower back, tucking me into his side as he spoke directly in my ear. "I said you look amazing."

I looked down at my dress. Leigh had used my credit card to rent it just before she'd left. I hadn't known what to expect given her "celebrate your body" philosophy and my commitment to hiding my flaws, but I'd been overwhelmed by her selection. In a good way. It was a metallic gown in shades of red and copper that reflected and refracted the light so that I looked like a living flame. There was a little more cleavage than I would have liked, but it also had a daring split that gave the illusion of proportion.

I felt like a goddess.

"Thank you." I pulled back just in time to see his gaze slide from my cleavage to my face. "Really. But are your eyes going to be on my chest all night?"

He hesitated, then nodded. "Why lie? Yup."

I whacked his arm with my clutch. "I'm already self-conscious. Please behave."

His brows lifted. "Why? Where's the fun in that?" A pretty young woman bearing a tray of hors d'oeuvres wandered over. Jackson stroked his chin as he considered the offerings. "Do we get to eat real food at this thing? Or is this it?"

I cracked up at his pained expression. "This is it for us. Tavia and Walker will be at the formal dinner tomorrow night so they can do the networking. I hate this shit. I'm just here to say a few polite words and hand over the check for the photo. We can get real food after this."

His face fell in mock disappointment. "You hear that," he said in a friendly aside to the server, lightly elbowing her free arm. She blushed under his teasing regard. "This is how she treats her dates. Drags 'em to fancy venues where they only have . . ." He peered at the tray's contents. "What is that, exactly?"

She grinned up at him, her gaze moving over his face and tuxedoed chest. "Canapés."

"What kind of canapés?"

"Mascarpone, sprouts with pickled onion, smoked sesame seeds, and wine salt."

His brows pulled low as he turned to me. "What the hell is wine salt?"

I rolled my eyes. "Either you want one or not, Jackson. Stop torturing her."

I blinked at the blinding smile she gifted him. "It's alright. He's okay. I don't mind."

Of course she didn't.

I ignored them both as I turned to survey the room, mentally calculating how to avoid as much social interaction as possible. There was what's-her-name with the insurance agency in town. She loved to pull my father aside for endless jawing whenever she saw him around town. I'd need to avoid her like the plague. Ditto for tonight's speaker, a colleague of mine who loved to wax on for at least an hour after *every* departmental meeting while his gaze intermittently melted down to my chest.

My head filled with what looked like football plays as I scanned the room, mentally charting blocks, evasions, and a route of escape. I had to get the hell out of here. There were too many people, period, and I knew way too many. Too many potential conversations. That I would say something inappropriate or embarrassing was an inevitability. I needed a hiding place until we got closer to the time to present the stupid check.

Jackson's voice sounded near my head again. "Just what I thought. Tastes like my ma pulled some of the weeds from her garden and put it on a Ritz cracker. Who puts sesame seeds on a cracker and thinks they're doing something? And what are 'smoked' sesame seeds anyway? How would you even taste the difference? If this isn't the emperor's new clothes—"

"Jackson."

"What?"

I took a moment to fully appreciate him in his formal wear. His freshly cut blond hair fell in neat layers and his beard was freshly trimmed. "I'm beginning to wish I came to this thing alone."

"Don't think you're just gonna use me as arm candy. You owe me a good time. I have standards." He flicked another glance in my direction. "So this is what you've hiding been under your clothes all this time? I mean, it was impossible to miss, but I've just . . . never seen the full extent of it. Damn."

"Jackson James." I punched him in the arm.

"You're just in a pissy mood because you hate these things. Let's see if we can scare off someone at one of these standing tables. I want you across from me so I can enjoy this view, and I'm gonna need somewhere to put my beer. Once I figure out where the beer is."

"How are we friends?"

"I'm trying not to get offended, knowing you didn't get all fancy for me."

I reared back. "And who, exactly, do you think I got 'all fancy' for? If not to make the best possible impression for my family's business?"

His face grew impassive. "I think I see one of the officers I know from Knoxville. I'll go over and say hi."

I shook my head as I watched him disappear into the crowd, clutching a handful of the offensive canapés.

I pulled my phone from my dainty clutch, groaning when I noted the time. Great. According to the itinerary, I had another ninety minutes before I could hand over the check and disappear. More than an hour of awkward small talk with strangers, pretending interest in inane chatter.

Kill me now. I craned my neck, scanning for an unoccupied corner or hiding spot.

My gaze fell on the recessed handle on the opposite partition wall.

Bingo.

∾

Nick

Despite listening attentively to a researcher drone on about telomeres and cancer cells, I was hyper-aware of Zora's arrival.

More than a few heads turned to take in the sight of her in that gold dress. She'd been oblivious, of course, clearly preoccupied with wrangling her date.

Jackson James.

I'd forced myself to relax, to unclench my fists, as I watched Jackson James shamelessly flirt with a waiter. With Zora less than was three feet away.

Synchrony, indeed.

Of all the fuckery.

I'd known Leffersbee Financial would have a presence at the ACS gala. I also had an inkling it wouldn't be prudent to mention my recent invitation, especially after learning Zora would be presenting a donation on the bank's behalf.

We hadn't spoken since the truth came out in her kitchen over a week ago. Instinct told me to leave it, to give her space, but I had to come tonight. As a business entity intent on investing in the community, I needed to have a presence.

And I wanted to see Zora in action.

When she and Tavia were ten, her father decided it would be "cute" for them to star in a print campaign advertising the bank's free checking accounts.

It hadn't gone as planned. In the end, only Tavia was the star of the campaign. Zora and I still laughed over the rejected proofs with both twins. Zora laughed, but I knew better. Deep down, she'd always craved her father's approval. Ezra's initial insistence that she participate showed he lacked insight about his quieter, introspective daughter. The ordeal hadn't improved their relationship, to say the least. And there was only so much Ellie could fix.

But Zora was no longer that little girl. She was a badass. Smart as hell. Sexy. I wanted to see Researcher Zora in action, in this setting.

I wanted to learn her.

Consume her.

But my money was on her escaping first, before she had to play the public game. My gaze tracked her as she finally decided on a course of escape. Light reflected off the gold of her dress, giving her the appearance of a tongue of fire as she moved toward the door. Everything in me strained to follow the enticing twitch of her hips. To find her. To beg for another beginning.

It was fucking impossible to breathe without her.

But I needed to wait.

So I fielded additional conversations, most layered with pointed references to the need for financial support. Then I gave up on being patient.

I needed to see her.

I'd nearly made it to the doorway of the ballroom when a hand closed around my arm, halting my progress.

I came way too close to knocking that toothy grin off Jackson James's goddamn face.

"Nick! Funny seeing you here."

The band switched to a new number, one I recognized as a favorite of Zora's dad. "Tears of a Clown" by Smokey Robinson & The Miracles.

I regarded him silently. I had no small talk for him, and I was about five seconds away from losing my patience.

"You know, the tabloids ran a story not too ago about that woman you're dating now. What's her name? The one with the red hair, starred in that horror movie with the haunted house?" A hint of the devilment I remembered entered into his expression. "Tell me, just between us guys. Is her hair red all over, or—"

"What do you want, Jackson?"

His eyebrows shot up. "We didn't get a chance to talk much in the bakery, what with your bear of a dog crop-dusting the place."

I made to move past him and felt his hand reattach itself to my arm. "What are you doing here, Nick?"

I fought the urge to restore appropriate distance between us, with whatever degree of force was necessary.

I'd grown, too. I wasn't that same kid swinging a bat into the motorcycles of my mother's dealers. I was in control of myself.

Besides, there were too many witnesses.

"Listen to me." I took a deep breath. Calm. I would stay calm. "The only reason why I haven't pulled you aside is out of respect for your father, and that uniform. But if you don't get your hand off my arm, that's going to change."

He drew himself up to his full height. "I don't need my badge to promise I'll make your life a living hell if you even *think* of causing Zora any trouble."

"Because you love her so much, right?"

He didn't hesitate. Huh. "That's right."

"And that's why you've had your head down the tits of every woman you've come across tonight?"

He stiffened.

"Spare me, Jackson. You were a slick little runt back then and you're not much better now. Now, are you gonna get outta my way or I am gonna have to help you?"

His hand tightened reflexively, then fell away again. "You haven't changed either, Nick. Only this time she'll see you for what you are."

"Unless you have official business with me, get out of my way." I looked back at his grip on my elbow. "And I'd move my hand if I were you. Wouldn't want there to be any misunderstandings."

I wouldn't have imagined Jackson capable of the threat I now saw glittering in his gaze. He stepped toward me, gaze hard. "I'm always gonna be there for Zora. She's making a mistake with you, and you'll prove me right on that count. But if she calls, I'm going to come running."

I didn't bother to mask my contempt. "Get the fuck out of my way."

CHAPTER TWENTY-FOUR

Zora

I'd almost topped my highest score in Tetris when the door swung open in a wide arc, admitting Nick.

I wasn't surprised. A part of me had expected his arrival. And even in the midst of all the hurt and shock of the previous days, I wasn't all that disappointed to see him.

Best not to examine those feelings too closely.

My common sense took leave as I took him in, once again unexpectedly framed in a doorway. My mouth watered as I took in his large frame, now resplendent in dark formalwear. Impeccable tailoring followed the lines of his barreled chest, broad shoulders, and muscled thighs, exploiting his uncivilized roughneck build. My gaze caught on the tanned skin of his throat, crawled upwards to the prominent cords of his neck. His bearded had thickened.

I wondered how that beard would feel against my face.

I wondered how that beard would feel against other body parts.

Help me, God.

Teenage Zora had once dreamed there'd be an evening like this, with Nick and I dressed to the nines, married. I'd imagined the landscape of our future lives as one endless ball, an endless slow dance of love and sensuality.

And now, all these years later . . . here we were. Two greatly changed people, searching for any clue on how to surmount the distance of so many years.

Nick's gaze traveled over my seated form. He held a glass of white wine in one hand, a snifter of a dark liquid in the other. His mouth opened, then closed.

"You're beautiful."

"Thank you." I made a last desperate yank at my neckline.

"I mean it. You're stunning, and you always were. But there's no escaping your beauty tonight. It's overwhelming."

"You look pretty too," I said shyly. *And you look like a tree I'd like to climb. Again and again. A beautifully suited tree. I'd like to scratch my itch on your bark.*

"How did you know where to find me?" The tenor of my thoughts betrayed me, coloring my voice with an unexpected huskiness.

Nick's brows lowered, his head tilting ever so slightly. He gestured with the wineglass he held, kicking the door closed as he pushed off the doorway.

"I thought you might like a drink. I know you hate these things. Thought that might not have changed."

He raised an eyebrow at the stacks of chairs on either side of me. "You mind if I join you?"

I lifted a shoulder. I'd been delighted to find the adjoining room empty. The sliding partitions on this side created a smaller conference space. Chairs formed regimented lines on either side of an aisle. I'd dragged a chair to the corner of the room and planted myself among the towering stacks, happy to take refuge in my phone. Proceedings from the ballroom were still audible through the partition wall. Registering the band's transition to a new Motown hit, I'd reasoned I could easily keep track of the program's progress.

Nick stood directly in front of me, apparently awaiting my verdict.

"Sure, you can join me. But I don't want you to miss out. Isn't this your element?"

He handed me the wine glass, along with the snifter. "Hold these, would you?"

I accepted both, unable to tear my eyes away when he shrugged out of his jacket and wrestled a chair from the top of a stack.

I redirected my eyes as he settled the chair nearby and draped his jacket over the back before he sat. His long legs extended toward me, his knee grazing mine.

My fingers itched to restore order to the thick, unruly strands of his dark hair.

"I don't know if it's my scene. It's business. Necessary evil."

"So I've learned. Getting older is all about realizing you can't escape those necessary evils, isn't it?"

"Whiskey's mine. You keep the wine." He leaned forward, fists clenched over his knees.

I took a hesitant sip from the snifter, grimaced at the bitter bite. "Yeah, that's whiskey, all right." I extended the wine glass to him. "The whiskey is your price for entry. You keep the wine."

I risked a gulp, gasping as the whiskey seared a trail down my esophagus.

"Why don't you keep both. You might need something to wash the whiskey down." He laughed.

"You were always good at this," I rasped, when I could breathe again.

He frowned. "Good at what?"

"The people, the politics, the noise." I waved at the wall, indicating all that was on the other side. "Schmoozing. Pretending to be interested in boring things. Wheeling and dealing. Remember when you used to go with my dad to those conferences?"

"I do. I used to wonder why he insisted on dragging me along to those banking conferences. I thought they were the most boring thing in the world. I didn't mind humoring him because I liked spending time with him and Walker. Then one day I finally understood what he was trying to teach me, in his own way. He'd explain the objective, what he was trying to maneuver around or accomplish before we went into the event. Then he'd do the post-mortem with

Walker and I during the drive home. He taught me some of the most profound business lessons I still use to this day."

"Like what?"

His temple pulsed. "That the most important element of a sound strategy is knowing your opponent, your own weaknesses, and how far you're willing to go to get what you want." He nodded to himself. "Those words, those lessons, helped me start my first company."

"Dad always said you had a head for business."

"I owe your dad and your mother everything."

I shifted, suddenly uncomfortable. The truth, newly unearthed, still smarted. As a grown woman, I understood he'd done the best he could as a scared eighteen-year-old. But it wasn't quite so easy to swallow the reality that the truth had been kept from me for so long. By him. By my own parents.

"Speaking of a head for business, is your sister running things yet?" I looked up to see Nick's eyeing me, his face soft.

He understood.

I breathed a bit easier at the topic change. It felt as if I'd lost my footing somewhere in the conversation.

"What do you mean?"

"Don't play coy. Out of all of us, your sister was the most creative thinker, business-wise. I know your dad had plans for Walker to rule, but . . ." He trailed off. "Walker . . ."

"Is just trying to fill the role we all expected of him," I supplied. "Still is. Whether he wants to or not. They have these take-no-prisoner fights—"

"Competition breeds success, separates those who are willing to fight from those that would prefer to watch. Your father knows that."

I bristled on my brother's behalf. "I hardly think Walker just wants to watch. He just—"

"He's not cut out for it," Nick said bluntly, lacing his hands behind his head. "The same way you're not. Neither you nor Walker is prepared to hunt down and kill your competitors for food. Now, Tavia—"

"She'll do anything," I said, remembering my sister's tense expression at lunch a few weeks ago. "Whatever it takes. She's like a comic book villain. She wanted to talk to you, get advice. Benefit from some of your relationships."

His expression grew cautious. "I'd be more than willing to talk to her, though I'd hesitate to make any promises. Capital and influence, above all else, is what she needs. Those are the most important things, the drivers that will take her and Leffersbee Financial to the next level. She's not there yet, but with a little more time, she will be."

I considered this. "Is that what's most important to you now?"

His face took on a hard cast. "Should it not be important?"

"I don't know. I guess it's just not what I expected. The Nick I knew wouldn't have thought that way."

"The Nick you knew almost threw his life away because one impulsive mistake. I learned."

I was almost at the end of the metaphorical limb, but I couldn't help myself. I wanted to know. "And what did your mistakes teach you?"

"Never to lose control. To always have the upper hand. Show no mercy when the deal is at stake."

"That sounds a little mercenary."

His mouth twisted. "Twelve years ago, our lives changed because I couldn't be the man you needed me to be. I got into trouble I couldn't get myself out of—"

"Nick, stop." I couldn't take it, couldn't take his self-recriminations anymore. Compassion surpassed my hurt and all I wanted to do was comfort him. To make it better, even if it was twelve years later. "You were *eighteen*. You weren't responsible for me and you weren't responsible for your mother. You did the only thing you could."

He looked away but I saw the flush along his neck. "I ruined us."

"You idiot, you made a mistake by making the choice for me." *Indoor voice, Zora.* "I never would have left you alone to deal with all of that, never—"

"Which is why I had to make the decision for you. There was no way you'd leave me, wherever I was. You deserved your own life. I'd do the same thing again."

Now *that* pissed me off. "You really don't get it, do you? That by making the decision alone, you took my choice away?"

"Isn't what love is? Making a sacrifice? Being willing to sacrifice yourself?"

My heart skipped at that word. "Love is informed consent. It's giving someone all the available information, all the potential risks and benefits, so they can make an informed decision. I don't want anyone making a decision for me. If you don't see how . . . arrogant and patriarchal that is—"

"We were both idiots at eighteen, Zora."

I stood, whiskey in hand. "I don't want to argue. It won't help either of us at this point and I've got to at least pretend to be in a less feral mood to give away the damn check—"

"Zora."

"Thanks for the drink, Nick. Let's pick this up another time."

He was quick, somehow cutting across a significant distance to capture my hand as I started toward the door.

"Zora." He resumed his seat, gaze steady on mine as he retained his leading grip on my hand. My heart hammered in my ears. I gripped the glass of whiskey, fighting to not become unmoored, to not surrender to the insane pull. Seated, Nick's head was flush with my chest as I stood within the widespread V of his legs. My lungs filled with the scent of clean male skin and expensive musk. Nick said nothing, his green eyes dark.

I stared down at him, suffused with contradictory impulses. I hurt from all I'd learned the previous week during his disclosure. But all I'd once felt for this man was still there. He still had a claim on my heart. I recognized the challenge in those vivid green eyes, saw the same strong-willed, headstrong boy I'd fallen in love with. The boy who'd wanted my dreams for me as I much as I'd wanted them for myself.

His grip tightened on my hand.

"What's this charade you're playing with Jackson James?"

"Is that what this is about? Your opinion—"

"Don't play games with me, Zora." His jaw tightened. "If I thought, even for a minute, that you were actually with that asshat, I'd have already taken his head off."

"He's not an asshat. I love him and you need to respect who he is to me, and the role he has in my life."

His eyes never left mine. "You love him. But you don't love him like you love me."

My mouth opened, closed. I was mute, trapped in that unholy green gaze.

"You're always a polite distance from each other. He doesn't touch you like a lover. You don't look at him like he knows your secrets. He somehow takes his eyes off you in that dress. Jackson James doesn't know you, doesn't love you like I do. He didn't then, and he doesn't now."

I was hypnotized by the low pitch of his voice, the dark intensity in his eyes. His thumb traced the same circuitous arc along the sensitive crease of my thumb. The unbearably light touch shot streamers of sensation up my arm, agitating my nerves.

The air grew dense, heavy.

"You're not with him." Below the strong column of his neck, his pulse beat an erratic rhythm. "You never once asked for him or thought of him when I was with you. You wouldn't have let me in your bed if you were with Jackson James."

I couldn't argue with that.

"I'm not the same girl I was, Nick. I traded my love of fairy tales for pragmatism."

"That's not who you are."

"What, it's who *you* are? You've spent the last twelve years waiting for True Love's Kiss?"

I startled as Nick's hand closed over mine, secured my grip on the snifter. Slowly, ever so slowly, his eyes hot on mine, he brought the glass to his mouth and took a healthy swallow. My fingers glanced against the silken skin of his lower lip and were abraded by the coarse stubble below.

My nipples tightened against the silk of my bra.

Trapped in the glowing heat of those green eyes, I barely registered when he gently disengaged the glass from our grip and set it on the floor beside him.

"I don't care about anyone else right now. This is about me and you."

"There . . . there can't be a me and you."

I fought the inclination to pant, feeling my chest rise and fall faster than was merited for standing still.

Steady, Zora. Steady.

Warm weight settled on either side of my hips as his hands claimed my waist. His long fingers splayed wide in all directions, exerting delicious pressure.

"Z. There's never been a time when there wasn't a me and you."

Before I could I sternly interrogate myself and my motives, I'd instinctively stepped closer between his spread thighs. My back arched as I steadied myself with my hands on the width of his shoulders.

Nick's gaze fell to my cleavage, now only inches away from his face. From his mouth.

Not so in control now, I mused, exulting in the feel of his shoulders rising and falling with increased respiration. *Maybe you don't have all the power now.*

His voice, when he spoke again, wasn't all the way steady. Some measure of his cocksure attitude fled.

"It will *never* be over. Not when I still remember how you bite your lip when you're worried and how you hide when you're around too many people. I know you always saved your tears for me because you didn't trust your feelings with anyone else. I remember being the first man to touch you, to discover what you wanted, what you like. I haven't forgotten what kind of touch makes you wild."

"I've changed."

"I still remember how you taste."

The breath in my lungs stalled.

Jesus. What did he just say?

He bit his lip, his gaze on my mouth.

We were both breathing like spent runners, worn down and winded at the end of a marathon.

On the other side of the partition, the band transitioned to a new song. The lead singer grooved her way into Smokey Robinson & The Miracles' *"You Really Got a Hold on Me."*

I gathered the courage to ask what I'd been wanting to ask since he appeared in my doorway weeks ago. "What do you want from me, Nick?"

His grip at my hips tightened, drawing me even closer to the solid wall of his chest. "Baby, I just want you to take what you want."

Looking into his eyes, surrounded by those tensed, powerful limbs, feeling his proprietary grip, I remembered.

I remembered another Nick. Seventeen-year-old Nick. Seated. Not as powerfully built but impressive in size even then, his hold at my waist tentative as he searched my face in the darkness of his bedroom. *"Whatever you want,"* he'd said, with a hushed reverence that had only solidified my decision that yes, this was what I wanted, and who I'd wanted it with. *"I only want whatever you want. You decide. You're in charge."*

To this day, despite having been just eighteen the last time we were together, he still held the record as the best partner I'd ever had. He was the only man to apply himself so thoroughly to knowing me, and what I wanted. It'd been sublime, partnering with him. Long before we'd stumbled onto his mattress and made the mutual decision to go all the way, to consummate our commitment to each other, we'd been each other's compass and roadmap.

He'd been my sanctuary.

And now, looking down into his dear face, somehow both the same and weathered with time, I contemplated if I could take another risk on the boy that I'd once loved with complete, selfless abandon.

I could no longer map the contents of his heart, or anticipate the contents of his soul. But there was no denying the echo of that same boy in the man before me, who gripped me as if his own life depended on my decision.

He was a man who would sit with me, holding my hand and offering comfort, in the same hospital where his mother overdosed.

Even if it pained him.

"I only want what you want," echoed in my head, merging with his challenge to take what I wanted.

I looked into those evergreen eyes, not breathing, balancing on the edge of a precipice, of a decision that would alter both of us once again.

And I fell.

∼

Our mouths collided.

Finally.

My hands sought the warmth of Nick's scalp. Thick, silken layers of hair ran through the sieve of my fingers. His hands coasted to my back, arms banding behind me until there was no room between us.

I moaned as his fingers anchored in my hair, craning my neck and holding it in place. I shivered, helpless against the twin sensations of wet heat and prickled stubble dragging along the sensitive skin of my neck. I whimpered, desperate for more.

"Come here," he murmured against my skin. Drunk with pleasure, I couldn't muster the words to ask what he meant, how we could possibly get any closer.

He removed all confusion, fisting my tight-fitting gown with his free hand and easing it upward by slow degrees.

And I actually helped him, as if there wasn't only a wall separating us from hundreds of people.

I reached back with one hand, working to peel the close-fitting dress upwards.

Nick gave a huff, then briefly relinquished his hold on my neck to tug at the dress with both hands, tugging and pulling with all the delicacy of a corn husker.

Cold air bathed my nude legs as the dress cleared my waist. He grunted, boosting my legs and guiding them until they clasped around his lean waist.

"That's better," he breathed, hands still busy, fingers awakening nerves all along my arms and thighs.

"Yes." I moaned it, yanking until I successfully slid the black tie free from around his neck.

"What do you want, Zora?" His tongue traced a trail down my chest to the tops of my breasts.

Was that me, moaning that loudly? Lower, my body clenched on its own emptiness while my thighs slid along the unbearably soft fabric of his trousers. Some wild instinct seized and my hips canted forward to meet his hardness, easily taking up a lurid rhythm, tightly circling on his lap.

He swore.

"Give me your mouth," I said, shameless in my grinding now.

He obeyed, capturing my face between his hands as I tasted his lips, then chased the whiskey flavor of his tongue. I readjusted my grip on his shoulders while my lower body sought greater friction against his solid heat.

"Shit, Zora." His breath was shallow and strangled, as if he too suddenly found air in short supply. "I can't . . . I can't . . ."

"You wanted me to take what I want." I gave a perverse laugh. "What, you scared?"

He pulled back just enough to meet my gaze. His mouth turned up in the cocky grin I recognized from our schoolyard days, and my heart turned over.

"I'm just making sure you're ready, baby."

"Stop calling me baby," I huffed, then gasped when cold air met my left breast, closely followed by the strong, warm suction of his mouth.

"Oh, God."

"You were saying?"

I gripped the back of his head, desperate for the clever exploration of his tongue again, and he gave a low laugh.

"I'm okay with it now. I'll be baby if you keep doing that with your tongue."

He rewarded me with a swirl that launched me into spasms of delight.

His hand slid between our bodies, past my mons, fingers seeking. "Zora?"

"Huh?" I was so hot, so out of my mind with lust, I might have answered to any name.

"What the hell is this? Why can't I get to you?"

"Spanx," I laughed, and he joined in, his rising chest jostling me.

"Why'd you have to go and do that?"

"I didn't see this in the forecast," I said, deciding to test out my own free access to all the rigid pleasure I'd been riding over his pants.

Our arms jockeyed for position as we frantically worked at each other. Nick caught my breast in his mouth again and I shuddered, momentarily stymied in my attempt to discover just how far his length extended outside the constraints of his trousers.

"I can't wait," I admitted, feeling my hips take on a life of their own.

"Me either," Nick breathed. "Although I think my heart's gonna stop if you keep squirming on me like that."

We both laughed and then I stopped, jarred by a realization.

The music. It had stopped.

"Oh, my God! Oh no!" I pushed off of Nick's chest and stumbled upright, now painfully aware of the fact that I was half-dressed.

Was this the second time I'd found myself half-naked in his presence? What was *wrong* with me?

"What's happened?" He seemed distracted, his eyes unfocused as they tracked my desperate efforts at shoving my breasts into my strapless bra which—spoiler alert—didn't work nearly as well in the reverse.

"The music," I hissed, panic turning my hands into ineffectual blocks. "They're about to start the awards presentation! I'm slated to go on first."

That seemed to snap him out of this haze. His eyes widened

briefly before he stood and joined me, his gaze moving over me with newly-sharpened awareness. "Alright, everything's fine. You've got this. They're not gonna start without you. Just let me help you."

We worked together, both of us pulling and tugging my dress into place. Nick was in the process of zipping my dress closed, with me simultaneously holding my breasts aloft for best placement, when the door unexpectedly swung open.

And Jackson James entered the room.

"Dear God," I sighed in utter defeat, just as Nick swiftly pulled me partly behind him and blocking Jackson's view, even though I was already fully clothed.

Several beats of silence passed before Jackson finally spoke.

"Well, well, well," he drawled, and even I would have laughed at his wicked grin if the circumstances weren't so dire. "What have we *here*? Is this where my *date* for the evening, who also abandoned me in that big ballroom, has been hiding all night? While I was left all *alone*, having to fend for myself?"

"Listen, Jackson—" Nick didn't sound as if he found Jackson as entertaining as I did, but I could also tell he no longer identified Jackson as a threat. His posture was loose and relaxed, shoulders low, as he faced Jackson.

"No, *you* listen, Nick. We all need to get our asses back in that room in less than five minutes so she can hand over that check." After a deliberate pause, Jackson added, "That is, if y'all are quite done?"

My cheeks warmed. I cleared my throat and reached up to place a hand on Nick's solid shoulder. "Nick, do you mind? I'll see you out there in a minute."

Nick turned back toward me, slowly scanning my face again before he leaned in to kiss me. Softly, gently, as if reminding me of what had transpired and all that was now inevitable.

"Okay, baby," he said, his voice low. "I'll see you in there. You look great. You'll *be* great."

God, my heart.

Nick didn't spare Jackson a glance as he left. Jackson waited until

Nick was gone until he made his way over to me, all while shaking his head.

"Oh, I don't want to hear it," I said wearily, searching for the shoes that had somehow come off during my . . . *interaction* with Nick.

Jackson leaned against the nearby wall, arms crossed. "The other one's under the chair." He pointed. "There."

"Thanks." I kicked the missing low-heeled shoe into my reach.

"Zora."

"Yeah?" I looked up to see Jackson watching me closely, his brown eyes serious. "Do you know what you're doing? With him?"

I shoved my foot into my shoe. "Well . . ."

"No, I need you to look at me." He paused and waited for me to meet his eyes before he continued.

"I need to know that you're okay, that you're comfortable with the decision you seem hell-bent on making with him. I'm not here to be your daddy, no matter how many bad jokes I may make about that. But I am your friend, and we've always been there for each other. So, I need you to let me know if you want me to back him off, slow this down, give you more time to think. Because I will do whatever you need, with no problem."

How lucky was I? To have this beautiful, loyal man as my friend?

"Jackson, you are gonna make some woman incredibly lucky one day. If you ever slow down long enough."

He frowned. "Stop chasing rabbit trails and answer my question, woman. Do you know what you're doing?"

I pulled Jackson into a hug and felt his arms reluctantly fold around me. "Yeah. I do. It's time, and I'm ready to see this through, wherever it takes me."

"I'm here if you need me," he said into my hair. "I've got your back no matter what happens. You just say the word, and I will throw that guy in the deepest, darkest pit—"

I huffed with laughter and he joined in. "Come on." I whacked his side as I pulled away and towed him to the doorway. "I've got a check to give away."

"Fine." There was no mistaking the mischief in his voice when he added, "But I want a formal apology, for all the times you called me a horny goat. Cause even in my wildest days, I never got down and dirty in the middle of a fancy—"

"Shut up, Jackson."

"In writing, Zora, I want it *in writing*."

"Shut up."

CHAPTER TWENTY-FIVE

Zora

I turned in a circle, wide-eyed at the lake view from Nick's Bandit Lake rental. The location itself was unparalleled, tucked away along a bend of the river I'd never known existed. Nick's driver dropped us off just as twilight coaxed the last bit of splendor from the dying sunlight, painting the horizon in a stunning display of purples and pinks. The lake teemed with life and the air filled with the cacophony of cave crickets, katydids and cicadas. Splashes sounded as beavers, ducks, and all forms of wildlife frolicked in the lake.

The interior of the open-concept home was even more impressive with a solid, two-story glass wall that provided a jaw-dropping view of the river.

I paced the length of the living room, pretending to take an interest in the rustic furnishings, the expansive skylight overhead and its unfettered view of the heavens.

I resisted the urge to bite my nails.

I was terrified.

It had seemed simple enough when I agreed to accompany Nick back to his house. Hell, I'd had my breast in his mouth and been shamelessly grinding all over his lap only a few hours before.

I'd presented my award to the ACS muckety-mucks, endured about an hour of small talk, and patiently addressed all of Jackson's concerns when I told him I was going home with Nick.

Nick held my hand the entire ride back to Green Valley. We'd behaved ourselves behind the opaque partition separating us from the driver, but the air was swollen with the weight of expectation. There was no mistaking the lascivious gleam in Nick's eyes.

"I can't wait," he'd said, his teeth catching deliciously on my earlobe in a way that produced a clenching in my underwear.

And that's when the panic hit.

I wanted this. I wanted Nick. I wanted his body. I wanted to connect with him in that way again. I wanted all the sexy things to happen tonight.

But a dark voice intruded into my thoughts, pricked my confidence and the sumptuous lust cloud I'd been riding. The same voice that always pointed out I would never have the same thighs or waistline as the model on the Peloton commercials.

So when Nick ushered me in and invited me to get comfortable while he took Sir Duke out for the dog's evening constitutional, I'd been relieved.

Then I'd abruptly panicked again when the tortuous internal whispering resumed. My mind whirred through the Google results list of all the women Nick had dated. Actresses. Models. Heiresses. All tight-bodied, with perfect skin, TV hair, and dainty features.

It was almost a certainty that none of those women wore a size ten shoe.

Or an eight double-wide.

Whatever.

By the time Nick and Sir Duke came back, I was downright terrified.

Nick gave Sir Duke a command I only half heard, and the dog scampered off to another room.

We both listened as canine feet skittered away into the adjoining rooms. Our gazes connected.

Sweat dripped down my back.

Great, Zora. You're off to a great start, before the action even starts.
Nick frowned at me and started forward.
I took a step back.
"Zora, is everything okay?" His expression softened as he took another step closer. I willed myself to stay still. "Are you nervous? You don't have to be. I know we got off to a, er, good start at the party, but we don't have to do anything tonight. We don't have to do anything you don't want to do. I'd be happy to just hold you again."

I nodded maniacally, my gaze still on Nick as he took quiet, stealthy steps forward until he was directly in front of me.

"I want to do this. I do. I've been wanting it, thinking about it for a while now," I admitted, shivering when Nick's eyes darkened at my admission. "I just got to thinking."

Slowly, he reached for me, hands settling on my back, pulling me into the hard surface of him. Clever fingertips dug into the taut muscles around my neck, dipped into the reef of my spine, elicited pleasurable spasms.

"What are you thinking, baby?"

I blinked. "Baby?"

You know, it could just work. I could get used to that.

"My asshole isn't bleached."

His hands and all their clever machinations stilled.

He burst out laughing and pulled me to into his shaking chest.

"I'm serious," I said. My hands went around him too, coasted along the planes of his back and all that hard, striated muscle. *Whew.* Hot.

Down, Celeste.

"Zora . . ." He wiped a tear from his eye, then dissolved into another round of laughing. "Why on *earth* is that on your mind right now?"

I shrugged. "It's the truth. I just wanted to make it clear, upfront. Before this gets started and you have buyer's remorse."

Any trace of mirth suddenly fled his expression.

"I would *never*—"

"No, I'm serious. Listen. The last time were together, I was eighteen. My breasts had more giddy-up and less 'Swing Low, Sweet Chariot.' I'm wider in certain places, I've got stretch marks. There's a few dimples on my thighs. I'm not what I used to be, what you remember." I let out a shuddery breath. "What you're used to." I looked away from him, painfully self-conscious.

"I need you to listen to me."

He cupped my chin and turned it until I met his gaze.

"All these years, you're all I've ever wanted. All I ever dreamed about. The thought of you, of living this very moment one day, is what propelled me through every hardship, every hoop, every hill that ever stood between me and what I wanted. I built the company, the empire, the *life* that I have today knowing it would only have meaning if you stood in this dream beside me. For twelve years, I've walked this earth missing my other half, afraid to hope that you'd give me another chance and make me whole again. You're the only woman I want."

His expression was infinitely kind and gentle when he added, "And I'm perfectly happy to prove I don't care whether your asshole is bleached or not, I'm sure we can—"

I slapped a hand over his mouth, feeling my face heat. "Okay. I hear you."

His head tilted to the side. "Nah. You know what? You're a researcher. A scientist. A scientist with a lab full of cameras. A woman who likes to *watch*. I think the best thing I could do is provide you with a little of the observational data I've collected. How does that sound?"

"Uhhh . . ."

"Yeah. I think that's what we need. You need a data-driven approach to quiet all those doubts in your mind. And lucky for you, I'm a committed scholar of all things pertaining to you."

He ducked his head to kiss me. It was sweet and chaste to start, then long and lewd as his tongue plumbed the depths of my mouth until I was hot and helpless. Gripping handfuls of his shirtfront. Leaning against him for balance. He gave my bottom lip a last lick, then bit it just enough that my inner muscles contracted.

"Do you know what I thought when I first saw you again?" He whispered it in my ear, then turned his face to lick the silken skin behind my ear.

I gasped. His beard abraded the sensitive skin of my neck and sent rivers of sensation streaming to all my secret places. My nipples tightened in my strapless bra.

Dimly, I registered we were moving. He walked us backward, legs between mine, arms banded against my back, steadying me.

"I thought, 'Damn, how can she be even more beautiful after all this time?' I saw your face, then all those damn curves and I couldn't breathe." He chuckled against my neck. "And then you got on your hands and knees to chase that battery. And I wanted to punish you for making me hard, for making me want you that badly in a room full of people." Sharp teeth nipped at my neck, followed by the soothing swipe of his tongue. "I'm going to make you pay for that."

I tried not to moan like a shameless hussy. "I hated you when I saw you. Hated that I wanted you despite what you'd done to me."

Nimble fingers worked along my back. Cold air met the newly exposed skin of my back.

"It's alright." He straightened to look at me. The burnished color in his cheeks made his green eyes even greener. "You can work out all that hatred on me. I can take it. I'm not going anywhere."

He tugged at the dress until it fell, leaving me in my underwear, then lifted me out of the circle of it.

"Then you fell asleep on top of me on the plane." His head lowered to the skin right above my breasts, his tongue tracing an indiscernible pattern. My hands opened, closed involuntarily. "I had to spend that whole plane ride hard, trying to think about my grandmother so I wouldn't be some pervert. But Zora? Fair warning. I'm a pervert."

We made slow backwards progress down a hallway decorated in muted tones. I barely noticed. My head, my heart, all of my senses swam with hyper-awareness of him. Of his hands on me. Of all I wanted to do with him.

Of how much I loved him.

My bra fell away. His hands immediately went to my nipples, tweaking, rubbing, pulling.

"Were you trying to kill me, that day in your office? Those thighs, that ass . . ."

I barely registered what he was saying, cocooned as I was in his sensual spell, floating on a current of bliss as we backed into a room.

His hands cupped my ass, gave it a proprietary squeeze.

He groaned.

I groaned, my hips unconsciously seeking him and his hardness.

My panties melted away. The backs of my legs hit a bed.

Just like that, I sat on his bed. Laid back.

Nick stood before me. His gaze moved over my body. Even in the dark, I read the hunger in his expression.

And I wasn't nervous anymore.

I felt powerful under his gaze.

A wicked smile curved my lips as I beckoned for him to come closer, to join me.

He didn't hesitate. Before I knew it, he was over me, biceps bulging as his forearms caged either side of my head. My nipples rubbed against the cold, smooth surface of his shirt and tightened unbearably. One of his hands moved, trailing a path of fire down, down the undersides of my breasts, over the small hill of my stomach, tangling in crisp hair before parting my lips. Broad fingers tested my wetness, dipped and danced around my clit, dived in my tight channel until I was squirming under him. Moaning. Cursing.

"Somehow, I don't think you're nervous anymore." He sounded insufferably smug.

"Dear God, shut up and *do* me already."

He laughed, swallowing my moans, his delving tongue mirroring the sly ministrations of his fingers below, his free hand insistently pulling at my nipple.

I bucked against him, sensation tightening and tightening, my hands clawing at his back, clutching his stone shoulders.

Until it all detonated and snatched my awareness, obliterated the whole world. I laid on the coverlet, legs spread, arms akimbo. Melted. Deconstructed.

Then the slide of a zipper penetrated my lust fog and I remembered.

I remembered what I wanted.

And I was going to take it.

"My turn."

I pushed at his chest until he was under me. I straddled him, my thighs spread wide across him.

"Zora." The timbre of his dropped, his eyes unbearably soft as he cupped my face. "I dreamed of this."

I grinned. "Me too. But I don't think I can be gentle."

His smile was wolfish as his hand shifted up until it was buried in my hair. "Promise?"

"No, you'll just have to be brave."

I took his mouth while I tore at his shirt, ripped at buttons until the front was open. I hated severing our connection even for the brief time it took to pull his undershirt over his head. He wriggled out his pants. I helped to peel his boxers down his legs.

Until he was finally naked.

All that hard muscle was on display, from the muscled terrain of his chest to the deeply indented grooves of his Adonis belt.

And the beautiful, curving dick in my hand.

"There's your empirical evidence," Nick choked out.

I didn't think Nick breathed as I ran my hand from the base to the tip, squeezing, milking.

His hands ran up my body until they settled on my breasts. His voice, when he spoke, was rusty. "Hey, Zora? Remember what you said, about just doing it? I would like to put in a vote for that. Right now. Please. Please put me inside you. Please let me feel that wet pussy coming all over me."

I was delirious with need, flirting with danger, canting against his dick until it nestled sweetly against my lips. I wanted to feel him inside me with no barriers, nothing between us.

Jesus. Leigh had not been too far off when inquiring about my current use of birth control.

"Where are your condoms?"

"Bedside table. Here." He commenced with an awkward shuffle up the bed, pulling me along, until we were at the head of the bed. I leaned over, opened the drawer, and snatched out the unopened three-pack.

"Unless," I began, unable to stop myself from sliding along his thick length.

His eyes widened. "Yes? You were saying? Unless?"

I closed my eyes, relishing the thrill of him, under me, in just the right place. Just a little more to the right and he'd be right where I needed him. "Unless . . . I have an IUD."

"That's wonderful news," Nick gasped out, his voice faltering as he exerted gentle pressure with his hands to still my grinding hips. "I news, too. Good news. Oh, *fuck me*, I can't think."

"I'm clean." I leaned forward to whisper it in his ear, then enjoyed the involuntary twitch of his hips when I bit his earlobe.

"Me too, me too," he rasped. "I get tested on a regular basis, I can send you the results."

"Mmmm." I chased the scent of him, tasted the thin skin of his neck. "Me too. I'm clean, you're clean. Sounds like we're both safe."

"So, we're doing this," Nick asked, and I'd have laughed at the near-octave his voice jumped if I hadn't been so out of my mind with lust.

"Yeah. I wanna feel you without anything between us."

"Dear God, yes. Yes, let's make that happen then."

I shifted and lowered myself on him slowly, delicious centimeter by delicious centimeter, relishing the pleasure-pain of this impalement. Loving the way Nick writhed as if on a torture rack, fisted the sheets, swore.

Begged.

And then I finally took all of him, feeling our pelvises touch.

Nick gave a sharp intake of breath as I squeezed him experimentally.

Yes.

"This is mine," I told him, feeling rich with power, brimming with the certainty that this, us, we, were meant to be.

Always had been.

"I thought I could go slow," I moaned, feeling my hips quicken, the flashpoint of my orgasm that much closer. "I wanted to savor this."

"We'll go for slow next time." He reared up, fastened his mouth to my nipple, his hips pistoning beneath me. "We've got time. We've got forever."

We both came together, on the same breath, every part of our bodies entangled and pulsing. He pulled me into him, leaving our connection intact.

"This is forever," he repeated in my ear, and I relaxed into him. Pliant.

Perfectly willing to wait for forever.

CHAPTER TWENTY-SIX

Zora

"No, Sir Duke. Let her sleep. We can't convince her to stay if she doesn't get her rest."

I cracked open an eye and aimed a glare at the handsome man and dog in the doorway.

"Am I supposed to fall for this sham act?"

Sir Duke's ear perked up when he heard my voice. Less than a second later, I was covered by over 150 pounds of greyhound. I shrieked as the dog's coarse, wet tongue laved my face.

Nick laughed, then he was there too, sliding alongside me on the bed.

"You two suck," I managed. Nick's searching fingers found all my sensitive spots under the covers and tickled me until I begged for mercy.

Sir Duke howled along with my squeals.

It was a mess.

A wonderful, messy, loud mess. And it was all mine.

They both were.

Nick maneuvered my prone body until it was under his, his mouth sliding hotly against mine.

"Nick," I protested, feeling mortified when I tasted the fresh mint on his breath and realized I hadn't brushed. "You're both animals! Licking me—"

"I didn't hear you complaining last night," he rasped in my ear, his hand sliding down to make mischief. "When I got you so wet with my mouth that you drenched the sheets—"

"Shh!"

Humor lit his eyes. I stared into those green eyes, arrested by the difference in him. He looked younger. Well-rested. Happy, with the hard edges gone.

"Who's going to hear me?"

"Don't corrupt Sir Duke."

He rolled his eyes. "Oh, please. You weren't thinking about any of that when you were screaming—"

"Okay, fine. I'm up, I'll get up now." I laughed. Nick gave Sir Duke a signal and they both clambered off the bed. "Are you both always up this early?"

He arched a brow at me. "Well, yes, if you considered noon early."

I threw back the covers in panic. "Oh, my God. It's noon? I have to get into work."

"It's also Saturday, baby. Hopefully you're not planning to go in on a Saturday."

Baby. I could get used to this, I decided.

"Well, I *should* go in, but if it's Saturday that changes things."

"Sir Duke and I have already been out on our morning run. We're hungry. We should get breakfast. It was his idea."

God. How had I gotten so lucky?

"I could eat."

He made a show of covering both Sir Duke's ears with his hands. "We should take a shower. You especially. You've got me all over you." I grinned at his self-satisfied smirk. He looked so damn happy for the first time since he'd arrived in Green Valley.

So was I.

"I think you've had me just about every way." He raised brows significantly. "If you still want to test out that theory about my preference for bleached or unbleached—"

"Nick!"

"Alright, alright."

I pushed back the covers, winding the sheet around me. I loved the hushed, wide-eyed look he gave me as I headed into the bathroom. I turned back and gave him my best seductress smile. "Aren't you coming?"

It was the longest, most pleasurable shower I'd ever had in my life.

We were getting ready to head out the house, me in his comically large T-shirt and pair of shorts, dress folded over my arm, when a knock sounded at his door.

He looked back at me. "You expecting anyone?"

"Nope. I hadn't had any plans to be here."

He flashed me a grin. "What a difference twenty-four hours makes."

With a protective hand on my arm, he moved ahead of me to answer the door. At his height, he had to stoop to use the peephole. His shoulders rose, stiffened. Something like regret colored his expression when he turned back to me.

"I'm sorry, Zora."

"What? Why?"

He opened the door, revealing my mother on the other side of the door. She held her third-best cake stand and wore her snarkiest smile.

∽

"I just wanted to check on you, Nick."

We sat around the kitchen table, plated slices of cake in front of each of us.

None of us had taken a bite yet.

I wasn't fooled by my mother or this cake. Everyone in Green Valley knew a freshly baked cake was the best tool, the most effective weapon, for prying the choicest bits of gossip from even the most close-mouthed neighbor. She came to ply with him cake and blackmail him for details about my reaction to their shared secret.

"I knew you and Zora needed to have The Talk. Walker told me he saw the two of you having an . . . intense conversation at the coffee shop. I thought I'd just check in." Her swift perusal of me lingered at my shoulder, which peeped from the neck of Nick's oversized shirt. "I see I didn't need to worry."

Oh, God. Kill me now.

Nothing ruined the afterglow more than your mother showing up for post-coital conversation, and no one was better skilled at low-key shade than Ellie Leffersbee.

Nick swallowed a smile. "Yes, ma'am, we've talked. I think we've worked things out between each other."

My mother gave me her shadiest side-eye. "Uh-huh. I see."

Nick's mouth twitched.

"I'm glad you came by," I said, meeting her gaze and raising the stakes. "I've been wanting to learn more about this secret you've been keeping all these years. From your own daughter."

She and Nick exchanged a quick glance.

"I understand you're upset." My mother laced her fingers together on the table, always a signal she was about to employ her famous diplomacy. "You have every right to be upset, I would be too. But I hope—"

I held up a hand. "I'm not angry. It hurts more than a little, yes, knowing you and Dad kept this from me all these years, even when you saw how upset I was."

My mother suddenly looked tired. "It weighed on us, on all of us." She exchanged another look with Nick. "But I gave my word—"

"You don't have to explain. I don't want to put you in the position of having to explain that you love us both. I know. More than anything, I'm grateful you and Dad were able to help him. I wouldn't have wanted him alone in the world, without our help, whether I'd known or not. So, thank you for taking care of him, and loving him the way I couldn't at the time."

Nick reached for my hand across the table, squeezed.

My mother looked at our joined hands at the table and a faint smile curved her lips. "How I wish Bethany had been here to see this.

It would have done her heart glad to see one of life's injustices righted. Privately, the two of us always rooted for you two."

Nick let out a sigh. "I wish she was here, too."

My mother eyed our untouched plates. "What, y'all aren't hungry?"

My stomach picked that unfortunate moment to loudly growl. "Yes, but we haven't eaten breakfast yet."

Her mouth twisted, eyes going small with sarcasm. "Looks like you're more than used to having your dessert first, from where I'm sitting."

My jaw dropped.

Nick ducked his head. A smothered guffaw escaped him.

"Mama, you're gonna call me out like that? Imply that I'm—"

"What, carrying on, unmarried, in broad daylight?" She made her face innocent. "Never."

She rose from the table and Nick stood. "Please, you don't have to go, Mrs. Leffersbee."

"Nick, I can see the filthy thoughts in my daughter's eyes. I best head out before she has a chance to act on them." Inwardly, I laughed at the twinkle in her eye. Right. As if I could entertain any prurient interest in Nick with my mother sitting right there. "God knows what these walls have seen."

"I wouldn't know, ma'am."

If I'd had something to throw at him, I would have.

She snorted. "Of course you wouldn't, dear."

She gathered her purse. "You two be good to each other, take care of each other. The love you have for each other has always been so pure, so rare. Protect it. Decide you'll hang on to each other, no matter what happens."

I stood and hugged her. "Thank you, Mama."

"Zora, hear me in this moment. I worry about all my children in equal measure. It's my job as a mother and one day you'll see. I worry Audre will fall in with the wrong crowd at UCLA and that Tavia won't ever slow down long enough to learn herself, let alone allow someone to love her. That Walker won't ever find the courage to face his own secrets and live in his truth. And that his peter will finally get sick and fall off from him sticking it into everything that moves."

Nick failed to mask a snort of laughter.

"But do you know what I worry about for you?"

I was afraid of her answer. "No, I don't."

She squeezed my shoulder. "I worry you'll never take the leap, the plunge, that will make you happy. That you'll spend your life living the life you *think* you should, for everyone else. If there was one thing I could tell you, now that you're on this new path, it would be this: it's easier to save the world than to save yourself. I hope you work up the courage to do it, though, because you're worth it." She gave me another hug. "Love you, baby."

She turned to Nick, arms open. "And you, my giant baby." He bent to embrace her, and their hug lasted much longer, with her murmuring something in his ear as he nodded along.

I thought I detected a bit of moisture in his eyes when they straightened.

"Alright, I'll see you children soon," she declared, marching to the door like the little dictator she was. "Nick, I want that cake plate back when you're done. And I hope one of you thinks to let Jackson know the little ruse he had going with Zora is up. Preferably before she's expecting your first child."

CHAPTER TWENTY-SEVEN

Nick

"You rat bastard."

I blinked in surprise.

Although, I wasn't completely surprised. During our drive to her house, Zora warned me that Leigh would be back in town. I remembered that it was Leigh who'd driven Zora out to Michigan all those years ago and witnessed Rebecca's kiss in the coffee shop.

I knew I had inroads to make with her best friend.

What I hadn't expected was Leigh crossing the porch to greet me as soon as Zora and I ascended the steps to her house. She was clearly battle-ready.

I didn't want to risk shaking hands. She looked mad enough to hack my arm off.

"And *you*." She fixed Zora with a look that raised my hackles a bit. I pulled Zora behind me; better to face her small friend's impressive fury myself.

"I realize a lot has changed since you left town—"

"Don't you hide behind him," Leigh barked, looking around me as if I wasn't a full foot taller than her. "Face me like a woman." Leigh ran a quick glance over me, sucked her teeth with a disdainful sound.

Zora peeked from around me. "We went to the gala, and—"

Leigh shook her head, lips pursed. "And let me guess. You ended up on top."

I whirled around just in time to see Zora's tiny nod. She looked proud of herself.

That's right, baby.

She'd done magnificent work on top.

Wait a minute, how did Leigh know—

"We talked," Zora told Leigh. "About what happened in Michigan. When we saw him that day in the coffee shop."

"I didn't cheat on her," I informed Leigh.

Her face twisted up at me. "Let me guess. You heard the Shaggy song, too. It wasn't you."

I extracted my wallet and pulled out a thrice folded envelope. "I thought it might come to this. This is for you."

She didn't take it. "What's that?"

"It's a notarized letter from that coworker, the one you saw kiss me. Who I did not kiss back, for the record. My security team located her and obtained this signed statement."

"You paid her for her statement?" Her voice dripped with scorn.

Damn, she was tough. She'd fit right in with the legal team at Rocket.

"I most certainly did not. She also offered her phone number, it's all in there. She's agreed to answer any questions you may have for her."

She snatched the envelope out of my hand. "I'll take a look."

Zora grimaced. "We're going to get breakfast. You want to come with?"

The screen door on Leigh's side banged closed in response.

Zora and I exchanged glances.

"It'll be alright. I'm not surprised. If I thought someone cheated on my best friend, well, I'd do everything in my power to make her pay."

"Rightfully so," she agreed.

"Alright. My stomach is eating my back at this point. Please, can we take you inside and get some clothes on you so we can go?"

"Sure." But she stood there smiling, her gaze stuck to mine. "Thanks, by the way."

"For what?"

"For contacting The Redhead. Putting her in contact with Leigh, who is definitely going to call her, by the way. I believed you, but this helps."

I wrapped my arms around her, happy that I could now. "What do I keep telling you? There's nothing I wouldn't do for you."

Responding to the dark intent in her eyes, I boosted her up until her legs wrapped around me. She'd just kissed me when another voice sounded behind me.

"Now I see what was so important in Green Acres."

"Valley," I corrected automatically, then turned, unable to believe my own ears.

"Eddie?"

"One and the same," he confirmed, his gaze bouncing between me and Zora. "So. Are you going to introduce me?"

CHAPTER TWENTY-EIGHT
Nick

"The trick to throwing an axe is knowing when to let go."

At that, our Axe Master hefted the axe behind his head until his elbow was skyward, then released it in a smooth downward arc.

The ax bit into the innermost circle of the bullseye. Perfect.

Zora stood at his elbow, tracking every nuance of his movement. "Okay. Can you do it again?"

Leigh snickered. I shot her a look.

Zora glared back at her friend. "Quiet from the peanut gallery, please."

Eddie shifted closer to me and said, just loud enough for me to hear, "He could do it fifty more times and—"

"Shut it."

He snorted with laughter. "You're really gone over this girl."

Leigh wandered over to us from her corner, her expression pained. "Listen. I know you probably like having sex with her, but it's not healthy to support delusional behavior. She sucks at this and that's not going to change today. We can't keep slowing down the game for these long tutorials every time it's her turn."

"We've got the lane until this place closes." I ignored them both, watching the Axe Master sneak a quick glance at Zora's ass.

This fucker.

Eddie murmured something to Leigh. They both cracked up.

Our plans for the day had changed once Eddie showed up. Leigh was determined to spend time with him after learning he was my closest friend. She'd cornered Eddie for most of our time in the throwing lane, pumping him for information.

And kicking our asses in competition.

I shouldn't have been surprised that it was her idea to come here. Or that she mimed chopping off my nuts when she made the suggestion.

I didn't care. I would do whatever it took to get along with Leigh's crazy ass. It was clear she and Zora were extremely close and protective of each other. Now that I had Zora back, I'd deal with whatever happened, no matter the obstacle.

Even if it was this bitingly sarcastic woman with scarily accurate aim.

Knoxville Axe was a relatively new establishment and a favorite after-work hangout of the hospital staff, apparently.

"I should buy one of these," Eddie had said, taking in the high-ceilinged renovated warehouse. In addition to its throwing lanes, Knoxville Axe offered a full bar and restaurant with cutesy amenities like a cereal bar and board games for diners. I'd expected the place to be swarming with students this time of day, but it was relatively slow. We easily snagged our own throwing lane as well as a supervising Axe Master named Chase, who sported a beard even Gimli the dwarf would have envied. Chase reviewed safety protocols, demonstrated the basics of axe throwing, and led us in what was supposed to be friendly competition.

But Zora was anything but friendly after watching the hash marks pile up under everyone else's names. I would defend her to the end against anyone that talked trash about her, but privately, I wondered if she was throwing with both eyes closed. Every axe she threw was destined to ricochet off the bottom of the wooden board.

Leigh planted a hand on her hip. I hadn't known her long, but I knew more shit talk was coming. "You know," she called to Zora, who was flinging the axe in dangerous practice arcs, "It's okay. Not everyone can be good at everything. You're unfairly talented at a number of things. Who cares if axe throwing isn't—"

"Shut up and stay in your corner," Zora said, and I saw the blood in her eyes. I eased back, mindful of the axe in her hand.

"Don't pay her any attention," Chase said soothingly. "I think you're doing better. Give it a shot, now that your arm placement's better."

Eddie sent me a sly look, his eyes bright with mischief. I'd known him long enough to discern its meaning.

I planned to get rid of Gimli in short order. I just couldn't do it in a way that would lead to Zora delivering another Beyoncé/Independent Women speech.

"Let's make one last change to your stance for a sec," Gimli said. He lifted a hand as if he meant to place it at her waist. "Do you mind if I make a few adjustments?"

I pushed off the wall. "That's it. You're done here. Get the fuck out."

He turned to find me less than a foot away, ready to dismember him.

"No disrespect intended. I was just trying to help." But I saw the cunning in his smirk.

"Get the fuck outta here."

He scampered out.

Zora glowered at me.

I shook my head. "Nope. Just . . . nope."

"So you like Neanderthals," I overheard Leigh say to Zora.

Zora ignored her and came to me, draping her arms around my waist.

I calculated how long it would take us to get back to Green Valley and back in one of our beds. Where had all these damn *people* come from? Shouldn't Zora and I be busy, *reuniting*?

"Hey," she said, looking up at me with wicked eyes. I pushed away a mental flashback of the previous night.

There were other people around.

"I need to catch up with Leigh and find out what happened while she was back home. I'm sure you wouldn't mind gossiping about us with Eddie when we're out of earshot."

Eddie snickered.

"We're gonna get drinks, then grab a table for dinner. You stay here, catch up with Eddie. Talk about whatever it is CEOs talk about. Meet us on the other side in an hour."

She puckered up and I met her, relieved to taste her again.

It had been too damn long.

Eddie watched the two of them leave the lane, then turned to me with a grin.

"Man, Nick. I never thought I'd live to see this day."

"What day?"

"The day you got whipped. You're in love, man. She just worked the hell out of you."

I frowned. "She didn't—"

"She just sashayed over there, calmed you down, and then told you what was going to happen." He bent over, laughing. "Man, I wish some of the people in the office could see this. Mr. Demanding has been taken down."

That didn't sit quite right with me.

"So, my expectation that the people we pay hit the mark makes me, what? A tyrant?" I picked up a discarded axe from the nearby table and assumed the position behind the line.

Eddie stood beside me, his own axe in hand. "Everyone's committed to doing their jobs, man. You know that. The problem is that you have impossibly high expectations for yourself. Which then get passed on to everyone else. You're always charging into the next thing, taking on the next challenge, jumping into the next project, then insisting we all fall in line to accommodate the almost impossible circumstances you drag us in. You're inexhaustible. Yes, you've built this company into an industry leader. We've prospered beyond what I ever thought possible. But when is it *enough?* Would you even recognize when you've hit the limit?"

He scrubbed a hand over his brow.

I hurled the axe at the board. It clattered off, completely missing the target.

Eddie and I switched places.

He lifted the axe, then lowered it, looked over his shoulder at me.

"I talked to Aunt Nan for a while."

Awww, shit.

"Did you?"

"Yeah, I did. Just wondered what connection you might have to this little dusty town in Tennessee, the way you just up and disappeared and pushed the team to pilot the app here."

"What did she tell you?"

"What I wish you'd told me. About your growing up here. What happened with your mom. How you had to leave."

Thanks, Aunt Nan.

I looked at him and found him watching me, frowning.

"Why'd I have to hear all that from Nan? How is it that, in all the years we've known each other, you've never told me your origin story?"

"Origin story? Dude, my life is not a comic book."

He smirked. "But you're trying to be a superhero, aren't you? Trying to avenge all the stuff that went wrong in your life?"

He threw the axe. It slammed into the board, right into the target.

He threw up his hands. "Why didn't that happen when Leigh was still here?"

I snorted. "In love too, huh?"

His eyes widened. "Man, I think she might kill me. Like those female praying mantises that bite their man's head off during sex. But I also think it might be worth it."

"Take your chances, then. Just make sure HR has all your next of kin information on file."

He snickered. "Seriously, though. You and Zora. She's amazing.

Gorgeous. Smart as hell. You've been in love with that girl all your life? I can see why now."

"My whole life, man."

"That why you never settled down?"

I took a deep breath, feeling relieved down to my toes. It was a gift to be on the other side now, the other side of all that sadness and longing.

"I think so. It's always been her for me."

He dug the axe out of the board and returned. "Then don't fuck it up."

"How would I do that?"

His head tilted. "I don't know. But this is the happiest and most relaxed I've seen you since we met. I'd like to know what it's like to work with Disney Nick."

"Get outta here, I'm still the same guy."

"I mean it. Don't fuck it up. And fix it if you do."

I stood behind the line, prepared to throw.

"And don't do that controlling, 'I know what's best for you' thing you do."

I looked back. "What are you talking about?"

He studied his shoes, axe dangling in one hand. "That thing you do, where you decide you know what's best for someone, what they should do. Then push and manipulate to that end."

I turned to face him fully. "I don't do that. I don't think so. Do I?"

"Constantly. I used to be confused by it. You're not a dick generally, not all the time."

I flipped him off.

"But talking to your Aunt Nan, I get it now. She thinks you're compensating for the earlier years in your life when you didn't have much control."

I closed my eyes, gritting my teeth. "It's nice to know my aunt is putting her profession to use by psychoanalyzing me for others."

"Don't be mad. It gave me great insight into you. It'll help me have better patience the next time you do it."

"I don't want you to have patience. I like you worrying that I'm steps away from crazy. Fosters a healthy reverence."

"I'm serious," Eddie said, all joking now gone from his face. "I see how much she means to you. Don't try to manage her life for her. That works for friends and family who can cuss you out, tell you to fuck off. Won't work in a new relationship with your dream girl."

I considered his words, studying the edge of the blade.

I knew Eddie and knew he wanted the best for me. He had no reason to lie to me.

And he may have had a point.

Especially considering what I'd done that very morning.

"Oh oh." Eddie shook his head, eyes closed. "What the hell did you do?"

I set the axe down on the nearby table, too preoccupied to throw it.

"Well..."

"Well, what?"

Briefly, I broke down Zora's funding and tenure dilemma, and Nellie's dogged pursuit of a donation.

Truth be told, I'd planned on making a gift anyway. I thought my mother would have gotten a kick out of having a conference room or building named after her. But after last night? After all that happened between Zora and me...

After finally having her back after all these years, seeing in her eyes how much I meant to her too...

I'd just wanted her to win.

And fuck anybody who stood in the way of that. My woman wasn't going to navigate this harsh world alone.

"So, you blackmailed the development lady?"

"That's not what I did."

"Offering someone something, contingent upon their actions in return. That's not blackmail?"

"I don't think it falls under that, no."

"You don't think dangling that kind of money under that woman's nose in exchange for Zora's tenure and secret funding doesn't fall under that definition?" He ran a hand over his head. "You're already fucking up."

I groaned, leaned back against the wall.

Had I? Had I fucked up?

"Tell her." Eddie's tone bit into my thoughts. "Now. Immediately. Before she finds out on her own, before it's worse."

I hesitated. "What if she never finds out? She may not have to, right? If it works out, if they want the money bad enough she'll never have to know. She'll just know she doesn't have to worry anymore. Not about tenure, not about saving the jobs of all her employees."

But I read the doom on Eddie's face.

And I worried.

CHAPTER TWENTY-NINE
Zora

I shivered, caught, floating on the thinnest wisp of consciousness. Breaths from reality, suspended in the indistinct shadows of a dream world.

Wicked fingers slid, drifted, cupped my breast, plucked at the berried stem of my nipple. I moaned, clenched my legs against the gathering heat below. Heat and warmth curled around me, blanketed me. Moist, hot, spearmint breaths collected in my ear. I captured the muscled arm stealthily traversing my hip, snaking through the valley of my waist.

"You up?" The sleep coarsened voice sent an involuntary finger of delight racing up my spine.

I took my time answering, luxuriating in the slow exploration of his questing fingers in the soft slick of our previous lovemaking.

"No. I'm asleep."

His laughter, low and wicked, rolled over me. Bearded bramble dragged deliciously along my forehead as he shifted, his hand, fingers working my tightness in earnest. My hips lifted, churned, circled, slave to his spell.

"Well. What about Celeste?"

"Seems you two are already talking."

The groan in his whiskered throat vibrated against my neck. "Baby. You're so wet. Can I have you. Please?"

The words, and the clever torment of his fingers, tripped the wire. Ecstasy, blinding and stinging, stiffened all my limbs. Clamped me tight all around his fingers.

"That's right." Wet heat laved my nipple with excruciatingly light strikes. The added sensation seized my jerking hips, pushed a keening, indistinct sound from my throat.

"Please."

The sly licking paused. "You sure you're not asleep still?"

"I'm going to kill you."

"Promise?" He lifted my leg, adjusted our position until the wide, broad head of his dick nudged my opening.

I reached back, my fingers gripping his hair, panting. Ready to beg.

"Please."

He surged forward in an aggressive thrust just as his teeth sank into my neck. Our twin moans rose as I clenched around him, my hips desperate for every possible inch of him. He swore, turning and adjusting me until I was in the lewdest position possible, open and exposed to his bright eyes.

"You're insatiable," I accused, grasping for coherent language as his hips commenced a heavy roll that stretched me and stole all conscious thought.

When it was over, him limp and heavy atop me, me full and wet with him, I reflected I'd never known this quality of happiness existed.

"Breakfast is ready," he gasped on what sounded like a dying breath. "I'll bring it to you when I'm back on this planet."

"That's okay." I smiled against his cheek, relishing the scrape. Loving that he was mine. "Let's put on clothes and sit at a table like civilized people. For once."

∼

Less than an hour later, I met him in the kitchen. Now freshly showered, I smiled at the slight sting from the abrasive beard burn between my thighs.

God. There couldn't be a happier woman on the planet. It wasn't possible.

Nick shot me a heavy-lidded glance from across the kitchen table. "What are you over there smiling about?"

I lowered into my seat, unable to help the grin spreading across my face. "Wouldn't you like to know."

He leaned forward, his gaze darting to my cleavage and the punctuation of my nipples beneath the coral silk robe.

The heat in his gaze, the flare of his nostrils, made me feel powerful.

"As a matter of fact, I would like to know. I can move this food and we can—"

I laughed, lowering my arms to encircle the plates. "No, sir, you won't. I'm hungry and Celeste is on a time out. You've worn her out. Now, what is this?"

He eyed me for several beats before responding. "Looks like some kind of quiche. Emilio didn't label it. Eggs, his favorite sweet potato hash—"

"Wait, who?"

"Emilio, my chef. He flew in yesterday, came in, and made a few meals for us while I was out."

"So you didn't make this? Your *chef* flew in? To make food for you?" I shook my head. "You have a chef?"

Nick handed the platter of bacon out to me. "Yeah, two. Emilio's East Coast. I've got another guy for when I'm in San— What's wrong?"

I stood up, went to the cabinet and opened the door so he wouldn't see my expression. God, what was I doing? How had I managed to forget who he was, all he had? What place would I have in his life when all this was over?

"Zora?"

"I'm just getting a glass."

"There's glasses here, on the table."

"Yeah, well. I want another one. Taller. For water."

"What's wrong?"

"Nothing."

"Liar."

I sighed, clenched the exterior cabinet pull in one hand. "I guess I just forgot."

"Forgot what?"

I pulled a glass down, steeled my nerves before turning.

And found Nick right behind me, so close I had no choice but to back against the counter.

His arms came around me, caged me in. "What's wrong, baby?"

I huffed. "Why do you call me that now?"

Dark swaths of hair swept across his forehead and almost obscured the view of those green eyes I loved so much. I reached up, pushed it back.

"You need a haircut."

He caught my arm, pressed a kiss against the sensitive skin right below my wrist. "I call you 'baby' because you're my baby. *Mine*. A few minutes ago, you held me inside you and told me I was yours. And now you've got that scared look in your eyes. So I need to know what's going on in your head."

I couldn't tear my eyes away from him, couldn't help but respond to the intimacy of his tone.

"Tell me."

"I forgot."

"Forgot what?"

"That you're rich. Really rich. *Rich*, rich."

He frowned. "That's a bad thing?"

I shrugged. "I guess I just forgot is all. It's been a while since we were in New York. I'm used to seeing you here. I guess I forgot who you are, what you do, what you have."

His forehead lowered to mine. "You want me to give it all away?"

I let out a short laugh. "No, I—"

"Zora, I've worked for this moment, with you in my arms, for a long time. I'm not giving you up for anything. The money's not who I am, baby. I think you already know that. Tell me what's really bothering you."

I lifted a shoulder, fought against the fear stirring in my belly. "You have an entire life, a way of being. Full of balls and events and *expectations,* all the things I'm no good at. You're in Green Valley for now, but you have to go back to that life."

He was quiet, but I wasn't fooled. I'd known him long enough to know his mind was busy behind the guileless expression.

"I've loved waking up to you every morning and Sir Duke. But—"
"But what?"
"My life is a mess right now. I barely know if I'm coming or going. With tenure and funding up in the air—"

He slid a hand behind my neck, wove his fingers into my thick curls. "There's only one question and one answer that matters here. Do you want me? Us? What we are?"

"Yes," I answered readily, immediately.
"That's all that matters. We will figure it out."
"But your travel—"
"I'll figure it out. I've got places all over. Though, maybe this isn't the time to talk about my international real estate." He grinned at me, then sobered, his gaze moving over my face. "If it comes through—tenure, funding—would you want to stay here?"

It was a damn good question.

Things were far different than they'd been when I'd accepted my position at the university and started conducting research at Knoxville Community Hospital. My mother was out of the woods. She'd be okay; I didn't have to live in close proximity to be assured of her well-being. I didn't feel the same inclination, the same pressure, to make a place for myself among my family anymore, to prove anything. I was okay with *me*, with the choices I'd made to get me to this point.

I was less certain about the career I'd spent so much time carving out, and my path forward. But suddenly, I felt . . . open to change.

"I don't know." It was the truth. "I honestly don't know what I'm doing. I think I'm open to exploring something else, for my sake. But I'm also not willing to just walk away from what I've built before I know how it all shakes out. Not without seeing it through."

His nodded, those bright eyes boring into mine. I didn't realize I was biting my lower lip until his thumb gently pulled it away from the torture of my teeth. "So, you want to wait? See how it shakes out?"

I sighed. I was eager to begin the future I hadn't even known I needed and yet . . . "Yes. I have to. It's one thing if I decide to change course. It's another thing if I fail. If I'm pushed out."

"But, that's not—"

I laid a finger against his lips when he shook his head, silencing his protestations. "No. Listen. It's true. *If* I decide to do something different, the way I leave all this matters. Especially then. I've got my staff to think about."

His gaze moved from mine and settled somewhere beside us. "I can wait with you. You'll know soon enough. I can easily fly back and forth for a month or two, you know that. And you know my offer to fund your employees still stands—"

"I know, and I'm grateful you would do that. For me, for them. But you've got to let me deal with this, my own way, however it shakes out. I know I'm a mess about it all right now—"

"You're not a mess—"

"But I really am capable of handling it all. I need you to know that. I don't want you to rush in and rescue me. But I damn sure could use a hug while I give it my all." I sent him my best seductive look from under my lashes. "Also, I've read that orgasms are incredibly effective for alleviating stress, even—"

His mouth was on mine and I responded before I really even registered it, my hands winding around his neck, then sliding along the strong planes of his back. His strong hands grasped my waist, planted me on the counter, and slid between my skin and the silk of the robe until my breasts were in his hands, his fingers tweaking my nipples. I cupped him though his pants, hunted for the zipper in the placket of his jeans.

It was so easy with him. I'd never imagined I could feel so free, so uninhibited, so much *myself* with a man. *This* man. My goofy, awkward, pain-in-the-ass self. It was a relief, and terrifying. The closeness, the naked intimacy he demanded left me unnerved, naked. Vulnerable.

It also left me certain now that I couldn't go back, didn't want to live life again without this quality of love that was at once steady, dependable, and exhilarating.

I bit his ear, then licked his neck as he slid my hips to the edge of the counter and tested my wetness with the tip of his dick. Shushed his hoarse murmur that he'd be gentle and whispered the words that were sure to drive him crazy, that made him slam home with an anguished groan, his hands digging into my back as he delivered deep-rooted thrusts that claimed my sanity.

Please God, I thought, wrapping my legs around his lean waist, clamping his dick in a vise grip, groaning as I felt the hot spill of him. *Please let it always be this way.*

CHAPTER THIRTY

Nick

"Where did you get this truck?"

Zora slid me that sly smile that warmed by blood, made my heart lighter.

"It's Walker's."

"You don't say." I admired her confident handling off the older F-250 truck and her deft negotiation of the stick shift.

I'd been suspicious when she insisted on picking me up from Knoxville's airport. Even more so when she pulled up in the aging truck, smiling that smile that meant she had something up her sleeve.

God, I loved her. How had we managed living apart all this time?

"What's that smell?" I sniffed the air of the truck's interior, searching after the vague scent of something delicious that hung in the air, but there was no food in sight.

"Would you stop asking questions?"

I loosened my tie and sat back, content to simply take in the view of her in snug jeans. The way her shirt clung to her curves.

After a stressful week working with our New York staff, I was relieved to be back home to her. Home.

How the hell had that happened? *Home.*

I missed the hell out of her. Without her in arm's reach, my bed was empty, cold. Sleep was elusive and I was cranky. Relief had swamped me when I climbed the steps to the plane on the return trip that would take me back to her, back to a Technicolor existence filled with laughter, lovemaking, cuddling, and dreaming.

I didn't want to go back to how things were before. I couldn't. Being without her for a week had shown me just how empty, lifeless, and grayscale my life had been without her.

"Fine," I said. "I'll stop asking questions. I'll let you carry out your plan without any further harassment."

"*Thank you*," she said, and that dimple winked at me. "I would think you'd be happy to relinquish a little control, given the week you had."

"And what would you know about that?"

She piloted the car around a familiar curve that made my heart beat that much faster.

Were we going to . . . ?

"I heard from Eddie," she said, and I groaned.

"He really went complaining to you?"

"He said you've been, and I quote, a 'narcissistic asshole' all week. Tormenting the staff, throwing wrenches in all their plans. Said he would've knocked you unconscious and sent you back to me if you hadn't already left."

The open road slowly transitioned into dense forest, muting the waning evening light. She slowed, prepared to cut into a place I'd once known very well. It was the setting of our horniest teenage years.

Cooper's Field.

"So I told him," she said, driving farther into the shadowy expanse, "to just send you home. 'Cause I knew what you needed."

I leaned over, rested my hand on the warmth of her upper thigh. God, it felt good to be able to touch her again.

"Uh-huh. And what was that?"

She aimed a full-on grin at me before returning her attention back to the windshield. "Me."

We both laughed. I unbuckled my seat belt and reached for her, unable to wait any longer. I loved seeing her this way, confident in the love I had for her and in the claim she'd staked on my heart. I needed her like I needed air and I loved that she knew it, owned it.

She pulled the truck past the middle of the clearing most often used by visitors and tucked the truck under a shadowed copse of trees.

As soon as the vehicle was properly parked I snatched her across the bench seat and held her against me, filled my lungs with the scent of her.

God. I'd needed this.

"You poor baby." She pulled back just enough to study me in the darkening interior of the car. "You haven't slept that well, have you?"

I didn't have to fake my piteous expression. "And I haven't been inside you in days."

She slapped at my hands when I hooked my thumbs in her jeans. "Down, boy. Let's eat."

Things were definitely looking up. "There's food?"

She jerked a thumb toward the window. "Get out."

I held her to me as I climbed down from the running board, ignored her squawking protests to put her down.

I just didn't want to let her out of my arms yet.

We rounded the back of the truck. I helped Zora clamber up and craned my neck to see what secrets awaited me in the truck's bed.

She climbed over to the supplies and blankets stacked neatly against one corner. I grinned when she stood and shook out a blanket.

"Really? A picnic?"

Zora busied herself with turning on several electric lanterns, strategically arranging them. "Yes. Get the food out of the cab. There's coolers. Behind your seat."

I returned to the cabin to find several coolers I hadn't noticed. By the time I'd rejoined her, she'd turned the bed into a makeshift lounge with bright pillows and a quilt.

I jumped up, set the food aside and tackled her in the middle of her efforts.

"Nick!"

"Zora." I turned us until she was under me, slid my hands into her hair and gripped the thick roots of it. I looked down into her face, thinking this was all I ever wanted or needed, ever again.

"I can't live without you." I surprised myself with the admission. I couldn't help my raw delivery, the flare of panic I felt at the idea that anything might separate us again. Even I could admit that I was a pain in the ass without her.

Her expression softened as her gaze moved over mine. She pulled my head until our lips met.

"You don't have to. Because I sure as hell don't want to live without you."

Our eyes met. Something in me settled, quieted to calm.

This was real. We were doing this.

We were *we*.

Zora and I sat up and worked together, unpacking the food and plating it. I grinned at the sight of a familiar, age-old thermos.

"Is that what I think it is?"

She rolled her eyes as she set out camping bowls. "Yes. It's my mother's gumbo."

That did it. This was one of the best days I'd had, ever.

"You're so spoiled. I told her I was picking you up and bringing you here. She threatened me with death if I didn't pick up this up. She made it just for you. Walker's jealous. You'll be hearing from him."

I rubbed my hands together gleefully as she poured a healthy portion into the bowl. The air was immediately saturated with the scent of slow cooked meats, seafood, and spices.

Poor Walker. He really was missing out. Mrs. Leffersbee had rarely made this when I was a kid, but she'd always busted it out for special occasions like my birthday. I *did* feel rather spoiled.

"I took his food and you took his truck? Between the two of us, I'd say I'm faring much better than him. My day just got a million times better."

She smirked as she unloaded squares of cornbread. "He's feeling a bit of sibling rivalry. Suddenly, he's not the only son around for my mother to fawn over. It's for the best. It'll keep him humble."

My breath caught on the word "son" and my chest tightened. My mother could never be replaced, I knew that. But to be back in the arms of this family . . . to once again be a treated as a son . . . I hadn't imagined this moment would be possible all those years ago.

"Why'd you borrow Walker's truck?" I kept the emotion from my voice.

"He comes here all the time. Keeps a readymade kit in the back. And I didn't want mud caked on my tires."

I flicked an apprehensive glance at the blanket we sat on. "This isn't Walker's, is it?"

She punched my arm, cackling. "Gross. Don't make me think about strangers' bodily fluids."

I cracked up. "Is it?"

"No."

"So it occurred to you already."

"You're disgusting."

"Nah, I know Walker."

We settled against the pillows, arms gently bumping as we ate while watching the constellations gain greater luminosity in the darkening sky. We talked about everything and nothing. Zora told me about her success in cleaning her office, filled me in on the most recent round of Walker v. Tavia and caught me up on town gossip. I let her pry the details of my week out of me while she watched me with slitted, all-knowing eyes.

"You *have* been some variety of asshole."

"What?"

She shook her head at me. "You get this way when you're bored."

I raised an eyebrow at her. "Excuse me. I'm not—"

"Yes, you are. You're bored. You did the same thing in school, remember? Before they finally understood that you were too advanced for the material? You'd cause trouble, disrupt class, get fascinated with random, bizarre things. It exhausted everyone around you."

I stilled, considering her words.

She chuffed, popped a piece of cornbread in her mouth. "It's okay. You don't have to say it. I know I'm right."

Jesus. *Was she?*

"I realized it the longer I listened to Eddie. The way you keep dragging the team into things, how you're always searching for the next, near-impossible thrill like an adrenaline junkie? The short-lived victory when you pull it off before you're moving on to the next thing? Same as before, I remember it. You're bored."

Words escaped me. Had she really summed up my discontent, the thing that kept me in near-constant conflict with our staff that easily? That she knew me so well, still, after all these years, brought a wave of affection. Now I'd have to grapple with her hypothesis, because there was enough evidence to support it.

Damn. *I was bored.* The realization was blunted by the fact that I was eating what was still the best gumbo I'd ever had in my life. This evening was already full of revelations.

"I forgot how good her gumbo is." Zora sounded thoughtful as she examined the spoon she'd just licked clean. I looked away, thinking I'd give her an opportunity to finish eating before I mauled her in the back of the truck. "She hasn't made it in years."

"I'm bored." I stared at her in the gathering darkness, heard the ring of truth in the words once I spoke them aloud. "That's what's wrong with me."

She tilted her bowl to get the last of the gumbo. "Yes. I'm surprised it took you this long to figure it out."

I dug an elbow into her thigh and she shrieked, then laughed.

"Okay, okay. I won't be so smug. But I'm not surprised."

"You're not?"

"Nope." Melancholy sat heavy in her voice. "It's how it works, I think. You put everything you have into something, you throw all your effort behind a goal. And then, years later, you reach your goal and discover things are different than you thought they'd be."

I considered her words as I poured myself more gumbo. "I can see that. When Eddie and I started this business in undergrad, my goals were to help people, but also to be first in everything we brought to the market. To win, to make all the money, to crush the competition."

"Not bad goals."

I shrugged. "Well, I guess not. We're first in introducing products most of the time, sure enough. Eddie keeps telling we've made enough money, which I don't know if I'll ever agree with. But, yeah, I guess I miss that thrill of the chase. It's not enough to just be first anymore. I guess I have been restless, looking for that next thing that would give me that *buzz*, you know? Haven't had enough new challenges, apparently." I snuck at look at her. "Is that what happened to you too?"

She sighed, sliding down until she was almost horizontal in the truck's bed. "Maybe. I don't know what's wrong with me."

I kept my tone casual. "Would getting tenure, getting the grant, fix things for you? Make you excited about your work again?"

She took a long time answering. By the time she spoke again, I barely made out her face in the gathering shadows. "It's not that I'm not *excited* about my work, per se. I just don't know if it's the thing I want to focus on forever, from here on out."

"Yes, but would you feel the same discontent if you got tenure and enough funding to take care of your employees for the long term?"

I made out her crumpled forehead in the gathering darkness. "I think so."

I poured another refill of gumbo. "Alright."

"It's just . . . When you're trying to solve a problem, you can never account for all the contributing factors, the complexities of the issue. You know why I started the clinician communication training at the hospital?"

"Tell me."

"It wasn't about helping the hospital meet their metrics. That was an important benefit. It helped us measure outcomes and incentivized the hospital to support my work. But why I really did it was because I met and talked to our doctors, nurses, and nurse practitioners. I saw how burnt out they were, how badly they wanted to help their patients, wanted to spend more time with them. Among all of them, one of the most common themes that emerged was that they didn't expect practicing medicine to be this way. Most of them became clinicians because they wanted to help people. They wanted to make a change, be the difference. Just like I did."

I groped for her hand, found it in the darkness and held on.

"They weren't prepared for the reality of practicing medicine in our deeply-flawed system. They hadn't anticipated how the industry would cripple them, how the *machine* of medicine and all the chains of bureaucracy would squeeze them, demand all their time, keep them up night and weekends charting. How their clinics were so full, with barely enough time to say hello to their patients, let alone prepare for a meaningful exchange. The people I work with and train, they're not apathetic monsters. If anything, they're most injured by their own dismay, by their disappointment that they often aren't supported in delivering the kind of care that motivated them to become clinicians in the first place. The training we offer? It helps. It gives them tools to connect, to facilitate the meaningful interactions with patients they dreamed of having as medical students. It shows them a way back to practicing medicine the way they dreamed of, even in the midst of all the bullshit, the noise."

I set down my empty bowl and slid down next to her, pulled her to me.

"What about you? What's the shot in the arm, the solution, that would help you remember why you got into this work?"

Her exhale warmed my neck. "I don't know. It's all so much. It's so big. I don't know if it's enough to address just the individual, interpersonal level barriers like I am. Yes, we're trying to address disparities in care by improving the quality of communication that takes place between doctors and patients. It does help, it does work. Our data clearly show that patients are getting better information provisioning, more high quality discussions of information related to diagnosis, treatment and ongoing care, they're actively included in decision making about treatment plans, next steps. They feel empowered to take care of themselves, to advocate and press for the information they need to manage their health. But now I see how glaring the other barriers are."

I sat back and folded my arms as I studied her in the near-dark, moved by her agitation and passion.

"What are the other barriers?"

Her arm lifted, then fell limply against the truck. "*So many.* We're not adequately addressing all the social determinants of health. I can coach and teach a patient and their doctor to have the most open, collaborative conversation possible. But what happens outside that clinic door has such a huge effect on what ultimately happens to that patient and their health."

"Like what? Give me an example."

"The other day, we had a lady come in, fresh from a surgery to remove a lump from her breast. The doc wants to explain a test he's recommending that will take a closer look at the pathology of her tumor to help determine if chemo will be helpful for her or not in the long run. The conversation goes well. The doc really digs in, probes to try to understand why she's objecting to this really important test. You know what the issue is?"

"What?"

"She has insurance, but she's *under*-insured. When she ranks all the financial needs in her household, that test comes in last. She's gotta think about the roof she can't afford to replace, the income she's lost as a result of not working during her treatment, the fact that the financial assistance she's gotten to keep her afloat during treatment is so miniscule it barely scratches the surface of what she needs. So, when a doc comes to her and proposes a test that will leave her with an astronomical out-of-pocket expense, what decision do you think she makes? Even after she's had a great conversation with her doctor about all the risks and benefits, and how this test can improve her outcome after identifying the best treatment option?"

I let out a sigh, pained by the anguish I heard in her voice, and the fact that another human being would be placed in such a heart-rending position, with so much already at stake.

"That's terrible, Z. I'm sorry. You're right. Those barriers do need to be addressed, and they do have a direct relationship on folks' health outcomes. Are you thinking that you, your research and training, don't matter in light of that?"

"No, it's just that the world needs so much more. What I'm doing isn't enough."

I weighed my words carefully. "I don't want you to just think about what the world needs. I want you to think about what *you* want. You got into the work you do now to address a problem you learned about during your mother's cancer diagnosis."

Her chest lifted against mine. "Yeah."

"My team told me about another grant you got to improve communication between patients and doctors when they talk about pain and opioid use."

She started to pull away. I held firm.

"You were thinking about *my* mom. Weren't you?"

Her words were muffled against me. "It's a well-documented disparity in care. There's ample evidence demonstrating African-American patients are undertreated for pain—"

"Zora."

"Yes." Her sigh hissed out into the open air. I pulled the quilt over us.

"I'm sure that's true. But I'm willing to bet that's not all that motivated you to explore that topic."

"It's not a bad thing." There was no mistaking her defensive tone. "To be inspired by the people, the problems you see around you—"

"It is when you're not motivated by what genuinely excites you anymore. What makes your soul sing. Then, baby—" I captured her chin. "Then you end up feeling like you're living for everybody else. Like you do now. Your mother said it to you, and I'll add to her voice. Take your time. Find that thing that excites you. Even if it leads you to a different path, don't be scared. Maybe the way you're looking at it, the way I've been looking at my own goals, is wrong. Maybe the journey isn't linear. Maybe the real deal is we never really find all the parts to ourselves, not wholly and completely, without a good deal of continued searching. Maybe life's just a meandering path we keep chasing in pursuit of learning all our selves. We're both still learning, growing, changing, and our paths may change to reflect that. I want you to know though," I pressed a kiss to her forehead, "I'm with you for this journey. I'm not going anywhere. I'll be with you every step of the way."

Her fingers pressed into my back. When she spoke, her words were lost to the wind.

"What's that, baby?"

"I'm scared."

I laughed, wrapped my arms around her. "Why? Have *you* met you? I'm excited. I'm gonna buy us pith helmets for this journey. I can't wait to see where we end up."

"What if I don't know who I am without my job? Without all I've worked so hard to build all this time?"

I found her lips in the darkness. "Here's the beauty of that. You get to find *yourself*. Another part of yourself. Your namesake, Zora Neale Hurston, said that research was 'formalized curiosity.' She said, 'It's poking and prying with a purpose.' Listening to you, I hear that curiosity. I hear the new questions you're asking, and I know you can't help but find new solutions in all the poking and prodding that's bound to follow. That sounds pretty damn exciting, doesn't it?"

We were quiet for an interminable moment, absorbing the dense quiet all around us.

"Nick?"

"Yeah?"

"I'm so glad you're back. Don't leave again. Okay?"

Damn. This woman. As if I *could* leave.

"I won't. This? Us? We're forever."

"Promise?"

"I do," I said, feeling the truth of it resonate down to my very marrow. "I'm so glad you brought me here. I've been a lot of places, seen most of the world. But I wouldn't trade any of it for this moment right here, back in Cooper's Field, stomach full of your mama's gumbo. Holding the girl I love."

Her breath hitched.

"I do love you, you know."

She sniffled. "I do, too. Still. Even after all this time."

"Good. Glad we're on the same page. You know something we need to do?"

Her smooth fingertips glided along my arm, unseen in the darkness. "What's that?"

"Finally go all the way. Here."

"Oh, God."

"You remember coming here before, hiding what we were doing under the blanket all those times?"

She gave a laugh. "Those were the days. Sneaking to kiss and touch each other before someone pulled up or Sheriff James came to run us all out."

"But we're grown now, and as your mama would say, this is grown folks' business."

She shivered. "Please don't bring my mother up right now."

"I'm definitely not thinking about your mama right now. I'm thinking about finally fulfilling my teenage fantasy. You, naked, in the back of a pickup. With nobody around to stop us."

Her voice was rich with laughter. "I'm not naked."

"Stay tuned. You're about to be."

Her smooth palm slid across my cheek, under my jaw. "Do what you will. Have your way with me. It *is* your fantasy, after all."

Her words electrified me, freed me of a fraying leash.

It was all the more exciting in the near darkness.

I ran my nose along her neck, hunted for her scent. Tasted. Grasped the edge of her shirt. She worked with me, our hands, forearms tangling in the dark as I pulled her bra down, tongued her nipple, fumbled with the clasps beneath her.

"Nick." Her gasp was low and throaty. It made my dick even harder, ran my blood even hotter as I turned her over. I stripped her of her jeans and underwear, then ran my fingers along the sensitive skin of inner thighs. Her legs parted naturally as I settled between them.

"Yes?"

"I can't believe we're actually doing this."

A quick tug and I had her right where I wanted her. Under me. Panting. Ready. My hands coasted up her abdomen and along all that smooth, warm skin. I felt the rise and fall of her frantic, excited breaths.

I smiled and pressed kisses against her hip bones.

Hooked her legs over my shoulders, spread her thighs as far I could.

And tasted her.

I smiled against all that wet, soft flesh. Lapped at it. Buried my face, my nose in her. Inhaled her scent as her hoarse, exultant cry rang out across the open field. Laved at her clit until her thighs closed around my head, muffling her shrieks.

She yanked at my hair.

I didn't let up. The telltale circling of her hips began and I sent a searching hand up her body until my palm found her breast and the hard point of her nipple.

"Nick . . ."

"Come for me, baby. I don't want you to have make any more videos about how you can't come. Not when you're with me."

She slapped at my shoulder, laughing, then shuddered as I slipped one, then two fingers into her.

She came in a rush of sound and wetness, gripping me with everything she had. I unbuttoned my pants, shoved them down in a fever to get back to her. To get inside her.

"Now," she choked out. Her hand caught my dick, gripped, squeezed, while the other slid around to my ass. Prodded me forward.

I'd just slid into the heaven of her tightness, gritting my teeth, fighting not to explode, when a loud voice cut across the field. Blinding white light flooded the truck's bed. I fell forward over Zora, hiding her from whatever was there.

"Walker Leffersbee? Is that you out there?"

The sound of an engine reached us, followed by a door slamming.

I didn't have time to do much more than tuck Zora under the

quilt before Jackson James's face appeared next to the flashlight he held at his ear.

He took in the sight of us in one sweeping glance, then turned with a curse.

"Jesus, Zora!"

Beneath me, she covered her eyes.

"Go away, Jackson!"

"What are y'all doing out here? You know we're cracking down on vehicles parked out here all times of night. I thought this was Walker's truck. Last thing I expected to see was Nick's ass looking back at me."

"Just go."

"I'm going."

Something fluttered into the bed. I snatched it up once the intrusive light was removed and peered at it in the scant light from the lanterns.

"Did you—did you just write out a ticket? For what?"

"I imagine you both have an idea." Laughter choked Jackson's voice. "I'll see you later. Y'all have a good night."

CHAPTER THIRTY-ONE

Nick

How ow was it possible to feel two extremely different emotions at the same time?

I was due at Zora's office in ten minutes. She wouldn't say what we were doing or where we were going, but I figured it must have been important. She'd reminded me to show up at the appointed time twice over the last two days, which wasn't like her.

And strange, considering we saw each other every night now.

Knowing I'd soon see her and her smile quickened my step across campus.

I wasn't entirely surprised that we'd fallen into our current rhythm so easily, but it was not at all what I'd expected prior to arriving in Green Valley.

It was far more than I'd even dared to hope for.

Being with Zora, laughing with Zora, making love to Zora—it was like stepping back into a favorite dream, or reliving a perfect memory.

It was also exciting, like discovering new terrain on a well-worn path, and realizing the opportunity for a new, divergent adventure.

My feelings for Zora were far from small or insignificant. In a very short amount of time, she'd reclaimed the reins to my heart.

I didn't want anyone else. I'd be perfectly content to spend the rest of my days with her. Learning her. Loving her.

Knowing she felt the same about me made me feel like the luckiest man in the world.

Eighteen-year-old Nick, dejected and despondent as he boarded a plane for Michigan and the unknown, would have been thrilled with this development.

I was happy.

Happy.

I turned the word around in my mind, examined it for flaws in logic or conclusion.

It was true.

For the first time in as long as I could remember, I thought the wolf might not be waiting outside my door anymore. Everything was fine. Better than fine, really.

I had Zora back.

However, a grim premonition wound itself around that hope and threatened to choke the life out of it.

I still hadn't told Zora about the deal I'd offered Nellie. The part of me that always waited for the other shoe to drop, for the boom to lower, worried. Eddie's words ran through my mind on a constant loop. It was true; I should have told her what I'd done, but now I'd waited too long. I knew her well enough to anticipate her response. She'd be pissed. Beyond angry.

Yet there was no way I could live without her again.

My mind fought against the reality of my impending doom even as my feet brought me closer to her.

If there was a way out of this, I hadn't found it yet. All I could do was hope she never found out. The deception of it didn't sit right with me, but my intentions were pure. There was hardly anything I wouldn't do for her.

I reached the open doorway of her office. Counseled myself to mentally reshelve the matter. I'd retrieve and re-examine the dilemma with a tactician's perspective later. When dread wasn't knotting my gut.

I took a moment to observe her. Her back was to me, just as it had been when I first showed up here. She sat at her newly cleared desk, chin propped up on her fist, gazing at her computer with a pained expression. A few curls had escaped the back of her ponytail and grazed the back of her neck. My groin tightened, remembering the previous night. I'd taken her from behind, one steadying hand on her hip while the fingers of my other hand plumbed the softest part of her. Then she'd looked over her shoulder at me—

Shit. It was early, but maybe there weren't that many people around . . . I cast a hasty look up and down the halls before heading in her office and pulling the door closed behind me.

Zora wasn't quiet, but we could probably find a way around that.

She looked up at the sound of the door closing. The hugest grin spread across her face as she turned to face me.

I heard the thud my heart made as it fell.

Fuck. I fucking loved her.

There had to be a way to make this work.

"Hey, you." She bit her lip as her gaze ran from my feet and then back up again. I wondered if her thoughts had also taken a turn into Naughtyville. "You're looking mighty official. Big meeting this afternoon?"

"Yeah. Focus group with the docs went well."

"How are things going? I'm sorry I haven't been very helpful."

"It's okay. We've got it." I came closer, fighting against a rising tide of guilt, trying not to stare at her mouth for too long. "Everything's fine. How're things on your end?"

She frowned, pushing back from her desk. "Don't ask."

I hesitated. "Literally? Or—"

"Literally." She stood, sexiness personified in jeans and a T-shirt that read, *Have You Hugged a Communication Major Today?* I took inventory of the stress lines between her brows, the pinched twist to her mouth. I'd get it out of her later, in bed, when she was relaxed and less likely to resist.

"No, but I'd like to." Seeing her head shake in confusion, I pointed to the slogan on her shirt. *Have You* was delightfully stretched.

Jesus, Nick, get your cock under control.

Her lips curved into an expression I'd become more and more acquainted with. The Hungry Zora look.

"I'd like that, too. I can never pass up a handsome man in a sexy suit." She stepped into my space, wound her hands past my suit coat and around my waist. I lowered my head, taking in the fruity fragrance of her hair as the strands tickled my nose. Then, without fail, my mouth slid against hers as I coaxed her to share her taste.

I walked her backwards until the backs of her legs hit the desk, then lifted her to its surface.

Her mouth never left mine, even as she moaned in the way that drove me crazy.

"We've gotta be quiet," I warned, my hand now full of the heft of her breast, thumb circling her nipple. When her hand wandered down to my zipper I groaned. I wondered if I could take my own advice.

I slid a hand against her skin of her stomach, impatient with the barriers of her shirt and bra. I wanted the heat of her softness spilling out of my hand. I wanted the sweetness of her flesh in my mouth.

Zora's fingertips had just, *finally, thank God*, hurried up and walked past my fly when a sharp knock sounded on the door.

She reacted as if a bucket of cold water had been thrown over her head, pulling her mouth and hand away simultaneously.

"Can we ignore them?"

She looked as disappointed as I felt. "No."

"No, don't put that away," I said, watching as she readjusted her bra. "I'll do it. I'll make them go."

She shook her head, pushing past me to slide off the desk. "Really? You're going to answer the door with that erection?"

The whole world was a cockblock. First Jackson James, now whoever was on the other side of that door.

I watched as she collected herself, then strode to the door where she cracked it open the barest sliver.

I didn't hear the other side of the conversation, but her response was clear. "Oh, it's time, isn't it? We'll be right down."

She turned back to me with a sigh, running a hand over her forehead. "Nick. You are going to be the death of me."

I willed my dick to accept defeat.

"You promise?"

"Get yourself together. We have to go."

Ten minutes later we made our way down the hallway. She'd still refused to tell me where we were going, which raised my hackles a bit.

When we reached the conference room, I was on full alert.

The last thing I'd expected to find was a room of middle-aged women sitting around the kidney-shaped conference room. I looked to Zora and found her gaze on me, her eyes wide as she gestured for me to proceed into the conference room.

What the hell was this?

"Hi, Nick," one of the gray-haired women said, smiling wide. I studied her, head tilted, trying to place her face, that smile. "You probably don't remember me. That's okay. I've changed a lot, too."

My feet were stuck to the floor. "Ms. Camille?"

She whooped. "You do remember! Alright!" She looked to the woman opposite her, who observed our exchange with a grin. "You see that, Maria? Maybe I haven't gotten that old. I'm going to go home and tell Dennis how Nick recognized me right off."

The other woman rolled her eyes. "You know Dennis. He's going to make some crack about whether anyone recognized how much your ass spread." Her voice had the guttural, metal on metal grind of a chain smoker. "How you've stayed married to that asshole all these years, I'll never understand."

Zora's hand closed around my arm but I barely felt it; I didn't hear whatever she was saying.

I remembered.

I remembered my mother taking me into the clinic where she worked, behind the door of the waiting room to see the "girls" she worked with during the week. She'd had to hold my hand when we visited Ms. Camille and her grumpy counterpart, Ms. Jackie, because I'd been pretty young. Looking around the table, I recognized the other three ladies more quickly, now that they were in context. I'd regaled them with my middle school exploits before I judged myself too old to accompany my mother on her visits to work friends.

The five women went around the table, introducing themselves, reminding me of who they were. Zora stood to the side, biting her lip in the way that meant she was *extremely* nervous.

I nodded politely through their chorus of how big I'd gotten, how I had my mother's eyes.

Zora cleared her throat. "I know you were interested in the pictures my parents had in the kitchen, and I thought it might be helpful if you had others. So, I checked in with these ladies, your mom's old coworkers, to see if they had their own photos. And it turns out they did."

"And stories," someone added. "We've gotta tell you some of these stories."

I looked back at the door, contemplating an escape. What in creation was this? A memorial?

I didn't know if I could do this.

Missing my mother, the pain of that wound . . . the only way I managed it was by not thinking about it, cramming that hurt deep, not letting it or the memories sneak up on me. Memories were the hardest for me. They had the deepest edges and sliced me open so easily.

God, I missed my mother.

Zora's hand pressed into my back. I let her nudge me toward an unoccupied chair. I worked up a pleasant expression for the women while Zora stood behind me, her hand a comforting weight at the back of my neck.

Ms. Camille picked up a plastic sandwich bag. It was full of photos.

"I had more than a fair amount," she said, shaking the stack into her hand, "because our old nurse manager loved any excuse to take pictures. I hated it at the time. Times like this, though, you appreciate it."

She slid photos across the slick surface of the table toward me, one by one.

I caught the first one, then stopped. More photos slid in my direction but I couldn't look away from what was in front of me: my mother in scrubs, arms crossed around my neck and beaming. Judging by the digitally rendered date in the corner, I'd been ten.

I traced our faces in the picture.

"Take Your Son to Work Day. Remember?" Camille grinned. "You made us promise we wouldn't make you watch babies being born."

The women laughed.

More photos came my way, mostly of my mother with her coworkers, at work and at get-togethers. At some point, while listening to one of the women recount the story of my mother singing a Beatles song to a laboring patient, I realized Zora had left without my noticing.

I sat back, taking in the room and my mother's friends.

The magnitude of this, the gift Zora had given me, was staggering. So few of my Green Valley memories were positive. Seeing the past this way, not through the prism of my last days in Green Valley, changed everything, reminded me that not all of my past was shitty.

We talked for another ninety minutes, chatting and laughing, until Camille signaled a topic change. "We wanted you to have something," she said, exchanging glances with the other women.

She rose from her seat and brought me a large plastic bag bearing the logo from a local crafts shop.

I opened it slowly, aware of five sets of eyes on me.

It was a quilt. A quilt of pictures. Of me, my mother, her coworkers. Group shots of us with the entire Leffersbee, Payton, and Winston clans.

"We all picked our favorites," Camille said, and the other women nodded along. "And Ellie Leffersee had so many. Zora raided her stash."

My throat was dry. "Thank you. Thank you all so much."

"See, I told you he would like it." One of the women stuck her tongue out, childishly.

"I wasn't arguing with you, Dorothy. I was just saying, he's a man and he wouldn't want any of that frilly shit you like."

I laughed despite myself. I could easily imagine my mother right along with them. She'd have kept the smartass comments coming, raising the stakes by further instigating their mock conflict.

"One more thing," Camille said. She was apparently the leader of the group, though I couldn't help but wonder if it was by self-nomination.

The ladies passed another plastic bag down to me. I fished out a small box.

It was a jewelry box.

My nerves felt too raw and exposed to joke, but I gave it a try anyway. "Are one of you ladies proposing?"

"Open it."

"Don't act like you're scared of it, open the gosh darn box!"

It was almost comical, seeing all of their craned necks and wide-eyed gazes trained on the box.

I eased the velvet box open.

And stopped breathing.

Camille got up and came around the table. She laid a hesitant hand on my shoulder. "You know what it is, then?"

I nodded. I didn't trust myself to speak.

Out of the corner of my eye, another chair pushed back. I kept my gaze down, trained on the glossy wood table and away from the contents of the box, fighting for control. I fought desperately against the heat of sadness and loss in my throat.

A new hand settled on my arm.

"Lila planned on getting it for you. She was going to surprise you before you left for college. She had it pinned up on the wall and told us all about it. She was saving for it but then she . . . left the job. We talked again, got reconnected when she was back in Michigan. We didn't talk a great deal more, but in one of the conversations, I remember her saying she'd meant to get you this, but it got lost in all the transitions. I know she'd have wanted you to finally have it." Camille's hand kept patting my shoulder.

"She was going to have it engraved," another voice said. "We'd all teased her about it back then. But we didn't forget."

I shook my head, sniffing past the stinging sensation in my nose. "How did you all even do this? All these years later?"

"Wasn't that hard. High school had the ring style from that year still on file. It wasn't nothing for the company to fire up one with the right year. Money talks—you know that."

A finger poked in my back. "What, are you trying to kill us with the suspense? Try it on!"

I reached into the box and retrieved the class ring. It bore my graduating year of high school on either side. The school's name was neatly printed around the perimeter of the stone.

I angled the band and, sure enough, made out an inscription inside. After tilting it to take advantage of the overhead lighting, I was almost unmanned by the engraved words.

It was from one of our favorite Dr. Seuss books. My mother read it to me a million times. Never told me she was sick of reading it, never skipped pages.

Oh, the places you'll go.

Her voice sounded in my head, repeating the familiar words.

Oh, Mom.

I gave it up, then, lowering my face to one hand, clenching the ring in the other.

A set of arms wrapped around my neck from behind, while that same hand kept patting me on the shoulder.

I shuddered, unable to hold back the emotion. I was gratified. Full. For the first time since arriving back in Green Valley, it wasn't my mother's absence I felt, but her presence.

CHAPTER THIRTY-TWO

Zora

One Month Later

"Zora! Right on time. Good to see you."

"Peter."

"Don't just stand there. Come in, have a seat."

I pushed off the doorway, walked into his office and pulled out a chair.

Please, I told the sick, anxious cramping that had started in my gut as soon as I'd gotten his email invite for this meeting today. *Please stop, cease, go away.*

Please let me have my dignity intact when I met this end. I can't start this thing out seconds away from vomiting.

I settled in the chair, forced myself to meet Dean Gould's eyes. I couldn't read his expression one way of the other.

I casted a vaguely interested glance around his office. It was one of the nicest on campus. Floor to ceiling window, fancy cherry furniture. A picture of a smiling young girl sat on his desk, angled toward him. I wondered who the little girl was and if he found it easier to smile at her.

"Thanks for coming in on such short notice."

"Sure."

He folded his hands on the desk and raised one bushy brow at me. "I know you've had quite a bit going on for the last month or two."

I nodded politely.

C'mon. Just hand me my metaphorical box so we can get this over with.

He gave me an appraising look. "You look great, though. Well-rested."

I nodded again. No good would come of my extolling the virtues of daily orgasms with him, right before he outlined an exit plan.

I decided I couldn't take any more of his silence, the probing stare he aimed at me as if trying to see the inside of my brain. Enough of the suspense; I just needed to *know* already.

"Why'd you ask me to come in, Peter?"

His usual, haughty expression slid into place. "Dr. Leffersbee, I need to make you aware of a . . . delicate situation."

Please, just hurry up and fire me.

"This is about my tenure. Right?"

"Well. Yes. In a way."

"Okay . . ."

He leaned back against the high-backed leather chair, clasping his hands just above his pin-striped covered paunch. "I have become aware of a situation in which a vendor, Nick Rossi, has presented us with a peculiar dilemma."

Oh, hurry the fuck up. I could tell he was enjoying this in his own perverse way, drawing out his words, studying the surface of his highly shined nails. "Please, Peter. Could you just . . . say it? Whatever it is?"

"Mr. Rossi has generously offered a very significant donation. *Very* significant. To be split between the School of Medicine and the hospital."

Some of the tension left my shoulders. That didn't sound bad at all. It sounded like a good development, as a matter of fact. "Okay."

But what did this have to do with my tenure?

As if reading my thoughts, he continued. "We are all very excited about this development, as you may imagine. There's just one problem. The gift is contingent on the School of Medicine granting you tenure. And funding your existing research. Without your knowledge."

I took in a breath and it got stuck.

I couldn't breathe.

"I thought you'd want to know." His gaze moved over mine, searching. "Especially if you've . . . elected to strike up a continued acquaintance with Mr. Rossi."

I sat still. Petrified. Unable to move, breathe or speak.

Had he really just said that? Had Nick really, what, *blackmailed* them? After I'd told him I had it under control, that I'd handle it?

"We are, of course, in a quandary. The money would certainly solve many of our problems. And yet we still have an obligation to uphold our ethical standards. Therefore, I decided you should know." His head lowered and he peered at me from under his brows. His eyes suddenly took on a decidedly flinty glint. "Unless you already knew?"

That woke me up.

"Of course I didn't know. What are you suggesting?"

He spread his hands wide. "I'm merely the messenger, Dr. Leffersbee. I know about as much as you do."

Nick.

Nick had extorted them, pressured them to grant me tenure. Asked them to lie to me about him funding my studies.

He'd never believed in me. Never thought me capable of earning this on my own.

How could I trust him, knowing he'd deceive me this way? That he'd go behind my back and try to pay my way? But hadn't he already done it, with my help? Hadn't I just fallen in line, given myself over as soon as he showed up to town?

Now, I really did feel sick, sick enough to throw up on my own shoes.

"We turned him down," Dean Gould said, his gaze on mine. I buried my head in my hands, reeling from emotional whiplash. "Because three days prior to Mr. Rossi approaching Nellie with his offer, the committee here voted to approve your tenure."

"Wait . . . What?" My head snapped up and my eyes went wide as I searched his face for any hint that he was toying with me. "What did you say? I got tenure?"

"You did." His face cracked with the rarest of smiles. "Congratulations. We were aware, of course, of the requirement to obtain an R01 within this period of time. But we're hardly ignorant of the fact that your work, your research, has greatly contributed to clinician training and education here. And while you did not obtain the designated grant, you've been extremely productive and brought in other forms of grant funding. So, I'm pleased to be the first person to congratulate you on this promotion."

He extended his hand across the desk.

I shook it.

I'd never imagined that this moment, one that I'd worried and agonized over for so long, would end so positively. I'd spent so long imagining every possible calamitous end that would befall my employees that I'd stopped entertaining the idea that I would actually make it.

The moment I'd been afraid to dream for, a victory, a triumph, had finally arrived. All while I choked back hot tears.

"I imagine this is a bittersweet moment for you." Dean Gould's look was warmer than I thought him capable of, and sympathetic. "But I thought it was important to tell you. You should have all the information you need before making any . . . significant decisions in the future."

Anger mounted, billowed in my chest.

Hadn't I said that very thing to Nick? When he'd justified making a decision on my behalf twelve years ago? A decision that separated us for all this time?

I'd excused it, forgiven it of the eighteen-year-old with limited resources and fewer choices. But how could I justify this behavior from the man I intended to spend the rest of my life with? Could I accept being managed, manipulated, and controlled behind my back? All in the name of love?

I'd *earned* tenure. Legitimately. But the victory tasted like ash in my mouth.

Because losing Nick again, letting go of the dream and the life I'd anticipated with him, devastated me in a way that tenure would never come close to fixing.

CHAPTER THIRTY-THREE

Zora

The smell of something wonderful met me as soon as I threw open my front door.

God. Nick was here.

I'd driven home, wanting to avoid him and the lake house until I thought through what I wanted to say. I'd forgotten we'd planned to meet me here so we could discuss our weekend in San Francisco.

I'd been so busy sniffling and sniveling during the drive home that, like an idiot, I must have missed Nick's car in the driveway.

A joyful bark sounded from within in, then the thunderous noise of Sir Duke bounding to the door followed. He pranced in a circle, tail wagging, tongue lolling.

I stroked a hand down his back, fighting back a fresh surge of tears.

How was I going to do this? I loved Nick and I loved this dog.

But I had to be strong.

"Zora? Baby, that you?"

Baby, I thought spitefully.

I made it into the kitchen, bag in hand.

Nick straightened from the kitchen table where he'd placed a plate on a placemat.

"You're back—"

He stiffened, his gaze moving over my face.

Several beats of silence passed as we stared at each other over the table. The air crackled with the anticipation of conflict, swelled with impending doom and disaster.

I watched as knowledge entered his eyes and something like resignation unlocked his shoulders from around his ears.

"You know."

I threw my bag on the counter, slammed my keys alongside it, fought to keep my hysteria and voice low. I didn't want to scare Sir Duke, and I didn't want to give way to the panic fluttering in my chest like captive butterfly wings. Giving in to the terror would make it true, right? Best to stay calm, to figure out how this was all a joke, to embrace the relief of knowing the sun wasn't about to set on the greatest love of my life.

Calm, Zora. Steady.

"That's the best you can do? 'You know?'"

He blinked, said nothing.

My chest heaved. "I just got my teeth kicked in by Dean Gould. I just heard that the man that I love went behind my back and orchestrated a deal, made me a charity case—"

"Zora, that wasn't my intention."

"What *was* your intention, then? If not to make me look like a fool. *Again.* If not to make it clear that you didn't have any confidence in me, or my ability."

"It wasn't you I doubted." He spoke very quietly, his gaze locked on mine. "It was never you. It was the unfair system they had in place. You trusted them to do the right thing—"

I held up a shaking hand. "Wait a minute. This is about me, now? Me being too stupid?"

"I never used that word," he said, sharply. "And this was not about you, it was all about them and the joke of a standard they were holding you to. I wasn't going to stand around and wait to see if they did what was right by you. After all that you've done for these people, why should you be a puppet, dancing on their strings, just to keep your job?" He shook his head and his lips thinned. "No. *No one* is going to take advantage of you, use you, on *my* watch. I just cut the strings—that's all—so you could keep doing what you wanted to do, but on *your* terms this time."

"So, you took it upon yourself to what? Deliver your own justice?"

"I saw how hard you worked. Not just for the job, but for the people. For your patients, for your employees, for the causes you want to advance. All while you neglected yourself. I wasn't going to wait around for them to acknowledge you and what you've done."

"Well, they did."

"What?" He frowned.

"They did see my effort. Peter said they voted to approve my tenure three days before you approached them."

His derisive laughter sent a chill down my spine. "And you believe that?"

"Why wouldn't I?"

"It's a clever solution, I'll give him that. He tells you they were already set to give you tenure just to cover all the bases. Just in case. Meanwhile, they still cash in on the money. He says he's not taking it, but just wait. You'll see."

Stricken, I grasped the back of my neck. It hadn't even occurred to me that Peter's explanation might have been his own volley in a mercenary battle.

Was Nick right? Had I really earned it, or was it just a strategic move on Peter's part?

"Zora, I love you, but you've got to see this the way I do, the way the other folks at the table do when they're gambling away your life and livelihood. Life, winning, it's all about having control. Having the upper hand. Being the strongest negotiator at the table. It's a test of wills. It's a game."

My stomach plummeted. "Was I a game?"

He frowned, his mouth working. "What do you mean?"

"Was I a game? You came back into town with the upper hand. All the power, all the money, all the influence. Knowing exactly what everyone needed. How hard up the school and hospital are for money, how worried I was. And look where we are today. All of us, eating out of your hand."

"No, that's not—"

"You've been gone all this time. You waited for years, *years,* until you showed up again and decided you wanted me back. And God, I just fell for it. I let you manipulate me again, just like you did all those years ago when I didn't even know it. You put me on the back burner, did whatever you wanted to do in the meantime, and then when you snapped your fingers . . ." I shook my head at my own gullibility. "I fell right in line."

Nick rushed over to me and I knocked his hands away.

"Do you realize what you've done? Asking my boss, my employer to *lie* to me? Trying to pay for my promotion? Do you realize how you've sullied my reputation? How those administrators, my colleagues, will look at me now?"

His lips thinned. "You don't even know that you want to stay there, and they don't deserve you. You've said yourself that you're starting to have second thoughts, new ideas about how you might—"

"Then why did you do it?" A horrible thought occurred to me. "Did you just plan on leaving again anyway? Was this all some sick experiment to see if I'd fall for you, then you'd go on your merry way? What was this? *Pity?*"

I looked at him as he stood before me, color high, breathing fast.

He'd never lied about who he was. He had told me that money and influence, power, were the most important things to him.

I loved this man, loved him more than I'd ever thought I was capable of loving someone not in my own family. He'd shown me a happiness, a possibility, a way of life I'd never thought possible. I hadn't even known how much I wanted it, craved it.

But I wanted myself, too. I wanted to excavate, to discover who Zora was and what she wanted, for once, finally.

I'd never be able to do that beside a man who would manipulate and lie to me. Even if he thought it was for my own good.

The words, when I finally spoke them, hurt. They tore my heart apart, wrenched my soul, sent all my newfound hopes crashing into a bottomless abyss.

"You need to leave."

He gaped at me. "Zora."

"Please. Please go."

Don't cry. Don't cry. Don't cry.

He dropped to his knees, planted his head against my stomach, wound his arms around my waist. I heard the genuine fear in his voice.

And it took everything I had not to rest my hand on his head, to run my fingers through those dark locks and tell him I understood, that it was okay.

I *wanted* it to be okay. I wanted there to be a rewind button where I could go back, where none of this happened and I could sit down and eat whatever dinner he'd brought over and laugh about our day, plan a lazy weekend in San Francisco.

But I couldn't. Because as much as I loved him, I couldn't betray myself. Or accept a lifetime of deception, no matter how benevolent it was.

Sir Duke came to my side, his wet nose nudging my hand.

God. I was not strong enough for this. I would not survive this.

"Please leave," I repeated, weeping now and hating myself for it.

He stood.

I averted my gaze as he moved around me. He made it all the way to the front door before I realized Sir Duke was still at my side, staring up at me with pleading eyes.

I bent, hugged his canine face to mine. "I'm sorry, sweet boy."

Nick called to him from the front door.

Sir Duke whined, not moving from away from me.

I pressed one last kiss against his snout, then released. "Go. You have to go."

He gave me one last sad look before he broke away, slowly meandering to Nick at the front door.

And just like that, they were gone.

It was over.

CHAPTER THIRTY-FOUR

Zora

Three Weeks Later

"So, you still haven't talked to him?"

I shook my head, dragged a fry through the mound of ketchup on the corner of my plate. "No."

Jackson cocked an eyebrow. "Any plans on talking to him soon?"

"No." Savagely, I suppressed the hiccup in my throat. Thinking about Nick, talking about him, was still hard. I never knew when I might start to cry.

And I was done crying. I needed to accept the truth.

"Have you guys talked at all since you asked him to leave?"

"He dropped off two letters."

"Letters? Really?"

"Yeah."

He shook his head, leaned back in the booth with a noisy whistle. "Poor bastard."

I sent him a glare. The waitress heading toward our table took one look at whatever was on my face and headed in the opposite direction.

I knew I wasn't the best company at present. Jackson, as

usual, had been a stellar friend and convinced me to quit my moping and enjoy an evening out to get my mind off of things. He was still buzzing with excitement, and more than a little latent lust, after watching a romantic comedy with one of his favorite stars, Raquel Ezra. I was somehow even deeper in my funk. I hadn't really been enjoying my lunch at the Front Porch anyway, but now Jackson's lack of sympathy further soured my stomach.

"I thought you were on my side."

He snickered. "Fine. I'm on your side. Is that what you want me to say?"

I was dangerously close to pouting. "No."

"He made a mistake, Zora."

"He was completely out of line. That's not just a mistake."

"Listen. All guys mess up. All of us. It's universal. Baked into our DNA. Even when we have the best intentions, we *are* gonna somehow mess it up. Now, his mess-up is directly proportional to the resources available to him. Meaning, a regular guy like me who sees someone messing with his girlfriend will use whatever tools he has on hand to address the issue, be it meeting up with the offender to give them a stern talking to, delivering threats, talking smack. As for beating someone up, I wouldn't recommend it. Not as an officer of the peace. But, you get the idea."

"Yeah, yeah."

"But our friend Nick? Well, he has money coming out of where the sun doesn't shine. When he sees someone jerking you around, he doesn't have to wait outside in the parking lot for a guy to leave work."

"That's awfully specific."

"Pay attention. Nick has the means to take on *the whole system*. And he did." He ate approximately one quarter of his hamburger in one bite. "And if you weren't so pissed at him, you'd be impressed. Hell, I'm impressed."

"Alright, Jackson."

"No, seriously. I am sitting here across from you, someone who was perfectly willing to pulverize the guy a month ago, and telling you I think that guy is completely badass. What he did was epic."

"And deceitful."

He acknowledged that with a shrug. "Yeah. But he did it for your own good."

"That sounds so condescending—"

"Life isn't fair, Zora. Nick would know that more than most people, especially given how far he's gotten from where he started. Good guys finish last, and girls don't like them until they're weightlifting in college. In real life, the nerdy girl doesn't just take off her glasses, put in contacts, and become popular."

"Why do I even talk to you? And what movies have you been watching?"

"Because you know I'll tell you the truth, even when you're going all Lisa Simpson on me." He caught my gaze, pointed at me. "And because that man loves the hell out of you."

"You don't even like him."

He waggled his head from side to side. "Eh. Well, for one thing, we weren't really in a position to like each other. I was standing in the way of what he wanted. And he was always such a smug, sly little—"

"What's the second thing?"

He put down his burger. "I talked to my dad."

"Huh?"

"My dad. He was there the night Mrs. Rossi overdosed and Nick got into it with the Iron Wraiths. Said he drove up on Nick getting his ass kicked by a mob of them." His gaze stayed on the surface of the table, fingers drumming. "Hearing how things went down that night, the state of mind Nick was in? I can't help but sympathize with what that guy's been through. Even if he was the smartest, cockiest kid in high school. I mean, so what? Yeah, he was taking college classes. Didn't make him that special."

"What did he tell you, your dad?"

Jackson hesitated. "Some of it you should let Nick tell you. But the one thing I feel comfortable telling you is something my dad said he was floored by. He said that even as worn out, scared, and shocked as Nick was, his first thoughts were about protecting you. Said he didn't think an eighteen-year-old could be capable of such selflessness, especially under the circumstances."

I sat back, mind racing.

"Can you blame him?"

"What?"

"Can you blame him if he did the exact same thing again, all these years later? I see how it's controlling, I see how you might call it manipulation. But I also see how the guy might act that way, seeing as he was backed in a corner all those years and figured out how to make it on top. Just so he could protect you again."

We sat in silence. Jackson stuffed his face with more burger, chased it with a beer.

"Besides," he said, "you gave up all *this*," he gestured to himself with a flourish, "to explore a relationship with this guy. You had to be in love to let a prize like me go. Admit it."

"Did you even chew any of that?"

"Admit it."

"I was trying to avoid a venereal disease, that's why I threw you back in."

"He's still in town, you know."

I'd wondered about that.

"How do you know?"

"Because I gave him a ticket this morning," he said, joy all over his face.

"Couldn't help yourself, huh?"

"Of course I couldn't. Broken heart's hard for a man, but it doesn't give you license to drive five miles over the speed limit."

"God, Jackson."

He reached across the table and clasped my hand. "I love you, Zora. I do. And I wouldn't be talking this way if I didn't think the guy had your best interests at heart. Or that he really loved you. I guess the only question is, what are you willing to do about it?"

CHAPTER THIRTY-FIVE

Nick

"No more conference calls for you. Not until you get this business with Zora resolved."

Eddie leaned over me and wrestled the headset of out my hand.

I took a calming breath. "You do realize, don't you, that conference calls work between remote callers? As in, there's no reason for you to be sitting next to me?"

He shrugged at me from the other side of the breakfast table I'd re-purposed into a desk. "Turns out I like it here. Clean, fresh air. Slower pace. A certain brunette across town. I'm following your example. There's no reason why I need to be sitting at my desk in New York or San Francisco. Not when I can stay here with you."

I loved Eddie, I did. I knew exactly why he'd decided to take over the house with me for the last three weeks.

Uninvited.

The lake house no longer held Zora's special touch. It didn't smell like pineapple or citrus in the bathroom anymore, or in the sheets. There was no more music, no Stevie Wonder, Aretha, Coldplay, Maroon 5. No more dancing in the kitchen while her pie cooled on the windowsill.

Just Eddie's shit all over every surface, his loud snoring from the guest room down the hall, and his insistence that I fix things with Zora.

As if it was that easy.

Even Sir Duke had been in a serious funk. He lifted his head from the corner of the kitchen, where he lounged on a cushy dog bed.

His canine expression clearly telegraphed, *How could you do this to us?*

I realized Eddie had turned my laptop around, typing something at full speed.

"What are you doing?"

"Done. Alright. Your secretary is clearing your schedule and having mine do the same."

I scowled. "Why?"

"Because you shouldn't be allowed around other humans until you figure your shit out. And I'm tired of waiting for you to figure it out, so I'm stepping in."

"Stay out of it."

"I've been deputized by Aunt Nan *and* Mrs. Leffersbee. Resist and it *will* get back to them. Now. Go get your ass in the car."

I was going to choke the life out of him. "Where are we going?"

He grabbed my keys off the wall.

"You're going to show me where you grew up."

∽

I guided the car down a vaguely familiar street. Gradually, the streets became increasingly familiar, with all the updates and modernizations twelve years brought. The parked cars along the streets got newer, the lawns and house exteriors more polished. What was a fledgling middle class neighborhood many years ago had clearly come up in the world.

I coasted to a stop in front of a ranch style home fronted by an immaculately manicured lawn. Precise diagonal stripes evidenced the current owner's care for the property. I slid the gear into park and just sat, taking in my childhood home.

My mother had saved for years to make the down payment. I still remembered when she'd surprised me as a kid one evening after baseball practice. *"Just taking a drive,"* she'd said when I'd asked her why we'd deviated from our normal route home. She'd worked hard to sound normal, but I'd spotted the telltale curl at the corner of her mouth.

I'd known her so well.

For a time.

She'd pulled into this same driveway and parked. My mouth had fallen open when she reached for the overhead visor, and just like magic, the garage door ahead of us began a slow ascent.

"You've got a yard to practice in now, baby," she'd said. As I sat there taking in the shy pride on her face, I'd known I'd never forget the moment. I'd flown out of the car, rounding to her side to hug her.

Then we'd cartwheeled all over the grass until our new neighbors came over and introduced themselves.

Thinking of it now, recalling the brightly colored plants that once filled the now-empty flower bed, an anchor dropped in my chest.

Damn, this hurt.

"Let's get out."

I'd forgotten Eddie was in the car.

"Why?"

"It's a rental now, and it's empty."

I frowned. "How do you know that?"

He fished in his pocket, pulled out a key ring. Separated a worn, silver key.

"I looked into it. The owner was fine with us taking a look around. You know, for old times sakes."

I gathered myself. Debated.

Did I really want to go back in there?

Eddie clapped a hand on my shoulder. "C'mon, man. You got this."

We got out, made our way to the house. Eddie handed me the key.

Just the act of sliding that key into the lock almost leveled me. I remembered to jiggle the key just right—the lock stuck at times—and winced at the familiar shape of the doorknob in my hand.

And then we were inside.

It was strange, seeing my childhood home this way. It was much smaller than I remembered. The interior was empty, but memories echoed back, filling my mind's eye with where things used to be.

Eddie asked questions. I took him on a tour. I pointed out my room, my mother's room.

He made me talk for almost an hour, answering his questions. About Christmases, birthdays, special events. Watching TV with my mother.

Remembering it all hurt, but I was surprised by the reluctant peace that settled over me as I remembered all that had happened in this house; the joy as well as the sorrow.

I looked around, took in all the little details I'd taken for granted back then, the ones I'd never thought that much about as a teenager. I studied the wood paneling my mother had always hated but never got around to removing, the tiny foundation crack above the living room window.

I thought about the life I'd had here in this house. Before things went to hell.

And I remembered Zora. When she'd come here as a kid with a book or game tucked under one arm. Or dragged me out to some festival or play I pretended to hate.

I remembered who I was before I lost everything here. And what Zora meant to me.

I remembered who Zora was, what excited her, what her dreams were, what she'd imagined for herself, me, the two of us together.

And I knew what I had to do.

CHAPTER THIRTY-SIX

Zora

"I told her, I couldn't care less about some tits. Don't get me wrong, hers were amazing. Always were. I used to salute 'em. But I love *her*, not her tits."

I bit back a smile as I watched the couple seated across from me in the examination room. I was certain the patient, Sheila, would have clobbered her husband if not for my presence. A deep flush spread from her face, down her neck. I caught the subtle kick she delivered to his ankle.

But Rick, her husband, remained intent on making his point. He leaned forward, jabbed his pointer finger at me. His other hand held his wife's hand in a tight, secure grip.

"And I know she's probably mad at me for saying it that way, probably wants me to use better words. She's always telling me how I could say something better."

Sheila closed her eyes.

"But not this time. All I can say is what I mean 'cause it's coming from the heart. I want you to hear it and I want her to hear it, too, 'cause she's the one who could probably stand to hear it a million more times before this is over."

I'd been working in my office when I'd gotten a frantic message from Carly. She was in a car accident several miles from campus and worried she wouldn't make it into the clinic in time for our participants' appointment, so she'd called me in a panic.

I'd been happy to go. It'd been a while since I'd gone to clinic to see a patient in person and done the work that was normally handled by my research staff. I also needed the distraction.

After Sheila completed the study's pre-survey and we talked through the intervention, we found ourselves chatting amiably. A nurse had already peeked in to warn us the oncologist was running behind. I was more than happy to help occupy their waiting time.

This was the visit where Sheila would learn if she needed chemo after a recent mastectomy. The stakes were high and the strain was showing on them both.

She already looked antsy enough. I sensed Rick was just as anxious, if not more, but found idle chatter an effective coping mechanism.

"I think that's a beautiful thing to hear. No matter how you say it, Rick." I smiled reassuringly at Sheila, letting her know I was in no way offended by Rick's brash delivery. I'd been raised by Ezra Leffersbee. Rick was tame in comparison.

"I mean it." His composure cracked a bit. "She's my entire life, my entire world. I've haven't spent a night away from this woman in over thirty-five years." He blinked back the wetness threatening to escape the corners of his eyes.

"Thirty-five years? God, that's amazing. What a massive accomplishment. How did you guys meet?"

Just as I hoped, Sheila warmed to the topic. She relayed the tale, giving Rick time to manfully blink away his tears.

"She was so mean to me," Rick said, interrupting Sheila's description of their meet-cute at their shared place of employment.

She pinned him with a severe look. "Trust me, you didn't need any encouragement."

Rick gave me an innocent expression I didn't trust in the least. "She was one of those independent types. You probably know what I mean—you got that look about you, too."

"Rick!" Sheila gaped at him, then turned to me with wide eyes.
"It's okay." I grinned. "You're spot on, Rick. I am that type."
He eyed me. "You married?"
I shook my head. "Nope."
He ran his free hand down his bald pate, eyeing me suspiciously. "Hope I'm not talking out of turn here, doc, but you're a good-looking woman. You ain't got a husband looking after you, it's probably your decision."
I shook my head at him, outright laughing now. Men were interesting creatures. He'd pronounced it as if it was common knowledge. "You think so, Rick?"
"You remind me of her," he said, lifting their joined heads. "Got that efficient look about you. Gotta open up and trust someone at some point, you know? Love's a beautiful thing. It ain't easy. Shit ain't always rosy. You know, I love her, but sometimes I could just—"
"You?" Sheila was looked at him in shock. "*You* 'could just?' I want to kill you at least once every day—"
"But I guess I love her more than the times I want to—"
"I could choke you," Sheila said. But she smiled. I saw her tighten her hold on his hand.
"Open yourself up to having somebody in your life," Rick said. "Beautiful woman like you, obviously as smart as you are, you don't want to go through life alone. And you know," he said, lowering his voice, "you're only getting older."
I laughed so hard I almost fell off the little stool I was sitting on. Sheila smacked him on the arm. I hadn't realized I'd missed this so much. Sitting and talking to the actual patients whose lives I was trying to change made it all feel so much more meaningful.
"Okay, Rick," I said. "Give me your pointers. I get it. I'm getting older. I need to open up, give love a chance?"
Rick hesitated. "You really want my pointers? 'Cause I'll give it to you straight, no chaser."
I flicked a glance at Sheila. She looked far more relaxed, no longer worried about what would come from Rick's mouth.
Good.

"Give it to me straight. No chaser. Maybe Sheila can help to balance things out if need be."

She caught my eye, then made a show of rolling hers.

"Okay." Rick leaned forward. "One. Change your mindset. This one here, she'd already made her mind up about how things were gonna be. Wasn't even open to the idea of a better life with my sexy ass."

We all cracked up a little. "And you got her past that?"

He nodded. "I slow-walked her. Wore her down, sneaky-like."

Sheila blushed, quiet.

"Okay, got it. Changed mindset. What's next?"

"Forgiveness. Gotta forgive yourself and the person you're with. Cause we're all still learning, aren't we?"

I swallowed past the lump on my throat. "Yes, sir, we are."

"Right. And if God can forgive, who are we, decidin' we won't forgive each other? Plus, you need each other, for the hard times. This woman right here? All them years ago she decided to walk this road with me. I decided the same. Now we're gonna face whatever happens. Together."

I heard the indistinct murmuring of the oncologist outside the door, likely in conversation with his fellow. I gathered the papers on the clipboard and stood. Gave them both a smile.

They were so brave.

"Well, I'm so grateful you both were willing to take your time to talk to me. I admire you both. And I got great advice out of the deal."

"I like you, doc," Rick said. He stuck out his hand. "I'll be praying good things happen to you."

I actually felt a lump rise to my throat. That these two, weighted with fear of all the possibilities that were just on the other side of the door, could think of a virtual stranger? I was always amazed by patients' endless capacity to process all of the difficult feelings that accompanied a tough diagnosis, while wanting so badly to help others.

I gave it a good shake, then shook Sheila's unoccupied hand. "I'll be praying for you both," I said. "That only the best things come to you."

Sheila beamed. When the door opened and I excused myself, I looked back just in time to see Sheila gift her husband with a small, tremulous smile. Then together, they faced their future.

I stood on the other side of the closed door. Lost in thought. Thinking through Rick's comments. Warm from the joy of that interaction.

And I knew what I needed to do.

CHAPTER THIRTY-SEVEN

Zora

"*I* know what I need to do."

Leigh looked up from her sideways perch in the armchair and lowered her magazine to face me.

"Now who's using someone's house key without warning, hmm?"

I ignored her and rushed in to sit on the opposite couch. "Listen. I know what I'm gonna do."

She tossed her magazine to the floor, peering up at me with mussed hair and mascara-smudged blue eyes. "About which part? There's so *many* things you need to address."

"I heard back from the NIH today, about that Hail Mary grant I submitted last month."

She sat up, her eyes wide. "What did they say?"

"The committee scored my grant. I got a great score. An amazing score. Way above the pay line. It's most likely going to be funded."

She jumped up from the chair. "Oh! Oh, my God!"

Then she screamed, arms in the air, and ran several laps around the living room.

I watched her, bemused, reflecting on how much I loved her. God, I was lucky to have her as a friend.

She made a victory lap back to me, frowning. "Okay . . . why are you not happy? I thought you'd be deliriously happy. Like, run-out-in-the-street-naked happy. What's going on?"

I sat back. For the first time since losing Nick, I felt a glimmer of hope that mixed with the ever-present pain.

I'd accepted the hurt would never go away. Someway, somehow, I'd have to live without Nick in my life.

Leaving him would always be my biggest regret. I now knew from experience I'd never get over this pain, but I had to carry on. Keep pushing on.

I took a breath, pushed down the sadness.

"I actually sat down with patients today. Carly was in a car accident—"

"She okay?"

"Yeah, thank goodness. But when I sat with them, I remembered what I loved so much about this kind of work. It reminded me of the days when I worked with the ladies in my mother's support group."

Leigh stared, silent.

"I realized what was wrong. Finally. The thing that got me into this work, the thing that I loved most? I don't do it anymore. I don't work with people one-on-one, I don't do any of the education, the coaching, the counseling. I got so caught up in the machine of it all that I lost touch."

Leigh looked cautious. "So, what does this mean?"

"I can't believe I'm saying this, but . . . I'm quitting my job. I'm not going to take on the grant. I checked with the grant administrator. Adesola is my co-investigator on it and they're reasonably sure she'll be able to keep it. My employees will have jobs, long-term funding. They'll be okay, thank God. I won't be there, but my employees will have jobs. That's the most important thing."

Leigh's mouth hung open. "You just said *what?*"

"Yep. I'm quitting."

"And you're *smiling* about it. But," Leigh spluttered, "You just got tenure. Finally. I've spent the last two years listening to you explore every possible doomsday scenario. How you would end up homeless and unloved if you didn't get a grant or didn't get tenure. And now what? You're just going to throw it all away?"

"Yes." Certainty that I'd finally done the right thing rushed through me.

But it was bittersweet.

Because the first person I'd wanted to tell?

Nick.

Even with the brave face I put on, inside I was bleeding.

She sat down, looking dazed. "Alright. Okay. Anything else?"

"Yes. I'm going to start a nonprofit. It'll be very small at first, just here in Green Valley. We'll focus on patient advocacy to start. I'll actually use all the patient materials, the decision aids, the question prompt lists, all the tools we developed to help patients better communicate with their doctors. I'll get help from other clinicians and educators to do education classes and teach people how to manage their chronic illnesses. We'll provide space for support groups, right here, so folks don't have to drive into Knoxville. Maybe even have a day where we get a volunteer nurse practitioner in to see folks, so they don't have to drive all the way to the hospital. That's just to start. Then, I'm going to work on advocacy at a national level, pick some of my colleagues' brains about advocacy work for burned-out clinicians, health care reform and getting those issues out there. I'm going to travel, try to learn more about what works in other health care systems. I can't lie, I don't have it all figured out at all. I'm sure I'm gonna mess up. But I'm excited to see where this takes me."

I was breathless, excited by the possibilities, eager to find another piece, another dimension of myself.

I was simultaneously heartbroken Nick wouldn't be by my side.

Leigh looked stunned. "You're serious."

"I am."

"Wow."

I lowered the last boom.

"And I'm going to London for a few weeks."

"Who *are* you?"

"Remember Christen, from grad school? The exchange student

from Oxford? Well, we kept in touch over the years. She'd been begging me to visit, and I finally said yes. She runs a patient advocacy organization out of London and said I could shadow her to learn more."

Leigh sighed. "That's why you're going to London?"

My smile faltered.

"Just be honest. It's me. You can always be honest with me."

"I miss him so much." I swiped away a tear. "Even now, when I should be so happy I've finally figured things out, all I want is him here with me." I sniffled. "No offense."

"None taken."

"I'm gonna call him when I get to London."

"Why do you have to wait until then?"

I let out a shuddery breath. "Because if I see him, if I lay eyes on him, I won't be able to help myself. And as much as I want him, and as much as I want a future with him, I need to be thinking clearly."

"Okay."

"Alright. Will you drop me off at the airport Wednesday?"

"That's two days away."

"I know." I shrugged. "It's hard being here. Getting some distance might help."

CHAPTER THIRTY-EIGHT

Zora

"You got your passport?"

Outside, the highway passed in a blur of green leaves, grass, and gray cement.

"Yes, Mother," I teased, trying to work myself up to a cheerful mood. It wasn't working.

Leigh was unusually quiet. I didn't think it was disapproval I sensed from her. More like nervousness.

Another equally viable possibility?

I'd projected my own anxiety onto her.

The farther we drove outside of Green Valley, the more my inner disquiet grew. It was a huge breakthrough to have finally figured out what I wanted and how I would get it.

I had a new career path to look forward to.

Yay.

The initial rush of assurance, the glow of satisfaction? It diminished more and more each day. My grief over losing Nick was like gangrene. It was slowly killing me, choking off all sensation. Blunting any joy. Rendering the world colorless.

London will be better, I told myself.

Right. Rainy, gray, Nick-less London will be better.
Sure.
God, my inner voice was a bully.
Signs announcing proximity to the airport caught my eye.
"Thank you for everything, Leigh."
She glanced at me. "What are you thanking me for?"
"Well, for being you. For being such a good friend. For putting up with me these past few months."
She shrugged. "You put up with me year-round. So."
I nodded. "So."
"You sure you wanna go?"
I turned my head in her direction, shocked by the question.
"We're already at the airport."
"That isn't what I asked you. I asked if you still wanted to go. That's what I want to know."
I felt her gaze on my face.
"Because I will turn this car around. We'll head right back to Green Valley. I'll take you to Nick myself, if that's you want."
The words sent a thrill of hope through me.
Back.
Back to Nick.
Yes, please.
No. Be a big girl. Stick to your guns.
But I'm so unhappy without him. I miss him so much.
"God, it's like I can hear your internal debate over there, like you're Sméagol and Gollum arguing over the Precious."
She took the exit for the airport.
My palms sweated.
"No." I sucked in a breath. "This is for the best. Just . . . just drop me off at Departures. I'll get my life together while I'm in London. I'll come back refreshed and confident and *sure*."
And miserable.
"You think *London* is going to do all that for you?"
"I thought you hated Nick."

"I did. I hated what he did to you. And then I met him. Really met him, talked to him. And I saw the two of you together. I understand a little better, I think, how close your bond is and why it hurt so much to be away. Plus, I called The Redhead."

I grinned. "Of course you did."

"You knew I would. Turns out she's not really a redhead, she's a gorgeous brunette like yours truly. And she's a state senator in Michigan."

"Really?!"

"Yes! She said she totally initiated it, and that she'd been laying down hints he'd been ignoring for over a year. Said she wanted to cheer him up because he was always so sad about the girlfriend he'd left."

My chest burned. "Damn."

"Plus, what he did? It really was a selfless act. He did it so you could win this thing. It's not like he wants to live in Green Valley full-time. He wanted you to have what you deserved. Even if it costs him."

She drove past the exit for my airline.

"No, wait. You wanna go that way." I gestured to the lane we were rapidly passing.

She kept driving, talking, as if she hadn't heard me.

"I saw how much he cared about you. You can't fake that, the love he has for you. What he did with the school? I agree, it was overstepping. But I can't fault him too much. Not when I had thoughts of burning that place down when you started sleeping in your office."

"Where are you going?"

"I decided to talk to him. I figured, what could it hurt?"

"Wait, you what?" I glanced between her and the unfamiliar path we drove along. "Where are we going? You *talked* to him?"

"And I decided you needed to have at least have one more conversation with him."

The car slowed and rounded a bend.

Ahead of us sat the hangars for private flights.

We pulled up to a fence and checkpoint. Leigh showed the uniformed guard a folded slip of paper from her jacket and he waved us forward.

"Leigh. What have you done?"

"You're my best friend and I love you. Just trust me. Please."

She pulled to a stop.

"Get out. I can't go any farther."

I looked around. Small, private planes crouched in the distance. The dark, open mouth of a huge hangar loomed ahead.

My heart beat a wild, unsteady rhythm. "What's going on?"

She leaned over. "Give me a hug."

I stared at her. "Who *are* you?"

"I'm your friend. And I want you to go hear him out. Please. Be brave."

I opened the door. Nausea sloshed through my stomach. I looked back at her.

"How will I get home?"

"I don't know. I did my part. Now get out of my car. I don't want to be late for my spin class."

I glared at her as I collected my purse and got out of the car.

She hit the gas as soon as I closed the door, executed a smooth three-point turn, and returned to the exit.

With my luggage in the back of the car.

I was stranded.

Just as I worked up the courage to walk ahead, I heard a familiar sound.

Barking.

Sir Duke.

He streaked out of the hangar, tongue lolling, legs a blur as he raced to me. I was relieved when he finally stopped in front of me. I petted him, cooed to him, as he did a joyous reunion dance.

"I missed you, boy."

"And I missed you."

Startled, I looked up. Nick stood less than five feet away.

He wore a dark suit, the crisp white shirt open at the throat.
I couldn't breathe.
"Nick."
"Zora." He smiled, but something in his eyes . . .
I went to him.

CHAPTER THIRTY-NINE

Zora

*I*n all the world, there existed no better place than the circle of Nick's arms.

I went to him, easily, naturally, without thinking.

Just as I'd always done.

He caught me up in his arms before I'd reached him, boosted my sweatpants-clad legs around him.

"I'm sorry," he breathed, his breath tickling the shell of my ear. "For everything. Can we talk?"

My breath stuttered. "Yeah."

He carried me to the hangar, Sir Duke trailing along.

Once on my feet, I turned in a circle. And gasped.

The massive space was filled with huge, life-size photos. Of me, of him, of us together.

He took my hand in his. "A few days ago, I had the opportunity to visit my old house."

I held onto his arm. "Did you? Are you okay?"

He nodded. "It was a good thing. I'm glad I did. I had some realizations. Important ones, I think. Sometimes it helps to remember the past when you want to find your way forward."

He gave a subtle nod.

Music from an unseen speaker filled the air. The opening strains of Coldplay's "Yellow" filled the air.

The smile he gave me was so slow, so tender, I thought I might die from it.

"May I take you on a tour of our past?"

I nodded.

He led me by the hand to the first photo. It was of the two of us. God, we were tiny. We both stood grinning at the camera, dressed in stained smocks with paintbrushes in hand. My two front teeth were missing. He was missing three on the bottom.

"That's third grade. Mrs. Beyer's class. Remember?"

I nodded.

"I went home and told my mother you were the most beautiful girl in the class and I was going to marry you."

I sniffled. "What did she say?"

"She said I wasn't allowed to get married until I learned how to do all my chores."

I cracked up. That sounded just like his mom.

We walked a few feet farther until we met the next picture. It featured middle-school aged versions of us. We sat at the kitchen table in Nick's house with a pizza and Monopoly board in front of us.

"You know what happened right after this picture?"

"No."

"You went to the teacher and the counselor and tattled on me."

I stared at him, taken aback.

"What?"

He smiled, his gaze soft. "You told them how bored I was in classes. That the work was too easy for me."

I laughed. "I did do that. I remember now."

"Yeah, and then I started taking community college classes. Because of you."

"I'd do it again."

"I know you would."

He pulled me along to the next picture. It wasn't a picture, really.

It was a photograph of a piece of paper. I squinted to make out the distorted lettering.

"It says 'Notice of Suspension.'"

"You got this from my mother. She took it out of the frame."

"I sure did. I'll never forget it. You kicked that girl's ass, right in the middle of social studies. Your first and last fight."

My blood heated at the memory. "She had no business talking about your mother like that, saying those things in front of the entire class. I gave her a warning, and she started it." The same anger I'd always felt about that event filled me and my free hand tightened into a fist. "She started it, but I sure finished it. She never said a word about you, your mother, or me again."

His hand tightened on mine.

"Over here."

We walked over to a picture of a young me.

God, I'd never appreciated myself when I was young. I remembered just turning eighteen and hating my imperfections so much.

And loving how Nick coaxed me into feeling comfortable in my skin.

I laid on a carpet of autumn leaves, my hair lost among the red, copper, and burnt orange leaves.

But there was no mistaking my grin. I held a chain up to the camera.

My ring dangled from the end.

"Remember that moment?" His voice sounded from behind me.

"You'd just proposed. And we decided I'd wear the ring around my neck so our parents wouldn't figure it out and freak."

He tugged me in a different direction. His footsteps echoed in the cavernous space. We toured all the in-between moments of our adolescence and teenage years until we reached the end of the timeline.

When we'd separated.

"After that, everything happened. We didn't have any more moments together. Not for a long while. Not until I got up the courage to come back. And all I could hope was that you'd give me the chance I'd been so desperate for during all those years."

"What if I'd gotten married? Had kids? How could you be so sure I'd still be here waiting for you?"

I'd wondered that more than once.

We stopped in front of a new picture Eddie had taken a month ago with his phone, at Knoxville Axe. Nick sat, one large arm extended along the booth. My head was on his shoulder, my hand on his chest. As if I wanted to absorb all his heat, all his energy. His free hand rested on top of my head, tangled in my curls.

God. Look at us.

I glanced up at Nick. He stared at the picture, chest lifting with an inhalation.

"Zora, that's us. It always has been. No matter what space, problems, or people were between us. We belong together. Fate wouldn't have it any other way."

He turned to face me, captured my other hand.

"You wanted to know if it was a game, a ploy, me coming back. Never. I came back because I couldn't breathe without you anymore, and I was tired of trying. I've come to understand why you're so angry about what I did. All I can tell you is that there will never be a day where I won't want to give you the world or correct whatever injustice you're experiencing if it's within my power. I can't promise it won't ever happen again. I'll do my best. But I do promise that I'll always respect your choices. I'll never step on your independence and I won't manipulate your path through life. Not ever again.

"I can be controlling. I realize that now. And I promise I'll work on it. One of the ways I want to do that is by being honest about the things that make me afraid, that make me fearful, that bring out the controlling part of me that needs to mask that fear.

"Today, I want to make a confession. I don't wanna make any more decisions for you, or without your knowledge. I'm done with that. I want you to know that I'm nothing without you. That I'm terrified of the idea of going through this world without my best friend. It scares me, you having this much power over me. But I'm helpless without you."

I shook my head at his earnest expression. God. My heart was going to explode.

"All I want is you. I want to live with you, laugh with you, make love with you. Have kids with your hair and heart. And then make up with you over all the stupid things I'm sure I'll do."

He took a breath.

Then lowered to one knee.

"So, I'm asking you to take me on. Full-time. I want to belong to you forever. No take-backs. Just you and me. And forever."

My vision blurred. I blinked away tears, regaining vision just in time to see him holding an open box out to me.

It couldn't be.

I reached in, pulled the ring out.

It was my ring. The one I'd returned to him all those years ago.

"Why do you still have this?" I wailed, and he smiled.

"Because I knew it was just a matter of time. Because forever does last always. It does when it's us."

I ugly cried, swiping at my falling tears with both hands.

Nick bit his lip, still on one knee. "So? Is it a yes?"

"Yes," I gasped, and behind us a door banged open and a crowd of people spilled around us, laughing, yelling, congratulating us.

I didn't even hear them. I only had eyes for Nick.

He surged to his feet, slid the ring on my hand. I kissed him with all I had, sliding my hand into his hair and holding him to me.

I never wanted to let go.

"Thank God," a familiar voice next to me said.

Leigh. She'd circled back.

"Welcome to the family, Nick. This is great news. Maybe we can sit down and talk soon? Here, I'm just going to slide my business card in your pocket. Zora knows how to get ahold me too."

Ugh, *Tavia*.

"This is wonderful, baby girl." My mother. "But save something for the wedding night, will y'all?"

I pulled away, reluctantly, already hungry for the next time we could be alone.

A short woman with a gray pageboy and snazzy red glasses claimed my arms. "Zora! I'm your new Aunt Nan! I can't wait to get to know you better."

Nick met my eyes over her head. *Forever*, he mouthed.

And my heart was glad.

CHAPTER FORTY

Zora

The community center was transformed again.
 But not for focus groups.
For our wedding reception.

Nick had flown in an ultra-expensive, ultra-pretentious wedding planner who ultimately drove us both crazy. But now, on this very special day, as I looked around the auditorium, I had to admit she was worth every penny and aggravation.

The auditorium was transformed into an enchanted, eternally fall forest. I grinned at the faux trees and their gorgeous, underlit fall foliage. Millions of twinkly fairy lights lent the darkened room an airy, ethereal feel. A rotation of Coldplay and Motown hits blasted from the hidden speakers.

I grinned at Nick. Less than an hour ago, I'd walked down an autumn leaves-lined aisle to meet him at the altar. I'd been bursting, full of so much love, certainty and anticipation I'd forced myself to maintain the dignified, measured pace on my father's arm.

"Forever," Nick had whispered in my ear as he took my arm, and I sealed that promise with my own vows.

I felt complete. I couldn't wait for our new life to start.

We sat at the couples' table at the foot of the room and watched the interesting side effects of our families, coworkers, and friends socializing.

It was comical.

Walker stalked bridesmaids. Tavia worked our reception like a networking event, and Audre made it clear we'd interrupted her life at UCLA by getting married mid-semester. My bridesman, Jackson, sniffed at the heels of one of Nick's employee as they shuffled along to the electric slide. Aunt Nan and my mother loudly discussed baby paraphernalia at the nearby table and negotiated visitation for grandchildren who did not yet exist.

We'd gotten married a month to the day after Nick proposed.

We just didn't want to wait any longer than we had to. We'd been separated long enough.

Finalizing the Nick and Zora Rossi Foundation would take slightly longer, but it would all be worth it. Nick had convinced me to partner with him to implement my ideas in Green Valley and far beyond. Thought leaders, policy makers, and clinicians had already pledged their services. We'd outlined our initiatives with great excitement, thrilled we would address barriers to care at personal, structural, cultural, and organizational levels. He was excited to learn more about lobbying and advocacy at a national level.

Maybe he'd be the politician he'd always wanted to be after all.

I was excited for what the future offered, what Nick and I could offer the world.

Nick loved to tease that I was excited to give away his money. He was only half-right. I was excited to live out my life's purpose with my best friend. And if his money helped lots of people, well, we were both more than okay with that.

Right now, though, I was counting down the minutes until I could be alone with Nick.

I rested a hand on his leg, let the edge of my nails tease the inside of his thigh.

He caught my hand, brought it to his mouth and kissed it.

"Nuh-uh. Whose idea was it to go without sex again, right before the wedding?"

"Mine."

"You know the deal. Not till we're back at the house."

I threw him a glance. "You are *so* not gonna last that long."

His cheek lifted in a smile. "You're right. No underwear allowed in the car."

My heart quickened. "Promise?"

He slid me a significant look. "Oh, *I do*."

"You think anything's going to come of Eddie chasing Leigh?"

I glanced over at our seated wedding party. Our best man and maid of honor sat next to each other, heads crowded together, talking. Eddie looked earnest, alit with joy, eager.

Leigh looked like a disinterested cat toying with a mouse.

Poor Eddie.

"Look this way!" We both turned to find my mother and Nan standing together, phones aimed at us. "Smile!"

We obliged them and they hustled over.

"You really won't tell me where y'all are going for the honeymoon?" My mother aimed a narrow look at Nick. "And you're gonna be gone for a whole month?"

I smiled at my mother. She'd been a little deflated since learning we planned to split our time between Green Valley, New York, and San Francisco.

She'd cheered up a bit when Nick promised we'd visit often, and that he'd send the plane for her whenever she wanted to be with us.

"Nope," Nick said in response to her question. "We'll send you a note when we arrive at each new place. You'll be surprised just like Zora."

Aunt Nan slapped at my mother's wrist.

These two had turned into quite the comedy duo.

"Ellie, would you leave these kids alone? Let them do what they need to do. We need grandbabies!"

My mother nodded back. "You're right, Nan." She gave me a sly smile. "Have fun on your honeymoon, baby girl. Now that you're married, I can tell you a Leffersbee secret: the sweetest nectar—"

"No." I widened my eyes at her. "Just . . . no."

She waved a hand at me, laughing, and Nan pulled her off to engage in other mischief.

"Zora."

I looked at my husband.

Wow. I had a *husband*.

Nick looked shell-shocked. "I think your mom might be kind of kinky."

I punched his arm.

"No, I'm just saying. Find out what she was going to tell you. Then tell me."

We laughed, and I realized my bladder was in danger of bursting. Nick helped me pull the enormous bustle out of the chair and set me on course to the bathroom.

"You need help?"

I pulled him down to plant a kiss on his whiskered chin. "I've got this. You don't need to follow me into the ladies' room."

He looked over at the now empty wedding party table. "I was gonna see if we could ask Leigh, but she's gone."

Along with Eddie, I noticed.

"I've got it." I made it a few steps, responded to well-wishers along the way, bladder clenching, and just caught a glimpse of Leigh and Eddie slipping around the corner ahead, past the bathrooms, into a rarely used storeroom.

Interesting.

I made into the bathroom. Right before the door closed, I caught sight of Walker following them into the storeroom, his face set.

Uh-oh.

That's grown folks' business, Zora.

I managed the heft of silk and tulle through all my ablutions, then headed out. I opened the bathroom door and immediately recognized Eddie's retreating back ahead of me as he returned to the auditorium.

Had Walker chased Eddie away? What was his problem? Leigh was single and Walker definitely had other prospects, not to mention zero desire to settle down. I loved my brother, but my best friend had been through far too much to be a victim of my brother's carelessness.

To my left, glass crashed in the adjoining storeroom.

Raised voices came from the other side of door. Leigh's voice was tight with . . . was that worry? Panic?

I rushed over and threw open the door.

Walker laid on the bare wooden floor. Splintered glass and liquid glittered by his head. Leigh straddled him in her copper dress, one arm planted above his head, her face inches from his. Tendrils of her dark hair fell over his face and her cleavage threatened to leave the low-cut bodice of her rust orange dress and visit Walker's face.

I scowled at them both. "Really? Out of the all times you could have picked, *finally,* you choose now?"

I left them, closing the door behind me.

I didn't have time to think of their tryst much more that night. Not with Nick slow dancing with me on the dance floor, his eyes full of everything he felt for me. Nan and I held each other and choked back sobs when Nick and my mother slow-danced to "Unforgettable" by Nat King Cole. Both he and my mother had wet cheeks when the song ended.

By the time the vintage Rolls Royce pulled up to take us home, I almost wanted to stay and celebrate with our friends.

Almost.

But not quite, not after that moment when we stood with fireworks over our heads and rice in our hair, and Nick framed my face in his hands. *"Forever,"* he said, and I saw my life, my future in his eyes.

And I pulled him to the car that would take us to our home.

To start forever.

ABOUT THE AUTHOR

Hope Ellis is a health outcomes researcher by day and writes romances featuring sexy nerds by night. She hopes to one day conquer her habit of compulsively binge-watching *The Office*.

~

Facebook: https://www.facebook.com/hopeelliswrites/
Goodreads: https://www.goodreads.com/author/show/19916500.Hope_Ellis
Twitter: https://twitter.com/HopeEllisWrites
Instagram: https://www.instagram.com/hopeelliswrites/

Find Smartypants Romance online:
Website: www.smartypantsromance.com
Facebook: www.facebook.com/smartypantsromance/
Goodreads: www.goodreads.com/smartypantsromance
Twitter: @smartypantsrom
Instagram: @smartypantsromance

ALSO BY SMARTYPANTS ROMANCE

Green Valley Chronicles
The Donner Bakery Series
Baking Me Crazy by Karla Sorensen (#1)
Stud Muffin by Jiffy Kate (#2)
No Whisk, No Reward by Ellie Kay (#3)
Beef Cake by Jiffy Kate (#4)
Batter of Wits by Karla Sorensen (#5)

The Green Valley Library Series
Love in Due Time by L.B. Dunbar (#1)
Crime and Periodicals by Nora Everly (#2)
Prose Before Bros by Cathy Yardley (#3)
Shelf Awareness by Katie Ashley (#4)
Carpentry and Cocktails by Nora Everly (#5)
Love in Deed by L.B. Dunbar (#6)

Scorned Women's Society Series
My Bare Lady by Piper Sheldon (#1)
The Treble with Men by Piper Sheldon (#2)

Park Ranger Series
Happy Trail by Daisy Prescott (#1)
Stranger Ranger by Daisy Prescott (#2)

The Leffersbee Series
Been There Done That by Hope Ellis (#1)

The Higher Learning Series

Upsy Daisy by Chelsie Edwards (#1)

Seduction in the City
Cipher Security Series

Code of Conduct by April White (#1)

Code of Honor by April White (#2)

Cipher Office Series

Weight Expectations by M.E. Carter (#1)

Sticking to the Script by Stella Weaver (#2)

Cutie and the Beast by M.E. Carter (#3)